THE NEW FOLGER LIBRARY SHAKESPEARE

Designed to make Shakespeare's great plays available to all readers, the New Folger Library edition of Shakespeare's plays provides accurate texts in modern spelling and punctuation, as well as scene-by-scene action summaries, full explanatory notes, many pictures clarifying Shakespeare's language, and notes recording all significant departures from the early printed versions. Each play is prefaced by a brief introduction, by a guide to reading Shakespeare's language, and by accounts of his life and theater. Each play is followed by an annotated list of further readings and by a "Modern Perspective" written by an expert on that particular play.

Barbara A. Mowat is Director of Research *emerita* at the Folger Shakespeare Library, Consulting Editor of *Shakespeare Quarterly*, and author of *The Dramaturgy of Shakespeare's Romances* and of essays on Shakespeare's plays and their editing.

Paul Werstine is Professor of English in the Graduate School and at King's University College at Western University. He is a general editor of the New Variorum Shakespeare and author of *Early Modern Playhouse Manuscripts and the Editing of Shakespeare,* as well as many papers and essays on the printing and editing of Shakespeare's plays.

The Folger Shakespeare Library

The Folger Shakespeare Library in Washington, D.C., a privately funded research library dedicated to Shakespeare and the civilization of early modern Europe, was founded in 1932 by Henry Clay and Emily Jordan Folger. In addition to its role as the world's preeminent Shakespeare collection and its emergence as a leading center for Renaissance studies, the Folger Library offers a wide array of cultural and educational programs and services for the general public.

EDITORS
BARBARA A. MOWAT
Director of Academic Programs
Folger Shakespeare Library

PAUL WERSTINE
Professor of English
King's College and the University of Western Ontario

FOLGER SHAKESPEARE LIBRARY

Cymbeline

By

WILLIAM SHAKESPEARE

EDITED BY BARBARA A. MOWAT
AND PAUL WERSTINE

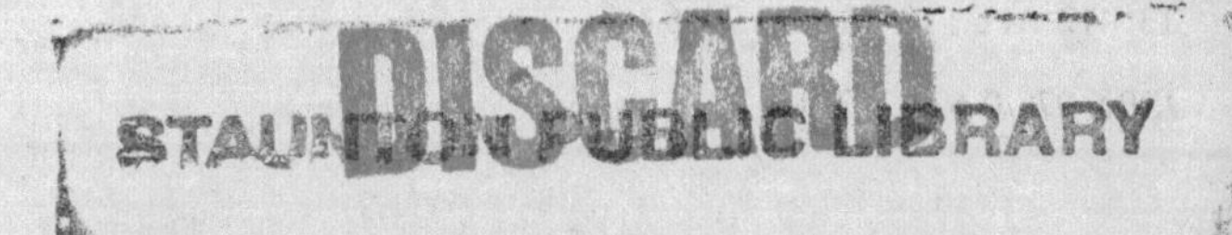

SIMON & SCHUSTER PAPERBACKS
NEW YORK LONDON TORONTO SYDNEY

Simon & Schuster Paperbacks
A Division of Simon & Schuster, Inc.
1230 Avenue of the Americas
New York, NY 10020

Washington Square Press New Folger Edition June 2003
This Simon & Schuster paperback edition March 2011

SIMON & SCHUSTER PAPERBACKS and colophon are registered trademarks of Simon & Schuster, Inc.

For information regarding special discounts for bulk purchases, please contact Simon & Schuster Special Sales at 1-866-506-1949 or business@simonandschuster.com.

The Simon & Schuster Speakers Bureau can bring authors to your live event. For more information or to book an event, contact the Simon & Schuster Speakers Bureau at 1-866-248-3049 or visit our website at www.simonspeakers.com.

Manufactured in the United States of America

13 12 11 10 9 8 7 6 5

ISBN 978-0-671-72259-3

From the Director of the Folger Shakespeare Library

It is hard to imagine a world without Shakespeare. Since their composition four hundred years ago, Shakespeare's plays and poems have traveled the globe, inviting those who see and read his works to make them their own.

Readers of the New Folger Editions are part of this ongoing process of "taking up Shakespeare," finding our own thoughts and feelings in language that strikes us as old or unusual and, for that very reason, new. We still struggle to keep up with a writer who could think a mile a minute, whose words paint pictures that shift like clouds. These expertly edited texts, presented here with accompanying explanatory notes and up-to-date critical essays, are distinctive because of what they do: they allow readers not simply to keep up, but to engage deeply with a writer whose works invite us to think, and think again.

These New Folger Editions of Shakespeare's plays are also special because of where they come from. The Folger Shakespeare Library in Washington, DC, where the Editions are produced, is the single greatest documentary source of Shakespeare's works. An unparalleled collection of early modern books, manuscripts, and artwork connected to Shakespeare, the Folger's holdings have been consulted extensively in the preparation of these texts. The Editions also reflect the expertise gained through the regular performance of Shakespeare's works in the Folger's Elizabethan Theater.

I want to express my deep thanks to editors Barbara Mowat and Paul Werstine for creating these indispensable editions of Shakespeare's works, which incorporate the best of textual scholarship with a richness of commentary that is both inspired and engaging. Readers who want to know more about Shakespeare and his plays can follow the paths these distinguished scholars have tread by visiting the Folger itself, where a range of physical and digital resources (available online) exist to supplement the material in these texts. I commend to you these words, and hope that they inspire.

Michael Witmore
Director, Folger Shakespeare Library

From the Director of the Folger Shakespeare Library

It is hard to imagine a world without Shakespeare. Since their composition four hundred years ago, Shakespeare's plays and poems have traveled the globe, inviting those who see and read his works to make them their own.

Readers of the New Folger Editions are part of this ongoing process of "taking up Shakespeare," finding our own thoughts and feelings in language that strikes us as old or unusual and, for that very reason, new. We still struggle to keep up with a writer who could think a mile a minute, whose words paint pictures that shift like clouds. These expertly edited texts, presented here with [illegible] notes and [illegible], give readers [illegible] what they do not know [illegible] to keep up [illegible] to engage deeply with a writer whose works invite us to think, and think again.

The New Folger Editions of Shakespeare's plays, which are the [illegible] of [illegible] the Folger Shakespeare Library in Washington, DC, where the edition was produced, is the [illegible] collection of Shakespeare [illegible] [illegible] and [illegible] make [illegible] [illegible] extensively in the [illegible] [illegible] Shakespeare's [illegible] the [illegible] Elizabethan theater.

I [illegible] Barbara Mowat and Paul Werstine [illegible] of Shakespeare's works, which incorporate [illegible] that is both [illegible] and [illegible] Shakespeare [illegible] the [illegible] [illegible] [illegible] [illegible]

[illegible]

Director, Folger Shakespeare Library

Contents

Editors' Preface

In recent years, ways of dealing with Shakespeare's texts and with the interpretation of his plays have been undergoing significant change. This edition, while retaining many of the features that have always made the Folger Shakespeare so attractive to the general reader, at the same time reflects these current ways of thinking about Shakespeare. For example, modern readers, actors, and teachers have become interested in the differences between, on the one hand, the early forms in which Shakespeare's plays were first published and, on the other hand, the forms in which editors through the centuries have presented them. In response to this interest, we have based our edition on what we consider the best early printed version of a particular play (explaining our rationale in a section called "An Introduction to This Text") and have marked our changes in the text—unobtrusively, we hope, but in such a way that the curious reader can be aware that a change has been made and can consult the "Textual Notes" to discover what appeared in the early printed version.

Current ways of looking at the plays are reflected in our brief prefaces, in many of the commentary notes, in the annotated lists of "Further Reading," and especially in each play's "Modern Perspective," an essay written by an outstanding scholar who brings to the reader his or her fresh assessment of the play in the light of today's interests and concerns.

As in the Folger Library General Reader's Shakespeare, which this edition replaces, we include explanatory notes designed to help make Shakespeare's language clearer to a modern reader, and we place the notes on the page facing the text that they explain. We also follow the earlier edition in including illustrations—of objects, of clothing, of mythological figures—from books and manuscripts in the Folger Library collection. We provide fresh accounts of the life of Shakespeare, of the publishing of his plays, and of the theaters in which his plays were performed, as well as an introduction to the text itself. We also include a section called "Reading Shakespeare's Language," in which we try to help readers learn to "break the code" of Elizabethan poetic language.

For each section of each volume, we are indebted to a host of generous experts and fellow scholars. The "Reading Shakespeare's Language" sections, for example, could not have been written had not Arthur King, of Brigham Young University, and Randall Robinson, author of *Unlocking Shakespeare's Language,* led the way in untangling Shakespearean language puzzles and shared their insights and methodologies generously with us. "Shakespeare's Life" profited by the careful reading given it by the late S. Schoenbaum; "Shakespeare's Theater" was read and strengthened by Andrew Gurr, John Astington, and William Ingram; and "The Publication of Shakespeare's Plays" is indebted to the comments of Peter W. M. Blayney. We, as editors, take sole responsibility for any errors in our editions.

We are grateful to the authors of the "Modern Perspectives"; to the late Susan Snyder for many helpful conversations about this play; to Leeds Barroll and David Bevington for their generous encouragement; to the Huntington and Newberry Libraries for fellowship support; to King's College for the grants it has provided to Paul Werstine; to the Social Sciences and Humanities Research Council of Canada, which provided him with a Research Time Stipend for 1990–91; to R. J. Shroyer of the University of Western Ontario for essential computer support; to the Folger Institute's Center for Shakespeare Studies for its sponsorship of a workshop on "Shakespeare's Texts for Students and Teachers" (funded by the National Endowment for the Humanities and led by Richard Knowles of the University of Wisconsin), a workshop from which we learned an enormous amount about what is wanted by college and high-school teachers of Shakespeare today; to Alice Falk for her expert copyediting; and especially to Steve Llano, our production editor at Pocket Books.

Our biggest debt is to the Folger Shakespeare Library—to Gail Kern Paster, Director of the Library, whose interest and support are unfailing, and to Werner Gundersheimer, the Library's Director from 1984 to 2002, who made possible our edition; to Deborah Curren-Aquino, who provides extensive editorial and production support; to Jean Miller, the Library's former Art Curator, who combs the Library holdings for illustrations, and to Julie Ainsworth, Head of the Photography Department, who carefully photographs them; to Peggy O'Brien, former Director of Education at the Folger and now Director of Education Programs at the Corporation for Public Broadcasting, who gave us expert advice about the needs being expressed by Shakespeare teachers and students (and to Martha Christian and other "master teachers" who used our texts in manuscript in their classrooms); to Allan Shnerson and Mary Bloodworth for their expert computer support; to the staff of the Academic Programs Division, especially Rachel Kunkle (whose help has been crucial), Solvei Robertson, Mary Tonkinson, Kathleen Lynch, Carol Brobeck, Liz Pohland, Sarah Werner, Owen Williams, and Dan Busey; and, finally, to the generously supportive staff of the Library's Reading Room.

Barbara A. Mowat and Paul Werstine

Shakespeare's *Cymbeline*

Cymbeline tells the story of an ancient British king and his three children. The king, Cymbeline, is mentioned in chronicles in Shakespeare's day, and may be historical or may be legendary. The chronicles say that he ruled at the time of Augustus Caesar, was brought up in Caesar's court, and had a peaceful reign. His children—although the two sons, Guiderius and Arviragus, also appear in the chronicles—are presented in the play as if they have stepped in from romance or fairy tales. And Cymbeline himself, with his marriage to a beautiful but wicked queen and his almost miraculous victory in his war against Rome, also partakes far more of romance than of history.

Much of the play focuses on the story of the king's daughter, Imogen, whose secret marriage to a gentleman named Posthumus Leonatus triggers a great deal of the play's action. Her father, outraged at the marriage, banishes Posthumus, who is then maneuvered into making a foolish wager on Imogen's chastity. The story that follows of villainous slander, homicidal jealousy, cross-gender disguise, a deathlike trance, the appearance of Jupiter in a vision, and final repentance, forgiveness, and reunion is the stuff of the popular fiction of the time, as well as of popular drama of an earlier period. The trials of Imogen, however, are also larger than life, reminding one of the sufferings of mythological heroines who anger powerful gods.

The story of Cymbeline's two sons, which intersects with that of Imogen, is even more deliberately fictional.

As the play tells it, Guiderius and Arviragus were kidnapped in infancy and raised in a cave in the Welsh mountains. (The play acknowledges the incredibleness of this part of the plot by having a gentleman say to a doubter: "Howsoe'er 'tis strange, / Or that the negligence may well be laughed at, / Yet is it true, sir" [1.1.75–77]). Knowing nothing of their heritage and remembering no life beyond their mountain cave and its environs, the young men yearn for adventure. In the course of the play, they rescue a starving young man (their sister Imogen in disguise); they kill and decapitate Cymbeline's stepson; and they go into battle against the Roman army and prove almost superhumanly valiant.

The fairy-tale-like stories of Imogen and of her brothers play against the somewhat more realistic story of King Cymbeline as he takes on a Roman invasion rather than pay the tribute agreed to by his ancestors. References to such personages as Augustus Caesar and Julius Caesar and his conquest of Britain appear to ground Cymbeline's story in history. But Cymbeline too is a familiar romance figure—a father who loses his children and after long years miraculously finds them; a king who, through what seems supernatural intervention, defeats an invading army and then grants pardon to all.

Shakespeare uses the long-ago-and-far-away fantasy quality of the stories dramatized in *Cymbeline* as the ground against which he displays unusually powerful human emotions. The play tells of love and loss, of jealousy and fury, of the joy of finding and the near-delirium of reuniting after heartrending separation; and the language in which the emotions accompanying these human states are expressed has never been more potent. The audience is seldom allowed to forget that the action is fictional; at the same time, the characters' ordeals and triumphs and their responses to those moments carry a tremendous charge. The resulting drama, while reminding us at many times of stories and situations explored in earlier Shakespearean plays, has a quality that links it to his other late work—especially *The Winter's Tale* and *The Tempest*—as a dramatization of improbable story lifted, through its characters and its language, into a realm that is nearly mythic in scope.

After you have read the play, we invite you to turn to the back of this book and read "*Cymbeline:* A Modern Perspective," by Professor Cynthia Marshall of Rhodes College.

Reading Shakespeare's Language: *Cymbeline*

For many people today, reading Shakespeare's language can be a problem—but it is a problem that can be solved. Those who have studied Latin (or even French or German or Spanish), and those who are used to reading poetry, will have little difficulty understanding the language of Shakespeare's poetic drama. Others, though, need to develop the skills of untangling unusual sentence structures and of recognizing and understanding poetic compressions, omissions, and wordplay. And even those skilled in reading unusual sentence structures may have occasional trouble with Shakespeare's words. Four hundred years of "static" intervene between his speaking and our hearing. Most of his immense vocabulary is still in use, but a few of his words are not—and many now have meanings quite different from those they had in the sixteenth and seventeenth centuries. In the theater, most of these difficulties are solved for us by actors who study the language and articulate it for us so that the essential meaning is heard—or, when combined with stage action, is at least *felt*. When we are reading on our own, we must do what each actor does: go over the lines (often with a dictionary close at hand) until the puzzles are solved and the lines yield up their poetry and the characters speak in words and phrases that are, suddenly, rewarding and wonderfully memorable.

Shakespeare's Words

As you begin to read the opening scenes of a play by Shakespeare, you may notice occasional unfamiliar words. Some are unfamiliar simply because we no longer use them. In the opening scenes of *Cymbeline,* for example, one finds the words *allayments* (i.e., antidotes, modifying agents), *liegers* (i.e., ambassadors), and *sluttery* (i.e., sluttishness). Words of this kind are explained in notes to the text and will become familiar the more of Shakespeare's plays you read.

In *Cymbeline,* as in all of Shakespeare's writing, more problematic are the words that are still in use but that now have a different meaning. In the opening scenes of *Cymbeline,* for example, the word *confounded* is used where we would say "killed," *convince* where we would say "vanquish," and *qualified* where we would say "accomplished." Such words will be explained in the notes to the text, but they, too, will become familiar as you continue to read Shakespeare's language.

Some words are strange not because of the "static" introduced by changes in language over the past centuries but because these are words that Shakespeare is using to build a dramatic world that has its own space, time, and history. In the opening scene of *Cymbeline,* for example, Shakespeare quickly constructs a background history for Cymbeline's royal family and for Posthumus Leonatus, Cymbeline's new, and unwanted, son-in-law. Shakespeare creates Posthumus's past through details about his father, Sicilius, who died before his son's birth. Sicilius had served the ancient British kings Cassibelan and Tenantius against the Romans and had, through his bravery, gained the "suraddition" of "Leonatus" (i.e., lion-born). Posthumus Leonatus was brought into the court by King Cymbeline himself, who made him "of his bedchamber"; there, Posthumus became "a sample to the youngest," a "glass" that "feated" the "more mature." The princess, Imogen, has chosen Posthumus as her husband, her "election" showing "what kind of man he is." Significant details about Cymbeline's own history focus, in the opening scene, on the remarkable story of the theft of his two sons, one still "i' th' swathing clothes," "conveyed" from the court some twenty years before, with no "guess in knowledge" how they were taken or where they went. Such language quickly constructs the world inhabited by Cymbeline and his family, a world that mixes legendary British history with deliberately improbable romance; the words and the world they create will become increasingly familiar as you get further into the play.

Shakespeare's Sentences

In an English sentence, meaning is quite dependent on the place given each word. "The dog bit the boy" and "The boy bit the dog" mean very different things, even though the individual words are the same. Because English places such importance on the positions of words in sentences, on the way words are arranged, unusual arrangements can puzzle a reader. Shakespeare frequently shifts his sentences away from "normal" English arrangements—often to create the rhythm he seeks, sometimes to use a line's poetic rhythm to emphasize a particular word, sometimes to give a character his or her own speech patterns or to allow the character to speak in a special way. When we attend a good performance of the play, the actors will have worked out the sentence structures and will articulate the sentences so that the meaning is clear. When reading the play, we need to do as the actor does: that is, when puzzled by a character's speech, check to see if words are being presented in an unusual sequence. (*Cymbeline,* like others of Shakespeare's very late plays, is written in language that sometimes steadfastly resists being reduced to any clear meaning. In performance the actors will clarify as far as the words and sentence structure allow, and we as readers will try to do the same.)

Often Shakespeare rearranges subjects and verbs (i.e., instead of "He goes" we find "Goes he"). In *Cymbeline,* when Imogen says "but most miserable / Is the desire that's glorious" (1.6.6–7), she is using such a construction. So is the Second Lord when he says "That such a crafty devil as is his mother / Should yield the world this ass" (2.1.52–53). The "normal" order would be "the desire that's glorious is most miserable" and "as his mother is." Shakespeare also frequently places the object before or between the subject and verb (i.e., instead of "I hit him," we might find "Him I hit" or "I him hit"). Posthumus provides an example of the first kind of inversion when he says to Iachimo "My ring I hold dear as my finger" (1.4.141) and an example of the second kind when he says to Imogen "I my poor self did exchange for you" (1.1.140). The "normal" order would be "I hold my ring" and "I did exchange my poor self."

Inversions are not the only unusual sentence structures in Shakespeare's language. Often in his sentences words that would normally appear together are separated from each other. Again, this is often done to create a particular rhythm or to stress a particular word, or else to draw attention to a needed piece of information. Take, for example, the First Gentleman's

For which their *father,*
Then old and fond of issue, *took* such sorrow
That he quit being; and his gentle *lady,*
Big of this gentleman our theme, *deceased*
As he was born.

(1.1.41–46)

Here the first subject ("father") is separated from its verb ("took") by the subject's modifiers, as is the second subject ("lady") from its verb ("deceased"). Each of the two interruptions draws our attention forcefully and concisely to the needed facts they provide. Or take Iachimo's lines to Imogen:

The cloyèd *will,*
That satiate yet unsatisfied desire, that tub
Both filled and running, ravening first the lamb,
Longs after for the garbage.
(1.6.53–56)

Here the subject and verb ("The will . . . longs") are separated by two appositive phrases ("that satiate yet unsatisfied desire, that tub both filled and running") and then by the participial phrase "ravening first the lamb," interruptions that emphasize the sordid greed of the "cloyèd will." In order to create sentences that seem more like the English of everyday speech, one can rearrange the words, putting together the word clusters ("father took sorrow," "lady deceased," "the cloyèd will longs for the garbage"). The result will usually be an increase in clarity but a loss of rhythm or a shift in emphasis.

Locating and rearranging words that "belong together" is especially necessary in passages that separate basic sentence elements by lengthy delaying or expanding interruptions, a common feature of dialogue in *Cymbeline.* One prominent example is Imogen's speech asking Pisanio to "say . . . how far it is to . . . Milford." Here, Imogen's excitement makes her interrupt herself so often and at such length that her request to Pisanio is almost unintelligible:

Then, true *Pisanio,*
Who long'st like me to see thy lord, who long'st—
O, let me bate—but not like me, yet long'st
But in a fainter kind—O, not like me,
For mine's beyond beyond—*say,* and speak thick—
Love's counselor should fill the bores of hearing

To th' smothering of the sense—*how far it is*
To this same blessèd *Milford.*
(3.2.55–62)

Often in *Cymbeline,* rather than separating basic sentence elements, Shakespeare simply holds them back, delaying them until other material to which he wants to give greater emphasis has been presented. Shakespeare puts this kind of construction in the mouth of Imogen as she explains why she parted with Posthumus without a proper leave-taking:

Ere I could tell him
How I would think on him at certain hours
Such thoughts and such; or I could make him swear
The shes of Italy should not betray
Mine interest and his honor; or have charged him
At the sixth hour of morn, at noon, at midnight
T' encounter me with orisons, for then
I am in heaven for him; or ere I could
Give him that parting kiss which I had set
Betwixt two charming words, *comes in my father,*
And like the tyrannous breathing of the north
Shakes all our buds from growing.
(1.3.33–44)

The basic sentence elements (an inverted form of "my father comes in") are here delayed while Imogen rehearses, in the form of a series of four adverbial clauses, the farewell lines that she had wanted to say to Posthumus. If one reverses the order, placing the basic sentence elements at the beginning of the sentence, the adverbial clauses lose interest and force, and one sees the power of Shakespeare's delaying strategy.

Finally, in many of Shakespeare's plays, sentences are sometimes complicated not because of unusual structures or interruptions but because Shakespeare omits words and parts of words that English sentences normally require. (In conversation, we, too, often omit words. We say, "Heard from him yet?" and our hearer supplies the missing "Have you.") Frequent reading of Shakespeare—and of other poets—trains us to supply such missing words. Even among Shakespeare's later plays, all of which frequently omit words, *Cymbeline* stands out for the compressed nature of its language. Ellipsis (omission of words) sometimes takes a familiar form—that is, words are simply left out. When, for example, Imogen begs Iachimo to "discover to me / What both you spur and stop" (1.6.117–18), her compressed language can be easily expanded by supplying the missing words: "both what you spur [on] and [what you then] stop [from being revealed]." In the same scene, when she says "Had I been thief-stol'n, / As my two brothers, happy" (5–6), she has, through simple ellipsis, condensed "As my two brothers [were,] [I would now be] happy"—though even this example becomes complicated when one notices that "As my two brothers, happy" might instead be expanded to read "As my two brothers [were,] [that would have been] happy (i.e., fortunate)," since the ellipsis is extensive and since "happy" has more than one meaning.

Complicated ellipsis and compression are characteristic of the language of *Cymbeline.* When Iachimo claims, at 1.6.135–37, "Not I, / Inclined to this intelligence, pronounce / The beggary of his change," one cannot simply restore omitted words; rather, if one wishes to expand, one must rearrange and paraphrase—perhaps as "I am not inclined to report this information regarding the base nature of his change." Again, when Imogen says, "If he should write / And I not have it, 'twere a paper lost / As offered mercy is" (1.3.2–4), the extreme compression of "'twere a paper lost as offered mercy is" forces a reader looking for a plausible expansion to paraphrase Imogen as perhaps saying "failure to receive a letter from Posthumus would be like failing to receive an offered divine or royal pardon." And when she says, a few lines later, "I would have broke mine eyestrings, cracked them, but / To look upon him till the diminution / Of space had pointed him sharp as my needle" (22–25), the phrase "the diminution of space" can be expanded only through such a paraphrase as "the apparent reduction in size caused by increasing distance." To take one final example: when Iachimo, slandering Posthumus, speaks of men who are blameworthy and Imogen responds, "Not he, I hope," Iachimo answers her cryptically "Not he—but yet heaven's bounty towards him might / Be used more thankfully. In himself 'tis much; / In you, which I account his, beyond all talents" (1.6.91–94). The phrase "In himself 'tis much" can be expanded to read "with regard to himself, heaven's bounty has provided him many gifts," and the phrase "In you . . . beyond all talents" can be paraphrased as "in giving him you, heaven's bounty has given him something beyond all talents." There are, of course, many other ways in which such compressed language can be expanded and paraphrased—though the variations seldom differ much in their larger sense. In the flow of theatrical performance, we as audience members catch the general meaning, and the emotion being conveyed pulls us into the illusion that we understand what is being said; as readers, however, trying to make sense of each speech, we must occasionally admit that some speeches in *Cymbeline* are written in a late-Shakespearean style that refuses to be fully paraphrased.

Shakespearean Wordplay

Shakespeare plays with language so often and so variously that entire books are written on the topic. Here we will mention only two kinds of wordplay, puns and metaphors. Puns in *Cymbeline* usually play on the multiple meanings of a single word. When, for example, at 1.1.114–16, Posthumus says to Imogen, "thither write, my queen, / And with mine eyes I'll drink the words you send, / Though ink be made of gall," he puns on two meanings of the word *gall* (bile, an intensely bitter substance; and oak-galls, used in making ink). When, at 1.2.9, a man's body is described, after a swordfight, as "a passable carcass," the phrase plays on the word *passable* as meaning (1) fairly good, and (2) easily pierced by a rapier.

Sometimes in *Cymbeline* puns are used more complexly, with a word introduced by one character answered by another character using the word in a different sense. When, for example, Cymbeline accuses Imogen of being "Past grace" and Imogen responds with "Past hope and in despair; that way past grace" (1.1.164–65), Cymbeline uses the word "grace" to mean "sense of duty or propriety," while Imogen's response shifts the meaning to "mercy" or "forgiveness," from which persistence in the sin of despair would bar her. And in the following exchange between Iachimo and Posthumus, the word "attempt" becomes the focus of the confrontation:

IACHIMO . . . I durst attempt it against any lady in the world.
POSTHUMUS You are a great deal abused in too bold a persuasion, and I doubt not you sustain what you're worthy of by your attempt.
IACHIMO What's that?
POSTHUMUS A repulse—though your attempt, as you call it, deserve more: a punishment, too.
(1.4.119–26)

Here, the word "attempt" is introduced by Iachimo as a verb whose primary meaning is "venture," though he probably hints at its secondary meaning of "try to ravish or seduce." It is that second meaning that Posthumus focuses on when he twice reiterates the word "attempt," using it as a noun that means "a personal assault on a woman's honor."

A metaphor is a play on words in which one object or idea is expressed as if it were something else, something with which it shares common features. For instance, when the First Gentleman says that young Posthumus "in 's spring became a harvest" (1.1.52), he is using metaphorical language to describe Posthumus as being simultaneously two seasons of the year—a springtime that yet yields the rich harvest of autumn. Posthumus, too, uses metaphor when, in declaring to Imogen that he will never seek a second wife, he exclaims: "cere up my embracements from a next [wife] / With bonds of death" (1.1.136–37). Since "cere up" means, literally, to wrap in a cerecloth, a waxed winding sheet for a corpse, his language transforms his future embraces into a body dead to anyone except his wife. When Imogen responds to her father's anguished "That mightst have had the sole son of my queen!" with "O blessèd that I might not! I chose an eagle / And did avoid a puttock" (1.1.166–68), she metaphorically contrasts Posthumus the eagle with Cloten the bird of prey (a kite, for instance, or a buzzard). Iachimo uses metaphor in a comparable way when he represents Posthumus choosing a prostitute instead of Imogen by saying: "What, / To hide me from the radiant sun and solace / I' th' dungeon by a snuff?" (1.6.102–4); here, Imogen is the sun and the prostitute the burned-out end of a candle.

Metaphor can, of course, be used more complexly, as it is when the Queen, trying to persuade Pisanio to desert Posthumus, says to him:

> What shalt thou expect,
> To be depender on a thing that leans,
> Who cannot be new built, nor has no friends
> So much as but to prop him?
>
> (1.5.66–69)

In this extended metaphor, Posthumus becomes a building or a wall that is falling down, that cannot be repaired, and that has nothing to prop it up.

Implied Stage Action

Finally, in reading Shakespeare's plays we should always remember that what we are reading is a performance script. The dialogue is written to be spoken by actors who, at the same time, are moving, gesturing, picking up objects, weeping, shaking their fists. Some stage action is described in what are called "stage directions"; some is signaled within the dialogue itself. We must learn to be alert to such signals as we stage the play in our imaginations. When Imogen says to Posthumus "Look here, love: / This diamond was my mother's. Take it, heart" (1.1.129–31) and Posthumus then addresses the diamond with "Remain, remain thou here, / While sense can keep it on" (138–39), it is reasonably clear that Imogen hands him a diamond ring that he places on his finger. A few lines later, when Posthumus says "For my sake, wear this. / It is a manacle of love. I'll place it / Upon this fairest prisoner" (142–44), it is again clear that he places on Imogen some object—presumably a bracelet, since he compares it to a manacle; later in the play we are told explicitly that his gift to her was indeed a bracelet. We can be fairly certain, then, that the stage gesture at 1.1.144 is his placing a bracelet on Imogen's wrist.

Occasionally in *Cymbeline,* signals to the reader are not so clear. In 1.5, for example, it is not possible to trace precisely the path of a box of drugs as it moves from the doctor Cornelius to the Queen and thence to Pisanio. Early in the scene, the Queen asks Cornelius, "Now, Master Doctor, have you brought those drugs?" He replies: "Pleaseth your Highness, ay. Here they are, madam" (1.5.5–6). We can assume he hands them to her at that point. Later in the scene, however, after Cornelius has exited, the Queen, speaking to Pisanio, interrupts herself in mid-speech to say,

> Thou tak'st up
> Thou know'st not what. But take it for thy labor.
> It is a thing I made which hath the King
> Five times redeemed from death. I do not know
> What is more cordial.
>
> (70–74)

The dialogue and action that follow leave no doubt that what Pisanio "takes up" is the same box that Cornelius earlier handed to the Queen. But why, and from where, does he take it up? It may be possible to stage this business in any number of ways, both onstage and in one's imagination. We as editors have inserted a (bracketed) stage direction that reads "*She drops the box and Pisanio picks it up,*" but this is merely our best guess. Directors and actors—and readers in their imaginations—may find much better ways to stage the scene.

Learning to read the language of stage action repays one many times over when one reaches scenes heavily dependent on stage business, such as scene 2.2, in which Iachimo suddenly emerges from a trunk in the bedroom of the sleeping Imogen; or scene 5.4, in which the ghosts of Posthumus's family appear and in which the god Jupiter descends seated on an eagle; or, perhaps most crucially, scene 5.5, the play's crowded final scene, in which the audience, sitting in a position of godlike knowledge, watches while multiple layers of misunderstanding are peeled away, the supposed dead return to life, betrayers confess and are forgiven, and numerous disguises are penetrated, abandoned, or removed.

It is immensely rewarding to work carefully with Shakespeare's language—with the words, the sentences, the wordplay, and the implied stage action—as readers for the past four centuries have discovered. It may be more pleasurable to attend a good performance of a play—though not everyone has thought so. But the joy of being able to stage one of Shakespeare's plays in one's imagination, to return to passages that continue to yield further meanings (or further questions) the more one reads them—these are pleasures that, for many, rival (or at least augment) those of the performed text, and certainly make it worth considerable effort to "break the code" of Elizabethan poetic drama and let free the remarkable language that makes up a Shakespeare text.

Shakespeare's Life

Surviving documents that give us glimpses into the life of William Shakespeare show us a playwright, poet, and actor who grew up in the market town of Stratford-upon-Avon, spent his professional life in London, and returned to Stratford a wealthy landowner. He was born in April 1564, died in April 1616, and is buried inside the chancel of Holy Trinity Church in Stratford.

We wish we could know more about the life of the world's greatest dramatist. His plays and poems are testaments to his wide reading—especially to his knowledge of Virgil, Ovid, Plutarch, Holinshed's *Chronicles,* and the Bible—and to his mastery of the English language, but we can only speculate about his education. We know that the King's New School in Stratford-upon-Avon was considered excellent. The school was one of the English "grammar schools" established to educate young men, primarily in Latin grammar and literature. As in other schools of the time, students began their studies at the age of four or five in the attached "petty school," and there learned to read and write in English, studying primarily the catechism from the Book of Common Prayer. After two years in the petty school, students entered the lower form (grade) of the grammar school, where they began the serious study of Latin grammar and Latin texts that would occupy most of the remainder of their school days. (Several Latin texts that Shakespeare used repeatedly in writing his plays and poems were texts that schoolboys memorized and recited.) Latin comedies were introduced early in the lower form; in the upper form, which the boys entered at age ten or eleven, students wrote their own Latin orations and declamations, studied Latin historians and rhetoricians, and began the study of Greek using the Greek New Testament.

Since the records of the Stratford "grammar school" do not survive, we cannot prove that William Shakespeare attended the school; however, every indication (his father's position as an alderman and bailiff of Stratford, the playwright's own knowledge of the Latin classics, scenes in the plays that recall grammar-school experiences—for example, *The Merry Wives of Windsor,* 4.1) suggests that he did. We also lack generally accepted documentation about Shakespeare's life after his schooling ended and his professional life in London began. His marriage in 1582 (at age eighteen) to Anne Hathaway and the subsequent births of his daughter Susanna (1583) and the twins Judith and Hamnet (1585) are recorded, but how he supported himself and where he lived are not known. Nor do we know when and why he left Stratford for the London theatrical world, nor how he rose to be the important figure in that world that he had become by the early 1590s.

We do know that by 1592 he had achieved some prominence in London as both an actor and a playwright. In that year was published a book by the playwright Robert Greene attacking an actor who had the audacity to write blank-verse drama and who was "in his own conceit [i.e., opinion] the only Shake-scene in a country." Since Greene's attack includes a parody of a line from one of Shakespeare's early plays, there is little doubt that it is Shakespeare to whom he refers, a "Shake-scene" who had aroused Greene's fury by successfully competing with university-educated dramatists like Greene himself. It was in 1593 that Shakespeare became a published poet. In that year he published his long narrative poem *Venus and Adonis;* in 1594, he followed it with *The Rape of Lucrece.* Both poems were dedicated to the young earl of Southampton (Henry Wriothesley), who may have become Shakespeare's patron.

It seems no coincidence that Shakespeare wrote these narrative poems at a time when the theaters were closed because of the plague, a contagious epidemic disease that devastated the population of London. When the theaters reopened in 1594, Shakespeare apparently resumed his double career of actor and playwright and began his long (and seemingly profitable) service as an acting-company shareholder. Records for December of 1594 show him to be a leading member of the Lord Chamberlain's Men. It was this company of actors, later named the King's Men, for whom he would be a principal actor, dramatist, and shareholder for the rest of his career.

So far as we can tell, that career spanned about twenty years. In the 1590s, he wrote his plays on English history as well as several comedies and at least two tragedies (*Titus Andronicus* and *Romeo and Juliet*). These histories, comedies, and tragedies are the plays credited to him in 1598 in a work, *Palladis Tamia,* that in one chapter compares English writers with "Greek, Latin, and Italian Poets." There the author, Francis Meres, claims that Shakespeare is comparable to the Latin dramatists Seneca for tragedy and Plautus for comedy, and calls him "the most excellent in both kinds for the stage." He also names him "Mellifluous and honey-tongued Shakespeare": "I say," writes Meres, "that the Muses would speak with Shakespeare's fine filed phrase, if they would speak English." Since Meres also mentions Shakespeare's "sugared sonnets among his private friends," it is assumed that many of Shakespeare's sonnets (not published until 1609) were also written in the 1590s.

In 1599, Shakespeare's company built a theater for themselves across the river from London, naming it the Globe. The plays that are considered by many to be Shakespeare's major tragedies (*Hamlet, Othello, King Lear,* and *Macbeth*) were written while the company was resident in this theater, as were such comedies as *Twelfth Night* and *Measure for Measure.* Many of Shakespeare's plays were performed at court (both for Queen Elizabeth I and, after her death in 1603, for King James I), some were presented at the Inns of Court (the residences of London's legal societies), and some were doubtless performed in other towns, at the universities, and at great houses when the King's Men went on tour; otherwise, his plays from 1599 to 1608 were, so far as we know, performed only at the Globe. Between 1608 and 1612, Shakespeare wrote several plays—among them *The Winter's Tale* and *The Tempest*—presumably for the company's new indoor Blackfriars theater, though the plays seem to have been performed also at the Globe and at court. Surviving documents describe a performance of *The Winter's Tale* in 1611 at the Globe, for example, and performances of *The Tempest* in 1611 and 1613 at the royal palace of Whitehall.

Shakespeare wrote very little after 1612, the year in which he probably wrote *King Henry VIII.* (It was at a performance of *Henry VIII* in 1613 that the Globe caught fire and burned to the ground.) Sometime between 1610 and 1613 he seems to have returned to live in Stratford-upon-Avon, where he owned a large house and considerable property, and where his wife and his two daughters and their husbands lived. (His son Hamnet had died in 1596.) During his professional years in London, Shakespeare had presumably derived income from the acting company's profits as well as from his own career as an actor, from the sale of his play manuscripts to the acting company, and, after 1599, from his shares as an owner of the Globe. It was presumably that income, carefully invested in land and other property, which made him the wealthy man that surviving documents show him to have become. It is also assumed that William Shakespeare's growing wealth and reputation played some part in inclining the crown, in 1596, to grant John Shakespeare, William's father, the coat of arms that he had so long sought. William Shakespeare died in Stratford on April 23, 1616 (according to the epitaph carved under his bust in Holy Trinity Church) and was buried on April 25. Seven years after his death, his collected plays were published as *Mr. William Shakespeares Comedies, Histories, & Tragedies* (the work now known as the First Folio).

The years in which Shakespeare wrote were among the most exciting in English history. Intellectually, the discovery, translation, and printing of Greek and Roman classics were making available a set of works and worldviews that interacted complexly with Christian texts and beliefs. The result was a questioning, a vital intellectual ferment, that provided energy for the period's amazing dramatic and literary output and that fed directly into Shakespeare's plays. The Ghost in *Hamlet,* for example, is

A stylized representation of the Globe theater.
From Claes Jansz Visscher, *Londinum florentissima Britanniae urbs* . . . [c. 1625].

wonderfully complicated in part because he is a figure from Roman tragedy—the spirit of the dead returning to seek revenge—who at the same time inhabits a Christian hell (or purgatory); Hamlet's description of humankind reflects at one moment the Neoplatonic wonderment at mankind ("What a piece of work is a man!") and, at the next, the Christian disparagement of human sinners ("And yet, to me, what is this quintessence of dust?").

As intellectual horizons expanded, so also did geographical and cosmological horizons. New worlds—both North and South America—were explored, and in them were found human beings who lived and worshiped in ways radically different from those of Renaissance Europeans and Englishmen. The universe during these years also seemed to shift and expand. Copernicus had earlier theorized that the earth was not the center of the cosmos but revolved as a planet around the sun. Galileo's telescope, created in 1609, allowed scientists to see that Copernicus had been correct; the universe was not organized with the earth at the center, nor was it so nicely circumscribed as people had, until that time, thought. In terms of expanding horizons, the impact of these discoveries on people's beliefs—religious, scientific, and philosophical—cannot be overstated.

London, too, rapidly expanded and changed during the years (from the early 1590s to around 1610) that Shakespeare lived there. London—the center of England's government, its economy, its royal court, its overseas trade—was, during these years, becoming an exciting metropolis, drawing to it thousands of new citizens every year. Troubled by overcrowding, by poverty, by recurring epidemics of the plague, London was also a mecca for the wealthy and the aristocratic, and for those who sought advancement at court, or power in government or finance or trade. One hears in Shakespeare's plays the voices of London—the struggles for power, the fear of venereal disease, the language of buying and selling. One hears as well the voices of Stratford-upon-Avon—references to the nearby Forest of Arden, to sheepherding, to small-town gossip, to village fairs and markets. Part of the richness of Shakespeare's work is the influence felt there of the various worlds in which he lived: the world of metropolitan London, the world of small-town and rural England, the world of the theater, and the worlds of craftsmen and shepherds.

That Shakespeare inhabited such worlds we know from surviving London and Stratford documents, as well as from the evidence of the plays and poems themselves. From such records we can sketch the dramatist's life. We know from his works that he was a voracious reader. We know from legal and business documents that he was a multifaceted theater man who became a wealthy landowner. We know a bit about his family life and a fair amount about his legal and financial dealings. Most scholars today depend upon such evidence as they draw their picture of the world's greatest playwright. Such, however, has not always been the case. Until the late eighteenth century, the William Shakespeare who lived in most biographies was the creation of legend and tradition. This was the Shakespeare who was supposedly caught poaching deer at Charlecote, the estate of Sir Thomas Lucy close by Stratford; this was the Shakespeare who fled from Sir Thomas's vengeance and made his way in London by taking care of horses outside a playhouse; this was the Shakespeare who reportedly could barely read but whose natural gifts were extraordinary, whose

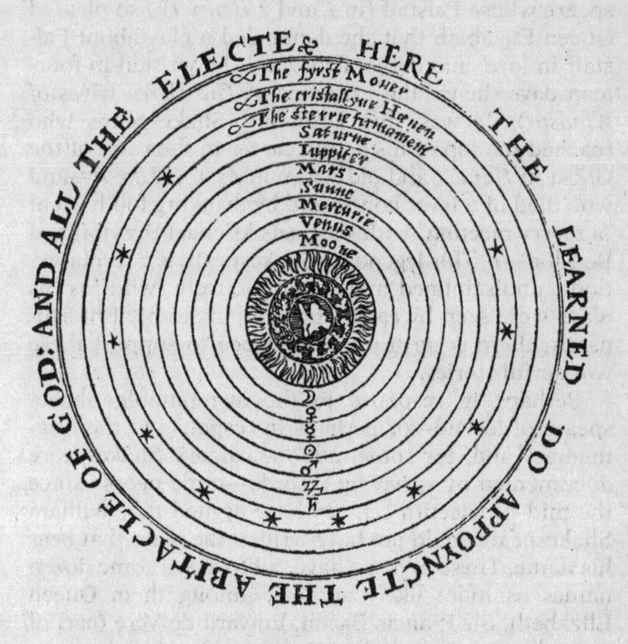

Ptolemaic universe.
From Leonard Digges, *A prognostication* . . . [1556].

father was a butcher who allowed his gifted son sometimes to help in the butcher shop, where William supposedly killed calves "in a high style," making a speech for the occasion. It was this legendary William Shakespeare whose Falstaff (in *1* and *2 Henry IV*) so pleased Queen Elizabeth that she demanded a play about Falstaff in love, and demanded that it be written in fourteen days (hence the existence of *The Merry Wives of Windsor*). It was this legendary Shakespeare who reached the top of his acting career in the roles of the Ghost in *Hamlet* and old Adam in *As You Like It*—and who died of a fever contracted by drinking too hard at "a merry meeting" with the poets Michael Drayton and Ben Jonson. This legendary Shakespeare is a rambunctious, undisciplined man, as attractively "wild" as his plays were seen by earlier generations to be. Unfortunately, there is no trace of evidence to support these wonderful stories.

Perhaps in response to the disreputable Shakespeare of legend—or perhaps in response to the fragmentary and, for some, all-too-ordinary Shakespeare documented by surviving records—some people since the mid-nineteenth century have argued that William Shakespeare could not have written the plays that bear his name. These persons have put forward some dozen names as more likely authors, among them Queen Elizabeth, Sir Francis Bacon, Edward de Vere (earl of Oxford), and Christopher Marlowe. Such attempts to find what for these people is a more believable author of the plays is a tribute to the regard in which the plays are held. Unfortunately for their claims, the documents that exist that provide evidence for the facts of Shakespeare's life tie him inextricably to the body of plays and poems that bear his name. Unlikely as it seems to those who want the works to have been written by an aristocrat, a university graduate, or an "important" person, the plays and poems seem clearly to have been produced by a man from Stratford-upon-Avon with a very good "grammar-school" education and a life of experience in London and in the world of the London theater. How this particular man produced the works that dominate the cultures of much of the world almost four hundred years after his death is one of life's mysteries—and one that will continue to tease our imaginations as we continue to delight in his plays and poems.

Shakespeare's Theater

The actors of Shakespeare's time performed plays in a great variety of locations. They played at court (that is, in the great halls of such royal residences as White-hall, Hampton Court, and Greenwich); they played in halls at the universities of Oxford and Cambridge, and at the Inns of Court (the residences in London of the legal societies); and they also played in the private houses of great lords and civic officials. Sometimes acting companies went on tour from London into the provinces, often (but not only) when outbreaks of bubonic plague in the capital forced the closing of the-aters to reduce the possibility of contagion in crowded audiences. In the provinces the actors usually staged their plays in churches (until around 1600) or in guild-halls. While surviving records show only a handful of occasions when actors played at inns while on tour, London inns were important playing places up until the 1590s.

The building of theaters in London had begun only shortly before Shakespeare wrote his first plays in the 1590s. These theaters were of two kinds: outdoor or public playhouses that could accommodate large numbers of playgoers, and indoor or private theaters for much smaller audiences. What is usually regarded as the first London outdoor public playhouse was called simply the Theatre. James Burbage—the father of Richard Burbage, who was perhaps the most famous actor in Shakespeare's company—built it in 1576 in an area north of the city of London called Shoreditch. Among the more famous of the other public playhouses that capitalized on the new fashion were the Curtain and the Fortune (both also built north of the city), the Rose, the Swan, the Globe, and the Hope (all located on the Bankside, a region just across the Thames south of the city of London). All these playhouses had to be built outside the jurisdiction of the city of London because many civic officials were hostile to the performance of drama and repeatedly petitioned the royal council to abolish it.

The theaters erected on the Bankside (a region under the authority of the Church of England, whose head was the monarch) shared the neighborhood with houses of prostitution and with the Paris Garden, where the blood sports of bearbaiting and bullbaiting were carried on. There may have been no clear distinction between playhouses and buildings for such sports, for the Hope was used for both plays and baiting, and Philip Henslowe, owner of the Rose and, later, partner in the ownership of the Fortune, was also a partner in a monopoly on baiting. All these forms of entertainment were easily accessible to Londoners by boat across the Thames or over London Bridge.

Evidently Shakespeare's company prospered on the Bankside. They moved there in 1599. Threatened by difficulties in renewing the lease on the land where their first playhouse (the Theatre) had been built, Shakespeare's company took advantage of the Christmas holiday in 1598 to dismantle the Theatre and transport its timbers across the Thames to the Bankside, where, in 1599, these timbers were used in the building of the Globe. The weather in late December 1598 is recorded as having been especially harsh. It was so cold that the Thames was "nigh [nearly] frozen," and there was heavy snow. Perhaps the weather aided Shakespeare's company in eluding their landlord, the snow hiding their activity and the freezing of the Thames allowing them to slide the timbers across to the Bankside without paying tolls for repeated trips over London Bridge. Attractive as this narrative is, it remains just as likely that the heavy snow hampered transport of the timbers in wagons through the London streets to the river. It also must be remembered that the Thames was, according to report, only "nigh frozen" and therefore as impassable as it ever was. Whatever the precise circumstances of this fascinating event in English theater history, Shakespeare's company was able to begin playing at their new Globe theater on the Bankside in 1599. After the first Globe burned down in 1613 during the staging of Shakespeare's *Henry VIII* (its thatch roof was set alight by cannon fire called for by the performance), Shakespeare's company immediately rebuilt on the same location. The second Globe seems to have been a grander structure than its predecessor. It remained in use until the beginning of the English Civil War in 1642, when Parliament officially closed the theaters. Soon thereafter it was pulled down.

The public theaters of Shakespeare's time were very different buildings from our theaters today. First of all, they were open-air playhouses. As recent exca-

A stage play.
From [William Alabaster,] *Roxana tragœdia* . . . (1632).

vations of the Rose and the Globe confirm, some were polygonal or roughly circular in shape; the Fortune, however, was square. The most recent estimates of their size put the diameter of these buildings at 72 feet (the Rose) to 100 feet (the Globe), but they were said to hold vast audiences of two or three thousand, who must have been squeezed together quite tightly. Some of these spectators paid extra to sit or stand in the two or three levels of roofed galleries that extended, on the upper levels, all the way around the theater and surrounded an open space. In this space were the stage and, perhaps, the tiring house (what we would call dressing rooms), as well as the so-called yard. In the yard stood the spectators who chose to pay less, the ones whom Hamlet contemptuously called "groundlings." For a roof they had only the sky, and so they were exposed to all kinds of weather. They stood on a floor that was sometimes made of mortar and sometimes of ash mixed with the shells of hazelnuts. The latter provided a porous and therefore dry footing for the crowd, and the shells may have been more comfortable to stand on because they were not as hard as mortar. Availability of shells may not have been a problem if hazelnuts were a favorite food for Shakespeare's audiences to munch on as they watched his plays. Archaeologists who are today unearthing the remains of theaters from this period have discovered quantities of these nutshells on theater sites.

Unlike the yard, the stage itself was covered by a roof. Its ceiling, called "the heavens," is thought to have been elaborately painted to depict the sun, moon, stars, and planets. Just how big the stage was remains hard to determine. We have a single sketch of part of the interior of the Swan. A Dutchman named Johannes de

Witt visited this theater around 1596 and sent a sketch of it back to his friend, Arend van Buchel. Because van Buchel found de Witt's letter and sketch of interest, he copied both into a book. It is van Buchel's copy, adapted, it seems, to the shape and size of the page in his book, that survives. In this sketch, the stage appears to be a large rectangular platform that thrusts far out into the yard, perhaps even as far as the center of the circle formed by the surrounding galleries. This drawing, combined with the specifications for the size of the stage in the building contract for the Fortune, has led scholars to conjecture that the stage on which Shakespeare's plays were performed must have measured approximately 43 feet in width and 27 feet in depth, a vast acting area. But the digging up of a large part of the Rose by archaeologists has provided evidence of a quite different stage design. The Rose stage was a platform tapered at the corners and much shallower than what seems to be depicted in the van Buchel sketch. Indeed, its measurements seem to be about 37.5 feet across at its widest point and only 15.5 feet deep. Because the surviving indications of stage size and design differ from each other so much, it is possible that the stages in other playhouses, like the Theatre, the Curtain, and the Globe (the outdoor playhouses where Shakespeare's plays were performed), were different from those at both the Swan and the Rose.

After about 1608 Shakespeare's plays were staged not only at the Globe but also at an indoor or private playhouse in Blackfriars. This theater had been constructed in 1596 by James Burbage in an upper hall of a former Dominican priory or monastic house. Although Henry VIII had dissolved all English monasteries in the 1530s (shortly after he had founded the Church of England), the area remained under church, rather than hostile civic, control. The hall that Burbage had purchased and renovated was a large one in which Parliament had once met. In the private theater that he constructed, the stage, lit by candles, was built across the narrow end of the hall, with boxes flanking it. The rest of the hall offered seating room only. Because there was no provision for standing room, the largest audience it could hold was less than a thousand, or about a quarter of what the Globe could accommodate. Admission to Blackfriars was correspondingly more expensive. Instead of a penny to stand in the yard at the Globe, it cost a minimum of sixpence to get into Blackfriars. The best seats at the Globe (in the Lords' Room in the gallery above and behind the stage) cost sixpence; but the boxes flanking the stage at Blackfriars were half a crown, or five times sixpence. Some spectators who were particularly interested in displaying themselves paid even more to sit on stools on the Blackfriars stage.

Whether in the outdoor or indoor playhouses, the stages of Shakespeare's time were different from ours. They were not separated from the audience by the dropping of a curtain between acts and scenes. Therefore the playwrights of the time had to find other ways of signaling to the audience that one scene (to be imagined as occurring in one location at a given time) had ended and the next (to be imagined at perhaps a different location at a later time) had begun. The customary way used by Shakespeare and many of his contemporaries was to have everyone onstage exit at the end of one scene and have one or more different characters enter to begin the next. In a few cases, where characters remain onstage from one scene to another, the dialogue or stage action makes the change of location clear, and the characters are generally to be imagined as having moved from one place to another. For example, in *Romeo and Juliet,* Romeo and his friends remain onstage in Act 1 from scene 4 to scene 5, but they are represented as having moved between scenes from the street that leads to Capulet's house into Capulet's house itself. The new location is signaled in part by the appearance onstage of Capulet's servingmen carrying napkins, something they would not take into the streets. Playwrights had to be quite resourceful in the use of hand properties, like the napkin, or in the use of dialogue to specify where the action was taking place in their plays because, in contrast to most of today's theaters, the playhouses of Shakespeare's time did not use movable scenery to dress the stage and make the setting precise. As another consequence of this difference, however, the playwrights of Shakespeare's time did not have to specify exactly where the action of their plays was set when they did not choose to do so, and much of the action of their plays is tied to no specific place.

Usually Shakespeare's stage is referred to as a "bare stage," to distinguish it from the stages of the last two or three centuries with their elaborate sets. But the stage in Shakespeare's time was not completely bare. Philip Henslowe, owner of the Rose, lists in his inventory of stage properties a rock, three tombs, and two mossy banks. Stage directions in plays of the time also call for such things as thrones (or "states"), banquets (presumably tables with plaster replicas of food on them), and beds and tombs to be pushed onto the stage. Thus the stage often held more than the actors.

The actors did not limit their performing to the stage alone. Occasionally they went beneath the stage, as the

Ghost appears to do in the first act of *Hamlet*. From there they could emerge onto the stage through a trapdoor. They could retire behind the hangings across the back of the stage (or the front of the tiring house), as, for example, the actor playing Polonius does when he hides behind the arras. Sometimes the hangings could be drawn back during a performance to "discover" one or more actors behind them. When performance required that an actor appear "above," as when Juliet is imagined to stand at the window of her chamber in the famous and misnamed "balcony scene," then the actor probably climbed the stairs to the gallery over the back of the stage and temporarily shared it with some of the spectators. The stage was also provided with ropes and winches so that actors could descend from, and reascend to, the "heavens."

Perhaps the greatest difference between dramatic performances in Shakespeare's time and ours was that in Shakespeare's England the roles of women were played by boys. (Some of these boys grew up to take male roles in their maturity.) There were no women in the acting companies, only in the audience. It had not always been so in the history of the English stage. There are records of women on English stages in the thirteenth and fourteenth centuries, two hundred years before Shakespeare's plays were performed. After the accession of James I in 1603, the queen of England and her ladies took part in entertainments at court called masques, and with the reopening of the theaters in 1660 at the restoration of Charles II, women again took their place on the public stage.

The chief competitors for the companies of adult actors such as the one to which Shakespeare belonged and for which he wrote were companies of exclusively boy actors. The competition was most intense in the early 1600s. There were then two principal children's companies: the Children of Paul's (the choirboys from St. Paul's Cathedral, whose private playhouse was near the cathedral); and the Children of the Chapel Royal (the choirboys from the monarch's private chapel, who performed at the Blackfriars theater built by Burbage in 1596, which Shakespeare's company had been stopped from using by local residents who objected to crowds). In *Hamlet* Shakespeare writes of "an aerie [nest] of children, little eyases [hawks], that cry out on the top of question and are most tyrannically clapped for 't. These are now the fashion and . . . berattle the common stages [attack the public theaters]." In the long run, the adult actors prevailed. The Children of Paul's dissolved around 1606. By about 1608 the Children of the Chapel Royal had been forced to stop playing at the Blackfriars theater, which was then taken over by the King's company of players, Shakespeare's own troupe.

Acting companies and theaters of Shakespeare's time were organized in different ways. For example, Philip Henslowe owned the Rose and leased it to companies of actors, who paid him from their takings. Henslowe would act as manager of these companies, initially paying playwrights for their plays and buying properties, recovering his outlay from the actors. With the building of the Globe, Shakespeare's company, however, managed itself, with the principal actors, Shakespeare among them, having the status of "sharers" and the right to a share in the takings, as well as the responsibility for a part of the expenses. Five of the sharers, including Shakespeare, owned the Globe. As actor, as sharer in an acting company and in ownership of theaters, and as playwright, Shakespeare was about as involved in the theatrical industry as one could imagine. Although Shakespeare and his fellows prospered, their status under the law was conditional upon the protection of powerful patrons. "Common players"—those who did not have patrons or masters—were classed in the language of the law with "vagabonds and sturdy beggars." So the actors had to secure for themselves the official rank of servants of patrons. Among the patrons under whose protection Shakespeare's company worked were the lord chamberlain and, after the accession of King James in 1603, the king himself.

We are now perhaps on the verge of learning a great deal more about the theaters in which Shakespeare and his contemporaries performed—or at least of opening up new questions about them. Already about 70 percent of the Rose has been excavated, as has about 10 percent of the second Globe, the one built in 1614. It is to be hoped that soon more will be available for study. These are exciting times for students of Shakespeare's stage.

The Publication of Shakespeare's Plays

Eighteen of Shakespeare's plays found their way into print during the playwright's lifetime, but there is nothing to suggest that he took any interest in their publication. These eighteen appeared separately in editions called quartos. Their pages were not much larger than the one you are now reading, and these little books were sold unbound for a few pence. The earliest of the quartos that still survive were printed in 1594, the year that both *Titus Andronicus* and a version of the play now called *2 King Henry VI* became available. While almost every one of these early quartos displays on its title page the name of the acting company that performed the play, only about half provide the name of the playwright, Shakespeare. The first quarto edition to bear the name Shakespeare on its title page is *Love's Labor's Lost* of 1598. A few of these quartos were popular with the book-buying public of Shakespeare's lifetime; for example, quarto *Richard II* went through five editions between 1597 and 1615. But most of the quartos were far from best-sellers; *Love's Labor's Lost* (1598), for instance, was not reprinted in quarto until 1631. After Shakespeare's death, two more of his plays appeared in quarto format: *Othello* in 1622 and *The Two Noble Kinsmen,* coauthored with John Fletcher, in 1634.

In 1623, seven years after Shakespeare's death, *Mr. William Shakespeares Comedies, Histories, & Tragedies* was published. This printing offered readers in a single book thirty-six of the thirty-eight plays now thought to have been written by Shakespeare, including eighteen that had never been printed before. And it offered them in a style that was then reserved for serious literature and scholarship. The plays were arranged in double columns on pages nearly a foot high. This large page size is called "folio," as opposed to the smaller "quarto," and the 1623 volume is usually called the Shakespeare First Folio. It is reputed to have sold for the lordly price of a pound. (One copy at the Folger Library is marked fifteen shillings—that is, three-quarters of a pound.)

In a preface to the First Folio entitled "To the great Variety of Readers," two of Shakespeare's former fellow actors in the King's Men, John Heminge and Henry Condell, wrote that they themselves had collected their dead companion's plays. They suggested that they had seen his own papers: "we have scarce received from him a blot in his papers." The title page of the Folio declared that the plays within it had been printed "according to the True Original Copies." Comparing the Folio to the quartos, Heminge and Condell disparaged the quartos, advising their readers that "before you were abused with divers stolen and surreptitious copies, maimed, and deformed by the frauds and stealths of injurious impostors." Many Shakespeareans of the eighteenth and nineteenth centuries believed Heminge and Condell and regarded the Folio plays as superior to anything in the quartos.

Once we begin to examine the Folio plays in detail, it becomes less easy to take at face value the word of Heminge and Condell about the superiority of the Folio texts. For example, of the first nine plays in the Folio (one-quarter of the entire collection), four were essentially reprinted from earlier quarto printings that Heminge and Condell had disparaged; and four have now been identified as printed from copies written in the hand of a professional scribe of the 1620s named Ralph Crane; the ninth, *The Comedy of Errors,* was apparently also printed from a manuscript, but one whose origin cannot be readily identified. Evidently then, eight of the first nine plays in the First Folio were not printed, in spite of what the Folio title page announces, "according to the True Original Copies," or Shakespeare's own papers, and the source of the ninth is unknown. Since today's editors have been forced to treat Heminge and Condell's pronouncements with skepticism, they must choose whether to base their own editions upon quartos or the Folio on grounds other than Heminge and Condell's story of where the quarto and Folio versions originated.

Editors have often fashioned their own narratives to explain what lies behind the quartos and Folio. They have said that Heminge and Condell meant to criticize only a few of the early quartos, the ones that offer much shorter and sometimes quite different, often garbled, versions of plays. Among the examples of these are the 1600 quarto of *Henry V* (the Folio offers a much fuller version) or the 1603 *Hamlet* quarto (in 1604 a different, much longer form of the play got into print as a quarto). Early-twentieth-century editors speculated that these questionable texts were produced when someone in the audience took notes from the plays' dialogue during performances and then employed "hack poets" to fill out the notes. The poor results were then sold to a publisher and presented in print as Shakespeare's plays. More recently this story has given way to another in which the shorter versions are said to be re-creations from memory of Shakespeare's plays by actors who wanted to stage them in the provinces but lacked manuscript copies. Most of the quartos offer much better texts than these so-called bad quartos. Indeed, in most of the quartos we find texts that are at least equal to or better than what is printed in the Folio. Many Shakespeare enthusiasts persuaded themselves that most of the quartos were set into type directly from Shakespeare's own papers, although there is nothing on which to base this conclusion except the desire for it to be true. Thus speculation continues about how the Shakespeare plays got to be printed. All that we have are the printed texts.

The book collector who was most successful in bringing together copies of the quartos and the First Folio was Henry Clay Folger, founder of the Folger Shakespeare Library in Washington, D.C. While it is estimated that there survive around the world only about 230 copies of the First Folio, Mr. Folger was able to acquire more than seventy-five copies, as well as a large number of fragments, for the library that bears his name. He also amassed a substantial number of quartos. For example, only fourteen copies of the First Quarto of *Love's Labor's Lost* are known to exist, and three are at the Folger Shakespeare Library. As a consequence of Mr. Folger's labors, scholars visiting the Folger Library have been able to learn a great deal about sixteenth- and seventeenth-century printing and, particularly, about the printing of Shakespeare's plays. And Mr. Folger did not stop at the First Folio, but collected many copies of later editions of Shakespeare, beginning with the Second Folio (1632), the Third (1663–64), and the Fourth (1685). Each of these later folios was based on its immediate predecessor and was edited anonymously. The first editor of Shakespeare whose name we know was Nicholas Rowe, whose first edition came out in 1709. Mr. Folger collected this edition and many, many more by Rowe's successors.

An Introduction to This Text

Cymbeline was first printed in the 1623 collection of Shakespeare's plays now known as the First Folio. The present edition is based directly upon that printing.*

---

*We have also consulted the computerized text of the First Folio provided by the Text Archive of the Oxford University Computing Centre, to which we are grateful.

For the convenience of the reader, we have modernized the punctuation and the spelling of the Folio. Sometimes we go so far as to modernize certain old forms of words; for example, usually when *a* means *he,* we change it to *he;* we change *mo* to *more,* and *ye* to *you.* But it is not our practice in editing any of the plays to modernize words that sound distinctly different from modern forms. For example, when the early printed texts read *sith* or *apricocks* or *porpentine,* we have not modernized to *since, apricots, porcupine.* When the forms *an, and,* or *and if* appear instead of the modern form *if,* we have reduced *and* to *an* but have not changed any of these forms to their modern equivalent, *if.* We also modernize and, where necessary, correct passages in foreign languages, unless an error in the early printed text can be reasonably explained as a joke.

Whenever we change the wording of the First Folio or add anything to its stage directions, we mark the change by enclosing it in superior half-brackets (⌜ ⌝). We want our readers to be immediately aware when we have intervened. (Only when we correct an obvious typographical error in the First Folio does the change not get marked.) Whenever we change either the First Folio's wording or its punctuation so that meaning changes, we list the change in the textual notes at the back of the book, even if all we have done is fix an obvious error.

We regularize spellings of a number of the proper names in the dialogue and stage directions, as is the usual practice in editions of the play. For example, the First Folio occasionally uses the forms "Clotten" and "Cymbaline," but our edition uses only the more usual Folio spellings "Cloten" and "Cymbeline."

This edition differs from many earlier ones in its efforts to aid the reader in imagining the play as a performance rather than as a series of actual events. Thus stage directions and speech prefixes are written with reference to the stage. For example, when one goes to a modern production of *Cymbeline,* one is always aware, after the actor playing Imogen has donned her disguise, that she no longer looks like the princess that she had first impersonated. Instead the actor playing Imogen looks like a boy, and is given the name "Fidele." In an effort to reproduce in our edition what an audience experiences, we have added her disguise name to the speech prefix, so that whenever she speaks as the boy Fidele, we give her the speech prefix "IMOGEN, ⌜*as* FIDELE⌝." With the addition of such a direction to the speech prefix, we hope to help our readers stage the play in their own imaginations in a way that more closely approximates an experience in the theater.

Whenever it is reasonably certain, in our view, that a speech is accompanied by a particular action, we provide a stage direction describing the action, setting the added direction in brackets to signal that it is not found in the Folio. (Occasional exceptions to this rule occur when the action is so obvious that to add a stage direction would insult the reader.) Stage directions for the entrance of a character in mid-scene are, with rare exceptions, placed so that they immediately precede the character's participation in the scene, even though these entrances may appear somewhat earlier in the early printed texts. Whenever we move a stage direction, we record this change in the textual notes. Latin stage directions (e.g., *Exeunt*) are translated into English (e.g., *They exit*).

We expand the often severely abbreviated forms of names used as speech headings in early printed texts into the full names of the characters. We also regularize the speakers' names in speech headings, using only a single designation for each character, even though the early printed texts sometimes use a variety of designations. Variations in the speech headings of the early printed texts are recorded in the textual notes.

In the present edition, as well, we mark with a dash any change of address within a speech, unless a stage direction intervenes. When the -ed ending of a word is to be pronounced, we mark it with an accent. Like editors for the past two centuries, we print metrically linked lines in the following way:

IMOGEN
When shall we see again?
POSTHUMUS Alack, the King.
(1.1.146–47)

However, when there are a number of short verse-lines that can be linked in more than one way, we do not, with rare exceptions, indent any of them.

The Explanatory Notes

The notes that appear on the pages facing the text are designed to provide readers with the help that they may need to enjoy the play. Whenever the meaning of a word in the text is not readily accessible in a good contemporary dictionary, we offer the meaning in a note. Sometimes we provide a note even when the relevant meaning is to be found in the dictionary but when the word has acquired since Shakespeare's time other potentially confusing meanings. In our notes, we try to offer modern synonyms for Shakespeare's words. We also try to indicate to the reader the connection between the word in the play and the modern synonym. For example, Shakespeare sometimes uses the word *head* to mean *source,* but, for modern readers, there may be no connection evident between these two words. We provide the connection by explaining Shakespeare's usage as follows: "**head:** fountainhead, source." On some occasions, a whole phrase or clause needs explanation. Then we rephrase in our own words the difficult passage, and add at the end synonyms for individual words in the passage. When scholars have been unable to determine the meaning of a word or phrase, we acknowledge the uncertainty.

mind. For example, Shakespeare sometimes uses the word *head* to mean *source*, but, for modern readers, there may be no connection evident between these two words. We provide the connection by explaining Shakespeare's usage as follows: "head: fountainhead, source." On some occasions, a whole phrase or clause needs explanation. Then we rephrase in our own words the difficult passage, and add at the end synonyms for individual words in the passage. When scholars have been unable to determine the meaning of a word or phrase, we acknowledge the uncertainty.

CYMBELINE

Characters in the Play

CYMBELINE, King of Britain
Cymbeline's QUEEN
IMOGEN, daughter to Cymbeline by his former queen
POSTHUMUS LEONATUS, husband to Imogen
CLOTEN, son to the present queen by a former husband

PISANIO, Posthumus's servant
CORNELIUS, a physician in Cymbeline's court

PHILARIO, Posthumus's host in Rome
IACHIMO, friend to Philario
A FRENCHMAN, friend to Philario

CAIUS LUCIUS, a Roman general

BELARIUS, an exiled nobleman
GUIDERIUS }
ARVIRAGUS } sons to Cymbeline by his former queen

Two LORDS attending Cloten
Two GENTLEMEN of Cymbeline's court
A LADY, Imogen's attendant
A LADY, the Queen's attendant
A Briton LORD
Two Briton CAPTAINS
Two JAILERS
Two MESSENGERS

Two Roman SENATORS
TRIBUNES
Roman CAPTAINS
A SOOTHSAYER

JUPITER
The Ghost of SICILIUS LEONATUS, Posthumus's father
The Ghost of Posthumus's MOTHER
The Ghosts of Posthumus's two BROTHERS

Lords, Ladies, Attendants, Musicians, a Dutchman, a Spaniard, Senators, Tribunes, Captains, and Soldiers

CYMBELINE

ACT 1

1.1 At the court of King Cymbeline, the princess, Imogen, has secretly married a gentleman named Posthumus Leonatus. Imogen is the king's only heir, since his two sons were stolen long ago, and the king had intended her to marry Cloten, the son of his present queen. The furious Cymbeline banishes Posthumus and, in effect, imprisons Imogen.

---

1. **but frowns:** i.e., who does not frown

1–3. **Our . . . King's:** i.e., just as human emotions (**our bloods**) are influenced by the planets (**the heavens**), so **our courtiers'** faces are governed by **the King's** **Still:** always

5. **of 's:** i.e., of his

6. **purposed to:** i.e., intended for

7. **late:** recently; **referred:** given

15. **to the bent:** i.e., according to the inclination

King Cymbeline.
From John Taylor, *All the workes of . . .* (1630).

ACT 1

Scene 1

Enter two Gentlemen.

FIRST GENTLEMAN
You do not meet a man but frowns. Our bloods
No more obey the heavens than our courtiers'
Still seem as does the King's.

SECOND GENTLEMAN But what's the matter?

FIRST GENTLEMAN
His daughter, and the heir of 's kingdom, whom 5
He purposed to his wife's sole son—a widow
That late he married—hath referred herself
Unto a poor but worthy gentleman. She's wedded,
Her husband banished, she imprisoned. All
Is outward sorrow, though I think the King 10
Be touched at very heart.

SECOND GENTLEMAN None but the King?

FIRST GENTLEMAN
He that hath lost her, too. So is the Queen,
That most desired the match. But not a courtier,
Although they wear their faces to the bent 15
Of the King's looks, hath a heart that is not
Glad at the thing they scowl at.

SECOND GENTLEMAN And why so?

FIRST GENTLEMAN
He that hath missed the Princess is a thing
Too bad for bad report, and he that hath her— 20

24. **his like:** i.e., who is his equal

25. **him that should compare:** i.e., any man who was compared (with the princess's husband)

28. **speak him far:** i.e., go **far** in praising **him**

29. **I do . . . himself:** i.e., he is himself larger than my representation of him

35, 36. **Cassibelan, Tenantius:** earlier British kings (See Historical Background, pages 285–86, and picture, page 10.)

38. **sur-addition:** i.e., additional name, surname; **Leonatus:** i.e., lion-born (Latin)

43. **fond of issue:** i.e., doting on his children

44. **gentle:** noble

45. **Big of:** i.e., pregnant with

46. **King he:** i.e., **King**

47. **Posthumus:** pronounced with the accent on the second syllable, as in general throughout the play

48. **Breeds:** educates; **of his bedchamber:** i.e., one of his "gentlemen of the **bedchamber,**" a sign of royal favor

49. **his time:** perhaps, **his** age, **his time** of life

54. **A sample:** i.e., an example

I mean, that married her, alack, good man!
And therefore banished—is a creature such
As, to seek through the regions of the earth
For one his like, there would be something failing
In him that should compare. I do not think 25
So fair an outward and such stuff within
Endows a man but he.

SECOND GENTLEMAN You speak him far.

FIRST GENTLEMAN
I do extend him, sir, within himself,
Crush him together rather than unfold 30
His measure duly.

SECOND GENTLEMAN What's his name and birth?

FIRST GENTLEMAN
I cannot delve him to the root. His father
Was called Sicilius, who did join his honor
Against the Romans with Cassibelan, 35
But had his titles by Tenantius, whom
He served with glory and admired success,
So gained the sur-addition Leonatus;
And had, besides this gentleman in question,
Two other sons, who in the wars o' th' time 40
Died with their swords in hand. For which their
father,
Then old and fond of issue, took such sorrow
That he quit being; and his gentle lady,
Big of this gentleman our theme, deceased 45
As he was born. The King he takes the babe
To his protection, calls him Posthumus Leonatus,
Breeds him and makes him of his bedchamber,
Puts to him all the learnings that his time
Could make him the receiver of, which he took 50
As we do air, fast as 'twas ministered,
And in 's spring became a harvest; lived in court—
Which rare it is to do—most praised, most loved,
A sample to the youngest, to th' more mature

55. **glass:** looking glass, mirror; **feated them:** perhaps, reflected them elegantly; or, perhaps, compelled them to live properly

57. **her own price:** perhaps, the **price** she was willing to pay; or, perhaps, **her own** worth or excellence

59. **election:** choice (of him)

62. **out of:** from; on account of

66. **Mark:** pay attention to

67. **I' th' swathing clothes:** i.e., a mere infant (literally, in swaddling clothes)

68. **guess in knowledge:** perhaps, credible **guess**

72. **conveyed:** stolen

75. **Howsoe'er 'tis strange:** i.e., however **strange** it seems

Cassibelan. (1.1.35; 3.1.5, 33, 44)
From John Taylor, *All the workes of . . .* (1630).

A glass that feated them, and to the graver 55
A child that guided dotards. To his mistress,
For whom he now is banished, her own price
Proclaims how she esteemed him; and his virtue
By her election may be truly read
What kind of man he is. 60

SECOND GENTLEMAN I honor him
Even out of your report. But pray you tell me,
Is she sole child to th' King?

FIRST GENTLEMAN His only child.
He had two sons—if this be worth your hearing, 65
Mark it—the eldest of them at three years old,
I' th' swathing clothes the other, from their nursery
Were stol'n, and to this hour no guess in knowledge
Which way they went.

SECOND GENTLEMAN How long is this ago? 70

FIRST GENTLEMAN Some twenty years.

SECOND GENTLEMAN
That a king's children should be so conveyed,
So slackly guarded, and the search so slow
That could not trace them!

FIRST GENTLEMAN Howsoe'er 'tis strange, 75
Or that the negligence may well be laughed at,
Yet is it true, sir.

SECOND GENTLEMAN I do well believe you.

FIRST GENTLEMAN
We must forbear. Here comes the gentleman,
The Queen and Princess. 80

They exit.

Enter the Queen, Posthumus, and Imogen.

QUEEN
No, be assured you shall not find me, daughter,
After the slander of most stepmothers,
Evil-eyed unto you. You're my prisoner, but
Your jailer shall deliver you the keys

85. **your restraint:** i.e., that which restrains you; **For:** i.e., as for; **Posthumus:** See note to line 47.

86. **win:** prevail upon

87. **Marry:** a mild oath (originally an oath derived from "By the Virgin Mary")

89. **leaned unto his sentence:** i.e., obeyed his command (literally, deferred to his opinion)

91. **Please:** i.e., if it **please** (a deferential phrase of request)

94. **fetch a turn:** i.e., walk back and forth, stroll

98. **fine:** subtly, delicately

100. **something:** somewhat, to some extent

101. **reserved my holy duty:** i.e., excepting the respect or deference I owe him (which is **holy** because of the biblical commandment to "honor thy father")

108. **give cause:** i.e., by weeping myself

111. **plight troth:** i.e., pledge his faith, engage himself to marry

116. **gall:** wordplay on **gall** as (1) bile, an intensely bitter substance; (2) oak-galls, used in making **ink**

That lock up your restraint.—For you, Posthumus, 85
So soon as I can win th' offended king,
I will be known your advocate. Marry, yet
The fire of rage is in him, and 'twere good
You leaned unto his sentence with what patience
Your wisdom may inform you. 90

POSTHUMUS Please your Highness,
I will from hence today.

QUEEN You know the peril.
I'll fetch a turn about the garden, pitying
The pangs of barred affections, though the King 95
Hath charged you should not speak together. *She exits.*

IMOGEN O,
Dissembling courtesy! How fine this tyrant
Can tickle where she wounds! My dearest husband,
I something fear my father's wrath, but nothing— 100
Always reserved my holy duty—what
His rage can do on me. You must be gone,
And I shall here abide the hourly shot
Of angry eyes, not comforted to live
But that there is this jewel in the world 105
That I may see again. ⌜*She weeps.*⌝

POSTHUMUS My queen, my mistress!
O lady, weep no more, lest I give cause
To be suspected of more tenderness
Than doth become a man. I will remain 110
The loyal'st husband that did e'er plight troth.
My residence in Rome at one Philario's,
Who to my father was a friend, to me
Known but by letter; thither write, my queen,
And with mine eyes I'll drink the words you send, 115
Though ink be made of gall.

Enter Queen.

QUEEN Be brief, I pray you.
If the King come, I shall incur I know not

119. **move:** prompt

121–22. **I never do him wrong / But:** i.e., whenever **I wrong him**

122. **injuries:** i.e., **offenses** (line 123)

126. **loathness:** reluctance

128. **but:** merely; **air yourself:** i.e., have some fresh air

131. **heart:** a term of endearment

132. **But:** only

134. **How:** i.e., what

136. **cere up:** i.e., seal (literally, wrap in a cerecloth, a waxed winding-sheet for a corpse) See below. **embracements:** i.e., embraces

138. **Remain . . . thou:** spoken to the ring

139. **sense:** ability to perceive or feel

142. **still win of:** i.e., continue to come out ahead (literally, always get the better of)

148. **avoid:** depart

149. **fraught:** i.e., burden (literally, load a ship with cargo)

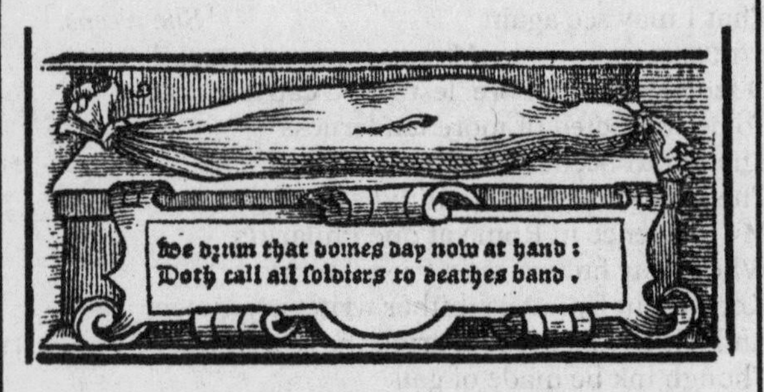

The drum that domes day now at hand :
Doth call all ſoldiers to deathes band .

A figure cered up for burial. (1.1.136)
From [Richard Day], *A booke of christian prayers . . .* (1578).

How much of his displeasure. (⌜*Aside.*⌝) Yet I'll move
him 120
To walk this way. I never do him wrong
But he does buy my injuries, to be friends,
Pays dear for my offenses. ⌜*She exits.*⌝

POSTHUMUS Should we be taking leave
As long a term as yet we have to live, 125
The loathness to depart would grow. Adieu.

IMOGEN Nay, stay a little!
Were you but riding forth to air yourself,
Such parting were too petty. Look here, love:
This diamond was my mother's. (⌜*She offers a* 130
ring.⌝) Take it, heart,
But keep it till you woo another wife
When Imogen is dead.

POSTHUMUS How, how? Another?
You gentle gods, give me but this I have, 135
And cere up my embracements from a next
With bonds of death. (⌜*He puts the ring on his finger.*⌝)
Remain, remain thou here,
While sense can keep it on.—And sweetest, fairest,
As I my poor self did exchange for you 140
To your so infinite loss, so in our trifles
I still win of you. For my sake, wear this.
⌜*He offers a bracelet.*⌝
It is a manacle of love. I'll place it
Upon this fairest prisoner. ⌜*He puts it on her wrist.*⌝

IMOGEN O the gods! 145
When shall we see again?

Enter Cymbeline and Lords.

POSTHUMUS Alack, the King.

CYMBELINE
Thou basest thing, avoid hence, from my sight!
If after this command thou fraught the court
With thy unworthiness, thou diest. Away! 150
Thou 'rt poison to my blood.

153. **the good remainders of:** i.e., those **good** people remaining at

155. **pinch:** torment

158. **repair:** restore

162. **senseless of:** insensible to; **touch:** feeling (In *Two Gentlemen of Verona,* Julia speaks of "the inly [i.e., inward, heartfelt] **touch** of love" [2.7.18].)

164. **grace:** Cymbeline uses the term to mean "sense of duty or propriety." Imogen's response shifts the meaning to "mercy" or "forgiveness," from which persistence in the sin of **despair** would bar her.

168. **puttock:** bird of prey (e.g., a kite or buzzard) See below.

176. **bred:** brought him up

177–78. **overbuys . . . pays:** i.e., what **he pays** for me (namely, himself) exceeds my worth by **almost the** entire **sum** he spends **overbuys:** buys at too high a price, pays too much for

181. **neatherd's:** cowherd's

A puttock. (1.1.168)
From Konrad Gesner, . . . *Historiae animalium* . . . (1585–1604).

POSTHUMUS The gods protect you,
And bless the good remainders of the court.
I am gone. *He exits.*

IMOGEN There cannot be a pinch in death 155
More sharp than this is.

CYMBELINE O disloyal thing
That shouldst repair my youth, thou heap'st
A year's age on me.

IMOGEN I beseech you, sir, 160
Harm not yourself with your vexation.
I am senseless of your wrath. A touch more rare
Subdues all pangs, all fears.

CYMBELINE Past grace? Obedience?

IMOGEN
Past hope and in despair; that way past grace. 165

CYMBELINE
That mightst have had the sole son of my queen!

IMOGEN
O, blessèd that I might not! I chose an eagle
And did avoid a puttock.

CYMBELINE
Thou took'st a beggar, wouldst have made my throne
A seat for baseness. 170

IMOGEN No, I rather added
A luster to it.

CYMBELINE O thou vile one!

IMOGEN Sir,
It is your fault that I have loved Posthumus. 175
You bred him as my playfellow, and he is
A man worth any woman, overbuys me
Almost the sum he pays.

CYMBELINE What, art thou mad?

IMOGEN
Almost, sir. Heaven restore me! Would I were 180
A neatherd's daughter, and my Leonatus
Our neighbor shepherd's son. ⌜*She weeps.*⌝

187. **Beseech:** i.e., I **beseech,** I urge

191. **advice:** perhaps, consideration; or, perhaps, counsel

192–93. **languish . . . blood:** Sighs were reputed to consume the heart's **blood.**

195. **Fie, you must give way:** It is unclear to whom the Queen addresses this rebuke. (See longer note, page 265.)

207. **Afric:** literally, Africa, but probably meaning any allegedly deserted place (In several plays, Shakespeare has characters wish they could confront an enemy in a wilderness or "desert.")

208. **by:** close at hand

210. **suffer:** allow

A shepherd. (1.1.182)
From *Hortus sanitatis* . . . (1536).

CYMBELINE Thou foolish thing!

Enter Queen.

They were again together. You have done
Not after our command. Away with her 185
And pen her up.

QUEEN Beseech your patience.—Peace,
Dear lady daughter, peace.—Sweet sovereign,
Leave us to ourselves, and make yourself some
comfort 190
Out of your best advice.

CYMBELINE Nay, let her languish
A drop of blood a day, and being aged
Die of this folly. *He exits,* ⌜*with Lords.*⌝

QUEEN Fie, you must give way. 195

Enter Pisanio.

Here is your servant.—How now, sir? What news?

PISANIO
My lord your son drew on my master.

QUEEN Ha?
No harm, I trust, is done?

PISANIO There might have been, 200
But that my master rather played than fought
And had no help of anger. They were parted
By gentlemen at hand.

QUEEN I am very glad on 't.

IMOGEN
Your son's my father's friend; he takes his part 205
To draw upon an exile. O, brave sir!
I would they were in Afric both together,
Myself by with a needle, that I might prick
The goer-back.—Why came you from your master?

PISANIO
On his command. He would not suffer me 210
To bring him to the haven, left these notes

215. **lay:** wager

1.2 An encounter between Cloten and Posthumus, reported in 1.1, is here discussed by Cloten and two lords.

---

1. **shift a:** i.e., change your
2. **action:** fighting; **as:** i.e., **as** if you were

3–4. **Where . . . vent:** i.e., whatever the state of the **air** that **comes out** (from Cloten), the **air abroad** that **comes in** is even less **wholesome** (the first of the First Lord's flatteries)

5. **to shift:** i.e., I'd change

7. **faith:** a mild oath

8. **patience:** forbearance

9. **passable:** wordplay on (1) tolerable or fairly good; (2) easily pierced by a rapier (See picture, page 138.)

10. **thoroughfare:** (1) a public highway; (2) a town through which traffic passes

12–13. **His steel . . . town:** Cloten's sword, which has missed Posthumus, was like a debtor who, to avoid his creditors, skirts the town by traveling through its backyards (**backside**).

14. **stand:** oppose, resist, face

15. **still:** always

Of what commands I should be subject to
When 't pleased you to employ me.

QUEEN, ⌜*to Imogen*⌝ This hath been
Your faithful servant. I dare lay mine honor 215
He will remain so.

PISANIO I humbly thank your Highness.

QUEEN, ⌜*to Imogen*⌝
Pray, walk awhile.

IMOGEN, ⌜*to Pisanio*⌝ About some half hour hence,
Pray you, speak with me. You shall at least 220
Go see my lord aboard. For this time leave me.

They exit.

Scene ⌜2⌝

Enter Cloten and two Lords.

FIRST LORD Sir, I would advise you to shift a shirt. The violence of action hath made you reek as a sacrifice. Where air comes out, air comes in. There's none abroad so wholesome as that you vent.

CLOTEN If my shirt were bloody, then to shift it. Have I 5 hurt him?

SECOND LORD, ⌜*aside*⌝ No, faith, not so much as his patience.

FIRST LORD Hurt him? His body's a passable carcass if he be not hurt. It is a thoroughfare for steel if it be 10 not hurt.

SECOND LORD, ⌜*aside*⌝ His steel was in debt; it went o' th' backside the town.

CLOTEN The villain would not stand me.

SECOND LORD, ⌜*aside*⌝ No, but he fled forward still, 15 toward your face.

FIRST LORD Stand you? You have land enough of your own, but he added to your having, gave you some ground.

20. **inches:** possible wordplay on the word's secondary sense of "small islands"

22. **would:** wish

27–28. **true election:** truly judicious selection (with possible wordplay on **election** as the exercise of God's will in choosing some in preference to others)

30. **sign:** show; mere semblance

31. **reflection:** i.e., indication (with wordplay in line 33 on **reflection** as the throwing back of light rays); **wit:** intelligence

39. **attend:** wait on

1.3 Posthumus's servant, Pisanio, describes to the grieving Imogen the departure of Posthumus toward Rome.

---

1. **would thou grew'st unto:** i.e., wish you were attached to; **haven:** harbor

4. **mercy:** perhaps, a royal or a divine pardon (The sense of the sentence is that failure to receive a letter from Posthumus would be like failing to receive some such pardon.)

SECOND LORD, ⌜*aside*⌝ As many inches as you have oceans. Puppies! 20

CLOTEN I would they had not come between us.

SECOND LORD, ⌜*aside*⌝ So would I, till you had measured how long a fool you were upon the ground.

CLOTEN And that she should love this fellow and refuse me! 25

SECOND LORD, ⌜*aside*⌝ If it be a sin to make a true election, she is damned.

FIRST LORD Sir, as I told you always, her beauty and her brain go not together. She's a good sign, but I have seen small reflection of her wit. 30

SECOND LORD, ⌜*aside*⌝ She shines not upon fools, lest the reflection should hurt her.

CLOTEN Come, I'll to my chamber. Would there had been some hurt done! 35

SECOND LORD, ⌜*aside*⌝ I wish not so, unless it had been the fall of an ass, which is no great hurt.

CLOTEN You'll go with us?

FIRST LORD I'll attend your Lordship.

CLOTEN Nay, come, let's go together. 40

SECOND LORD Well, my lord.

They exit.

Scene ⌜3⌝

Enter Imogen and Pisanio.

IMOGEN

I would thou grew'st unto the shores o' th' haven
And questionedst every sail. If he should write
And I not have it, 'twere a paper lost
As offered mercy is. What was the last
That he spake to thee? 5

PISANIO It was his queen, his queen!

9. **Senseless:** insensate

13. **keep:** remain on

15. **Still:** constantly; **stirs:** disturbances

19. **ere left:** before ceasing

20. **after-eye him:** follow him with your eyes, look after him

22. **eyestrings:** the supposed "strings" of the eye, the breaking or cracking of which was thought to end one's ability to see

23. **but:** merely

24–25. **diminution / Of space:** perhaps, the apparent reduction in size caused by increasing distance

25. **pointed him:** fashioned him to a point

31. **vantage:** chance, opportunity

32. **take my leave of:** i.e., (properly) bid farewell to

The white lily. (2.2.18; 4.2.257)
From John Gerard, *The herball* . . . (1597).

IMOGEN
Then waved his handkerchief?
PISANIO And kissed it, madam.
IMOGEN
Senseless linen, happier therein than I.
And that was all? 10
PISANIO No, madam. For so long
As he could make me with ⌜this⌝ eye or ear
Distinguish him from others, he did keep
The deck, with glove or hat or handkerchief
Still waving, as the fits and stirs of 's mind 15
Could best express how slow his soul sailed on,
How swift his ship.
IMOGEN Thou shouldst have made him
As little as a crow, or less, ere left
To after-eye him. 20
PISANIO Madam, so I did.
IMOGEN
I would have broke mine eyestrings, cracked them, but
To look upon him till the diminution
Of space had pointed him sharp as my needle; 25
Nay, followed him till he had melted from
The smallness of a gnat to air; and then
Have turned mine eye and wept. But, good Pisanio,
When shall we hear from him?
PISANIO Be assured, madam, 30
With his next vantage.
IMOGEN
I did not take my leave of him, but had
Most pretty things to say. Ere I could tell him
How I would think on him at certain hours
Such thoughts and such; or I could make him swear 35
The shes of Italy should not betray
Mine interest and his honor; or have charged him
At the sixth hour of morn, at noon, at midnight

39. **encounter:** go to meet

40. **for him:** i.e., on his behalf

43. **breathing of the north:** i.e., north wind

48. **attend the Queen:** i.e., obey the Queen's summons

1.4 Posthumus arrives in Rome, where an Italian gentleman, Iachimo, maneuvers him into placing a bet on Imogen's chastity. Posthumus bets the diamond ring given him by Imogen that Iachimo cannot seduce her.

---

2. **crescent:** increasing, waxing (like the moon); **note:** distinction, reputation

3. **allowed:** accorded, given

5. **admiration:** wonder, astonishment

6. **tabled:** listed

12–13. **could behold . . . he:** i.e., were as good **as he** (The allusion is to an eagle's ability to look at **the sun** with **eyes** that do not blink, one of the attributes that led the eagle to be considered the king of birds.)

15. **value:** worth in respect of rank or personal qualities

T' encounter me with orisons, for then
I am in heaven for him; or ere I could 40
Give him that parting kiss which I had set
Betwixt two charming words, comes in my father,
And like the tyrannous breathing of the north
Shakes all our buds from growing.

Enter a Lady.

LADY The Queen, madam, 45
Desires your Highness' company.

IMOGEN, ⌜*to Pisanio*⌝
Those things I bid you do, get them dispatched.
I will attend the Queen.

PISANIO Madam, I shall.

They exit.

Scene ⌜4⌝

Enter Philario, Iachimo, a Frenchman, a Dutchman, and a Spaniard.

IACHIMO Believe it, sir, I have seen him in Britain. He was then of a crescent note, expected to prove so worthy as since he hath been allowed the name of. But I could then have looked on him without the help of admiration, though the catalogue of his 5 endowments had been tabled by his side and I to peruse him by items.

PHILARIO You speak of him when he was less furnished than now he is with that which makes him both without and within. 10

FRENCHMAN I have seen him in France. We had very many there could behold the sun with as firm eyes as he.

IACHIMO This matter of marrying his king's daughter, wherein he must be weighed rather by her value 15

16–17. **words him . . . matter:** i.e., gives him a reputation far from the truth **words:** represents (as in **words**)

20. **divorce:** (forced) separation; **under her colors:** i.e., in her camp (**Colors** refers literally to the flag or ensign of a regiment or a ship, military imagery that continues in **fortify** [line 21] and **battery,** an artillery attack on a fortress or walled city [line 22].) The subject of **are** is "**banishment . . . and . . . approbation**" (lines 18, 19).

23. **without less quality:** a much-debated phrase that seems to mean "with even **less quality** than **a beggar**"

29. **entertained:** treated

30–31. **knowing:** i.e., discernment

31. **quality:** rank

35. **story him:** relate his history

36–37. **together:** each other

44–45. **importance . . . nature:** an affair of such **slight** consequence

47. **go even:** agree (It has been suggested that lines 47–49 should be interpreted as meaning "rather than appear to be **guided by others' experiences,** I avoided giving assent to **what I heard.**")

than his own, words him, I doubt not, a great deal from the matter.

FRENCHMAN And then his banishment.

IACHIMO Ay, and the approbation of those that weep this lamentable divorce under her colors are wonderfully to extend him, be it but to fortify her judgment, which else an easy battery might lay flat for taking a beggar without less quality.—But how comes it he is to sojourn with you? How creeps acquaintance? 20 25

PHILARIO His father and I were soldiers together, to whom I have been often bound for no less than my life.

Enter Posthumus.

Here comes the Briton. Let him be so entertained amongst you as suits, with gentlemen of your knowing, to a stranger of his quality.—I beseech you all, be better known to this gentleman, whom I commend to you as a noble friend of mine. How worthy he is I will leave to appear hereafter rather than story him in his own hearing. 30 35

FRENCHMAN, ⌜*to Posthumus*⌝ Sir, we have known together in Orleans.

POSTHUMUS Since when I have been debtor to you for courtesies which I will be ever to pay and yet pay still. 40

FRENCHMAN Sir, you o'errate my poor kindness. I was glad I did atone my countryman and you. It had been pity you should have been put together with so mortal a purpose as then each bore, upon importance of so slight and trivial a nature. 45

POSTHUMUS By your pardon, sir, I was then a young traveler, rather shunned to go even with what I heard than in my every action to be guided by others' experiences. But upon my mended judg-

54. **confounded:** killed

56–57. **difference:** disagreement; dispute

59–60. **suffer the report:** i.e., bear the telling

60. **fell out:** occurred, arose

61. **fell . . . of:** i.e., began to praise

61–62. **our country mistresses:** i.e., the women we love from our own nations

63. **vouching:** declaring

63–64. **upon . . . affirmation:** i.e., pledging that he would affirm it with bloodshed

64. **fair:** beautiful

65. **qualified:** accomplished, perfect; **attemptable:** open to seduction or temptation

68. **by this:** i.e., by now

73. **abate her nothing:** i.e., in no way lessen my estimation of her

74. **friend:** lover

75–76. **hand-in-hand comparison:** i.e., **comparison** that claimed equality, not superiority **hand-in-hand:** well-matched, side-by-side

76. **something:** somewhat

77. **went before:** were superior to

78. **that diamond:** i.e., the ring given Posthumus by Imogen

78–79. **outlusters:** outshines, surpasses in luster

ment—if I offend ⌜not⌝ to say it is mended—my quarrel was not altogether slight. 50

FRENCHMAN Faith, yes, to be put to the arbitrament of swords, and by such two that would by all likelihood have confounded one the other or have fall'n both. 55

IACHIMO Can we with manners ask what was the difference?

FRENCHMAN Safely, I think. 'Twas a contention in public, which may without contradiction suffer the report. It was much like an argument that fell out 60 last night, where each of us fell in praise of our country mistresses, this gentleman at that time vouching—and upon warrant of bloody affirmation—his to be more fair, virtuous, wise, chaste, constant, qualified, and less attemptable than any 65 the rarest of our ladies in France.

IACHIMO That lady is not now living, or this gentleman's opinion by this worn out.

POSTHUMUS She holds her virtue still, and I my mind.

IACHIMO You must not so far prefer her 'fore ours of 70 Italy.

POSTHUMUS Being so far provoked as I was in France, I would abate her nothing, though I profess myself her adorer, not her friend.

IACHIMO As fair and as good—a kind of hand-in-hand 75 comparison—had been something too fair and too good for any lady in Britain. If she went before others I have seen, as that diamond of yours outlusters many I have beheld, I could not ⌜but⌝ believe she excelled many. But I have not seen the 80 most precious diamond that is, nor you the lady.

POSTHUMUS I praised her as I rated her. So do I my stone.

IACHIMO What do you esteem it at?

POSTHUMUS More than the world enjoys. 85

86. **unparagoned:** unsurpassed, unexcelled

87. **outprized by a trifle:** surpassed in value **by a** trinket

89. **or if:** i.e., either **if**

91. **only the gift of the gods:** i.e., **the gift of the gods** alone

94. **You may wear her in title yours:** i.e., **you may** have legal right to **her**

96–97. **So your brace of unprizable estimations:** i.e., thus, of your two objects of inestimable value

98. **casual:** subject to chance or accident

102. **convince:** overcome, vanquish; **honor:** chastity

104. **nothing:** in no way; **store:** a sufficient supply, an abundance

105. **fear not:** am not apprehensive about

106. **leave: leave** off, cease

109. **familiar at first:** unceremonious from the **first**

111. **get ground:** obtain mastery (Like **go back** [lose ground] and **yielding** [line 112], this is a military expression used as sexual metaphor.)

113. **to friend:** as supporters, on my side

117. **something:** somewhat

118. **confidence:** perhaps used here in the sense of overconfidence, presumption

119. **attempt:** possible wordplay on (1) venture; (2) try to ravish or seduce. In Posthumus's response (lines 123 and 125), an **attempt** is a personal assault on a woman's honor.

121–22. **abused . . . a persuasion:** mistaken . . . an assurance

IACHIMO Either your unparagoned mistress is dead, or she's outprized by a trifle.

POSTHUMUS You are mistaken. The one may be sold or given, or if there were wealth enough for the ⌜purchase⌝ or merit for the gift. The other is not a thing 90 for sale, and only the gift of the gods.

IACHIMO Which the gods have given you?

POSTHUMUS Which, by their graces, I will keep.

IACHIMO You may wear her in title yours, but you know strange fowl light upon neighboring ponds. 95 Your ring may be stolen too. So your brace of unprizable estimations, the one is but frail and the other casual. A cunning thief or a that-way-accomplished courtier would hazard the winning both of first and last. 100

POSTHUMUS Your Italy contains none so accomplished a courtier to convince the honor of my mistress, if in the holding or loss of that, you term her frail. I do nothing doubt you have store of thieves; notwithstanding, I fear not my ring. 105

PHILARIO Let us leave here, gentlemen.

POSTHUMUS Sir, with all my heart. This worthy signior, I thank him, makes no stranger of me. We are familiar at first.

IACHIMO With five times so much conversation I 110 should get ground of your fair mistress, make her go back even to the yielding, had I admittance and opportunity to friend.

POSTHUMUS No, no.

IACHIMO I dare thereupon pawn the moiety of my 115 estate to your ring, which in my opinion o'ervalues it something. But I make my wager rather against your confidence than her reputation, and, to bar your offense herein too, I durst attempt it against any lady in the world. 120

POSTHUMUS You are a great deal abused in too bold a

122. **sustain:** i.e., will experience, will have to submit to

130. **Would I had put:** i.e., I wish I had wagered

131. **approbation:** confirmation, proof

133. **whom:** i.e., who

135. **commend me:** (if you) present me as worthy of regard

137. **conference:** meeting for conversation

139. **reserved:** possible wordplay on (1) set apart for you alone; (2) cold or distant

140. **wage:** pledge; **gold to it:** i.e., **gold to** (equal) **it**

142. **You . . . wiser:** perhaps, as her lover (and therefore one who knows her well), you are understandably reluctant to wager **your ring** on her chastity

143. **dram:** in apothecaries' weight, 1/8 of an ounce

145. **fear:** wordplay on religious **fear** (as in Psalm 111.10: "The beginning of wisdom is **fear** of the Lord") and on Posthumus's presumed **fear** of wagering his ring

149. **undergo:** undertake

151. **drawn:** formally written out

155. **lay:** wager, bet

persuasion, and I doubt not you sustain what you're worthy of by your attempt.

IACHIMO What's that?

POSTHUMUS A repulse—though your attempt, as you call it, deserve more: a punishment, too. 125

PHILARIO Gentlemen, enough of this. It came in too suddenly. Let it die as it was born, and, I pray you, be better acquainted.

IACHIMO Would I had put my estate and my neighbor's on th' approbation of what I have spoke. 130

POSTHUMUS What lady would you choose to assail?

IACHIMO Yours, whom in constancy you think stands so safe. I will lay you ten ⌜thousand⌝ ducats to your ring that, commend me to the court where your lady is, with no more advantage than the opportunity of a second conference, and I will bring from thence that honor of hers which you imagine so reserved. 135

POSTHUMUS I will wage against your gold, gold to it. My ring I hold dear as my finger; 'tis part of it. 140

IACHIMO You are a friend, and therein the wiser. If you buy ladies' flesh at a million a dram, you cannot preserve it from tainting. But I see you have some religion in you, that you fear. 145

POSTHUMUS This is but a custom in your tongue. You bear a graver purpose, I hope.

IACHIMO I am the master of my speeches and would undergo what's spoken, I swear.

POSTHUMUS Will you? I shall but lend my diamond till your return. Let there be covenants drawn between 's. My mistress exceeds in goodness the hugeness of your unworthy thinking. I dare you to this match. Here's my ring. 150

PHILARIO I will have it no lay. 155

IACHIMO By the gods, it is one!—If I bring you no sufficient testimony that I have enjoyed the dearest

159–60. **come off:** retire from the attempt (a military term)

162–63. **I have . . . entertainment:** i.e., you provide a letter that assures my warm reception

165. **articles:** i.e., a formal agreement; **you shall answer:** i.e., are you answerable, liable to be called to account

166. **make your voyage upon:** i.e., undertake this enterprise against

170. **ill:** bad, evil

175. **straight:** immediately

176. **starve:** die

180. **from it:** i.e., leave it, let it go

1.5 The queen obtains a box that she is told contains poison. (The audience is told that the box actually contains a sleeping potion that mimics death.) The queen gives the box of supposed poison to Pisanio, telling him it is a helpful medicine. Her hope is that with Posthumus's servant Pisanio dead, Imogen will be less likely to cling to her love for Posthumus.

---

4. **Dispatch:** make haste

bodily part of your mistress, my ten thousand ducats are yours; so is your diamond too. If I come off and leave her in such honor as you have trust 160 in, she your jewel, this your jewel, and my gold are yours, provided I have your commendation for my more free entertainment.

POSTHUMUS I embrace these conditions. Let us have articles betwixt us. Only thus far you shall answer: 165 if you make your voyage upon her and give me directly to understand you have prevailed, I am no further your enemy; she is not worth our debate. If she remain unseduced, you not making it appear otherwise, for your ill opinion and th' assault you 170 have made to her chastity, you shall answer me with your sword.

IACHIMO Your hand; a covenant. (⌜*They shake hands.*⌝) We will have these things set down by lawful counsel, and straight away for Britain, lest the bargain 175 should catch cold and starve. I will fetch my gold and have our two wagers recorded.

POSTHUMUS Agreed. ⌜*Iachimo and Posthumus exit.*⌝

FRENCHMAN Will this hold, think you?

PHILARIO Signior Iachimo will not from it. Pray, let us 180 follow 'em.

They exit.

Scene ⌜5⌝

Enter Queen, Ladies, and Cornelius.

QUEEN
Whiles yet the dew's on ground, gather those flowers.
Make haste. Who has the note of them?

LADY
I, madam.

QUEEN Dispatch. *Ladies exit.*
Now, Master Doctor, have you brought those drugs? 5

6. **Pleaseth your Highness:** a deferential phrase of address

7. **without offense:** i.e., **without** intending any **offense**

8. **wherefore:** why

11. **movers:** i.e., cause

15. **learned:** taught

18. **confections:** compounds, medicines

19. **meet:** appropriate, fitting

21. **conclusions:** experiments; **try the forces:** test the efficacy

24. **vigor of them:** i.e., intensity of their effects

25. **Allayments:** i.e., antidotes (literally, modifying agents)

26. **virtues:** powers

"To make perfumes, distil, preserve." (1.5.16)
From Hannah Woolley, *The queen-like closet* . . . (1675).

CORNELIUS
Pleaseth your Highness, ay. Here they are, madam.
⌜*He hands her a small box.*⌝
But I beseech your Grace, without offense—
My conscience bids me ask—wherefore you have
Commanded of me these most poisonous
compounds, 10
Which are the movers of a languishing death,
But though slow, deadly.

QUEEN I wonder, doctor,
Thou ask'st me such a question. Have I not been
Thy pupil long? Hast thou not learned me how 15
To make perfumes, distil, preserve—yea, so
That our great king himself doth woo me oft
For my confections? Having thus far proceeded,
Unless thou think'st me devilish, is 't not meet
That I did amplify my judgment in 20
Other conclusions? I will try the forces
Of these thy compounds on such creatures as
We count not worth the hanging—but none human—
To try the vigor of them and apply
Allayments to their act, and by them gather 25
Their several virtues and effects.

CORNELIUS Your Highness
Shall from this practice but make hard your heart.
Besides, the seeing these effects will be
Both noisome and infectious. 30

QUEEN O, content thee.

Enter Pisanio.

⌜*Aside.*⌝ Here comes a flattering rascal. Upon him
Will I first work. He's for his master
And enemy to my son.—How now, Pisanio?—
Doctor, your service for this time is ended. 35
Take your own way.

CORNELIUS, ⌜*aside*⌝ I do suspect you, madam,
But you shall do no harm.

45. **prove:** test, demonstrate
48. **a time:** i.e., for a while
56. **quench:** cool down
57. **possesses:** resides
61. **name:** reputation
63. **shift his being:** i.e., change locations
65. **decay:** waste, destroy
69. **but:** merely

Handfasting. (1.5.89)
From George Wither, *A collection of emblemes . . .* (1635).

QUEEN, ⌜*to Pisanio*⌝ Hark thee, a word.

CORNELIUS, ⌜*aside*⌝

I do not like her. She doth think she has 40
Strange ling'ring poisons. I do know her spirit,
And will not trust one of her malice with
A drug of such damned nature. Those she has
Will stupefy and dull the sense awhile,
Which first perchance she'll prove on cats and dogs, 45
Then afterward up higher. But there is
No danger in what show of death it makes,
More than the locking-up the spirits a time,
To be more fresh, reviving. She is fooled
With a most false effect, and I the truer 50
So to be false with her.

QUEEN No further service, doctor,
Until I send for thee.

CORNELIUS I humbly take my leave. *He exits.*

QUEEN

Weeps she still, sayst thou? Dost thou think in time 55
She will not quench and let instructions enter
Where folly now possesses? Do thou work.
When thou shalt bring me word she loves my son,
I'll tell thee on the instant thou art then
As great as is thy master; greater, for 60
His fortunes all lie speechless, and his name
Is at last gasp. Return he cannot, nor
Continue where he is. To shift his being
Is to exchange one misery with another,
And every day that comes comes to decay 65
A day's work in him. What shalt thou expect,
To be depender on a thing that leans,
Who cannot be new built, nor has no friends
So much as but to prop him? (⌜*She drops the box*
and Pisanio picks it up.⌝) Thou tak'st up 70
Thou know'st not what. But take it for thy labor.
It is a thing I made which hath the King

74. **cordial:** restorative, reviving

75. **an earnest:** a small payment to seal a bargain; thus, a promise of a greater reward to come

78. **chance thou changest on:** perhaps, good opportunity (this is) to change your fortune (The line may be defective.)

79. **to boot:** in addition

80. **move:** urge

83. **set thee on to this desert:** urged you to this meritorious action

88. **the remembrancer of her:** i.e., her appointed reminder

88–89. **hold / The handfast to her lord:** keep inviolate her marriage vow (See picture, page 40.)

91. **liegers:** i.e., ledgers, ambassadors; **sweet:** i.e., sweetheart, husband

92. **Except she bend her humor:** i.e., unless she relents

96. **closet:** private chamber

Cowslips. (1.5.95)
From John Gerard, *The herball* . . . (1597).

Five times redeemed from death. I do not know
What is more cordial. Nay, I prithee, take it.
It is an earnest of a farther good 75
That I mean to thee. Tell thy mistress how
The case stands with her. Do 't as from thyself.
Think what a chance thou changest on, but think
Thou hast thy mistress still; to boot, my son,
Who shall take notice of thee. I'll move the King 80
To any shape of thy preferment such
As thou'lt desire; and then myself, I chiefly,
That set thee on to this desert, am bound
To load thy merit richly. Call my women.
Think on my words. *Pisanio exits.* 85
A sly and constant knave,
Not to be shaked; the agent for his master
And the remembrancer of her to hold
The handfast to her lord. I have given him that
Which, if he take, shall quite unpeople her 90
Of liegers for her sweet, and which she after,
Except she bend her humor, shall be assured
To taste of too.

Enter Pisanio and Ladies ⌜carrying flowers.⌝

⌜*To the Ladies.*⌝ So, so. Well done, well done.
The violets, cowslips, and the primroses 95
Bear to my closet.—Fare thee well, Pisanio.
Think on my words. *Queen and Ladies exit.*

PISANIO And shall do.
But when to my good lord I prove untrue,
I'll choke myself; there's all I'll do for you. 100
He exits.

1.6 Iachimo arrives in Britain and begins his attempt to seduce Imogen by telling her that Posthumus is betraying her with prostitutes. She turns on Iachimo in fury when he advises her to take revenge on Posthumus by becoming Iachimo's lover. Iachimo then claims he slandered Posthumus only to test her. She forgives the slander and agrees to keep in her bedroom that night Iachimo's trunk that he says is filled with jewels and precious ornaments.

---

1. **stepdame:** stepmother

3. **That . . . banished:** i.e., whose **husband** has been **banished**

4. **repeated:** i.e., already recounted

7. **Is . . . glorious:** perhaps, **is** someone who desires, and therefore lacks, what is **glorious,** or splendid (i.e., Posthumus)

8. **How mean soe'er:** i.e., however lowly; **honest wills:** unsophisticated desires

9. **seasons:** adds savor to; **comfort:** pleasure

11. **letters:** i.e., a letter (from the Latin plural *litterae)*

12. **Change you:** i.e., does your complexion **change** (in alarm)

15. **dearly:** fondly

18. **out of door:** i.e., visible (literally, outside)

20. **alone th' Arabian bird:** i.e., unique (literally, the only phoenix, the mythical bird of which there was only one living at a given time, and which reproduced itself through reincarnation after burning itself to ashes) See picture, page 54.

(continued)

Scene ⌜6⌝

Enter Imogen alone.

IMOGEN
A father cruel and a stepdame false,
A foolish suitor to a wedded lady
That hath her husband banished. O, that husband,
My supreme crown of grief and those repeated
Vexations of it! Had I been thief-stol'n, 5
As my two brothers, happy; but most miserable
Is the ⌜desire⌝ that's glorious. Blessed be those,
How mean soe'er, that have their honest wills,
Which seasons comfort. Who may this be? Fie!

Enter Pisanio and Iachimo.

PISANIO
Madam, a noble gentleman of Rome 10
Comes from my lord with letters.

IACHIMO Change you, madam?
The worthy Leonatus is in safety
And greets your Highness dearly. 15
⌜*He gives her a letter.*⌝

IMOGEN Thanks, good sir.
You're kindly welcome.

IACHIMO, ⌜*aside*⌝
All of her that is out of door, most rich!
If she be furnished with a mind so rare,
She is alone th' Arabian bird, and I 20
Have lost the wager. Boldness be my friend.
Arm me, audacity, from head to foot,
Or like the Parthian I shall flying fight—
Rather, directly fly.

IMOGEN *reads*: *He is one of the noblest note, to whose* 25
kindnesses I am most infinitely tied. Reflect upon
him accordingly as you value your trust.
Leonatus.

23. **Parthian:** i.e., the mounted archer, or **Parthian** cavalryman, famous for firing backward as he fled or pretended to flee

24. **directly:** immediately

25. **note:** reputation

26. **Reflect:** bestow regard or attention

36. **What . . . mad:** With this line Iachimo begins to speak as if he were delivering soliloquies (lines 36–56), but these are designed to be overheard by Imogen.

37. **vaulted arch:** i.e., the sky, the heavens; **crop:** fruit, produce

38–40. **distinguish . . . beach:** i.e., tell the difference between the stars **above** and the pebbles on the **beach** (The paradoxical phrase **the numbered beach,** often emended by editors to "th' unnumbered beach," may be an allusion to Matthew 10.30: "the very hairs of your head are all **numbered,**" with hairs being indistinguishable from each other but **numbered** by God.)

41. **Partition:** distinction; **spectacles:** i.e., **eyes** (line 36)

43. **makes your admiration:** causes your wonder

45. **shes:** women; **this way:** i.e., when looking at one of them

46. **mows:** grimaces

47. **favor:** beauty

48. **definite:** certain, decisive

49. **Sluttery:** sluttishness; **neat:** fine, elegant; bright, clear

50. **emptiness:** i.e., until it had emptied itself

51. **so allured:** i.e., attracted by this

(continued)

So far I read aloud.
But even the very middle of my heart 30
Is warmed by th' rest and ⌜takes⌝ it thankfully.—
You are as welcome, worthy sir, as I
Have words to bid you, and shall find it so
In all that I can do.

IACHIMO Thanks, fairest lady.— 35
What, are men mad? Hath nature given them eyes
To see this vaulted arch and the rich crop
Of sea and land, which can distinguish 'twixt
The fiery orbs above and the twinned stones
Upon the numbered beach, and can we not 40
Partition make with spectacles so precious
'Twixt fair and foul?

IMOGEN What makes your admiration?

IACHIMO
It cannot be i' th' eye, for apes and monkeys
'Twixt two such shes would chatter this way and 45
Contemn with mows the other; nor i' th' judgment,
For idiots in this case of favor would
Be wisely definite; nor i' th' appetite—
Sluttery to such neat excellence opposed
Should make desire vomit emptiness, 50
Not so allured to feed.

IMOGEN
What is the matter, trow?

IACHIMO The cloyèd will,
That satiate yet unsatisfied desire, that tub
Both filled and running, ravening first the lamb, 55
Longs after for the garbage.

IMOGEN What, dear sir,
Thus raps you? Are you well?

IACHIMO Thanks, madam, well.
(⌜*To Pisanio.*⌝) Beseech you, sir, 60
Desire my man's abode where I did leave him.
He's strange and peevish.

52. **trow:** an expletive which means, perhaps, "I wonder"

53. **will:** carnal appetite, lust

54. **satiate:** glutted

55. **running:** i.e., emptying itself (literally, leaking)

58. **raps you:** transports you

60. **Beseech:** i.e., (I) beg

61. **Desire my man's abode:** request my servant to wait (for me)

62. **strange:** i.e., a foreigner

68. **pleasant:** cheerful; **None a stranger:** i.e., no other foreigner

69. **gamesome:** playful, inclined to joking (and to sex)

72. **sadness:** seriousness; melancholy

77. **Gallian:** Gallic, French; **furnaces:** exhales like a furnace

78. **The thick:** i.e., frequent

79. **from 's free lungs:** i.e., without the constraints of any such longing

81. **proof:** experience

83. **will 's: will** his; **languish:** waste away in longing

84. **Assurèd bondage:** (1) the **bondage** of betrothal; (2) certain **bondage**

90. **much to blame:** very blameworthy, deserving of **much** rebuke

93. **In himself 'tis much:** i.e., with regard to **himself, heaven's bounty** has provided **much** in the way of **talents** (line 94)

PISANIO I was going, sir,
To give him welcome. *He exits.*
IMOGEN
Continues well my lord? His health, beseech you? 65
IACHIMO Well, madam.
IMOGEN
Is he disposed to mirth? I hope he is.
IACHIMO
Exceeding pleasant. None a stranger there
So merry and so gamesome. He is called
The Briton Reveler. 70
IMOGEN When he was here
He did incline to sadness, and ofttimes
Not knowing why.
IACHIMO I never saw him sad.
There is a Frenchman his companion, one 75
An eminent monsieur that, it seems, much loves
A Gallian girl at home. He furnaces
The thick sighs from him, whiles the jolly Briton—
Your lord, I mean—laughs from 's free lungs, cries "O,
Can my sides hold to think that man who knows 80
By history, report, or his own proof
What woman is, yea, what she cannot choose
But must be, will 's free hours languish for
Assurèd bondage?"
IMOGEN Will my lord say so? 85
IACHIMO
Ay, madam, with his eyes in flood with laughter.
It is a recreation to be by
And hear him mock the Frenchman. But heavens
know
Some men are much to blame. 90
IMOGEN Not he, I hope.
IACHIMO
Not he—but yet heaven's bounty towards him might
Be used more thankfully. In himself 'tis much;

100. **wrack:** damage, impairment

102. **Lamentable:** accented on the first syllable; **What:** an interjection introducing a question (Iachimo returns to speaking in the form of quasi-soliloquy that he first adopted in line 36.)

103. **hide me:** i.e., **hide; solace:** i.e., seek enjoyment (literally, take enjoyment)

104. **snuff:** candle end

107. **demands:** questions

110. **office:** duty, function; **venge:** avenge

111. **on 't:** i.e., about it

114. **doubting:** i.e., fearing that, suspecting that

117. **discover:** reveal

118. **spur and stop:** i.e., **spur** on, or impel (to reveal itself) and then **stop** (from being revealed) The metaphor is from horseback riding.

126. **Capitol:** the great national temple of Rome, dedicated to Jupiter; **join gripes with:** clutch, grasp

127–28. **Made hard . . . labor:** hardened **with hourly falsehood** as much as they would be **with hourly labor**

128. **by-peeping:** glancing sidelong

In you, which I account his, beyond all talents.
Whilst I am bound to wonder, I am bound 95
To pity too.

IMOGEN What do you pity, sir?

IACHIMO
Two creatures heartily.

IMOGEN Am I one, sir?
You look on me. What wrack discern you in me 100
Deserves your pity?

IACHIMO Lamentable! What,
To hide me from the radiant sun and solace
I' th' dungeon by a snuff?

IMOGEN I pray you, sir, 105
Deliver with more openness your answers
To my demands. Why do you pity me?

IACHIMO That others do—
I was about to say, enjoy your—but
It is an office of the gods to venge it, 110
Not mine to speak on 't.

IMOGEN You do seem to know
Something of me or what concerns me. Pray you,
Since doubting things go ill often hurts more
Than to be sure they do—for certainties 115
Either are past remedies, or, timely knowing,
The remedy then born—discover to me
What both you spur and stop.

IACHIMO Had I this cheek
To bathe my lips upon; this hand, whose touch, 120
Whose every touch, would force the feeler's soul
To th' oath of loyalty; this object which
Takes prisoner the wild motion of mine eye,
⌜Fixing⌝ it only here; should I, damned then,
Slaver with lips as common as the stairs 125
That mount the Capitol, join gripes with hands
Made hard with hourly falsehood—falsehood as
With labor; then by-peeping in an eye

129. **illustrous:** dull, lackluster (See longer note, page 265.)

132. **revolt:** i.e., infidelity (literally, casting off of allegiance)

135–37. **Not I . . . his change:** i.e., **I** am not **inclined** to report this information regarding the base nature of **his change**

138. **mutest:** most silent; **conscience:** inmost thought

139. **Charms:** conjure

144. **Would:** i.e., which **would; partnered:** i.e., made a partner (by virtue of Posthumus's relations)

145. **tomboys:** immodest women; **self:** same; **exhibition:** allowance of money

146. **ventures:** venturers, prostitutes

148. **boiled stuff:** i.e., prostitutes (an allusion to the sweating tub, a treatment for venereal disease) See picture, page 94.

151. **Recoil:** fall away, degenerate

158. **Diana's priest:** i.e., the **priest** of the Roman goddess of chastity

159. **variable:** (1) various; (2) inconstant; **ramps:** vulgar women

160. **your despite:** contemptuous disregard of you; **upon your purse:** i.e., using your money

162. **runagate to:** (1) deserter from; (2) renegade from

Base and ⌜illustrous⌝ as the smoky light
That's fed with stinking tallow; it were fit 130
That all the plagues of hell should at one time
Encounter such revolt.

IMOGEN My lord, I fear,
Has forgot Britain.

IACHIMO And himself. Not I, 135
Inclined to this intelligence, pronounce
The beggary of his change, but 'tis your graces
That from my mutest conscience to my tongue
Charms this report out.

IMOGEN Let me hear no more. 140

IACHIMO
O dearest soul, your cause doth strike my heart
With pity that doth make me sick. A lady
So fair, and fastened to an empery
Would make the great'st king double, to be partnered
With tomboys hired with that self exhibition 145
Which your own coffers yield, with diseased ventures
That play with all infirmities for gold
Which rottenness can lend nature; such boiled stuff
As well might poison poison. Be revenged,
Or she that bore you was no queen, and you 150
Recoil from your great stock.

IMOGEN Revenged?
How should I be revenged? If this be true—
As I have such a heart that both mine ears
Must not in haste abuse—if it be true, 155
How should I be revenged?

IACHIMO Should he make me
Live like Diana's priest betwixt cold sheets,
Whiles he is vaulting variable ramps,
In your despite, upon your purse? Revenge it. 160
I dedicate myself to your sweet pleasure,
More noble than that runagate to your bed,

163. **fast:** constant, firm, steadfast

164. **Still close:** i.e., always as secret

166. **tender:** offer

168. **attended:** listened to

173. **Solicits:** i.e., you attempt to seduce (The correct verb form would be "solicit'st.")

177. **saucy:** (1) insolent; (2) lascivious; **stranger:** foreigner; **mart:** do business

178. **As in:** i.e., **as** if he were **in; Romish:** Roman; **stew:** brothel

183. **credit . . . of:** i.e., trust . . . in

185. **Her:** i.e., **deserves her**

186. **sir:** gentleman

187. **called his:** i.e., **called** its own; **mistress:** ladylove

189. **affiance:** fidelity

191–92. **one . . . mannered:** i.e., alone, of the best moral character

192. **witch:** magician, enchanter

193. **societies:** i.e., those in his company

The phoenix, or "th' Arabian bird." (1.6.20)
From Conrad Lycosthenes, *Prodigiorum* . . . [1557].

And will continue fast to your affection,
Still close as sure.

IMOGEN What ho, Pisanio! 165

IACHIMO
Let me my service tender on your lips.

IMOGEN
Away! I do condemn mine ears that have
So long attended thee. If thou wert honorable,
Thou wouldst have told this tale for virtue, not
For such an end thou seek'st, as base as strange. 170
Thou wrong'st a gentleman who is as far
From thy report as thou from honor, and
Solicits here a lady that disdains
Thee and the devil alike.—What ho, Pisanio!—
The King my father shall be made acquainted 175
Of thy assault. If he shall think it fit
A saucy stranger in his court to mart
As in a Romish stew and to expound
His beastly mind to us, he hath a court
He little cares for and a daughter who 180
He not respects at all.—What ho, Pisanio!

IACHIMO
O happy Leonatus! I may say
The credit that thy lady hath of thee
Deserves thy trust, and thy most perfect goodness
Her assured credit.—Blessèd live you long, 185
A lady to the worthiest sir that ever
Country called his; and you his mistress, only
For the most worthiest fit. Give me your pardon.
I have spoke this to know if your affiance
Were deeply rooted, and shall make your lord 190
That which he is, new o'er; and he is one
The truest mannered, such a holy witch
That he enchants societies into him.
Half all ⌜men's⌝ hearts are his.

IMOGEN You make amends. 195

197. **sets him off:** shows him to advantage

198. **More . . . seeming:** i.e., so that he seems **more** than merely human

202. **election:** choice

203. **Which:** i.e., who

204. **fan:** i.e., test (literally, winnow, separate the chaff or husks from the grain by means of a current of air)

209. **moment:** consequence; **concerns:** is of importance

216. **factor:** agent

217. **plate:** silver or gold (or silver- and gold-plated) utensils or ornaments; **jewels:** ornaments of gold, silver, or precious stones

219. **something curious:** somewhat concerned or anxious; **strange:** i.e., a foreigner

An Italian gentleman. (1.4.0 SD)
From Cesare Vecellio, *Habiti antichi et moderni* . . . [1598].

IACHIMO

He sits 'mongst men like a ⌜descended⌝ god.
He hath a kind of honor sets him off
More than a mortal seeming. Be not angry,
Most mighty princess, that I have adventured
To try your taking of a false report, which hath 200
Honored with confirmation your great judgment
In the election of a sir so rare,
Which you know cannot err. The love I bear him
Made me to fan you thus, but the gods made you,
Unlike all others, chaffless. Pray, your pardon. 205

IMOGEN

All's well, sir. Take my power i' th' court for yours.

IACHIMO

My humble thanks. I had almost forgot
T' entreat your Grace but in a small request,
And yet of moment too, for it concerns.
Your lord, myself, and other noble friends 210
Are partners in the business.

IMOGEN Pray, what is 't?

IACHIMO

Some dozen Romans of us and your lord—
The best feather of our wing—have mingled sums
To buy a present for the Emperor; 215
Which I, the factor for the rest, have done
In France. 'Tis plate of rare device and jewels
Of rich and exquisite form, their values great.
And I am something curious, being strange,
To have them in safe stowage. May it please you 220
To take them in protection?

IMOGEN Willingly;

And pawn mine honor for their safety. Since
My lord hath interest in them, I will keep them
In my bedchamber. 225

IACHIMO They are in a trunk

Attended by my men. I will make bold

231. **short:** fail to make good

232. **Gallia:** Gaul, a region in the ancient world comprising present-day France and Belgium

233. **on promise:** i.e., because I promised

238. **if you please:** i.e., **if** it is your wish

240. **outstood:** stayed beyond; **material:** (1) of much consequence; (2) pertinent, essential

241. **tender:** offer

244. **truly:** faithfully, duly

Sinon overlooking Troy. (3.4.62)
From Geoffrey Whitney, *A choice of emblemes* . . . (1586).

To send them to you, only for this night.
I must aboard tomorrow.

IMOGEN O no, no. 230

IACHIMO

Yes, I beseech, or I shall short my word
By length'ning my return. From Gallia
I crossed the seas on purpose and on promise
To see your Grace.

IMOGEN I thank you for your pains. 235
But not away tomorrow.

IACHIMO O, I must, madam.
Therefore I shall beseech you, if you please
To greet your lord with writing, do 't tonight.
I have outstood my time, which is material 240
To th' tender of our present.

IMOGEN I will write.
Send your trunk to me; it shall safe be kept
And truly yielded you. You're very welcome.

They exit.

CYMBELINE

ACT 2

2.1 Cloten and two lords discuss the arrival of Iachimo. The Second Lord, in soliloquy, expresses the hope that Imogen will remain safe and that she and Posthumus will one day rule in Britain.

---

2. **kissed the jack:** i.e., delivered my bowl so that it rested against **the jack** (the smaller bowl at which players aim); **an upcast:** a chance, an accident; **be hit away:** i.e., have my bowl knocked **away**

3. **whoreson:** vile, detestable (a coarsely abusive adjective)

4. **take me up:** rebuke or reprimand me

6. **at my pleasure:** at will

7–8. **broke his pate:** cut his scalp

9. **wit:** intellectual capacity; knowledge

13. **crop the ears:** wordplay on **curtail** (line 12), which also meant "cut off short, lop off" (The allusion might be to cropping a person's ears as a form of punishment or to docking asses' ears.)

15. **gave him satisfaction:** challenged him to satisfy his honor in a duel

16. **rank:** social standing (A social inferior could not offer or accept a challenge. Line 17 plays on **rank**'s adjectival sense, "offensively strong in smell.")

19. **A pox on 't:** an exclamation of irritation (Literally, **pox** is venereal disease.)

21. **jack-slave:** man of low or no social standing

ACT 2

Scene 1

Enter Cloten and the two Lords.

CLOTEN Was there ever man had such luck? When I kissed the jack, upon an upcast to be hit away? I had a hundred pound on 't. And then a whoreson jackanapes must take me up for swearing, as if I borrowed mine oaths of him and might not spend them at my pleasure. 5

FIRST LORD What got he by that? You have broke his pate with your bowl.

SECOND LORD, ⌜*aside*⌝ If his wit had been like him that broke it, it would have run all out. 10

CLOTEN When a gentleman is disposed to swear, it is not for any standers-by to curtail his oaths, ha?

SECOND LORD No, my lord, (⌜*aside*⌝) nor crop the ears of them.

CLOTEN Whoreson dog! I gave him satisfaction. Would he had been one of my rank. 15

SECOND LORD, ⌜*aside*⌝ To have smelled like a fool.

CLOTEN I am not vexed more at anything in th' earth. A pox on 't! I had rather not be so noble as I am. They dare not fight with me because of the Queen my mother. Every jack-slave hath his bellyful of fighting, and I must go up and down like a cock that nobody can match. 20

24–25. **capon . . . on:** i.e., also eunuch and fool (wordplay on [1] **capon** as castrated rooster and "cap on," and [2] "cock's **comb**" and coxcomb, the professional Fool's cap) See below.

26. **Sayest:** i.e., what **sayest**

27–28. **undertake:** enter into combat with

28. **companion:** fellow (a term of contempt); **give offense to:** offend, displease; disgust

29–30. **commit offense:** i.e., attack, assault

34. **tonight:** last night

44. **derogation in 't:** detraction from my honor or reputation (in going **to look upon** the foreigner)

45. **cannot derogate:** (1) are incapable of losing honor; (2) have no honor to lose

48. **issues:** actions, deeds; **derogate:** lessen your excellence

51. **attend:** wait upon

54. **Bears all down:** overwhelms everything

55. **for his heart:** i.e., if **his heart** (and therefore his life) depended on it

A man wearing a coxcomb. (2.1.24–25)
From George Wither, *A collection of emblemes . . .* (1635).

SECOND LORD, ⌜*aside*⌝ You are cock and capon too, and you crow cock with your comb on. 25

CLOTEN Sayest thou?

SECOND LORD It is not fit ⌜your⌝ Lordship should undertake every companion that you give offense to.

CLOTEN No, I know that, but it is fit I should commit offense to my inferiors. 30

SECOND LORD Ay, it is fit for your Lordship only.

CLOTEN Why, so I say.

FIRST LORD Did you hear of a stranger that's come to court ⌜tonight⌝?

CLOTEN A stranger, and I not know on 't? 35

SECOND LORD, ⌜*aside*⌝ He's a strange fellow himself and knows it not.

FIRST LORD There's an Italian come, and 'tis thought one of Leonatus' friends.

CLOTEN Leonatus? A banished rascal; and he's another, 40 whatsoever he be. Who told you of this stranger?

FIRST LORD One of your Lordship's pages.

CLOTEN Is it fit I went to look upon him? Is there no derogation in 't?

SECOND LORD You cannot derogate, my lord. 45

CLOTEN Not easily, I think.

SECOND LORD, ⌜*aside*⌝ You are a fool granted; therefore your issues, being foolish, do not derogate.

CLOTEN Come, I'll go see this Italian. What I have lost today at bowls I'll win tonight of him. Come, go. 50

SECOND LORD I'll attend your Lordship.

⌜*Cloten and First Lord*⌝ *exit.*

That such a crafty devil as is his mother
Should yield the world this ass! A woman that
Bears all down with her brain, and this her son
Cannot take two from twenty, for his heart, 55
And leave eighteen. Alas, poor princess,
Thou divine Imogen, what thou endur'st,
Betwixt a father by thy stepdame governed,

62. **he'd:** i.e., Cloten would

2.2 As Imogen sleeps, the trunk that she is keeping for Iachimo opens, and Iachimo emerges. Before climbing back into it, he examines the room and Imogen's sleeping body, and he steals Posthumus's bracelet from her wrist.

---

0 SD. **in her bed:** The **bed** might be "thrust out" onto the stage or might be revealed by pulling back a curtain.

2. **Please you:** i.e., may it **please you** (a deferential phrase of address)

6. **left:** stopped

14. **o'erlabored:** fatigued

15. **Our Tarquin:** Sextus Tarquinius, a Roman who, in the legendary past, raped Lucretia. (See Shakespeare's poem *The Rape of Lucrece,* and see picture, page 86.)

A mother hourly coining plots, a wooer
More hateful than the foul expulsion is 60
Of thy dear husband, than that horrid act
Of the divorce he'd make! The heavens hold firm
The walls of thy dear honor, keep unshaked
That temple, thy fair mind, that thou mayst stand
T' enjoy thy banished lord and this great land. 65
He exits.

Scene 2

⌜*A trunk is brought in.*⌝ *Enter Imogen,* ⌜*reading,*⌝ *in her bed, and a Lady.*

IMOGEN
Who's there? My woman Helen?

LADY
Please you, madam.

IMOGEN
What hour is it?

LADY
Almost midnight, madam.

IMOGEN
I have read three hours then. Mine eyes are weak. 5
⌜*She hands the Lady her book.*⌝
Fold down the leaf where I have left. To bed.
Take not away the taper; leave it burning.
And if thou canst awake by four o' th' clock,
I prithee, call me. (⌜*Lady exits.*⌝) Sleep hath seized
me wholly. 10
To your protection I commend me, gods.
From fairies and the tempters of the night
Guard me, beseech you. *Sleeps.*

Iachimo from the trunk.

IACHIMO
The crickets sing, and man's o'erlabored sense
Repairs itself by rest. Our Tarquin thus 15

16. **rushes:** standard floor covering in Shakespeare's England (although not in ancient Rome)

17. **Cytherea:** Aphrodite, Greek goddess of beauty and love

18. **bravely:** splendidly

20. **unparagoned:** matchless, incomparable

21. **do 't:** perhaps, **kiss** or **touch** (each other)

23. **underpeep:** peep under

25. **windows:** i.e., eyelids

26. **tinct:** color; **design:** scheme

29. **figures:** perhaps, the images woven into the tapestries (**arras**) hung along the walls; or, perhaps, the statues or paintings that decorate Imogen's chamber

30. **story:** perhaps, the narrative set out in pictorial form in the tapestries

31. **notes:** signs, marks

32. **meaner:** less important; **movables:** articles of furniture, clothing, etc.

34. **dull:** heavy

35. **sense:** i.e., five senses; **monument:** (recumbent) effigy (See picture, page 230.)

38. **slippery:** i.e., easily loosed (literally, having a surface so smooth that it slides easily); **Gordian knot:** in Greek mythology, a **knot** so intricate that no one could untie it (See picture, page 244.)

40. **conscience:** inmost thought

41. **madding:** maddening

42. **cinque-spotted:** i.e., with five spots

43. **voucher:** piece of evidence

Did softly press the rushes ere he wakened
The chastity he wounded.—Cytherea,
How bravely thou becom'st thy bed, fresh lily,
And whiter than the sheets.—That I might touch!
But kiss, one kiss! Rubies unparagoned, 20
How dearly they do 't. 'Tis her breathing that
Perfumes the chamber thus. The flame o' th' taper
Bows toward her and would underpeep her lids
To see th' enclosèd lights, now canopied
Under these windows, white and azure-laced 25
With blue of heaven's own tinct. But my design:
To note the chamber. I will write all down.

⌜*He begins to write.*⌝

Such and such pictures; there the window; such
Th' adornment of her bed; the arras, figures,
Why, such and such; and the contents o' th' story. 30

⌜*He continues to write.*⌝

Ah, but some natural notes about her body
Above ten thousand meaner movables
Would testify t' enrich mine inventory.
O sleep, thou ape of death, lie dull upon her,
And be her sense but as a monument 35
Thus in a chapel lying. (⌜*He begins to remove her bracelet.*⌝) Come off, come off;
As slippery as the Gordian knot was hard.
'Tis mine, and this will witness outwardly
As strongly as the conscience does within 40
To th' madding of her lord. On her left breast
A mole cinque-spotted, like the crimson drops
I' th' bottom of a cowslip. Here's a voucher
Stronger than ever law could make. This secret
Will force him think I have picked the lock and ta'en 45
The treasure of her honor. No more. To what end?
Why should I write this down that's riveted,
Screwed to my memory? She hath been reading late

49. **Tereus:** mythological king of Thrace who raped his sister-in-law Philomela (**Philomel** [line 50]) and then cut out her tongue so that she could not accuse him (The story is told in Ovid's *Metamorphoses* [6.527–854, in the 1567 translation by Arthur Golding].) See picture, page 76.

2.3 Cloten serenades Imogen in an attempt to win her love. Imogen enrages Cloten by saying that he is not as dear as Posthumus's "meanest garment." Cloten vows revenge. In the meantime, Imogen realizes that her bracelet is lost.

---

2. **most coldest: most** unimpassioned, coolest; **turned up ace:** perhaps, rolled the lowest score (one) in gambling with a die—one of a pair of dice; or, perhaps, **turned up** the card with the lowest value (an **ace**) in gambling at cards (with a pun on **ace** as *ass*)

3. **cold:** gloomy, dispirited

4. **after:** like, **after** the manner of

7. **put . . . courage:** hearten, encourage, cheer up anyone

11. **would this music:** i.e., wish these musicians

12. **a-mornings:** every morning

12–13. **penetrate:** i.e., touch her heart, affect her feelings

14–15. **your fingering:** playing your instruments with your fingers (with an obvious obscene pun, that begins with **penetrate** and continues in the next line with **tongue**)

(continued)

The tale of Tereus; here the leaf's turned down
Where Philomel gave up. I have enough. 50
To th' trunk again, and shut the spring of it.
Swift, swift, you dragons of the night, that dawning
May bare the raven's eye. I lodge in fear.
Though this a heavenly angel, hell is here.
Clock strikes.
One, two, three. Time, time! 55
He exits ⌜*into the trunk. The trunk and bed are removed.*⌝

Scene 3

Enter Cloten and Lords.

FIRST LORD Your Lordship is the most patient man in loss, the most coldest that ever turned up ace.

CLOTEN It would make any man cold to lose.

FIRST LORD But not every man patient after the noble temper of your Lordship. You are most hot and 5 furious when you win.

⌜CLOTEN⌝ Winning will put any man into courage. If I could get this foolish Imogen, I should have gold enough. It's almost morning, is 't not?

FIRST LORD Day, my lord. 10

CLOTEN I would this music would come. I am advised to give her music a-mornings; they say it will penetrate.

Enter Musicians.

Come on, tune. If you can penetrate her with your fingering, so. We'll try with tongue, too. If none 15 will do, let her remain, but I'll never give o'er. First, a very excellent good-conceited thing; after, a wonderful sweet air, with admirable rich words to it, and then let her consider.

15. **so:** i.e., let it be **so;** it is well; **tongue:** i.e., vocal music

16. **do:** succeed, suffice; **give o'er: give** up

17. **good-conceited:** clever, witty, ingenious

18. **air:** (1) solo, with or without accompaniment; (2) light tune; (3) part-song

21. **Phoebus gins arise:** i.e., the sun is rising **Phoebus:** the sun god, often pictured in a chariot pulled by horses (See picture, page 256.) **gins:** begins to

23. **chaliced:** cuplike; **lies:** i.e., lie

24. **winking Mary-buds:** closed marigold buds

30. **consider:** recompense

31. **vice:** imperfection; **horsehairs:** i.e., bowstrings

31–32. **calves' guts:** strings of lutes, viols, and other stringed instruments

32. **unpaved:** i.e., castrated (wordplay that connects "stone" as testicle, "unstoned" as castrated, and "stone" as paving stone, so that a **eunuch,** being "unstoned," is called **unpaved**)

41. **musics:** pieces of music

43. **minion:** darling, lover

45. **wear:** i.e., **wear** out, efface; **print:** image; vestige; **remembrance:** memory

48. **vantages:** opportunities, chances

⌜*Musicians begin to play.*⌝

Song.

Hark, hark, the lark at heaven's gate sings, 20
And Phoebus gins arise,
His steeds to water at those springs
On chaliced flowers that lies;
And winking Mary-buds begin
To ope their golden eyes. 25
With everything that pretty is,
My lady sweet, arise,
Arise, arise.

⌜CLOTEN⌝ So, get you gone. If this penetrate, I will consider your music the better. If it do not, it is a 30 ⌜vice⌝ in her ears which horsehairs and calves' guts, nor the voice of unpaved eunuch to boot, can never amend.

⌜*Musicians exit.*⌝

Enter Cymbeline and Queen, ⌜*with Attendants.*⌝

SECOND LORD Here comes the King.

CLOTEN I am glad I was up so late, for that's the reason 35 I was up so early. He cannot choose but take this service I have done fatherly.—Good morrow to your Majesty and to my gracious mother.

CYMBELINE
Attend you here the door of our stern daughter?
Will she not forth? 40

CLOTEN I have assailed her with musics, but she vouchsafes no notice.

CYMBELINE
The exile of her minion is too new;
She hath not yet forgot him. Some more time
Must wear the print of his remembrance on 't, 45
And then she's yours.

QUEEN, ⌜*to Cloten*⌝ You are most bound to th' King,
Who lets go by no vantages that may

49. **Prefer you:** settle you in marriage; recommend you; **Frame:** prepare; adapt

50. **To:** i.e., to make; **orderly:** regular; **solicits:** solicitations, entreaties

50–51. **friended . . . season:** i.e., assisted by appropriate timing or favorable occasion

54. **tender:** offer

55. **dismission:** rejection

56. **senseless:** i.e., incapable of hearing (Cloten's response [line 57] suggests that he interprets the word as meaning "stupid" or "foolish.")

58. **So like you:** i.e., if it please you

64. **his goodness forespent on us:** i.e., in recompense for the **goodness** he has previously expended **on us**

66. **mistress:** ladylove

74. **line:** i.e., fill with money

76. **Diana's rangers:** i.e., nymphs (literally, gamekeepers) in the service of Diana, the huntress-goddess of chastity (See picture, page 92.) **false themselves:** betray their trust; violate their oaths (to Diana)

77. **stand:** ambush; standing place from which a hunter or sportsman may shoot game

78. **true:** honest

Prefer you to his daughter. Frame yourself
To orderly solicits and be friended 50
With aptness of the season. Make denials
Increase your services. So seem as if
You were inspired to do those duties which
You tender to her; that you in all obey her,
Save when command to your dismission tends, 55
And therein you are senseless.

CLOTEN Senseless? Not so.

⌜*Enter a Messenger.*⌝

MESSENGER, ⌜*to Cymbeline*⌝
So like you, sir, ambassadors from Rome;
The one is Caius Lucius. ⌜*Messenger exits.*⌝

CYMBELINE A worthy fellow, 60
Albeit he comes on angry purpose now.
But that's no fault of his. We must receive him
According to the honor of his sender,
And towards himself, his goodness forespent on us,
We must extend our notice.—Our dear son, 65
When you have given good morning to your mistress,
Attend the Queen and us. We shall have need
T' employ you towards this Roman.—Come, our
queen.

⌜*Cymbeline and Queen*⌝ *exit,* ⌜*with Lords and Attendants.*⌝

CLOTEN
If she be up, I'll speak with her; if not, 70
Let her lie still and dream. (⌜*He knocks.*⌝) By your
leave, ho!—
I know her women are about her. What
If I do line one of their hands? 'Tis gold
Which buys admittance—oft it doth—yea, and makes 75
Diana's rangers false themselves, yield up
Their deer to th' stand o' th' stealer; and 'tis gold
Which makes the true man killed and saves the thief,

89. **dear:** expensive

91. **ready:** properly dressed (The Lady's reply [line 93] plays on **ready** as *inclined* or *disposed.*)

95. **good report:** i.e., favorable recommendation to your lady

96. **my good name:** wordplay on **report** (line 95) as *reputation*

Tereus, Philomel, and Philomel's sister depart for Tereus's kingdom. (2.2.49–50)
From Ovid, . . . *Metamorphoseon* . . . (1582).

Nay, sometime hangs both thief and true man. What
Can it not do and undo? I will make 80
One of her women lawyer to me, for
I yet not understand the case myself.
By your leave. *Knocks.*

Enter a Lady.

LADY
Who's there that knocks?

CLOTEN A gentleman. 85

LADY No more?

CLOTEN
Yes, and a gentlewoman's son.

LADY That's more
Than some whose tailors are as dear as yours
Can justly boast of. What's your Lordship's pleasure? 90

CLOTEN
Your lady's person. Is she ready?

LADY Ay,
To keep her chamber.

CLOTEN There is gold for you.
Sell me your good report. ⌜*He offers a purse.*⌝ 95

LADY
How, my good name? Or to report of you
What I shall think is good?

Enter Imogen.

The Princess.
⌜*Lady exits.*⌝

CLOTEN
Good morrow, fairest sister. Your sweet hand.

IMOGEN
Good morrow, sir. You lay out too much pains 100
For purchasing but trouble. The thanks I give
Is telling you that I am poor of thanks
And scarce can spare them.

105. **as deep:** i.e., of the same (grave) consequence

109. **But . . . silent:** i.e., if not for fear **you** would **say** my silence implies consent

111. **unfold equal discourtesy:** i.e., display rudeness **equal**

112. **knowing:** knowledge

116. **Fools . . . folks:** This line is so puzzling that editors often substitute "cure" for **are,** or they suggest that Cloten interrupts Imogen before she finishes her thought.

121. **put:** force, compel

122. **verbal:** verbose, talkative (From a conservative patriarchal perspective, women were ideally to be not only chaste and obedient but also silent.) **for all:** i.e., once and **for all**

123. **which:** who

125. **charity:** Christian love of all fellow human beings

126. **I hate:** i.e., of hating

127. **felt:** recognized or apprehended (without having to be explicitly informed)

129. **For:** i.e., as **for**

130. **contract:** i.e., private exchange of promises to marry (See longer note, page 265.) **pretend:** use as a pretext (for denying me); **base:** lowborn

131. **bred of alms:** brought up on charity

133. **in meaner parties:** i.e., among people of little or no social consequence

CLOTEN Still I swear I love you.

IMOGEN

If you but said so, 'twere as deep with me. 105
If you swear still, your recompense is still
That I regard it not.

CLOTEN This is no answer.

IMOGEN

But that you shall not say I yield being silent,
I would not speak. I pray you, spare me. Faith, 110
I shall unfold equal discourtesy
To your best kindness. One of your great knowing
Should learn, being taught, forbearance.

CLOTEN

To leave you in your madness 'twere my sin.
I will not. 115

IMOGEN

Fools are not mad folks.

CLOTEN Do you call me fool?

IMOGEN As I am mad, I do.
If you'll be patient, I'll no more be mad.
That cures us both. I am much sorry, sir, 120
You put me to forget a lady's manners
By being so verbal; and learn now for all
That I, which know my heart, do here pronounce,
By th' very truth of it, I care not for you,
And am so near the lack of charity 125
To accuse myself I hate you—which I had rather
You felt than make 't my boast.

CLOTEN You sin against
Obedience, which you owe your father. For
The contract you pretend with that base wretch— 130
One bred of alms and fostered with cold dishes,
With scraps o' th' court—it is no contract, none;
And though it be allowed in meaner parties—
Yet who than he more mean?—to knit their souls,
On whom there is no more dependency 135

136. **self-figured knot:** i.e., marriage of their own making, rather than one arranged for them by their elders

137. **enlargement:** freedom of action

138. **consequence . . . crown:** i.e., your status as successor to the **crown; foil:** pollute, defile

139. **note:** importance, reputation

140. **hilding:** contemptible person; **for a livery:** i.e., only fit to wear a servant's uniform; **squire's cloth:** attendant's clothing

141. **pantler:** servant in charge of the pantry

143. **Jupiter:** king of the Roman gods (also known as Jove, as often in this play) See picture, page 262.

144. **wert:** would be

145. **his:** i.e., Posthumus's; **dignified:** exalted in rank

146. **envy:** i.e., being envied by others

146–48. **if 'twere . . . kingdom:** i.e., if one were to award positions according to the difference in **your virtues,** he would be a king and you his assistant hangman **styled:** honored with the title

149. **preferred:** advanced in rank, promoted

150. **south fog:** The **south** wind was then regarded as a source of infectious disease.

152. **named of:** i.e., **named** by; **mean'st:** most worthless

153. **clipped:** encircled

154. **respect:** regard, consideration

157. **presently:** immediately

159. **sprighted with:** haunted by

161. **jewel:** costly ornament, piece of jewelry

162. **Shrew me:** i.e., may I be cursed

But brats and beggary, in self-figured knot;
Yet you are curbed from that enlargement by
The consequence o' th' crown, and must not foil
The precious note of it with a base slave,
A hilding for a livery, a squire's cloth, 140
A pantler—not so eminent.

IMOGEN Profane fellow,
Wert thou the son of Jupiter and no more
But what thou art besides, thou wert too base
To be his groom. Thou wert dignified enough, 145
Even to the point of envy, if 'twere made
Comparative for your virtues to be styled
The under-hangman of his kingdom and hated
For being preferred so well.

CLOTEN The south fog rot him! 150

IMOGEN
He never can meet more mischance than come
To be but named of thee. His mean'st garment
That ever hath but clipped his body is dearer
In my respect than all the hairs above thee,
Were they all made such men.—How now, Pisanio! 155

Enter Pisanio.

CLOTEN "His ⌜garment⌝"? Now the devil—

IMOGEN, ⌜*to Pisanio*⌝
To Dorothy, my woman, hie thee presently.

CLOTEN
"His garment"?

IMOGEN, ⌜*to Pisanio*⌝ I am sprighted with a fool,
Frighted and angered worse. Go bid my woman 160
Search for a jewel that too casually
Hath left mine arm. It was thy master's. Shrew me
If I would lose it for a revenue
Of any king's in Europe. I do think
I saw 't this morning. Confident I am 165
Last night 'twas on mine arm; I kissed it.

168. **aught:** anything

174. **action:** case at law, legal proceeding

177. **good lady:** i.e., **good** friend, benefactress (said ironically); **conceive:** think, imagine; **hope:** suspect; suppose

2.4 Iachimo returns to Rome with his proofs of Imogen's unfaithfulness: descriptions of her bedroom and of private marks on her body, and, most damaging, the bracelet that Posthumus had given her. Posthumus, enraged with jealousy, relinquishes his diamond ring to Iachimo and swears to take revenge on Imogen.

---

1. **would:** wish

2. **win the King:** i.e., prevail upon or persuade Cymbeline (to accept me); **bold:** confident; **honor:** chastity; reputation as a chaste woman

4. **means:** overtures

7–8. **feared hopes:** perhaps, **hopes** qualified by fear (Some editors print "seared **hopes.**")

9. **gratify:** requite, repay

I hope it be not gone to tell my lord
That I kiss aught but he.

PISANIO 'Twill not be lost.

IMOGEN
I hope so. Go and search. ⌜*Pisanio exits.*⌝ 170

CLOTEN You have abused me.
"His meanest garment"?

IMOGEN Ay, I said so, sir.
If you will make 't an action, call witness to 't.

CLOTEN
I will inform your father. 175

IMOGEN Your mother too.
She's my good lady and will conceive, I hope,
But the worst of me. So I leave ⌜you,⌝ sir,
To th' worst of discontent. *She exits.*

CLOTEN
I'll be revenged! "His mean'st garment"? Well. 180
He exits.

Scene 4

Enter Posthumus and Philario.

POSTHUMUS
Fear it not, sir. I would I were so sure
To win the King as I am bold her honor
Will remain hers.

PHILARIO What means do you make to him?

POSTHUMUS
Not any, but abide the change of time, 5
Quake in the present winter's state, and wish
That warmer days would come. In these feared
⌜hopes⌝
I barely gratify your love; they failing,
I must die much your debtor. 10

12. **this:** i.e., **this** time

13. **of:** from; **Augustus: Augustus** Caesar (63 B.C.E.–14 C.E.) was the first Roman emperor. See picture, page 140.

14. **throughly:** thoroughly

15. **He'll:** i.e., Cymbeline will

16. **whose remembrance:** i.e., the memory of whom

17. **their:** i.e., the Britons'

19. **Statist:** politician, statesman; **like:** likely

21. **legion:** sometimes emended to "legions" on the grounds that Rome would never invade Britain with a single **legion; Gallia:** See note to 1.6.232. **sooner:** is **sooner**

24. **more ordered:** better prepared; **Julius Caesar:** Roman general, politician, and author (100–44 B.C.E.), reputed to have conquered Britain in 54 B.C.E. (See picture, page 100.)

27. **wingèd with:** i.e., given wings by; **courages:** i.e., spirit, confidence, boldness

28. **their approvers:** i.e., those who test them

29. **mend upon the world:** perhaps, improve in the world's opinion

31. **posted you:** conveyed you swiftly (as if by post-horse)

32. **all the corners:** i.e., every region of the earth (See picture, page 246.)

35. **your answer:** i.e., the response Imogen made to you

40. **Look thorough a casement:** The allusion is to prostitutes displaying themselves at windows **to allure** customers. **thorough:** through

PHILARIO

Your very goodness and your company
O'erpays all I can do. By this, your king
Hath heard of great Augustus. Caius Lucius
Will do 's commission throughly. And I think
He'll grant the tribute, send th' arrearages, 15
Or look upon our Romans, whose remembrance
Is yet fresh in their grief.

POSTHUMUS I do believe,
Statist though I am none nor like to be,
That this will prove a war; and you shall hear 20
The legion now in Gallia sooner landed
In our not-fearing Britain than have tidings
Of any penny tribute paid. Our countrymen
Are men more ordered than when Julius Caesar
Smiled at their lack of skill but found their courage 25
Worthy his frowning at. Their discipline,
Now ⌜wingèd⌝ with their courages, will make known
To their approvers they are people such
That mend upon the world.

Enter Iachimo.

PHILARIO See, Iachimo! 30

POSTHUMUS

The swiftest harts have posted you by land,
And winds of all the corners kissed your sails
To make your vessel nimble.

PHILARIO Welcome, sir.

POSTHUMUS

I hope the briefness of your answer made 35
The speediness of your return.

IACHIMO Your lady
Is one of the fairest that I have looked upon.

POSTHUMUS

And therewithal the best, or let her beauty
Look thorough a casement to allure false hearts 40
And be false with them.

42. **are letters:** i.e., is a letter (from the Latin plural *litterae*)

44. **like:** likely, probable

59–60. **Make . . . sport:** i.e., do not **make** a joke of **your loss**

63. **keep covenant:** i.e., adhere to our contract

64. **knowledge:** i.e., carnal **knowledge**

Tarquin waking Lucrece. (2.2.15–17)
From [Jost Amman], *Icones Liuianae* . . . (1572).

IACHIMO, ⌜*handing him a paper*⌝ Here are letters for you.

POSTHUMUS
Their tenor good, I trust.

IACHIMO 'Tis very like.

⌜*Posthumus reads the letter.*⌝

⌜PHILARIO⌝
Was Caius Lucius in the Briton court 45
When you were there?

IACHIMO
He was expected then, but not approached.

POSTHUMUS All is well yet.
Sparkles this stone as it was wont, or is 't not
Too dull for your good wearing? 50

⌜*He indicates his ring.*⌝

IACHIMO If I have lost it,
I should have lost the worth of it in gold.
I'll make a journey twice as far t' enjoy
A second night of such sweet shortness which
Was mine in Britain, for the ring is won. 55

POSTHUMUS
The stone's too hard to come by.

IACHIMO Not a whit,
Your lady being so easy.

POSTHUMUS Make ⌜not,⌝ sir,
Your loss your sport. I hope you know that we 60
Must not continue friends.

IACHIMO Good sir, we must,
If you keep covenant. Had I not brought
The knowledge of your mistress home, I grant
We were to question farther; but I now 65
Profess myself the winner of her honor,
Together with your ring, and not the wronger
Of her or you, having proceeded but
By both your wills.

POSTHUMUS If you can make 't apparent 70
That ⌜you⌝ have tasted her in bed, my hand

74. **leave:** i.e., let it **leave**

76. **my circumstances:** i.e., the details that I will give

80. **spare:** omit

85. **that:** i.e., **that** which; **watching:** staying awake (for)

86. **the story:** i.e., **the story** it pictured was that of

87. **her Roman:** i.e., Antony (Shakespeare tells this story in *Antony and Cleopatra.*)

88. **Cydnus:** the river in Asia Minor where Cleopatra first met Antony (See *Antony and Cleopatra* 2.2.222–65.) **or for:** i.e., either because of

89. **pride:** i.e., through **pride**

90. **bravely:** splendidly

90–91. **it did strive / In workmanship and value:** i.e., its **workmanship and value** competed with each other for preeminence

92. **exactly wrought:** i.e., perfectly made

102. **chimney-piece:** an ornament placed over a fireplace (here, a piece of sculpture)

103. **Dian:** i.e., Diana, goddess of chastity (See longer note, page 266, and picture, page 92.)

104. **likely to report themselves:** perhaps, so like what they represented; or, perhaps, so lifelike that they seemed about to speak; **cutter:** sculptor or carver

105–6. **outwent her, / Motion and breath left out:** i.e., surpassed **Nature** except in failing to include movement and **breath**

And ring is yours. If not, the foul opinion
You had of her pure honor gains or loses
Your sword or mine, or masterless leave both
To who shall find them. 75

IACHIMO Sir, my circumstances,
Being so near the truth as I will make them,
Must first induce you to believe; whose strength
I will confirm with oath, which I doubt not
You'll give me leave to spare when you shall find 80
You need it not.

POSTHUMUS Proceed.

IACHIMO First, her bedchamber—
Where I confess I slept not, but profess
Had that was well worth watching—it was hanged 85
With tapestry of silk and silver, the story
Proud Cleopatra when she met her Roman
And Cydnus swelled above the banks, or for
The press of boats or pride. A piece of work
So bravely done, so rich, that it did strive 90
In workmanship and value, which I wondered
Could be so rarely and exactly wrought
Since the true life on 't was—

POSTHUMUS This is true,
And this you might have heard of here, by me 95
Or by some other.

IACHIMO More particulars
Must justify my knowledge.

POSTHUMUS So they must,
Or do your honor injury. 100

IACHIMO The chimney
Is south the chamber, and the chimney-piece
Chaste Dian bathing. Never saw I figures
So likely to report themselves; the cutter
Was as another Nature, dumb, outwent her, 105
Motion and breath left out.

108. **relation:** report

111. **cherubins:** cherubs (winged angels, depicted as infants with wings and rosy, smiling faces [See picture, below.]) **fretted:** adorned

112. **winking Cupids:** Cupid, the boy god of Love, is often pictured as blind, or blindfolded. **winking:** with the eyes shut, or blindfolded

114. **Depending:** i.e., leaning, resting; **brands:** perhaps, torches (Editors speculate that the **Cupids** here are very small and that they lean on large torches.)

115. **her honor:** i.e., evidence that sullies her reputation

117. **remembrance:** memory

124. **Jove:** an oath on the name of the king of the Roman gods (also known as **Jupiter** [lines 152–53])

129. **outsell her gift:** i.e., exceed the bracelet in value

136. **basilisk:** a mythical serpent whose look could kill (See picture, page 142.)

139. **The vows:** i.e., let **the vows**

Cherubins. (2.4.111)

From Martin Luther, *Der zwey und zwentzigste Psalm* . . . (1525).

POSTHUMUS This is a thing
Which you might from relation likewise reap,
Being, as it is, much spoke of.

IACHIMO The roof o' th' chamber 110
With golden cherubins is fretted. Her andirons—
I had forgot them—were two winking Cupids
Of silver, each on one foot standing, nicely
Depending on their brands.

POSTHUMUS This is her honor? 115
Let it be granted you have seen all this—and praise
Be given to your remembrance—the description
Of what is in her chamber nothing saves
The wager you have laid.

IACHIMO Then if you can 120
Be pale, I beg but leave to air this jewel. See—
⌜*He shows the bracelet.*⌝
And now 'tis up again. It must be married
To that your diamond. I'll keep them.

POSTHUMUS Jove!
Once more let me behold it. Is it that 125
Which I left with her?

IACHIMO Sir, I thank her, that.
She stripped it from her arm. I see her yet.
Her pretty action did outsell her gift
And yet enriched it too. She gave it me 130
And said she prized it once.

POSTHUMUS Maybe she plucked it off
To send it me.

IACHIMO She writes so to you, doth she?

POSTHUMUS
O, no, no, no, 'tis true. Here, take this too. 135
⌜*He gives Iachimo the ring.*⌝
It is a basilisk unto mine eye,
Kills me to look on 't. Let there be no honor
Where there is beauty, truth where semblance, love
Where there's another man. The vows of women

140. **bondage:** obligation, binding force; **where they:** i.e., those to whom **the vows**

141. **they:** i.e., the **women; nothing:** not at all

142. **above measure:** beyond all limits

146. **one her women:** i.e., **one** of **her women**

157. **sworn:** i.e., bound by an oath of fidelity

159–60. **The cognizance . . . this:** i.e., the bracelet identifies her as unfaithful **cognizance:** badge or token identifying a person as belonging to a particular group (a term from heraldry)

166. **persuaded:** thought

168. **colted:** Elsewhere in Shakespeare, this word means "tricked"; here, it seems to mean "mounted" (a word that Posthumus will use in 2.5 to refer to Iachimo's supposed copulation with Imogen).

Acteon sees "Chaste Dian bathing" with her "rangers." (2.4.103; 2.3.76)
From Ovid, . . . *Le metamorphosi* . . . (1538).

Of no more bondage be to where they are made 140
Than they are to their virtues, which is nothing.
O, above measure false!

PHILARIO Have patience, sir,
And take your ring again. 'Tis not yet won.
It may be probable she lost it; or 145
Who knows if one her women, being corrupted,
Hath stol'n it from her.

POSTHUMUS Very true,
And so I hope he came by 't.—Back, my ring!
⌜*He takes back the ring.*⌝
Render to me some corporal sign about her 150
More evident than this, for this was stol'n.

IACHIMO
By Jupiter, I had it from her arm.

POSTHUMUS
Hark you, he swears! By Jupiter he swears.
'Tis true—nay, keep the ring—'tis true.
⌜*He holds out the ring.*⌝
I am sure 155
She would not lose it. Her attendants are
All sworn and honorable. They induced to steal it?
And by a stranger? No, he hath enjoyed her.
The cognizance of her incontinency
Is this. She hath bought the name of whore thus 160
dearly.
There, take thy hire, and all the fiends of hell
Divide themselves between you!
⌜*He gives the ring to Iachimo.*⌝

PHILARIO Sir, be patient.
This is not strong enough to be believed 165
Of one persuaded well of.

POSTHUMUS Never talk on 't.
She hath been colted by him.

IACHIMO If you seek
For further satisfying, under her breast, 170

173. **present:** instant, immediate
188. **limb-meal:** limb from limb
192. **government:** control, rule
193. **pervert:** divert

2.5 Posthumus, in soliloquy, attacks women as the embodiment of all that is vicious.

---

1. **be:** come into existence

A sweating tub for the treatment of venereal disease. (1.6.146–49)
From Thomas Randolph, *Cornelianum dolium* . . . (1638).

Worthy ⌜the⌝ pressing, lies a mole, right proud
Of that most delicate lodging. By my life,
I kissed it, and it gave me present hunger
To feed again, though full. You do remember
This stain upon her? 175

POSTHUMUS Ay, and it doth confirm
Another stain as big as hell can hold,
Were there no more but it.

IACHIMO Will you hear more?

POSTHUMUS Spare your arithmetic; 180
Never count the turns. Once, and a million!

IACHIMO I'll be sworn—

POSTHUMUS No swearing.
If you will swear you have not done 't, you lie,
And I will kill thee if thou dost deny 185
Thou'st made me cuckold.

IACHIMO I'll deny nothing.

POSTHUMUS
O, that I had her here, to tear her limb-meal!
I will go there and do 't i' th' court, before
Her father. I'll do something. *He exits.* 190

PHILARIO Quite beside
The government of patience. You have won.
Let's follow him and pervert the present wrath
He hath against himself.

IACHIMO With all my heart. 195
They exit.

⌜Scene 5⌝

Enter Posthumus.

POSTHUMUS
Is there no way for men to be, but women
Must be half-workers? We are all bastards,
And that most venerable man which I

5. **stamped:** Human conception is here figured as the making of coins through the process of stamping. The metaphor continues in **coiner, tools,** and **counterfeit.**

12. **Saturn:** in Roman mythology, the father of Jupiter (In *The Two Noble Kinsmen* [5.4], one finds the phrase "Cold as **old Saturn.**")

15. **yellow:** perhaps referring to his sallow skin, or perhaps to his jaundiced view of the world

19. **what he looked for should oppose:** i.e., that which he expected to stop him (This may refer to her honor, but it has been argued that it refers to her hymen. If the second, the argument proposes that the marriage is unconsummated and that Posthumus's fury is therefore more explicable.)

21. **motion:** impulse, desire

25. **rank:** lewd, lascivious

26. **change of prides:** perhaps, exchanging one excess or display for another

27. **Nice:** wanton, lascivious

31. **still:** always

34. **'tis greater skill:** perhaps, is more just; or, perhaps, shows more understanding or reason

Did call my father was I know not where
When I was stamped. Some coiner with his tools 5
Made me a counterfeit; yet my mother seemed
The Dian of that time; so doth my wife
The nonpareil of this. O, vengeance, vengeance!
Me of my lawful pleasure she restrained
And prayed me oft forbearance; did it with 10
A pudency so rosy the sweet view on 't
Might well have warmed old Saturn, that I thought
her
As chaste as unsunned snow. O, all the devils!
This yellow Iachimo in an hour, was 't not? 15
Or less? At first? Perchance he spoke not, but,
Like a full-acorned boar, a German one,
Cried "O!" and mounted; found no opposition
But what he looked for should oppose and she
Should from encounter guard. Could I find out 20
The woman's part in me—for there's no motion
That tends to vice in man but I affirm
It is the woman's part: be it lying, note it,
The woman's; flattering, hers; deceiving, hers;
Lust and rank thoughts, hers, hers; revenges, hers; 25
Ambitions, covetings, change of prides, disdain,
Nice longing, slanders, mutability,
All faults that ⌜have a⌝ name, nay, that hell knows,
Why, hers, in part or all, but rather all.
For even to vice 30
They are not constant, but are changing still
One vice but of a minute old for one
Not half so old as that. I'll write against them,
Detest them, curse them. Yet 'tis greater skill
In a true hate to pray they have their will; 35
The very devils cannot plague them better.

He exits.

CYMBELINE

ACT 3

3.1 Caius Lucius arrives as ambassador from Augustus Caesar, demanding that Cymbeline pay the tribute Britain owes to Rome. With the encouragement of the queen and Cloten, Cymbeline refuses. Caius Lucius pronounces war between Rome and Britain.

---

0 SD. **in state:** with great pomp and solemnity

1–2. **Augustus Caesar, Julius Caesar:** See notes to 2.4.13, 24, page 84, and see picture below.

5. **Cassibelan:** See note to 1.1.35, page 8.

8. **succession:** successors, heirs

9. **pounds:** i.e., pound weights of silver

10. **untendered:** not offered

11. **marvel:** astonishment

13. **There:** i.e., **there** will

16. **our own:** i.e., rather than Roman (the bridges of which were famously prominent)

18–19. **to resume . . . again:** i.e., we must reassume

21. **bravery:** (1) splendor; (2) courage, fortitude

Julius Caesar. (2.4.24; 3.1.2, 39)
From Plutarch, *The liues of the noble Grecians and Romanes* . . . (1579).

ACT 3

Scene 1

Enter in state Cymbeline, Queen, Cloten, and Lords at one door, and, at another, Caius Lucius and Attendants.

CYMBELINE
Now say, what would Augustus Caesar with us?

LUCIUS
When Julius Caesar, whose remembrance yet
Lives in men's eyes and will to ears and tongues
Be theme and hearing ever, was in this Britain
And conquered it, Cassibelan, thine uncle, 5
Famous in Caesar's praises no whit less
Than in his feats deserving it, for him
And his succession granted Rome a tribute,
Yearly three thousand pounds, which by thee lately
Is left untendered. 10

QUEEN And, to kill the marvel,
Shall be so ever.

CLOTEN There be many Caesars
Ere such another Julius. Britain's a world
By itself, and we will nothing pay 15
For wearing our own noses.

QUEEN That opportunity
Which then they had to take from 's, to resume
We have again.—Remember, sir, my liege,
The Kings your ancestors, together with 20
The natural bravery of your isle, which stands

22. **Neptune's:** Neptune is the Roman god of the sea; **palèd:** fenced

27. **came . . . overcame:** This famous expression (*veni, vidi, vici*) is associated with Julius Caesar's success in battle, in 47 B.C.E., near Zela, in modern-day Turkey.

28. **touched:** affected; vexed

29. **shipping:** ships

30. **baubles:** i.e., toys, too small or weak to be seaworthy (See longer note, page 266.)

33. **at point:** i.e., just about

34. **giglet Fortune:** i.e., the goddess **Fortune,** the personification of chance or luck, here pictured as a **giglet**—a lewd, wanton woman (See longer note, page 266, and picture, page 232.) **master:** capture, possess

35. **Lud's Town:** i.e., London, named, according to a false etymology, after King Lud, Cymbeline's grandfather (See picture, page 116.)

40. **crooked noses:** See note to line 16 above. **owe:** own, possess

41. **straight:** steady (with obvious wordplay on its meaning of "not **crooked**")

48. **else:** otherwise; **pray you now:** i.e., if you please (here, a mocking deferential phrase)

50. **injurious:** insulting

53. **all color:** i.e., even the show or pretence of reason (Wordplay on *collar* is picked up in the word **yoke** [line 54].)

57. **Mulmutius:** a British king (See Historical Background, pages 284–85, and picture, page 104.)

As Neptune's park, ribbed and palèd in
With ⌜rocks⌝ unscalable and roaring waters,
With sands that will not bear your enemies' boats
But suck them up to th' topmast. A kind of conquest 25
Caesar made here, but made not here his brag
Of "came, and saw, and overcame." With shame—
The first that ever touched him—he was carried
From off our coast, twice beaten; and his shipping,
Poor ignorant baubles, on our terrible seas 30
Like eggshells moved upon their surges, cracked
As easily 'gainst our rocks. For joy whereof
The famed Cassibelan, who was once at point—
O, giglet Fortune!—to master Caesar's sword,
Made Lud's Town with rejoicing fires bright 35
And Britons strut with courage.

CLOTEN Come, there's no more tribute to be paid. Our kingdom is stronger than it was at that time, and, as I said, there is no more such Caesars. Other of them may have crooked noses, but to owe such 40 straight arms, none.

CYMBELINE Son, let your mother end.

CLOTEN We have yet many among us can grip as hard as Cassibelan. I do not say I am one, but I have a hand. Why tribute? Why should we pay tribute? If 45 Caesar can hide the sun from us with a blanket or put the moon in his pocket, we will pay him tribute for light; else, sir, no more tribute, pray you now.

CYMBELINE, ⌜*to Lucius*⌝ You must know,
Till the injurious Romans did extort 50
This tribute from us, we were free. Caesar's ambition,
Which swelled so much that it did almost stretch
The sides o' th' world, against all color here
Did put the yoke upon 's, which to shake off
Becomes a warlike people, whom we reckon 55
Ourselves to be. We do say, then, to Caesar,
Our ancestor was that Mulmutius which

58. **Ordained:** established, instituted; **whose use:** the application of which (**laws**)

59. **franchise:** exemption from this particular burden or exaction

70. **confusion:** destruction, ruin, overthrow

72. **not to be:** i.e., that cannot **be; Thus defied:** i.e., having **thus defied** (challenged) you (**in Caesar's name**)

75–76. **my youth . . . him:** i.e., **I spent much** of **my youth under** his direct command

76. **Of him:** i.e., from him

78. **keep at utterance:** to guard or preserve to the uttermost degree; **perfect:** certain

79. **Pannonians and Dalmatians:** Pannonia was an ancient region corresponding to modern-day Hungary; Dalmatia was a region on the Adriatic.

81. **cold:** indifferent, apathetic

83. **proof:** the result, issue, or effect

92. **the remain:** that which remains

THe Land vnguided, Kingleſſe did remaine,
Till great *Mulmutius* did the Wreathe obtaine:

King Mulmutius. (3.1.57–65)
From John Taylor, *All the workes of . . .* (1630).

Ordained our laws, whose use the sword of Caesar
Hath too much mangled, whose repair and franchise
Shall, by the power we hold, be our good deed, 60
Though Rome be therefore angry. Mulmutius made
our laws,
Who was the first of Britain which did put
His brows within a golden crown and called
Himself a king. 65

LUCIUS I am sorry, Cymbeline,
That I am to pronounce Augustus Caesar—
Caesar, that hath more kings his servants than
Thyself domestic officers—thine enemy.
Receive it from me, then: war and confusion 70
In Caesar's name pronounce I 'gainst thee. Look
For fury not to be resisted. Thus defied,
I thank thee for myself.

CYMBELINE Thou art welcome, Caius.
Thy Caesar knighted me; my youth I spent 75
Much under him. Of him I gathered honor,
Which he to seek of me again perforce
Behooves me keep at utterance. I am perfect
That the Pannonians and Dalmatians for
Their liberties are now in arms, a precedent 80
Which not to read would show the Britons cold.
So Caesar shall not find them.

LUCIUS Let proof speak.

CLOTEN His Majesty bids you welcome. Make pastime
with us a day or two, or longer. If you seek us after- 85
wards in other terms, you shall find us in our salt-
water girdle; if you beat us out of it, it is yours. If
you fall in the adventure, our crows shall fare the
better for you, and there's an end.

LUCIUS So, sir. 90

CYMBELINE
I know your master's pleasure, and he mine.
All the remain is welcome.

They exit.

3.2 Pisanio receives two letters from Posthumus—one in which Pisanio is instructed to kill Imogen, and another written to Imogen, telling her to leave the court and travel with Pisanio to Milford Haven, where Posthumus claims to be waiting for her. Imogen makes excited plans for the journey.

---

1. **How:** i.e., what (as also in line 11); **Wherefore:** why

5. **As poisonous-tongued as handed:** i.e., **as** gifted in spreading venomous words **as** in actual poisoning (an allusion to the reputation of the **Italian** as a poisoner)

7. **truth:** fidelity, constancy

9. **take in:** conquer

10. **to her:** i.e., compared with her

15. **serviceable:** diligent in service

17. **fact:** deed, crime

19. **by her own command:** i.e., through what she will tell you to do

21. **Senseless bauble:** i.e., trifle incapable of perception or sensation

22. **fedary for:** i.e., confederate or accomplice to

23. **without:** on the outside

24. **am ignorant in:** i.e., will pretend ignorance of

Scene 2

Enter Pisanio reading of a letter.

PISANIO

How? Of adultery? Wherefore write you not
What monsters her accuse? Leonatus,
O master, what a strange infection
Is fall'n into thy ear! What false Italian,
As poisonous-tongued as handed, hath prevailed 5
On thy too ready hearing? Disloyal? No.
She's punished for her truth and undergoes,
More goddesslike than wifelike, such assaults
As would take in some virtue. O my master,
Thy mind to her is now as low as were 10
Thy fortunes. How? That I should murder her,
Upon the love and truth and vows which I
Have made to thy command? I her? Her blood?
If it be so to do good service, never
Let me be counted serviceable. How look I 15
That I should seem to lack humanity
So much as this fact comes to? (⌜*He reads:*⌝) *Do 't!*
The letter
That I have sent her, by her own command
Shall give thee opportunity. O damned paper, 20
Black as the ink that's on thee! Senseless bauble,
Art thou a fedary for this act, and look'st
So virginlike without? Lo, here she comes.

Enter Imogen.

I am ignorant in what I am commanded.

IMOGEN How now, Pisanio? 25

PISANIO

Madam, here is a letter from my lord.

⌜*He gives her a paper.*⌝

IMOGEN

Who, thy lord that is my lord, Leonatus?

28. **astronomer:** i.e., astrologer (See picture, page 250.)

29. **characters:** i.e., handwriting

30. **He'd:** i.e., such an astrologer would

31. **relish:** taste

34. **med'cinable:** medicinal, healing, curative

35. **physic love:** i.e., make **love** stronger (literally, provide medicine to **love**)

36. **Good wax, thy leave:** her apology to the sealing **wax** before she breaks it

38. **locks of counsel:** i.e., wax seals pictured as **locks** protecting secrets (Lines 38–41 contrast **lovers,** who value such **locks,** with **men in dangerous bonds,** i.e., **men** bound [by legal documents also sealed in wax] either to repay debts or be confined in debtors' prison.)

41. **clasp young Cupid's tables:** i.e., secure love letters (as if the letters were table-books [**tables**] fastened with a clasp)

44. **as:** i.e., but that (See longer note, page 267.)

45. **Cambria:** i.e., Wales

46. **Milford Haven:** a port city in Wales

47. **advise you:** i.e., **advise you** to do; **follow:** act upon, obey

48–49. **and your increasing in love:** i.e., **and (he wishes)** that your **love** will continue to increase

53. **mean affairs:** unimportant business

57. **bate:** i.e., abate, calm down

59. **thick:** i.e., quickly

62. **by th' way:** i.e., as we travel

O, learned indeed were that astronomer
That knew the stars as I his characters!
He'd lay the future open. You good gods, 30
Let what is here contained relish of love,
Of my lord's health, of his content (yet not
That we two are asunder; let that grieve him.
Some griefs are med'cinable; that is one of them,
For it doth physic love) of his content 35
All but in that. Good wax, thy leave.
⌜*She opens the letter.*⌝
Blest be
You bees that make these locks of counsel. Lovers
And men in dangerous bonds pray not alike;
Though forfeiters you cast in prison, yet 40
You clasp young Cupid's tables. Good news, gods!

⌜*Reads.*⌝ *Justice and your father's wrath, should he take me in his dominion, could not be so cruel to me as you, O the dearest of creatures, would even renew me with your eyes. Take notice that I am in Cambria* 45 *at Milford Haven. What your own love will out of this advise you, follow. So he wishes you all happiness, that remains loyal to his vow, and your increasing in love.*

Leonatus Posthumus. 50

O, for a horse with wings! Hear'st thou, Pisanio?
He is at Milford Haven. Read, and tell me
How far 'tis thither. If one of mean affairs
May plod it in a week, why may not I
Glide thither in a day? Then, true Pisanio, 55
Who long'st like me to see thy lord, who long'st—
O, let me bate—but not like me, yet long'st
But in a fainter kind—O, not like me,
For mine's beyond beyond—say, and speak thick—
Love's counselor should fill the bores of hearing 60
To th' smothering of the sense—how far it is
To this same blessèd Milford. And by th' way

64. **T' inherit:** i.e., to come into possession of, to acquire

65–67. **for the gap . . . to excuse:** i.e., how we may justify or explain the time that we are away (from court)

68. **or ere begot:** i.e., before (the reason for the **excuse**) exists

70. **rid:** ride

75. **riding wagers:** i.e., horse races (on which people bet)

76–77. **the sands . . . behalf:** i.e., sand in an hourglass (See picture, page 236.) **i' th' clock's behalf:** i.e., serving in the place of a clock

79. **presently:** immediately

80. **fit:** be appropriate for

81. **huswife:** housewife (pronounced "hussif")

82. **you're best:** i.e., you had better

83–84. **Nor here . . . in them:** Since *to ensue* can mean either "to precede" or "to be subsequent to," these lines can have two opposing meanings. (1) There is **a fog** covering every direction except the one **before me;** or (2) There is **a fog** in every direction, so that the journey is into the unknown. **Nor . . . nor:** i.e., neither . . . nor

3.3 Three men enter as if from a cave, the two younger men protesting the limitations of their mountain lives. When they exit to pursue game for food, the older man reveals that they are actually the two lost princes, whom he stole in infancy in protest against unjust treatment he had received from Cymbeline. Belarius (who now calls himself

(continued)

Tell me how Wales was made so happy as
T' inherit such a haven. But first of all,
How we may steal from hence, and for the gap 65
That we shall make in time from our hence-going
And our return, to excuse. But first, how get hence?
Why should excuse be born or ere begot?
We'll talk of that hereafter. Prithee speak,
How many ⌜score⌝ of miles may we well rid 70
'Twixt hour and hour?

PISANIO One score 'twixt sun and sun,
Madam, 's enough for you, and too much too.

IMOGEN
Why, one that rode to 's execution, man,
Could never go so slow. I have heard of riding wagers 75
Where horses have been nimbler than the sands
That run i' th' clock's behalf. But this is fool'ry.
Go, bid my woman feign a sickness, say
She'll home to her father; and provide me presently
A riding suit no costlier than would fit 80
A franklin's huswife.

PISANIO Madam, you're best consider.

IMOGEN
I see before me, man. Nor here, ⌜nor⌝ here,
Nor what ensues, but have a fog in them
That I cannot look through. Away, I prithee. 85
Do as I bid thee. There's no more to say.
Accessible is none but Milford way.

They exit.

Scene 3

Enter, ⌜as from a cave,⌝ Belarius ⌜as Morgan,⌝ Guiderius ⌜as Polydor,⌝ and Arviragus ⌜as Cadwal.⌝

BELARIUS, ⌜*as* MORGAN⌝
A goodly day not to keep house with such

Morgan) has given Welsh names to Guiderius and Arviragus. They have no idea of their heritage, thinking Morgan their father.

---

1. **keep house:** stay indoors
2. **gate:** entrance way
3. **bows you:** i.e., forces you to bend
4. **morning's holy office:** i.e., morning prayer
5. **jet:** strut, stroll, parade
7. **Good morrow:** i.e., saying "good morning"
8. **i' th' rock:** i.e., in a cave; **hardly:** harshly (with wordplay on the hardness of **rock**)
14. **like a crow:** i.e., as if I were no larger than **a crow**
15. **place:** (1) relative physical positioning; (2) social rank; **lessens:** diminishes (someone); **sets off:** shows (someone) to advantage, makes (someone) prominent
16. **revolve:** ponder
17. **tricks:** stratagems
19. **allowed:** accepted as satisfactory, praised
22. **sharded beetle:** i.e., **beetle** with its scaly wings; or, **beetle** living in dung (Editors often strongly favor one of these very different meanings over the other.) **hold:** place of refuge
24. **attending for a check:** obediently waiting on (a powerful person) only to receive a reprimand
27. **gain . . . fine:** i.e., receive courteous gestures from his own tailor **the cap:** i.e., the deferential doffing of **the cap**

(continued)

Whose roof's as low as ours! ⌜Stoop,⌝ boys. This gate
Instructs you how t' adore the heavens and bows you
To a morning's holy office. The gates of monarchs
Are arched so high that giants may jet through 5
And keep their impious turbans on, without
Good morrow to the sun. Hail, thou fair heaven!
We house i' th' rock, yet use thee not so hardly
As prouder livers do.

GUIDERIUS, ⌜*as* POLYDOR⌝ Hail, heaven! 10

ARVIRAGUS, ⌜*as* CADWAL⌝ Hail, heaven!

BELARIUS, ⌜*as* MORGAN⌝

Now for our mountain sport. Up to yond hill;
Your legs are young. I'll tread these flats. Consider,
When you above perceive me like a crow,
That it is place which lessens and sets off, 15
And you may then revolve what tales I have told you
Of courts, of princes, of the tricks in war.
This service is not service, so being done,
But being so allowed. To apprehend thus
Draws us a profit from all things we see, 20
And often, to our comfort, shall we find
The sharded beetle in a safer hold
Than is the full-winged eagle. O, this life
Is nobler than attending for a check,
Richer than doing nothing for a ⌜robe,⌝ 25
Prouder than rustling in unpaid-for silk:
Such gain the cap of him that makes him fine
Yet keeps his book uncrossed. No life to ours.

GUIDERIUS, ⌜*as* POLYDOR⌝

Out of your proof you speak. We poor unfledged
Have never winged from view o' th' nest, nor ⌜know⌝ 30
not
What air 's from home. Haply this life is best
If quiet life be best, sweeter to you
That have a sharper known, well corresponding
With your stiff age; but unto us it is 35

28. **keeps his book uncrossed:** i.e., does not pay (cross off) the debts in **his** account **book; to ours:** i.e., compared **to ours**

29. **proof:** experience

32. **air 's from home:** i.e., **air** there is away from **home; Haply:** perhaps

36. **abed:** in bed (i.e., only in one's dreams)

38. **stride a limit:** step over a border (i.e., out of sanctuary and into a locale where the **debtor** [line 37] can be arrested for his unpaid debt)

41. **beat:** i.e., **beat** down in

42. **pinching:** narrow, confining

45. **Like:** i.e., as

46. **flies:** flees

55. **pain:** effort, labor

59. **ill deserve:** earn or win harm or misfortune

60. **curtsy at:** i.e., bow to

62. **report:** fame, reputation

63. **best of note:** most notable, those of greatest eminence

68. **hangings:** i.e., **fruit** (line 66)

A cell of ignorance, traveling abed,
A prison ⌜for⌝ a debtor that not dares
To stride a limit.

ARVIRAGUS, ⌜*as* CADWAL⌝ What should we speak of
When we are old as you? When we shall hear 40
The rain and wind beat dark December, how
In this our pinching cave shall we discourse
The freezing hours away? We have seen nothing.
We are beastly: subtle as the fox for prey,
Like warlike as the wolf for what we eat. 45
Our valor is to chase what flies. Our cage
We make a choir, as doth the prisoned bird,
And sing our bondage freely.

BELARIUS, ⌜*as* MORGAN⌝ How you speak!
Did you but know the city's usuries 50
And felt them knowingly; the art o' th' court,
As hard to leave as keep, whose top to climb
Is certain falling, or so slipp'ry that
The fear's as bad as falling; the toil o' th' war,
A pain that only seems to seek out danger 55
I' th' name of fame and honor, which dies i' th' search
And hath as oft a sland'rous epitaph
As record of fair act—nay, many times
Doth ill deserve by doing well; what's worse,
Must curtsy at the censure. O boys, this story 60
The world may read in me. My body's marked
With Roman swords, and my report was once
First with the best of note. Cymbeline loved me,
And when a soldier was the theme, my name
Was not far off. Then was I as a tree 65
Whose boughs did bend with fruit. But in one night
A storm or robbery, call it what you will,
Shook down my mellow hangings, nay, my leaves,
And left me bare to weather.

GUIDERIUS, ⌜*as* POLYDOR⌝ Uncertain favor! 70

76. **rock:** i.e., cave; **demesnes:** lands, territories

77. **at honest:** i.e., in **honest**

79. **fore-end:** early part

81. **venison:** animals hunted for food (not necessarily deer)

83. **attends:** awaits

84. **In place of greater state:** i.e., where there is **greater** ceremony

92. **prince it:** carry themselves like princes

93. **trick:** knack, art

101. **nerves:** sinews

103. **in as . . . figure:** i.e., acting a part just as apt **like:** apt, suitable **figure:** part enacted

King Lud. (3.1.35)
From John Taylor, *All the workes of . . .* (1630).

BELARIUS, ⌜*as* MORGAN⌝
My fault being nothing, as I have told you oft,
But that two villains, whose false oaths prevailed
Before my perfect honor, swore to Cymbeline
I was confederate with the Romans. So
Followed my banishment; and this twenty years 75
This rock and these demesnes have been my world,
Where I have lived at honest freedom, paid
More pious debts to heaven than in all
The fore-end of my time. But up to th' mountains!
This is not hunters' language. He that strikes 80
The venison first shall be the lord o' th' feast;
To him the other two shall minister,
And we will fear no poison, which attends
In place of greater state. I'll meet you in the valleys.
⌜*Guiderius and Arviragus*⌝ *exit.*

⌜BELARIUS⌝
How hard it is to hide the sparks of nature! 85
These boys know little they are sons to th' King,
Nor Cymbeline dreams that they are alive.
They think they are mine, and, though trained up
thus meanly,
I' th' cave ⌜wherein they⌝ bow, their thoughts do hit 90
The roofs of palaces, and nature prompts them
In simple and low things to prince it much
Beyond the trick of others. This Polydor,
The heir of Cymbeline and Britain, who
The King his father called Guiderius—Jove! 95
When on my three-foot stool I sit and tell
The warlike feats I have done, his spirits fly out
Into my story; say "Thus mine enemy fell,
And thus I set my foot on 's neck," even then
The princely blood flows in his cheek, he sweats, 100
Strains his young nerves, and puts himself in posture
That acts my words. The younger brother, Cadwal,
Once Arviragus, in as like a figure

105. **conceiving:** imagination

106. **knows:** i.e., know

109. **of succession:** i.e., from transmitting your crown (to your heirs)

110. **refts:** deprived, robbed; **Euriphile:** accent on second and fourth syllables

115. **up:** roused, started

3.4 On the journey to Milford Haven, Pisanio reveals to Imogen that he is supposed to kill her. She is so distraught at Posthumus's lack of faith in her that she encourages Pisanio to stab her immediately. Instead, he proposes that she disguise herself as a boy and serve Caius Lucius, who is soon to land at Milford Haven. When she agrees to this plan, he gives her the box containing what he thinks is a restorative medicine.

---

3. **have:** i.e., long

7. **but painted:** i.e., merely represented in a painting

8. **perplexed:** troubled

10. **havior of less fear:** i.e., less terrifying manner; **wildness:** panic

11. **senses:** mental faculties

12. **tender'st thou:** i.e., do you offer

15. **But:** only; **hand:** handwriting

Strikes life into my speech and shows much more
His own conceiving. Hark, the game is roused! 105
O Cymbeline, heaven and my conscience knows
Thou didst unjustly banish me; whereon,
At three and two years old I stole these babes,
Thinking to bar thee of succession as
Thou refts me of my lands. Euriphile, 110
Thou wast their nurse; they took thee for their
mother,
And every day do honor to her grave.
Myself, Belarius, that am Morgan called,
They take for natural father. The game is up! 115
He exits.

Scene 4

Enter Pisanio and Imogen.

IMOGEN
Thou told'st me, when we came from horse, the place
Was near at hand. Ne'er longed my mother so
To see me first as I have now. Pisanio, man,
Where is Posthumus? What is in thy mind
That makes thee stare thus? Wherefore breaks that 5
sigh
From th' inward of thee? One but painted thus
Would be interpreted a thing perplexed
Beyond self-explication. Put thyself
Into a havior of less fear, ere wildness 10
Vanquish my staider senses. What's the matter?
⌜*Pisanio hands her a paper.*⌝
Why tender'st thou that paper to me with
A look untender? If 't be summer news,
Smile to 't before; if winterly, thou need'st
But keep that count'nance still. My husband's hand! 15

16. **drug-damned:** i.e., cursed because of its use of poisons (For Italians as poisoners, see note to 3.2.5.) **out-craftied:** outwitted

18. **take off some extremity:** i.e., lessen the intensity of something in the letter

20. **Please you:** a deferential phrase of request ("may it **please you** to")

24. **lies:** i.e., lie

28. **faith:** loyalty, fidelity; **with the breach:** i.e., along **with the** breaking

34. **What:** i.e., why, for what reason

35. **'tis slander:** i.e., it is **slander** that has **cut her throat**

37. **worms:** serpents (See picture, page 164.)

38. **posting:** swift, rapidly moving

38–39. **belie . . . world:** perhaps, fills all **the world** with lies

39. **states:** dignitaries; nobles

41. **What cheer:** i.e., how are you? (literally, what is your mood or disposition?)

43. **in watch:** i.e., awake; **think on:** i.e., **think** about

44. **'twixt clock and clock:** i.e., from hour to hour (literally, between the hours as struck by the **clock**); **If sleep charge nature:** i.e., **if** I fall asleep (**Charge** has its sense of weighing down, placing a load on.)

45. **fearful:** anxious, frightening

48. **Thy:** presumably addressed to Posthumus (as she openly addresses him at lines 57, 64, and 94)

That drug-damned Italy hath out-craftied him,
And he's at some hard point. Speak, man! Thy tongue
May take off some extremity, which to read
Would be even mortal to me.

PISANIO Please you read, 20
And you shall find me, wretched man, a thing
The most disdained of fortune.

IMOGEN *reads: Thy mistress, Pisanio, hath played the strumpet in my bed, the testimonies whereof lies bleeding in me. I speak not out of weak surmises but* 25 *from proof as strong as my grief and as certain as I expect my revenge. That part thou, Pisanio, must act for me, if thy faith be not tainted with the breach of hers. Let thine own hands take away her life. I shall give thee opportunity at Milford Haven—she hath* 30 *my letter for the purpose—where, if thou fear to strike and to make me certain it is done, thou art the pander to her dishonor and equally to me disloyal.*

PISANIO, ⌜*aside*⌝
What shall I need to draw my sword? The paper
Hath cut her throat already. No, 'tis slander, 35
Whose edge is sharper than the sword, whose tongue
Outvenoms all the worms of Nile, whose breath
Rides on the posting winds and doth belie
All corners of the world. Kings, queens, and states,
Maids, matrons, nay, the secrets of the grave 40
This viperous slander enters.—What cheer, madam?

IMOGEN
False to his bed? What is it to be false?
To lie in watch there and to think on him?
To weep 'twixt clock and clock? If sleep charge nature,
To break it with a fearful dream of him 45
And cry myself awake? That's false to 's bed, is it?

PISANIO Alas, good lady!

IMOGEN
I false? Thy conscience witness! Iachimo,

49. **incontinency:** sexual indulgence

51. **favor's:** i.e., appearance is; **jay:** i.e., woman in flashy clothing, prostitute (called such after the European **jay,** a bird with striking plumage), in contrast to Imogen, **a garment out of fashion** (line 53)

52. **Whose mother was her painting:** perhaps, who derives her beauty not from nature (her **mother**) but from cosmetics (This line has been much debated.) **betrayed him:** seduced him, led him astray (See picture, page 126.)

53. **stale:** no longer new, out of date

54. **richer than to hang by th' walls:** i.e., too fine to be simply discarded (Out-of-fashion garments were hung on pegs or **ripped** [line 55] into cloth to use for other purposes.)

56. **seeming:** appearance (Lines 56–64 describe how the actions of hypocrites and liars have made **good seeming**—the appearance of honesty, penitence, devoutness, genuine distress—look spurious, as if **put on for villainy** [line 58].)

57. **revolt:** casting off of allegiance, changing sides

61. **Aeneas:** The hero of Virgil's *Aeneid* betrayed Dido, queen of Carthage, through **false** protestations of his love.

62. **Sinon's weeping:** The hypocritically **weeping** Sinon persuaded the Trojans to allow the wooden horse (filled with Greek soldiers) inside the walls of Troy. **Sinon's** false tears are mentioned several times in Shakespeare's *The Rape of Lucrece.* See picture, page 58.

63. **scandal:** bring into disrepute

63–64. **took pity / From most true wretchedness:** i.e., **took** sympathy away from genuine distress

(continued)

Thou didst accuse him of incontinency.
Thou then looked'st like a villain. Now methinks 50
Thy favor's good enough. Some jay of Italy,
Whose mother was her painting, hath betrayed him.
Poor I am stale, a garment out of fashion,
And, for I am richer than to hang by th' walls,
I must be ripped. To pieces with me! O, 55
Men's vows are women's traitors! All good seeming,
By thy revolt, O husband, shall be thought
Put on for villainy, not born where 't grows,
But worn a bait for ladies.

PISANIO Good madam, hear me. 60

IMOGEN
True honest men, being heard like false Aeneas,
Were in his time thought false, and Sinon's weeping
Did scandal many a holy tear, took pity
From most true wretchedness. So thou, Posthumus,
Wilt lay the leaven on all proper men; 65
Goodly and gallant shall be false and perjured
From thy great fail.—Come, fellow, be thou honest;
Do thou thy master's bidding. When thou seest him,
A little witness my obedience. Look,
I draw the sword myself. 70

⌜*She draws Pisanio's sword from its scabbard and hands it to him.*⌝

Take it, and hit
The innocent mansion of my love, my heart.
Fear not; 'tis empty of all things but grief.
Thy master is not there, who was indeed
The riches of it. Do his bidding; strike. 75
Thou mayst be valiant in a better cause,
But now thou seem'st a coward.

PISANIO, ⌜*throwing down the sword*⌝ Hence, vile instrument!
Thou shalt not damn my hand. 80

IMOGEN Why, I must die,

65. **lay the leaven on:** i.e., taint the reputation of (Almost all biblical references to **leaven** associate it with sin, deception, and corruption.) **proper:** honest

66. **Goodly:** admirable, excellent; **gallant:** praiseworthy; **be:** i.e., **be** perceived as

67. **From thy great fail:** i.e., because of your failure; **honest:** honorable

69. **A little witness:** i.e., testify **a little** to

85. **cravens:** makes cowardly

86. **afore 't:** in front of it; **Soft:** i.e., wait a minute; **We'll no defense:** i.e., I want no protective armor

88. **scriptures:** i.e., letters (with wordplay on [1] writings; [2] sacred texts)

95. **set up:** urge on, instigate

98. **princely fellows:** i.e., Imogen's **princely** equals

99–100. **It is . . . rareness:** i.e., what I have done is no ordinary action, but (comes from) rare qualities in me (with possible puns on **strain** as pedigree or lineage, in contrast to Posthumus's **common** status)

101. **disedged:** dulled, blunted (i.e., sexually sated)

102. **tirest on:** greedily feed on (language from falconry)

103. **panged:** tormented; **dispatch:** make haste, hurry

And if I do not by thy hand, thou art
No servant of thy master's. Against self-slaughter
There is a prohibition so divine
That cravens my weak hand. Come, here's my heart— 85
Something's ⌜afore 't⌝. Soft, soft! We'll no defense—
Obedient as the scabbard. What is here?
⌜*She takes papers from her bodice.*⌝
The scriptures of the loyal Leonatus,
All turned to heresy? Away, away!
⌜*She throws away the letters.*⌝
Corrupters of my faith, you shall no more 90
Be stomachers to my heart. Thus may poor fools
Believe false teachers. Though those that are betrayed
Do feel the treason sharply, yet the traitor
Stands in worse case of woe. And thou, Posthumus,
That didst set up 95
My disobedience 'gainst the King my father
And ⌜make⌝ me put into contempt the suits
Of princely fellows, shalt hereafter find
It is no act of common passage, but
A strain of rareness: and I grieve myself 100
To think, when thou shalt be disedged by her
That now thou tirest on, how thy memory
Will then be panged by me.—Prithee, dispatch.
The lamb entreats the butcher. Where's thy knife?
Thou art too slow to do thy master's bidding 105
When I desire it too.

PISANIO O gracious lady,
Since I received command to do this business
I have not slept one wink.

IMOGEN Do 't, and to bed, then. 110

PISANIO
I'll wake mine eyeballs ⌜out⌝ first.

IMOGEN Wherefore then
Didst undertake it? Why hast thou abused
So many miles with a pretense? This place?

118. **Purpose:** propose to

119. **To be unbent:** i.e., only to lose your readiness to act (The term **unbent** is from archery, describing a bow.) **stand:** i.e., standing place for shooting game

120. **elected:** chosen

122. **the which:** i.e., **which time**

129. **Nor tent to bottom that:** i.e., **nor** probe **that wound** (line 128) to its **bottom**

131. **back:** i.e., be going **back** (to the court)

132. **like:** i.e., likely, probably

137. **abused:** deceived

138. **singular:** remarkable, extraordinary; **art:** skill

142. **give but:** i.e., just **give**

147. **the while:** in the meantime, meanwhile; **bide:** dwell, reside

A woman at "her painting." (3.4.52)
From Hannah Woolley, *The accomplish'd ladies delight* . . . (1684).

Mine action and thine own? Our horses' labor? 115
The time inviting thee? The perturbed court
For my being absent, whereunto I never
Purpose return? Why hast thou gone so far
To be unbent when thou hast ta'en thy stand,
Th' elected deer before thee? 120

PISANIO But to win time
To lose so bad employment, in the which
I have considered of a course. Good lady,
Hear me with patience.

IMOGEN Talk thy tongue weary. 125
Speak.
I have heard I am a strumpet, and mine ear,
Therein false struck, can take no greater wound,
Nor tent to bottom that. But speak.

PISANIO Then, madam, 130
I thought you would not back again.

IMOGEN Most like,
Bringing me here to kill me.

PISANIO Not so, neither.
But if I were as wise as honest, then 135
My purpose would prove well. It cannot be
But that my master is abused. Some villain,
Ay, and singular in his art, hath done
You both this cursèd injury.

IMOGEN
Some Roman courtesan? 140

PISANIO No, on my life.
I'll give but notice you are dead, and send him
Some bloody sign of it, for 'tis commanded
I should do so. You shall be missed at court,
And that will well confirm it. 145

IMOGEN Why, good fellow,
What shall I do the while? Where bide? How live?
Or in my life what comfort when I am
Dead to my husband?

152. **noble:** high-ranking

159. **Are they not but:** i.e., do they exist only

160. **of it, but not in 't:** perhaps, part **of it but** separated from it

162. **livers:** living creatures

164. **ambassador:** envoy, official messenger

167. **Dark:** wordplay on (1) hidden, secretive; (2) dismal

168. **t' appear:** to reveal

169. **But by:** i.e., without; **should:** could

170. **Pretty and full of view:** perhaps, pleasing and with good prospects; **haply:** perhaps

176. **modesty:** womanly propriety, chastity; **death on 't:** i.e., its destruction

180. **Command:** i.e., her powerful role as princess; **niceness:** shyness, reserve

182. **it:** i.e., its; **waggish:** i.e., boyish, roguish (A **wag** was a mischievous boy or a young man.)

". . . doublet, hat, hose." (3.4.196)
From [Robert Greene], *A quip for an vpstart courtier . . .* (1620).

PISANIO If you'll back to th' court— 150

IMOGEN
No court, no father, nor no more ado
With that harsh, noble, simple nothing,
That Cloten, whose love suit hath been to me
As fearful as a siege.

PISANIO If not at court, 155
Then not in Britain must you bide.

IMOGEN Where, then?
Hath Britain all the sun that shines? Day, night,
Are they not but in Britain? I' th' world's volume
Our Britain seems as of it, but not in 't, 160
In a great pool a swan's nest. Prithee think
There's livers out of Britain.

PISANIO I am most glad
You think of other place. Th' ambassador,
Lucius the Roman, comes to Milford Haven 165
Tomorrow. Now, if you could wear a mind
Dark as your fortune is, and but disguise
That which t' appear itself must not yet be
But by self-danger, you should tread a course
Pretty and full of view: yea, haply near 170
The residence of Posthumus; so nigh, at least,
That though his actions were not visible, yet
Report should render him hourly to your ear
As truly as he moves.

IMOGEN O, for such means, 175
Though peril to my modesty, not death on 't,
I would adventure.

PISANIO Well then, here's the point:
You must forget to be a woman; change
Command into obedience, fear and niceness— 180
The handmaids of all women, or, more truly,
Woman it pretty self—into a waggish courage,
Ready in gibes, quick-answered, saucy, and

184. **quarrelous:** quarrelsome, contentious

188. **common-kissing Titan:** In poetry, **Titan** is the personification of the sun, which kisses everything.

189. **trims:** adornments, outfits

190. **You . . . angry:** Pisanio implies that, as with many mythological heroes, Imogen's suffering comes from having angered **Juno,** queen of the Roman gods.

195. **Forethinking this:** considering this beforehand; **fit:** prepared

196. **doublet:** close-fitting men's jacket; **hose:** breeches (See picture, page 128.)

197. **answer to:** match, go along with; **Would . . . serving:** if you should, with their assistance

199. **of such a season:** i.e., of the age you are imitating

200. **desire his service:** i.e., ask to be taken into **his service**

201. **happy:** favored, i.e., gifted; **make him know:** i.e., convince him

203. **embrace you:** take you into his service

206. **supplyment:** the act of supplying or what is supplied

208. **diet:** feed; **Prithee:** I pray thee, please

209. **even:** keep pace with

215. **carriage:** conveyance

As quarrelous as the weasel. Nay, you must
Forget that rarest treasure of your cheek, 185
Exposing it—but O, the harder heart!
Alack, no remedy—to the greedy touch
Of common-kissing Titan, and forget
Your laborsome and dainty trims, wherein
You made great Juno angry. 190

IMOGEN Nay, be brief.
I see into thy end and am almost
A man already.

PISANIO First, make yourself but like one.
Forethinking this, I have already fit— 195
'Tis in my cloakbag—doublet, hat, hose, all
That answer to them. Would you, in their serving,
And with what imitation you can borrow
From youth of such a season, 'fore noble Lucius
Present yourself, desire his service, tell him 200
Wherein you're happy—which will make him know,
If that his head have ear in music—doubtless
With joy he will embrace you, for he's honorable
And, doubling that, most holy. Your means abroad:
You have me, rich, and I will never fail 205
Beginning nor supplyment.

IMOGEN, ⌜*taking the cloakbag*⌝ Thou art all the comfort
The gods will diet me with. Prithee, away.
There's more to be considered, but we'll even
All that good time will give us. This attempt 210
I am soldier to, and will abide it with
A prince's courage. Away, I prithee.

PISANIO
Well, madam, we must take a short farewell,
Lest, being missed, I be suspected of
Your carriage from the court. My noble mistress, 215
Here is a box. I had it from the Queen.

⌜*He hands her the box.*⌝

218. **stomach-qualmed:** i.e., nauseated; **dram:** small draft

219. **distemper:** illness, ill health; **To some shade:** i.e., go to a secluded spot

220. **fit you to:** i.e., clothe yourself for

3.5 When Imogen's absence from court is discovered, Cloten forces Pisanio to tell him where she is. Pisanio shows him the letter instructing Imogen to go to Milford Haven to meet Posthumus. Cloten demands that Pisanio provide him with Posthumus's clothing, so that, dressed in Posthumus's garments, he may take revenge on Imogen by killing Posthumus, raping Imogen, and then dragging her back to court.

---

3. **wrote:** i.e., written

4. **right:** extremely

11. **conduct:** safe-conduct; company of attendants appointed to escort me

14. **point:** detail

What's in 't is precious. If you are sick at sea
Or stomach-qualmed at land, a dram of this
Will drive away distemper. To some shade,
And fit you to your manhood. May the gods 220
Direct you to the best.

IMOGEN Amen. I thank thee.

They exit.

Scene 5

Enter Cymbeline, Queen, Cloten, Lucius, Lords, ⌜*and Attendants.*⌝

CYMBELINE
Thus far, and so farewell.

LUCIUS Thanks, royal sir.
My emperor hath wrote I must from hence,
And am right sorry that I must report you
My master's enemy. 5

CYMBELINE Our subjects, sir,
Will not endure his yoke, and for ourself
To show less sovereignty than they must needs
Appear unkinglike.

LUCIUS So, sir. I desire of you 10
A conduct overland to Milford Haven.—
Madam, all joy befall your Grace—and you.

CYMBELINE, ⌜*to Lords*⌝
My lords, you are appointed for that office.
The due of honor in no point omit.—
So, farewell, noble Lucius. 15

LUCIUS, ⌜*to Cloten*⌝ Your hand, my lord.

CLOTEN
Receive it friendly, but from this time forth
I wear it as your enemy.

LUCIUS Sir, the event
Is yet to name the winner. Fare you well. 20

22. **Severn:** a principal British river that originates in Wales

28. **fits . . . ripely:** i.e., is thus fitting that quickly

30. **powers:** armed forces

31. **drawn to head:** i.e., brought together

36. **forward:** ready, prompt

38–39. **to us . . . day:** i.e., greeted **us,** as is her **duty** every day to do

39. **looks us:** i.e., **looks** or seems to **us**

42. **slight in sufferance:** weak in (our) indulgence or toleration

48. **tender of:** sensitive to

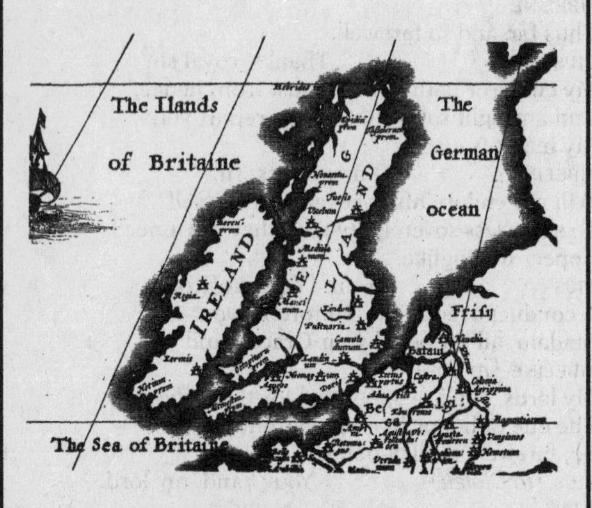

A map of Roman Britain.
From John Speed, *A prospect of the most famous parts of the world . . .* (1631).

CYMBELINE
Leave not the worthy Lucius, good my lords,
Till he have crossed the Severn. Happiness!
Exit Lucius ⌜and Lords.⌝

QUEEN
He goes hence frowning, but it honors us
That we have given him cause.

CLOTEN 'Tis all the better. 25
Your valiant Britons have their wishes in it.

CYMBELINE
Lucius hath wrote already to the Emperor
How it goes here. It fits us therefore ripely
Our chariots and our horsemen be in readiness.
The powers that he already hath in Gallia 30
Will soon be drawn to head, from whence he moves
His war for Britain.

QUEEN 'Tis not sleepy business,
But must be looked to speedily and strongly.

CYMBELINE
Our expectation that it would be thus 35
Hath made us forward. But, my gentle queen,
Where is our daughter? She hath not appeared
Before the Roman, nor to us hath tendered
The duty of the day. She ⌜looks⌝ us like
A thing more made of malice than of duty. 40
We have noted it.—Call her before us, for
We have been too slight in sufferance.
⌜An Attendant exits.⌝

QUEEN Royal sir,
Since the exile of Posthumus, most retired
Hath her life been, the cure whereof, my lord, 45
'Tis time must do. Beseech your Majesty,
Forbear sharp speeches to her. She's a lady
So tender of rebukes that words are ⌜strokes⌝
And strokes death to her.
Enter ⌜Attendant.⌝

51. **answered:** justified
56. **close:** secluded, private
60. **great court:** important business at **court**
61. **to blame:** blameworthy, culpable
69. **stand'st so for:** i.e., **so** strongly supports
71. **by swallowing:** i.e., from **swallowing**
73. **Haply:** perhaps

"O, for a horse with wings!" (3.2.51)
From August Casimir Redel, *Apophtegmata symbolica* . . . [n.d.].

CYMBELINE Where is she, sir? How 50
Can her contempt be answered?

⌜ATTENDANT⌝ Please you, sir,
Her chambers are all locked, and there's no answer
That will be given to th' ⌜loud'st⌝ noise we make.

QUEEN
My lord, when last I went to visit her, 55
She prayed me to excuse her keeping close;
Whereto constrained by her infirmity,
She should that duty leave unpaid to you
Which daily she was bound to proffer. This
She wished me to make known, but our great court 60
Made me to blame in memory.

CYMBELINE Her doors locked?
Not seen of late? Grant, heavens, that which I
Fear prove false! *He exits ⌜with Attendant.⌝*

QUEEN Son, I say, follow the King. 65

CLOTEN
That man of hers, Pisanio, her old servant
I have not seen these two days.

QUEEN Go, look after.
⌜Cloten⌝ exits.
⌜*Aside.*⌝ Pisanio, thou that stand'st so for Posthumus—
He hath a drug of mine. I pray his absence 70
Proceed by swallowing that, for he believes
It is a thing most precious. But for her,
Where is she gone? Haply despair hath seized her,
Or, winged with fervor of her love, she's flown
To her desired Posthumus. Gone she is 75
To death or to dishonor, and my end
Can make good use of either. She being down,
I have the placing of the British crown.

Enter Cloten.

How now, my son?

CLOTEN 'Tis certain she is fled. 80

84. **forestall:** deprive
85. **for:** because; **fair:** beautiful
86. **that:** because; **parts:** qualities, talents, gifts
89. **Outsells:** exceeds in value
91. **low:** socially inferior; **slanders:** disgraces, discredits
92. **else rare:** otherwise excellent; **in that point:** because of **that** determination (on her part)
96. **What:** an interjection introducing a question; **packing:** plotting; **sirrah:** a form of address to a male social inferior
99. **straightway:** immediately
102. **Close:** uncommunicative
106. **drawn:** extracted

"His body's . . . a thoroughfare for steel." (1.2.9–10)
From Sebastian Heussler, *Künstliches Abprobirtes* . . . (1665).

Go in and cheer the King. He rages; none
Dare come about him.

QUEEN, ⌜*aside*⌝ All the better. May
This night forestall him of the coming day!

Queen exits, ⌜*with Attendants.*⌝

CLOTEN
I love and hate her, for she's fair and royal, 85
And that she hath all courtly parts more exquisite
Than lady, ladies, woman. From every one
The best she hath, and she, of all compounded,
Outsells them all. I love her therefore, but
Disdaining me and throwing favors on 90
The low Posthumus slanders so her judgment
That what's else rare is choked. And in that point
I will conclude to hate her, nay, indeed,
To be revenged upon her. For, when fools
Shall— 95

Enter Pisanio.

Who is here? What, are you packing, sirrah?
Come hither. Ah, you precious pander! Villain,
Where is thy lady? In a word, or else
Thou art straightway with the fiends.

⌜*He draws his sword.*⌝

PISANIO O, good my lord— 100

CLOTEN
Where is thy lady? Or, by Jupiter—
I will not ask again. Close villain,
I'll have this secret from thy heart or rip
Thy heart to find it. Is she with Posthumus,
From whose so many weights of baseness cannot 105
A dram of worth be drawn?

PISANIO Alas, my lord,
How can she be with him? When was she missed?
He is in Rome.

CLOTEN Where is she, sir? Come nearer. 110

111. **home:** directly, thoroughly

115. **Discover:** disclose, reveal

120. **This paper:** This is apparently Posthumus's letter asking Imogen to meet him at Milford Haven. We may imagine it as one of the letters discarded by Imogen at 3.4.88–89 and presumably picked up and kept by Pisanio.

124. **Or . . . or:** i.e., Either . . . or

126. **travail:** (1) journey; (2) painful labor (These two senses were then not yet separated from each other.)

132. **hand:** i.e., handwriting

134. **undergo:** undertake, perform

138. **want:** lack

139. **relief:** sustenance

Augustus Caesar. (2.4.13; 3.1.1)
Thomas Treterus, *Romanorum imperatorum effigies* . . . (1590).

No farther halting. Satisfy me home
What is become of her.

PISANIO
O, my all-worthy lord!

CLOTEN All-worthy villain!
Discover where thy mistress is at once, 115
At the next word. No more of "worthy lord"!
Speak, or thy silence on the instant is
Thy condemnation and thy death.

PISANIO Then, sir,
This paper is the history of my knowledge 120
Touching her flight. ⌜*He gives Cloten a paper.*⌝

CLOTEN Let's see 't. I will pursue her
Even to Augustus' throne.

PISANIO, ⌜*aside*⌝ Or this or perish.
She's far enough, and what he learns by this 125
May prove his travail, not her danger.

CLOTEN Humh!

PISANIO, ⌜*aside*⌝
I'll write to my lord she's dead. O Imogen,
Safe mayst thou wander, safe return again!

CLOTEN Sirrah, is this letter true? 130

PISANIO Sir, as I think.

CLOTEN It is Posthumus' hand, I know 't. Sirrah, if thou wouldst not be a villain, but do me true service, undergo those employments wherein I should have cause to use thee with a serious industry— 135 that is, what villainy soe'er I bid thee do to perform it directly and truly—I would think thee an honest man. Thou shouldst neither want my means for thy relief nor my voice for thy preferment.

PISANIO Well, my good lord. 140

CLOTEN Wilt thou serve me? For since patiently and constantly thou hast stuck to the bare fortune of that beggar Posthumus, thou canst not in the course of gratitude but be a diligent follower of mine. Wilt thou serve me? 145

148. **late:** recent
156. **anon:** soon
157. **would:** wish
158. **upon a time:** i.e., once
161. **more:** i.e., greater
164. **in her eyes:** i.e., before **her eyes**
166. **insultment:** insult, contemptuous triumph
168. **vex:** torment
170. **foot:** kick
179. **be a voluntary mute to:** i.e., voluntarily or willingly **be** quiet about

A basilisk. (2.4.136)
From Edward Topsell, *The history of four-footed beasts and serpents* . . . (1658).

PISANIO Sir, I will.

CLOTEN Give me thy hand. Here's my purse. ⌜*Gives him money.*⌝ Hast any of thy late master's garments in thy possession?

PISANIO I have, my lord, at my lodging the same suit he wore when he took leave of my lady and mistress. 150

CLOTEN The first service thou dost me, fetch that suit hither. Let it be thy first service. Go.

PISANIO I shall, my lord. *He exits.*

CLOTEN Meet thee at Milford Haven!—I forgot to ask him one thing; I'll remember 't anon. Even there, thou villain Posthumus, will I kill thee. I would these garments were come. She said upon a time—the bitterness of it I now belch from my heart—that she held the very garment of Posthumus in more respect than my noble and natural person, together with the adornment of my qualities. With that suit upon my back will I ravish her. First, kill him, and in her eyes. There shall she see my valor, which will then be a torment to her contempt. He on the ground, my speech of insultment ended on his dead body, and when my lust hath dined—which, as I say, to vex her I will execute in the clothes that she so praised—to the court I'll knock her back, foot her home again. She hath despised me rejoicingly, and I'll be merry in my revenge. 155 160 165 170

Enter Pisanio ⌜*with the clothes.*⌝

Be those the garments?

PISANIO Ay, my noble lord.

CLOTEN How long is 't since she went to Milford Haven? 175

PISANIO She can scarce be there yet.

CLOTEN Bring this apparel to my chamber; that is the second thing that I have commanded thee. The third is that thou wilt be a voluntary mute to my

182. **be true: be** loyal

183. **true:** i.e., to be **true**

185. **most true: most** honorable

187. **This fool's:** i.e., may **this fool's; speed:** (1) swiftness; (2) success

188. **crossed:** thwarted; **meed:** reward

3.6 Imogen, disguised as a boy named Fidele, stumbles, exhausted and famished, into the cave of Belarius and the two young mountaineers. They welcome the "boy."

---

0 SD. **Fidele:** The word means "faithful one" in the Romance languages. (The name is pronounced as three syllables.)

6. **within a ken:** i.e., within sight

7. **Foundations:** i.e., charitable religious houses (with possible wordplay on "the lowest parts of buildings"—like those of Milford Haven—or on "security" or "fixed places")

11. **trial:** test (perhaps of virtue)

12. **lapse:** sin; **in fullness:** i.e., when one's needs are plentifully supplied

13. **sorer:** more serious

16. **but even before:** i.e., only a moment ago

17. **At point:** ready; **for:** i.e., **for** lack of

18. **hold:** refuge, shelter

design. Be but duteous, and true preferment shall 180
tender itself to thee. My revenge is now at Milford.
Would I had wings to follow it! Come, and be true.

He exits.

PISANIO

Thou bidd'st me to my loss, for true to thee
Were to prove false, which I will never be,
To him that is most true. To Milford go, 185
And find not her whom thou pursuest. Flow, flow,
You heavenly blessings, on her. This fool's speed
Be crossed with slowness. Labor be his meed.

He exits.

Scene 6

Enter Imogen alone, ⌜*dressed as a boy, Fidele.*⌝

IMOGEN

I see a man's life is a tedious one.
I have tired myself, and for two nights together
Have made the ground my bed. I should be sick
But that my resolution helps me. Milford,
When from the mountain top Pisanio showed thee, 5
Thou wast within a ken. O Jove, I think
Foundations fly the wretched—such, I mean,
Where they should be relieved. Two beggars told me
I could not miss my way. Will poor folks lie,
That have afflictions on them, knowing 'tis 10
A punishment or trial? Yes. No wonder,
When rich ones scarce tell true. To lapse in fullness
Is sorer than to lie for need, and falsehood
Is worse in kings than beggars. My dear lord,
Thou art one o' th' false ones. Now I think on thee, 15
My hunger's gone; but even before, I was
At point to sink for food. But what is this?
Here is a path to 't. 'Tis some savage hold.

21. **breeds:** i.e., breed; **hardness:** hardship

23. **civil:** civilized

24. **Take or lend:** i.e., seize (whatever I have) or grant (me food or help)

25. **an if:** i.e., **if**

27. **Such . . . heavens:** i.e., I pray that the **good heavens** present **a foe** as fearful as I

28. **woodman:** hunter

30. **match:** agreement, bargain

31–32. **The sweat . . . works to:** i.e., strenuous exertion would disappear **and die** if it were not for its intended purpose

32–33. **our stomachs . . . savory:** Proverbial: "Hunger is the best sauce."

34. **resty:** lazy, sluggish

37. **throughly:** thoroughly

39. **meat:** food; **browse:** feed (customarily used only with reference to animals)

43. **But:** i.e., except for the fact

Guiderius, Cymbeline's elder son and future king of Britain.
From John Taylor, *All the workes of . . .* (1630).

I were best not call; I dare not call. Yet famine,
Ere clean it o'erthrow nature, makes it valiant. 20
Plenty and peace breeds cowards; hardness ever
Of hardiness is mother.—Ho! Who's here?
If anything that's civil, speak; if savage,
Take or lend. Ho!—No answer? Then I'll enter.
Best draw my sword; an if mine enemy 25
But fear the sword like me, he'll scarcely look on 't.

⌜*She draws her sword.*⌝

Such a foe, good heavens!

She exits, ⌜*as into the cave.*⌝

Enter Belarius ⌜*as Morgan,*⌝ *Guiderius* ⌜*as Polydor,*⌝ *and Arviragus* ⌜*as Cadwal.*⌝

BELARIUS, ⌜*as* MORGAN⌝
You, Polydor, have proved best woodman and
Are master of the feast. Cadwal and I
Will play the cook and servant; 'tis our match. 30
The sweat of industry would dry and die
But for the end it works to. Come, our stomachs
Will make what's homely savory. Weariness
Can snore upon the flint when resty sloth
Finds the down pillow hard. Now peace be here, 35
Poor house, that keep'st thyself.

GUIDERIUS, ⌜*as* POLYDOR⌝ I am throughly weary.

ARVIRAGUS, ⌜*as* CADWAL⌝
I am weak with toil, yet strong in appetite.

GUIDERIUS, ⌜*as* POLYDOR⌝
There is cold meat i' th' cave. We'll browse on that
Whilst what we have killed be cooked. 40

BELARIUS, ⌜*as* MORGAN, *looking into the cave*⌝
Stay, come
not in!
But that it eats our victuals, I should think
Here were a fairy.

GUIDERIUS, ⌜*as* POLYDOR⌝ What's the matter, sir? 45

49. **masters:** sirs, gentlemen
50. **thought:** meant, intended
51. **took:** i.e., taken
51–52. **Good troth:** a mild oath
55. **meat:** food
56. **so soon:** i.e., as **soon**
57. **made:** finished
60. **All gold:** i.e., may **all gold**
61. **but of:** i.e., except by
65. **made:** committed
72. **in this:** i.e., into **this**
76. **cheer:** refreshment, provisions

Arviragus, Cymbeline's younger son and future king of Britain.
From John Taylor, *All the workes of* . . . (1630).

BELARIUS, ⌜*as* MORGAN⌝
By Jupiter, an angel! Or, if not,
An earthly paragon. Behold divineness
No elder than a boy.

Enter Imogen ⌜as Fidele.⌝

IMOGEN, ⌜*as* FIDELE⌝ Good masters, harm me not.
Before I entered here, I called, and thought 50
To have begged or bought what I have took. Good troth,
I have stol'n naught, nor would not, though I had found
Gold strewed i' th' floor. Here's money for my meat. 55
⌜*She offers money.*⌝
I would have left it on the board so soon
As I had made my meal, and parted
With prayers for the provider.

GUIDERIUS, ⌜*as* POLYDOR⌝ Money, youth?

ARVIRAGUS, ⌜*as* CADWAL⌝
All gold and silver rather turn to dirt, 60
As 'tis no better reckoned but of those
Who worship dirty gods.

IMOGEN, ⌜*as* FIDELE⌝ I see you're angry.
Know, if you kill me for my fault, I should
Have died had I not made it. 65

BELARIUS, ⌜*as* MORGAN⌝ Whither bound?

IMOGEN, ⌜*as* FIDELE⌝ To Milford Haven.

BELARIUS, ⌜*as* MORGAN⌝ What's your name?

IMOGEN, ⌜*as* FIDELE⌝
Fidele, sir. I have a kinsman who
Is bound for Italy. He embarked at Milford, 70
To whom being going, almost spent with hunger,
I am fall'n in this offense.

BELARIUS, ⌜*as* MORGAN⌝ Prithee, fair youth,
Think us no churls, nor measure our good minds
By this rude place we live in. Well encountered! 75
'Tis almost night; you shall have better cheer

80. **but:** i.e., in order to; **groom:** bridegroom; **in honesty:** i.e., honorably

81. **as I do buy:** perhaps, (in the honorable way) I always transact purchases; or, perhaps, as if **I** fully intended to **buy** (you)

86. **sprightly:** cheerful

90. **prize:** valuation (with possible wordplay on "ship captured as booty," picked up in the image of **ballasting** in line 91)

91. **ballasting:** i.e., weight (literally, ballast, weight added to the hold of a ship to prevent it from capsizing)

93. **wrings:** writhes, struggles in pain

96. **What . . . what:** i.e., Whatever . . . whatever

100. **attend themselves:** i.e., function as their own attendants or servants

101. **sealed:** confirmed (The metaphor is that of affixing a seal to a document so as to authenticate it.) **laying by:** dismissing from consideration

102. **nothing-gift of differing multitudes:** i.e., worthless **gift** (of flattery) from the fickle **multitudes**

103. **outpeer:** excel; **these twain:** this pair

107. **hunt:** game killed in hunting

108. **Discourse:** conversation; **heavy:** dull, tedious

109. **demand:** ask

Ere you depart, and thanks to stay and eat it.—
Boys, bid him welcome.

GUIDERIUS, ⌜*as* POLYDOR⌝ Were you a woman, youth,
I should woo hard but be your groom in honesty, 80
Ay, bid for you as I do buy.

ARVIRAGUS, ⌜*as* CADWAL⌝ I'll make 't my comfort
He is a man. I'll love him as my brother.—
And such a welcome as I'd give to him
After long absence, such is yours. Most welcome. 85
Be sprightly, for you fall 'mongst friends.

IMOGEN, ⌜*as* FIDELE⌝ 'Mongst friends?
If brothers—(⌜*aside*⌝) Would it had been so, that they
Had been my father's sons! Then had my prize 90
Been less, and so more equal ballasting
To thee, Posthumus.

BELARIUS, ⌜*as* MORGAN⌝ He wrings at some distress.

GUIDERIUS, ⌜*as* POLYDOR⌝
Would I could free 't!

ARVIRAGUS, ⌜*as* CADWAL⌝ Or I, whate'er it be, 95
What pain it cost, what danger. Gods!

BELARIUS, ⌜*as* MORGAN⌝ Hark, boys.
⌜*They talk aside.*⌝

IMOGEN Great men
That had a court no bigger than this cave,
That did attend themselves and had the virtue 100
Which their own conscience sealed them, laying by
That nothing-gift of differing multitudes,
Could not outpeer these twain. Pardon me, gods!
I'd change my sex to be companion with them,
Since Leonatus false. 105

BELARIUS, ⌜*as* MORGAN⌝ It shall be so.
Boys, we'll go dress our hunt.—Fair youth, come in.
Discourse is heavy, fasting. When we have supped,
We'll mannerly demand thee of thy story
So far as thou wilt speak it. 110

3.7 A Roman senator announces that the Roman army attacking Britain will be under the control of Caius Lucius and that it will be augmented by Roman gentry.

---

1. **writ:** written command
3. **Pannonians and Dalmatians:** See note to 3.1.79.
5. **Full:** exceedingly, very
6. **fall'n-off:** rebellious
9. **commends:** entrusts
16. **supplyant:** i.e., auxiliary, supplementary

An ancient Briton.
From John Speed, *The history of Great Britaine under the conquests* . . . (1611).

GUIDERIUS, ⌜*as* POLYDOR⌝ Pray, draw near.
ARVIRAGUS, ⌜*as* CADWAL⌝
The night to th' owl and morn to th' lark less
welcome.
IMOGEN, ⌜*as* FIDELE⌝ Thanks, sir.
ARVIRAGUS, ⌜*as* CADWAL⌝ I pray, draw near. 115
They exit.

Scene ⌜7⌝

Enter two Roman Senators, and Tribunes.

FIRST SENATOR
This is the tenor of the Emperor's writ:
That since the common men are now in action
'Gainst the Pannonians and Dalmatians,
And that the legions now in Gallia are
Full weak to undertake our wars against 5
The fall'n-off Britons, that we do incite
The gentry to this business. He creates
Lucius proconsul; and to you the tribunes
For this immediate levy, he commends
His absolute commission. Long live Caesar! 10
TRIBUNE
Is Lucius general of the forces?
SECOND SENATOR Ay.
TRIBUNE
Remaining now in Gallia?
FIRST SENATOR With those legions
Which I have spoke of, whereunto your levy 15
Must be supplyant. The words of your commission
Will tie you to the numbers and the time
Of their dispatch.
TRIBUNE We will discharge our duty.
They exit.

CYMBELINE

ACT 4

4.1 Cloten, dressed in Posthumus's garments, arrives at the spot where he plans to cut off Posthumus's head and rape Imogen.

---

2. **fit:** becomingly (This word begins a series of puns that continues in lines 4 and 6.)

4. **fit:** appropriate (for me), with wordplay on "(sexually) compatible"

5. **The rather:** i.e., (even) more so; **saving reverence:** an apologetic phrase (for the bawdy puns)

6. **fitness:** readiness; (sexual) inclination; **by fits:** i.e., **by fits** and starts, by irregular impulses

7. **workman:** skilled or expert craftsman

8. **glass:** looking glass, mirror

11. **beyond:** i.e., superior to

12. **advantage:** i.e., favoring circumstances

13. **alike conversant:** equally experienced; **services:** perhaps, military actions

14. **single oppositions:** i.e., duels, **single** combats

14–15. **imperceiverant:** undiscerning (See longer note, page 267.)

15. **my despite:** i.e., in contemptuous disregard of me

16. **mortality:** mortal existence, life

18. **enforced:** raped

19. **spurn:** kick

20. **haply:** perhaps

22. **power of:** command over

24. **sore:** fierce, violent

ACT 4

Scene 1

Enter Cloten alone, ⌜*dressed in Posthumus's garments.*⌝

CLOTEN I am near to th' place where they should meet, if Pisanio have mapped it truly. How fit his garments serve me! Why should his mistress, who was made by him that made the tailor, not be fit too? The rather, saving reverence of the word, for 5 'tis said a woman's fitness comes by fits. Therein I must play the workman. I dare speak it to myself, for it is not vainglory for a man and his glass to confer in his own chamber. I mean, the lines of my body are as well drawn as his, no less young, more 10 strong; not beneath him in fortunes, beyond him in the advantage of the time, above him in birth, alike conversant in general services, and more remarkable in single oppositions. Yet this imperceiverant thing loves him in my despite. What 15 mortality is! Posthumus, thy head, which now is growing upon thy shoulders, shall within this hour be off, thy mistress enforced, thy garments cut to pieces before thy face; and all this done, spurn her home to her father, who may haply be a little angry 20 for my so rough usage. But my mother, having power of his testiness, shall turn all into my commendations. My horse is tied up safe. Out, sword, and to a sore purpose. Fortune, put them into my

4.2 Imogen, not feeling well, takes the potion given her by Pisanio, thinking it is a restorative; the potion puts her into a deathlike trance. Cloten confronts Belarius and his two "sons" and, in the ensuing fight with Guiderius, is killed and his head cut off. The body of "Fidele" is discovered and mourned, and the headless body of Cloten placed beside it. When Imogen wakes, she thinks the body is that of Posthumus. As she grieves, Caius Lucius enters; she tells him that the body is that of her former master and asks to become Caius's page. He welcomes "Fidele" into his service.

---

6. **clay:** human being (literally, the human body, as in Genesis 2.7: "The Lord God . . . made man of the **dust** of the ground.") **dignity:** rank

7. **dust:** See note to line 6.

10. **citizen:** city-bred; **wanton:** pampered person

11. **So please you:** i.e., **please** (a polite phrase)

12. **journal:** daily

13. **by:** i.e., near

14. **amend:** cure; **Society:** company

16. **reason of:** talk (rationally) about

18. **so poorly:** perhaps, from one **so** poor (as **myself**)

20. **How . . . weight:** i.e., in **quantity** and **weight**

hand! This is the very description of their meeting place, and the fellow dares not deceive me. 25

He ⌜draws his sword and⌝ exits.

Scene 2

Enter Belarius ⌜as Morgan,⌝ Guiderius ⌜as Polydor,⌝ Arviragus ⌜as Cadwal,⌝ and Imogen ⌜as Fidele,⌝ from the cave.

BELARIUS, ⌜*as* MORGAN, *to Fidele*⌝
You are not well. Remain here in the cave.
We'll come to you after hunting.
ARVIRAGUS, ⌜*as* CADWAL, *to Fidele*⌝ Brother, stay here.
Are we not brothers?
IMOGEN, ⌜*as* FIDELE⌝ So man and man should be, 5
But clay and clay differs in dignity,
Whose dust is both alike. I am very sick.
GUIDERIUS, ⌜*as* POLYDOR, *to Morgan and Cadwal*⌝
Go you to hunting. I'll abide with him.
IMOGEN, ⌜*as* FIDELE⌝
So sick I am not, yet I am not well;
But not so citizen a wanton as 10
To seem to die ere sick. So please you, leave me.
Stick to your journal course. The breach of custom
Is breach of all. I am ill, but your being by me
Cannot amend me. Society is no comfort
To one not sociable. I am not very sick, 15
Since I can reason of it. Pray you trust me here—
I'll rob none but myself—and let me die,
Stealing so poorly.
GUIDERIUS, ⌜*as* POLYDOR⌝
I love thee—I have spoke it—
How much the quantity, the weight as much 20
As I do love my father.
BELARIUS, ⌜*as* MORGAN⌝ What? How, how?

23. **me:** i.e., myself

26. **Love's . . . reason:** Proverbial: "Love is without reason."

27. **demand:** peremptory asking; question

29. **strain:** inherited character or constitution

32. **meal and bran:** i.e., the edible part of grain **and** the husks

33–34. **who this . . . me:** i.e., whoever this person is, it is miraculous that he is **loved** more than I

37. **sport:** pleasant pastime, recreation

38. **So please you:** a deferential phrase of address or request

41. **report:** common talk, what is generally believed

42–43. **Th' imperious . . . fish:** i.e., the court can be treacherous, while out-of-the-way places can provide things as good as the court's (See longer note, page 267.)

46. **stir him:** i.e., persuade or entreat him (to speak of himself)

47. **gentle:** wellborn (i.e., a gentleman)

48. **Dishonestly:** (1) with dishonor or disgrace; (2) fraudulently; **honest:** honorable

ARVIRAGUS, ⌜*as* CADWAL⌝
If it be sin to say so, sir, I yoke me
In my good brother's fault. I know not why
I love this youth, and I have heard you say 25
Love's reason's without reason. The bier at door,
And a demand who is 't shall die, I'd say
"My father, not this youth."

BELARIUS, ⌜*aside*⌝ O, noble strain!
O, worthiness of nature, breed of greatness! 30
Cowards father cowards and base things sire base;
Nature hath meal and bran, contempt and grace.
I'm not their father, yet who this should be
Doth miracle itself, loved before me.—
'Tis the ninth hour o' th' morn. 35

ARVIRAGUS, ⌜*as* CADWAL, *to Fidele*⌝ Brother, farewell.

IMOGEN, ⌜*as* FIDELE⌝
I wish you sport.

ARVIRAGUS, ⌜*as* CADWAL⌝ You health.—So please you, sir.

IMOGEN, ⌜*aside*⌝
These are kind creatures. Gods, what lies I have heard!
Our courtiers say all's savage but at court; 40
Experience, O, thou disprov'st report!
Th' imperious seas breeds monsters; for the dish
Poor tributary rivers as sweet fish.
I am sick still, heart-sick. Pisanio,
I'll now taste of thy drug. ⌜*She swallows the drug.*⌝ 45

GUIDERIUS, ⌜*as* POLYDOR, *to Morgan and Cadwal*⌝
I could not stir him.
He said he was gentle but unfortunate,
Dishonestly afflicted but yet honest.

ARVIRAGUS, ⌜*as* CADWAL⌝
Thus did he answer me, yet said hereafter
I might know more. 50

BELARIUS, ⌜*as* MORGAN⌝ To th' field, to th' field!

56. **huswife:** manager of our household (pronounced "hussif")

58. **bound:** obligated (Belarius replies as if to the sense "**bound** by mutual affection" [line 59].)

60. **distressed:** impoverished

63. **neat:** dainty, elegant; **characters:** symbols, figures (e.g., letters of the alphabet or numerals)

64. **as:** i.e., **as** if

65. **her dieter:** regulator of her diet

68. **that:** i.e., **that** which

70. **commix:** blend, mingle

73. **them both:** i.e., **both** the **smile** and the **sigh**

74. **spurs:** roots

76. **stinking elder:** elder tree, which has a pungent odor (This tree was also maligned because of the tradition that Judas Iscariot, betrayer of Christ, had hanged himself on an **elder.**) **untwine:** release by untwisting

77. **His:** i.e., its; **perishing:** dying and deadly; **with . . . vine:** i.e., as **the vine** (which represents **patience** [line 73]) grows

78. **great morning:** fully **morning** (i.e., the sun is all the way up)

79. **runagates:** runaways

80. **mocked:** deceived

⌜*To Fidele.*⌝ We'll leave you for this time. Go in and
rest.

ARVIRAGUS, ⌜*as* CADWAL⌝
We'll not be long away.

BELARIUS, ⌜*as* MORGAN⌝ Pray, be not sick, 55
For you must be our huswife.

IMOGEN, ⌜*as* FIDELE⌝ Well or ill,
I am bound to you.

BELARIUS, ⌜*as* MORGAN⌝ And shalt be ever.

⌜*Imogen*⌝ *exits* ⌜*as into the cave.*⌝

This youth, howe'er distressed, appears he hath had 60
Good ancestors.

ARVIRAGUS, ⌜*as* CADWAL⌝ How angel-like he sings!

GUIDERIUS, ⌜*as* POLYDOR⌝
But his neat cookery! He cut our roots in characters
And sauced our broths as Juno had been sick
And he her dieter. 65

ARVIRAGUS, ⌜*as* CADWAL⌝ Nobly he yokes
A smiling with a sigh, as if the sigh
Was that it was for not being such a smile,
The smile mocking the sigh that it would fly
From so divine a temple to commix 70
With winds that sailors rail at.

GUIDERIUS, ⌜*as* POLYDOR⌝ I do note
That grief and patience, rooted in them both,
Mingle their spurs together.

ARVIRAGUS, ⌜*as* CADWAL⌝ Grow, ⌜patience,⌝ 75
And let the stinking elder, grief, untwine
His perishing root with the increasing vine!

BELARIUS, ⌜*as* MORGAN⌝
It is great morning. Come, away. Who's there?

Enter Cloten.

CLOTEN, ⌜*to himself*⌝
I cannot find those runagates. That villain
Hath mocked me. I am faint. 80

85. **held:** regarded

87. **companies:** possibly, companions (of Cloten's); or, possibly, troops, bodies of soldiers

89. **Soft:** i.e., wait, stay

90. **fly:** flee; **mountaineers:** mountain people

94. **a knock:** i.e., giving him a blow

99. **bigger:** more haughty, more boastful

100. **what:** i.e., who

106–7. **Who . . . thee:** Wordplay on the proverbs "**Clothes make** the man" and "The **tailor** makes the man" (Cloten's **tailor** is his **grandfather** in that the **tailor** made the clothes that in turn, according to the proverb, make the man Cloten.)

108. **precious:** utterly worthless; or, out-and-out; **varlet:** rascal

113. **injurious thief:** insulting villain

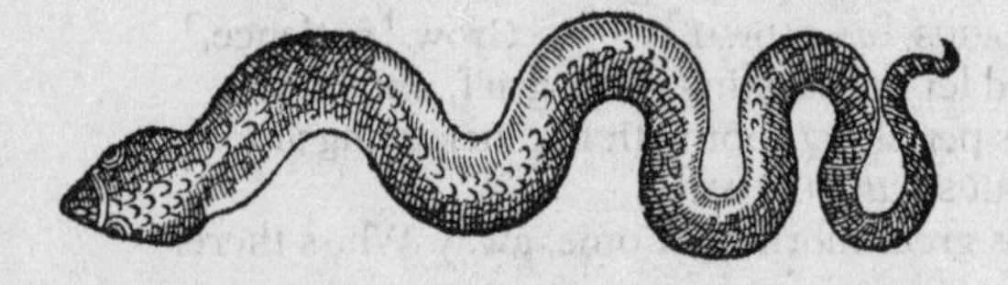

A "worm" or serpent. (3.4.37–39)
From Edward Topsell, *The historie of serpents . . .* (1608).

BELARIUS, ⌜*as* MORGAN, *to Polydor and Cadwal*⌝
"Those runagates"?
Means he not us? I partly know him. 'Tis
Cloten, the son o' th' Queen. I fear some ambush.
I saw him not these many years, and yet
I know 'tis he. We are held as outlaws. Hence. 85

GUIDERIUS, ⌜*as* POLYDOR⌝
He is but one. You and my brother search
What companies are near. Pray you, away.
Let me alone with him. ⌜*Belarius and Arviragus exit.*⌝

CLOTEN Soft, what are you
That fly me thus? Some villain mountaineers? 90
I have heard of such.—What slave art thou?

GUIDERIUS, ⌜*as* POLYDOR⌝ A thing
More slavish did I ne'er than answering
A slave without a knock.

CLOTEN Thou art a robber, 95
A lawbreaker, a villain. Yield thee, thief.

GUIDERIUS, ⌜*as* POLYDOR⌝
To who? To thee? What art thou? Have not I
An arm as big as thine? A heart as big?
Thy words, I grant, are bigger, for I wear not
My dagger in my mouth. Say what thou art, 100
Why I should yield to thee.

CLOTEN Thou villain base,
Know'st me not by my clothes?

GUIDERIUS, ⌜*as* POLYDOR⌝ No, nor thy tailor,
rascal. 105
Who is thy grandfather? He made those clothes,
Which, as it seems, make thee.

CLOTEN Thou precious varlet,
My tailor made them not.

GUIDERIUS, ⌜*as* POLYDOR⌝ Hence then, and thank 110
The man that gave them thee. Thou art some fool.
I am loath to beat thee.

CLOTEN Thou injurious thief,
Hear but my name, and tremble.

117. **Cloten . . . name:** i.e., even if "**Cloten, thou double villain**" is your **name**

119. **move me sooner:** more easily trouble me

121. **mere confusion:** utter confounding; or, possibly, destruction

123. **not seeming:** i.e., because you do not seem

125. **afeard:** afraid

129. **proper:** own

136. **lines of favor:** distinctive facial features

137. **snatches:** catches, hesitations

138. **absolute:** perfectly certain

139. **very:** truly, really

141. **make good time:** i.e., shortly finish

GUIDERIUS, ⌜*as* POLYDOR⌝ What's thy name? 115

CLOTEN Cloten, thou villain.

GUIDERIUS, ⌜*as* POLYDOR⌝
Cloten, thou double villain, be thy name,
I cannot tremble at it. Were it Toad, or Adder, Spider,
'Twould move me sooner.

CLOTEN To thy further fear, 120
Nay, to thy mere confusion, thou shalt know
I am son to th' Queen.

GUIDERIUS, ⌜*as* POLYDOR⌝ I am sorry for 't, not seeming
So worthy as thy birth.

CLOTEN Art not afeard? 125

GUIDERIUS, ⌜*as* POLYDOR⌝
Those that I reverence, those I fear—the wise;
At fools I laugh, not fear them.

CLOTEN Die the death!
When I have slain thee with my proper hand,
I'll follow those that even now fled hence 130
And on the gates of Lud's Town set your heads.
Yield, rustic mountaineer!

They fight and exit.

Enter Belarius ⌜as Morgan⌝ and Arviragus ⌜as Cadwal⌝.

BELARIUS, ⌜*as* MORGAN⌝ No company's abroad?

ARVIRAGUS, ⌜*as* CADWAL⌝
None in the world. You did mistake him sure.

BELARIUS, ⌜*as* MORGAN⌝
I cannot tell. Long is it since I saw him, 135
But time hath nothing blurred those lines of favor
Which then he wore. The snatches in his voice
And burst of speaking were as his. I am absolute
'Twas very Cloten.

ARVIRAGUS, ⌜*as* CADWAL⌝ In this place we left them. 140
I wish my brother make good time with him,
You say he is so fell.

143. **scarce:** scarcely, barely; **made up:** grown

144. **apprehension:** conscious perception, understanding

145–46. **for defect . . . fear:** See longer note, page 268.

148. **an empty purse:** In performance, Guiderius often holds up the head to show how **empty** it is.

149. **Hercules:** in classical mythology, a hero who, at the command of the goddess Juno, carried out twelve seemingly impossible labors (See picture, page 170.)

151. **I not doing this:** i.e., had **I** not done **this**

154. **perfect:** certain, fully informed

155. **after:** according to

157. **take us in: take us** prisoner, conquer **us**

158. **where:** i.e., from **where**

161. **undone:** ruined, destroyed

163. **that:** i.e., **that** which

164. **tender:** i.e., so mild as

165. **threat:** i.e., threaten

167. **For:** because

170. **safe:** sane

171. **humor:** inclination, disposition, mood

BELARIUS, ⌜*as* MORGAN⌝ Being scarce made up,
I mean to man, he had not apprehension
Of roaring terrors; for defect of judgment 145
Is oft the cause of fear.

Enter Guiderius ⌜as Polydor, carrying Cloten's head.⌝

But see, thy brother.

GUIDERIUS, ⌜*as* POLYDOR⌝
This Cloten was a fool, an empty purse;
There was no money in 't. Not Hercules
Could have knocked out his brains, for he had none. 150
Yet I not doing this, the fool had borne
My head as I do his.

BELARIUS, ⌜*as* MORGAN⌝ What hast thou done?

GUIDERIUS, ⌜*as* POLYDOR⌝
I am perfect what: cut off one Cloten's head,
Son to the Queen, after his own report, 155
Who called me traitor mountaineer, and swore
With his own single hand he'd take us in,
Displace our heads where, ⌜thank⌝ the gods, they
grow,
And set them on Lud's Town. 160

BELARIUS, ⌜*as* MORGAN⌝ We are all undone.

GUIDERIUS, ⌜*as* POLYDOR⌝
Why, worthy father, what have we to lose
But that he swore to take, our lives? The law
Protects not us. Then why should we be tender
To let an arrogant piece of flesh threat us, 165
Play judge and executioner all himself,
For we do fear the law? What company
Discover you abroad?

BELARIUS, ⌜*as* MORGAN⌝ No single soul
Can we set eye on, but in all safe reason 170
He must have some attendants. Though his ⌜humor⌝
Was nothing but mutation—ay, and that
From one bad thing to worse—not frenzy,

174. **so far have raved:** i.e., **have** been **so** insane
177. **Cave:** live in caves
178. **make . . . head:** i.e., gather a **stronger** force
180. **break out:** i.e., burst into speech
181. **fetch us in:** i.e., capture us
183. **suffering:** allowing
186. **ord'nance:** destiny, providence
187. **foresay:** foretell
191. **Did make . . . forth:** i.e., made **my** journey seem long (literally, protracted or prolonged **my way**)
195. **rock:** i.e., cave; **it to:** i.e., **it** go **to**
197. **reck:** care
202. **alone pursued me:** i.e., **pursued me** only
204–7. **I would . . . answer:** i.e., I wish that avengers whom our strength is sufficient to oppose would search for us and force us to confront them **meet:** oppose in battle **through:** thoroughly **answer:** responsive action

Hercules. (4.2.149, 384)
From Vincenzo Cartari, *Le vere e noue imagini* . . . (1615).

Not absolute madness could so far have raved
To bring him here alone. Although perhaps 175
It may be heard at court that such as we
Cave here, hunt here, are outlaws, and in time
May make some stronger head, the which he
hearing—
As it is like him—might break out and swear 180
He'd fetch us in, yet is 't not probable
To come alone, either he so undertaking
Or they so suffering. Then on good ground we fear,
If we do fear this body hath a tail
More perilous than the head. 185

ARVIRAGUS, ⌜*as* CADWAL⌝ Let ord'nance
Come as the gods foresay it. Howsoe'er,
My brother hath done well.

BELARIUS, ⌜*as* MORGAN⌝ I had no mind
To hunt this day. The boy Fidele's sickness 190
Did make my way long forth.

GUIDERIUS, ⌜*as* POLYDOR⌝ With his own sword,
Which he did wave against my throat, I have ta'en
His head from him. I'll throw 't into the creek
Behind our rock, and let it to the sea 195
And tell the fishes he's the Queen's son, Cloten.
That's all I reck. *He exits.*

BELARIUS, ⌜*as* MORGAN⌝ I fear 'twill be revenged.
Would, Polydor, thou hadst not done 't, though valor
Becomes thee well enough. 200

ARVIRAGUS, ⌜*as* CADWAL⌝ Would I had done 't,
So the revenge alone pursued me. Polydor,
I love thee brotherly, but envy much
Thou hast robbed me of this deed. I would revenges
That possible strength might meet would seek us 205
through
And put us to our answer.

BELARIUS, ⌜*as* MORGAN⌝ Well, 'tis done.
We'll hunt no more today, nor seek for danger

215. **to:** i.e., go **to; gain:** i.e., help him regain

216. **let . . . blood:** i.e., cause a whole **parish** full of Clotens to bleed (with wordplay on "letting blood" as a surgical procedure)

219. **blazon'st:** proclaims (with wordplay on displaying lineage by means of a coat of arms)

222. **his:** its

223. **enchafed:** furious, excited; **rud'st:** roughest

225. **him:** i.e., it

226. **frame:** shape, fashion, form

234. **clotpole:** thick or wooden head

236. **his:** its

237. **ingenious instrument:** Mechanical musical devices existed in Shakespeare's day, but the assumption is that in performance, a consort of viols or other musical instruments played **solemn music** offstage.

239. **give it motion:** i.e., make **it** play; or, play **it** (literally, set **it** in **motion**)

Violets. (1.5.95)
From John Gerard, *The herball* . . . (1597).

Where there's no profit. I prithee, to our rock. 210
You and Fidele play the cooks. I'll stay
Till hasty Polydor return, and bring him
To dinner presently.

ARVIRAGUS, ⌜*as* CADWAL⌝ Poor sick Fidele.
I'll willingly to him. To gain his color 215
I'd let a parish of such Clotens blood,
And praise myself for charity. *He exits.*

BELARIUS O thou goddess,
Thou divine Nature, thou thyself thou blazon'st
In these two princely boys! They are as gentle 220
As zephyrs blowing below the violet,
Not wagging his sweet head; and yet as rough,
Their royal blood enchafed, as the rud'st wind
That by the top doth take the mountain pine
And make him stoop to th' vale. 'Tis wonder 225
That an invisible instinct should frame them
To royalty unlearned, honor untaught,
Civility not seen from other, valor
That wildly grows in them but yields a crop
As if it had been sowed. Yet still it's strange 230
What Cloten's being here to us portends,
Or what his death will bring us.

Enter Guiderius ⌜as Polydor.⌝

GUIDERIUS, ⌜*as* POLYDOR⌝ Where's my brother?
I have sent Cloten's clotpole down the stream
In embassy to his mother. His body's hostage 235
For his return. *Solemn music.*

BELARIUS, ⌜*as* MORGAN⌝ My ⌜ingenious⌝ instrument!
Hark, Polydor, it sounds! But what occasion
Hath Cadwal now to give it motion? Hark.

GUIDERIUS, ⌜*as* POLYDOR⌝
Is he at home? 240

BELARIUS, ⌜*as* MORGAN⌝ He went hence even now.

244. **All solemn things:** with reference to the **solemn music** (line 236 SD)

245. **accidents:** incidents, events; **The matter:** i.e., what do you suppose is **the matter**

246. **Triumphs for nothing:** elation or joy for no reason; **lamenting toys:** i.e., passionate grief over trifles

247. **apes:** perhaps, fools (though the word might be meant literally)

253. **much on:** i.e., **much** of

261. **sound thy bottom:** i.e., measure your depths (as with a sounding or fathom line)

262. **crare:** small sailing vessel

264. **but I:** i.e., **but I** know

267. **Stark:** rigid, stiff (in death)

268. **as some:** i.e., **as** if **some**

269. **Not . . . at:** i.e., **not as** though he were laughing **at Death's** spear

273. **leagued:** joined; i.e., folded

GUIDERIUS, ⌜*as* POLYDOR⌝
What does he mean? Since death of my dear'st
mother
It did not speak before. All solemn things
Should answer solemn accidents. The matter? 245
Triumphs for nothing and lamenting toys
Is jollity for apes and grief for boys.
Is Cadwal mad?

Enter Arviragus ⌜as Cadwal,⌝ with Imogen ⌜as⌝ dead, bearing her in his arms.

BELARIUS, ⌜*as* MORGAN⌝ Look, here he comes,
And brings the dire occasion in his arms 250
Of what we blame him for.
ARVIRAGUS, ⌜*as* CADWAL⌝ The bird is dead
That we have made so much on. I had rather
Have skipped from sixteen years of age to sixty,
To have turned my leaping time into a crutch, 255
Than have seen this.
GUIDERIUS, ⌜*as* POLYDOR⌝ O sweetest, fairest lily!
My brother wears thee not the one half so well
As when thou grew'st thyself.
BELARIUS, ⌜*as* MORGAN⌝ O melancholy, 260
Whoever yet could sound thy bottom, find
The ooze, to show what coast thy sluggish ⌜crare⌝
⌜Might⌝ eas'liest harbor in?—Thou blessèd thing,
Jove knows what man thou mightst have made; but I,
Thou died'st, a most rare boy, of melancholy.— 265
How found you him?
ARVIRAGUS, ⌜*as* CADWAL⌝ Stark, as you see;
Thus smiling, as some fly had tickled slumber,
Not as Death's dart being laughed at; his right cheek
Reposing on a cushion. 270
GUIDERIUS, ⌜*as* POLYDOR⌝ Where?
ARVIRAGUS, ⌜*as* CADWAL⌝ O' th' floor,
His arms thus leagued. I thought he slept, and put

274. **clouted brogues:** hobnailed boots; **rudeness:** roughness (with possible wordplay on "bad manners")

275. **Answered:** echoed; **loud:** i.e., loudly

284. **harebell:** bluebell, wild hyacinth (See picture, page 260.)

286. **ruddock:** robin (Folklore credits the robin with bringing **flowers, moss** [line 290], etc. to cover dead bodies.) See below.

291. **winter-ground:** a word unrecorded elsewhere and thus of unknown meaning; **corse:** corpse

295. **admiration:** marveling; astonishment

296. **due debt:** i.e., unpaid **debt** already **due**

297. **shall 's:** i.e., ought we (literally, "shall us")

302. **Have . . . crack:** i.e., **have** broken (i.e., no longer sing soprano)

303. **like note:** the same tune or melody

306. **word:** speak (as opposed to sing)

308. **fanes:** temples (perhaps, oracles issuing from temples)

A ruddock, or robin. (4.2.286)
From Konrad Gesner, . . . *Historiae animalium* . . . (1585–1604).

My clouted brogues from off my feet, whose rudeness
Answered my steps too loud. 275

GUIDERIUS, ⌜*as* POLYDOR⌝ Why, he but sleeps.
If he be gone, he'll make his grave a bed;
With female fairies will his tomb be haunted—
And worms will not come to thee.

ARVIRAGUS, ⌜*as* CADWAL⌝ With fairest flowers, 280
Whilst summer lasts and I live here, Fidele,
I'll sweeten thy sad grave. Thou shalt not lack
The flower that's like thy face, pale primrose; nor
The azured harebell, like thy veins; no, nor
The leaf of eglantine whom, not to slander, 285
Out-sweetened not thy breath. The ruddock would
With charitable bill—O bill, sore shaming
Those rich-left heirs that let their fathers lie
Without a monument—bring thee all this,
Yea, and furred moss besides, when flowers are none 290
To winter-ground thy corse.

GUIDERIUS, ⌜*as* POLYDOR⌝ Prithee, have done,
And do not play in wench-like words with that
Which is so serious. Let us bury him
And not protract with admiration what 295
Is now due debt. To th' grave.

ARVIRAGUS, ⌜*as* CADWAL⌝ Say, where shall 's lay
him?

GUIDERIUS, ⌜*as* POLYDOR⌝
By good Euriphile, our mother.

ARVIRAGUS, ⌜*as* CADWAL⌝ Be 't so. 300
And let us, Polydor, though now our voices
Have got the mannish crack, sing him to th' ground
As once to our mother; use like note and words,
Save that "Euriphile" must be "Fidele."

GUIDERIUS, ⌜*as* POLYDOR⌝ Cadwal, 305
I cannot sing. I'll weep, and word it with thee,
For notes of sorrow, out of tune, are worse
Than priests and fanes that lie.

ARVIRAGUS, ⌜*as* CADWAL⌝ We'll speak it then.

310. **Great . . . less:** Proverbial: "The greater grief drives out **the less.**" **med'cine:** heal, cure

313–14. **mean . . . dust:** Proverbial: "All have **one dust.**" **mean:** i.e., those of low social rank

314. **reverence:** due respect shown to a person on account of his or her social position

321. **Thersites' . . . Ajax':** In Homer's *Iliad* Thersites is a crippled Greek whose only weapon is abusive language, Ajax a powerful hero in the Greek forces. (Here, they represent the **low** and the **high** [line 316], though both are satirically presented in Shakespeare's *Troilus and Cressida.*)

325. **the whilst:** in the meantime

326. **to th' east:** This custom is consistent with the worship of the morning sun in 3.3.

329. **remove him:** i.e., change the way he is placed

336. **As:** like

Primroses. (1.5.95; 4.2.283)
From John Gerard, *The herball* . . . (1597).

BELARIUS, ⌜*as* MORGAN⌝
Great griefs, I see, med'cine the less, for Cloten 310
Is quite forgot. He was a queen's son, boys,
And though he came our enemy, remember
He was paid for that. Though mean and mighty,
Rotting together, have one dust, yet reverence,
That angel of the world, doth make distinction 315
Of place 'tween high and low. Our foe was princely,
And though you took his life as being our foe,
Yet bury him as a prince.

GUIDERIUS, ⌜*as* POLYDOR, *to Morgan*⌝ Pray you fetch him
hither. 320
Thersites' body is as good as Ajax'
When neither are alive.

ARVIRAGUS, ⌜*as* CADWAL, *to Morgan*⌝ If you'll go fetch
him,
We'll say our song the whilst.—Brother, begin. 325
⌜*Belarius exits.*⌝

GUIDERIUS, ⌜*as* POLYDOR⌝
Nay, Cadwal, we must lay his head to th' east;
My father hath a reason for 't.

ARVIRAGUS, ⌜*as* CADWAL⌝ 'Tis true.

GUIDERIUS, ⌜*as* POLYDOR⌝
Come on then, and remove him.
⌜*They move Imogen's body.*⌝

ARVIRAGUS, ⌜*as* CADWAL⌝ So, begin. 330

Song.

GUIDERIUS, ⌜*as* POLYDOR⌝
Fear no more the heat o' th' sun,
Nor the furious winter's rages;
Thou thy worldly task hast done,
Home art gone and ta'en thy wages.
Golden lads and girls all must, 335
As chimney-sweepers, come to dust.

ARVIRAGUS, ⌜*as* CADWAL⌝
Fear no more the frown o' th' great;
Thou art past the tyrant's stroke.

340. **the reed is as the oak: The reed** often represents fragility and flexibility, **the oak** strength and rigidity. (See picture, page 254.)

341. **scepter, learning, physic:** i.e., those possessing regal power, knowledge, and medical science (See picture, page 228.)

344. **thunderstone:** i.e., the supposed bolt thought to cause the destruction when lightning strikes

348. **Consign to:** In Shakespeare's time, **consign** usually means "confirm," "subscribe," or "entrust." The eighteenth-century Shakespeare editor George Steevens suggested that here **consign to** means "seal the same contract with," i.e., submit to the same terms with.

349. **exorciser:** conjurer of spirits

351. **unlaid:** i.e., walking, appearing (not laid to rest); **forbear thee:** leave you alone

352. **ill:** evil

353. **consummation:** ending, death

358. **Upon their faces:** See longer note, page 268.

Care no more to clothe and eat;
To thee the reed is as the oak. 340
The scepter, learning, physic must
All follow this and come to dust.

GUIDERIUS, ⌜*as* POLYDOR⌝
Fear no more the lightning flash.

ARVIRAGUS, ⌜*as* CADWAL⌝
Nor th' all-dreaded thunderstone.

GUIDERIUS, ⌜*as* POLYDOR⌝
Fear not slander, censure rash; 345

ARVIRAGUS, ⌜*as* CADWAL⌝
Thou hast finished joy and moan.

BOTH *All lovers young, all lovers must*
Consign to thee and come to dust.

GUIDERIUS, ⌜*as* POLYDOR⌝
No exorciser harm thee,

ARVIRAGUS, ⌜*as* CADWAL⌝
Nor no witchcraft charm thee. 350

GUIDERIUS, ⌜*as* POLYDOR⌝
Ghost unlaid forbear thee.

ARVIRAGUS, ⌜*as* CADWAL⌝
Nothing ill come near thee.

BOTH *Quiet consummation have,*
And renownèd be thy grave.

Enter Belarius ⌜*as Morgan,*⌝ *with the body of Cloten.*

GUIDERIUS, ⌜*as* POLYDOR⌝
We have done our obsequies. Come, lay him down. 355
⌜*Cloten's body is placed by Imogen's.*⌝

BELARIUS, ⌜*as* MORGAN⌝
Here's a few flowers, but 'bout midnight more.
The herbs that have on them cold dew o' th' night
Are strewings fitt'st for graves. Upon their faces.—
You were as flowers, now withered. Even so

360. **herblets:** little flowering plants; **shall:** i.e., **shall** wither (See reference to the **withered flowers** in line 359.)

361. **apart upon our knees:** perhaps, let us leave and go pray

362. **The ground . . . again:** i.e., they have returned to **dust** (See notes to lines 6 and 7 above.)

366. **Ods pittikins:** i.e., by God's pity (a mild oath)

367. **gone:** walked

368. **soft:** wait

370. **care:** sorrow, trouble; **on 't:** i.e., in it

371. **cave-keeper:** cave dweller (with possible wordplay on "housekeeper")

373. **bolt:** i.e., arrow made

378. **a part:** i.e., give me **a part**

380. **Without:** outside of

382. **of 's:** i.e., of his

383. **Mercurial:** like that of Mercury, the winged-heeled messenger god of mythology (See picture, page 196.) **Martial:** like that of Mars, the powerful god of war

384. **brawns:** muscles (See picture of **Hercules,** page 170.) **Jovial:** like that of Jove or Jupiter, king of the gods

386. **madded:** i.e., which the maddened; **Hecuba:** queen of Troy who witnessed the slaughter of her husband and people and the destruction of her city by **the Greeks**

387. **to boot:** in addition

388. **Conspired:** i.e., conspiring; **irregulous:** unlawful (a word derived by Shakespeare from the Latin word *regula,* meaning "rule")

(continued)

These herblets shall, which we upon you strew.— 360
Come on, away; apart upon our knees.
The ground that gave them first has them again.
Their pleasures here are past; so ⌜is⌝ their pain.
They exit.

Imogen awakes.

⌜IMOGEN⌝
Yes, sir, to Milford Haven. Which is the way?
I thank you. By yond bush? Pray, how far thither? 365
Ods pittikins, can it be six mile yet?
I have gone all night. Faith, I'll lie down and sleep.
⌜*She sees Cloten's headless body.*⌝
But soft! No bedfellow? O gods and goddesses!
These flowers are like the pleasures of the world,
This bloody man the care on 't. I hope I dream, 370
For so I thought I was a cave-keeper
And cook to honest creatures. But 'tis not so.
'Twas but a bolt of nothing, shot at nothing,
Which the brain makes of fumes. Our very eyes
Are sometimes like our judgments, blind. Good faith, 375
I tremble still with fear; but if there be
Yet left in heaven as small a drop of pity
As a wren's eye, feared gods, a part of it!
The dream's here still. Even when I wake it is
Without me as within me, not imagined, felt. 380
A headless man? The garments of Posthumus?
I know the shape of 's leg. This is his hand,
His foot Mercurial, his Martial thigh,
The brawns of Hercules; but his Jovial face—
Murder in heaven! How? 'Tis gone. Pisanio, 385
All curses madded Hecuba gave the Greeks,
And mine to boot, be darted on thee! Thou,
Conspired with that irregulous devil Cloten,
Hath here cut off my lord. To write and read

389. **cut off:** put to death suddenly and prematurely

392. **bravest:** splendid

393. **Struck:** (1) taken down; (2) removed with a blow; **maintop:** top of the mainmast

397. **lucre:** i.e., desire for gain or profit (presumably, on Pisanio's part)

398. **pregnant:** clear, obvious

400. **cordial:** stimulating, restorative, reviving

401. **home:** completely

402. **Cloten:** i.e., Cloten's

405. **Which:** i.e., who

406. **To them:** perhaps, in addition **to them** (See longer note, page 268.)

407. **After:** according to; **will:** orders, command; **attending:** waiting for

411. **confiners:** inhabitants

414. **conduct:** command, leadership

415. **Siena's:** i.e., the duke of **Siena's**

417. **With . . . wind:** i.e., as soon as the **wind** is advantageous

418. **forwardness:** promptness

Be henceforth treacherous. Damned Pisanio 390
Hath with his forgèd letters—damned Pisanio—
From this most bravest vessel of the world
Struck the maintop. O Posthumus, alas,
Where is thy head? Where's that? Ay me, where's that?
Pisanio might have killed thee at the heart 395
And left this head on. How should this be? Pisanio?
'Tis he and Cloten. Malice and lucre in them
Have laid this woe here. O, 'tis pregnant, pregnant!
The drug he gave me, which he said was precious
And cordial to me, have I not found it 400
Murd'rous to th' senses? That confirms it home.
This is Pisanio's deed, and Cloten. O,
Give color to my pale cheek with thy blood,
That we the horrider may seem to those
Which chance to find us. O my lord! My lord! 405

Enter Lucius, Captains, ⌜Soldiers,⌝ and a Soothsayer.

CAPTAIN
To them the legions garrisoned in Gallia,
After your will, have crossed the sea, attending
You here at Milford Haven with your ships.
They are here in readiness.

LUCIUS But what from Rome? 410

CAPTAIN
The Senate hath stirred up the confiners
And gentlemen of Italy, most willing spirits
That promise noble service, and they come
Under the conduct of bold Iachimo,
Siena's brother. 415

LUCIUS When expect you them?

CAPTAIN
With the next benefit o' th' wind.

LUCIUS This forwardness
Makes our hopes fair. Command our present numbers

421. **of this war's purpose:** i.e., regarding the outcome we seek in fighting **this war**

422. **the very gods: the gods** themselves (**Very** is simply emphatic.)

423. **fast:** i.e., fasted; **intelligence:** information

427. **my sins . . . divination:** i.e., because of **my sins** I am unable to prophesy

430. **false:** i.e., falsely; **Soft:** wait

431. **sometime:** once

433. **Or . . . or:** i.e., either . . . or

434. **his:** i.e., its

442. **did:** i.e., painted this **picture** (line 443)

444. **wrack:** ruin

450. **is:** i.e., are

451. **service:** i.e., the opportunity to serve a master

". . . Jove's bird, the Roman eagle." (4.2.424)
From Claude Paradin, *Deuises heroiques* . . . (1557).

Be mustered; bid the Captains look to 't.—Now, sir, 420
What have you dreamed of late of this war's purpose?

SOOTHSAYER
Last night the very gods showed me a vision—
I fast and prayed for their intelligence—thus:
I saw Jove's bird, the Roman eagle, winged
From the spongy south to this part of the west, 425
There vanished in the sunbeams, which portends—
Unless my sins abuse my divination—
Success to th' Roman host.

LUCIUS Dream often so,
And never false.—Soft, ho, what trunk is here 430
Without his top? The ruin speaks that sometime
It was a worthy building. How, a page?
Or dead or sleeping on him? But dead rather,
For nature doth abhor to make his bed
With the defunct or sleep upon the dead. 435
Let's see the boy's face.

CAPTAIN He's alive, my lord.

LUCIUS
He'll then instruct us of this body.—Young one,
Inform us of thy fortunes, for it seems
They crave to be demanded. Who is this 440
Thou mak'st thy bloody pillow? Or who was he
That, otherwise than noble nature did,
Hath altered that good picture? What's thy interest
In this sad wrack? How came 't? Who is 't?
What art thou? 445

IMOGEN, ⌜*as* FIDELE⌝ I am nothing; or if not,
Nothing to be were better. This was my master,
A very valiant Briton, and a good,
That here by mountaineers lies slain. Alas,
There is no more such masters. I may wander 450
From east to occident, cry out for service,
Try many, all good, serve truly, never
Find such another master.

454. **'Lack:** i.e., alack

455. **Thou mov'st:** i.e., you stir (my pity)

457. **Richard du Champ:** i.e., Richard of the Field (See longer note, page 269.)

462. **approve:** prove, demonstrate

463. **faith:** faithfulness (See note to 3.6.0 SD.)

468. **prefer:** recommend

471. **pickaxes:** i.e., hands

474. **century of:** hundred

477. **So please you:** i.e., if it **please you** to; **entertain me:** employ me as your servant

482. **partisans:** long-handled bladed weapons (See below.)

483. **arm him:** i.e., lift him up; **preferred:** recommended

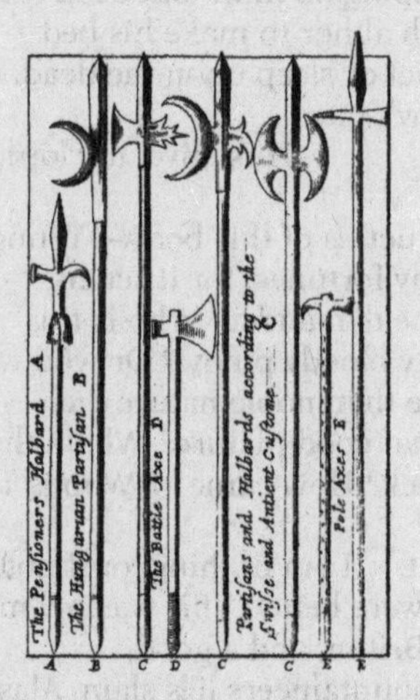

"Pikes and partisans." (4.2.482)
From Louis de Gaya, *A treatise of the arms . . .* (1678).

LUCIUS 'Lack, good youth,
Thou mov'st no less with thy complaining than 455
Thy master in bleeding. Say his name, good friend.

IMOGEN, ⌜*as* FIDELE⌝
Richard du Champ. ⌜*Aside.*⌝ If I do lie and do
No harm by it, though the gods hear, I hope
They'll pardon it.—Say you, sir?

LUCIUS Thy name? 460

IMOGEN, ⌜*as* FIDELE⌝ Fidele, sir.

LUCIUS
Thou dost approve thyself the very same;
Thy name well fits thy faith, thy faith thy name.
Wilt take thy chance with me? I will not say
Thou shalt be so well mastered, but be sure 465
No less beloved. The Roman Emperor's letters
Sent by a consul to me should not sooner
Than thine own worth prefer thee. Go with me.

IMOGEN, ⌜*as* FIDELE⌝
I'll follow, sir. But first, an 't please the gods,
I'll hide my master from the flies as deep 470
As these poor pickaxes can dig; and when
With wild-wood leaves and weeds I ha' strewed his
grave
And on it said a century of prayers,
Such as I can, twice o'er, I'll weep and sigh, 475
And leaving so his service, follow you,
So please you entertain me.

LUCIUS Ay, good youth,
And rather father thee than master thee.—My friends,
The boy hath taught us manly duties. Let us 480
Find out the prettiest daisied plot we can,
And make him with our pikes and partisans
A grave. Come, arm him.—Boy, he's preferred
By thee to us, and he shall be interred
As soldiers can. Be cheerful; wipe thine eyes. 485
Some falls are means the happier to arise.

They exit, ⌜the Soldiers carrying Cloten's body.⌝

4.3 Cymbeline finds himself alone in the face of the Roman attack, with Imogen and Cloten both missing and the queen desperately ill.

---

1. **Again:** i.e., go back **again**
2. **with:** i.e., because of
4. **at once:** at one stroke, with one sweep; **touch:** hurt, wound
6. **Upon a desperate bed:** i.e., so sick as to be given up as hopeless **bed:** sickbed
8. **needful:** indispensable; **this present:** i.e., **this present** moment
9. **for:** i.e., as **for**
11. **we'll:** Note the shift from the first-person singular to the royal "we."
15. **nothing know:** i.e., do not **know** at all
16. **purposes:** intends
18. **Hold me:** consider me as, regard me as
22. **subjection:** obligations as a subject; **For:** i.e., as **for**
23. **wants:** lacks
24. **will:** i.e., he **will**
25. **troublesome:** filled with distress
26. **slip you:** i.e., let you go, turn you loose; **for a season:** i.e., for a while; **our jealousy:** my wrath
27. **Does yet depend:** perhaps, still hangs (over you)
30. **a supply:** reinforcements

Scene 3

Enter Cymbeline, Lords, Pisanio, ⌜*and Attendants.*⌝

CYMBELINE

Again, and bring me word how 'tis with her.

⌜*An Attendant exits.*⌝

A fever, with the absence of her son;
A madness, of which her life's in danger. Heavens,
How deeply you at once do touch me! Imogen,
The great part of my comfort, gone; my queen 5
Upon a desperate bed, and in a time
When fearful wars point at me; her son gone,
So needful for this present. It strikes me past
The hope of comfort.—But for thee, fellow,
Who needs must know of her departure and 10
Dost seem so ignorant, we'll enforce it from thee
By a sharp torture.

PISANIO Sir, my life is yours.
I humbly set it at your will. But for my mistress,
I nothing know where she remains, why gone, 15
Nor when she purposes return. Beseech your
Highness,
Hold me your loyal servant.

LORD Good my liege,
The day that she was missing, he was here. 20
I dare be bound he's true and shall perform
All parts of his subjection loyally. For Cloten,
There wants no diligence in seeking him,
And will no doubt be found.

CYMBELINE The time is troublesome. 25
⌜*To Pisanio.*⌝ We'll slip you for a season, but our jealousy
Does yet depend.

LORD So please your Majesty,
The Roman legions, all from Gallia drawn,
Are landed on your coast with a supply 30
Of Roman gentlemen by the Senate sent.

33. **amazed with matter:** i.e., overwhelmed by the course of events

35. **preparation:** military force

35–36. **affront no less / Than:** i.e., confront (an army) as large as

38. **The want is but:** i.e., all that is lacking is; **powers:** armies

42. **annoy:** hurt, injure

43. **chances:** events; mishaps

48. **is betid to:** i.e., has become of

49. **Perplexed:** troubled, bewildered

50. **to be:** i.e., in order **to be**

52. **note:** notice, attention

53. **doubts:** uncertainties, difficulties

4.4 The young princes persuade Belarius that the three of them should join with the Britons against Rome.

---

2. **from it:** i.e., move away **from it**

CYMBELINE
Now for the counsel of my son and queen!
I am amazed with matter.

LORD Good my liege,
Your preparation can affront no less 35
Than what you hear of. Come more, for more you're ready.
The want is but to put those powers in motion
That long to move.

CYMBELINE I thank you. Let's withdraw, 40
And meet the time as it seeks us. We fear not
What can from Italy annoy us, but
We grieve at chances here. Away.

They exit. ⌜*Pisanio remains.*⌝

PISANIO
I heard no letter from my master since
I wrote him Imogen was slain. 'Tis strange. 45
Nor hear I from my mistress, who did promise
To yield me often tidings. Neither know I
What is ⌜betid⌝ to Cloten, but remain
Perplexed in all. The heavens still must work.
Wherein I am false I am honest; not true, to be true. 50
These present wars shall find I love my country,
Even to the note o' th' King, or I'll fall in them.
All other doubts, by time let them be cleared.
Fortune brings in some boats that are not steered.

He exits.

Scene 4

Enter Belarius ⌜*as Morgan,*⌝ *Guiderius* ⌜*as Polydor,*⌝ *and Arviragus* ⌜*as Cadwal.*⌝

GUIDERIUS, ⌜*as* POLYDOR⌝
The noise is round about us.

BELARIUS, ⌜*as* MORGAN⌝ Let us from it.

6. **This way:** i.e., if we try to hide

7. **Must or:** i.e., **must** either; **receive:** regard; harbor

8. **revolts:** rebels (against Britain)

9. **During their use:** i.e., while we are useful to them

14. **bands:** organized companies, troops; **render:** rendering of an account of

16. **whose answer:** the response to which

17. **Drawn on with:** brought on by (though with echoes of "**drawn** out, prolonged" and of *to draw* as meaning "to disembowel," part of the torture and execution of traitors)

18. **doubt:** apprehension, fear

19. **nothing:** not at all

23. **their quartered fires:** i.e., the watch **fires** in their quarters or camps

24. **cloyed importantly:** i.e., filled (literally, clogged) with urgent or important matters

25. **upon our note:** i.e., noting or observing us

28. **Of many:** i.e., to **many**

29. **not wore him:** i.e., did **not** wear **him**

30. **remembrance:** memory

32. **want:** lack

33. **certainty:** i.e., certain continuance; **aye:** forever

35. **still:** always; **tanlings:** tanned people (In Shakespeare's time, the upper classes avoided exposure to the sun.)

ARVIRAGUS, ⌜*as* CADWAL⌝
What pleasure, sir, ⌜find we⌝ in life, to lock it
From action and adventure?
GUIDERIUS, ⌜*as* POLYDOR⌝ Nay, what hope 5
Have we in hiding us? This way the Romans
Must or for Britons slay us or receive us
For barbarous and unnatural revolts
During their use, and slay us after.
BELARIUS, ⌜*as* MORGAN⌝ Sons, 10
We'll higher to the mountains, there secure us.
To the King's party there's no going. Newness
Of Cloten's death—we being not known, not mustered
Among the bands—may drive us to a render
Where we have lived, and so extort from 's that 15
Which we have done, whose answer would be death
Drawn on with torture.
GUIDERIUS, ⌜*as* POLYDOR⌝ This is, sir, a doubt
In such a time nothing becoming you
Nor satisfying us. 20
ARVIRAGUS, ⌜*as* CADWAL⌝ It is not likely
That when they hear ⌜the⌝ Roman horses neigh,
Behold their quartered fires, have both their eyes
And ears so cloyed importantly as now,
That they will waste their time upon our note, 25
To know from whence we are.
BELARIUS, ⌜*as* MORGAN⌝ O, I am known
Of many in the army. Many years,
Though Cloten then but young, you see not wore him
From my remembrance. And besides, the King 30
Hath not deserved my service nor your loves,
Who find in my exile the want of breeding,
The certainty of this hard life, aye hopeless
To have the courtesy your cradle promised,
But to be still hot summer's tanlings and 35
The shrinking slaves of winter.
GUIDERIUS, ⌜*as* POLYDOR⌝ Than be so

40. **thereto:** in addition to that, besides; **o'ergrown:** perhaps, with hair and beard; perhaps, with age

43. **What thing:** i.e., **what** a shameful **thing**

45. **hot:** lecherous

47. **rowel:** i.e., spur (literally, the wheel of a spur)

50. **his:** i.e., its

55. **hazard therefore due:** i.e., peril I deserve to endure because of my disobedience

60. **cracked:** i.e., impaired (by age); **Have with you:** i.e., come on

61. **country:** i.e., country's

64. **thinks scorn:** disdains (itself)

The god Mercury. (4.2.383)
From Innocenzio Ringhieri, *Cento giuochi liberali . . .* (1580).

Better to cease to be. Pray, sir, to th' army.
I and my brother are not known; yourself
So out of thought, and thereto so o'ergrown, 40
Cannot be questioned.

ARVIRAGUS, ⌜*as* CADWAL⌝ By this sun that shines,
I'll thither. What thing is 't that I never
Did see man die, scarce ever looked on blood
But that of coward hares, hot goats, and venison! 45
Never bestrid a horse save one that had
A rider like myself, who ne'er wore rowel
Nor iron on his heel! I am ashamed
To look upon the holy sun, to have
The benefit of his blest beams, remaining 50
So long a poor unknown.

GUIDERIUS, ⌜*as* POLYDOR⌝ By heavens, I'll go!
If you will bless me, sir, and give me leave,
I'll take the better care, but if you will not,
The hazard therefore due fall on me by 55
The hands of Romans.

ARVIRAGUS, ⌜*as* CADWAL⌝ So say I. Amen.

BELARIUS, ⌜*as* MORGAN⌝
No reason I—since of your lives you set
So slight a valuation—should reserve
My cracked one to more care. Have with you, boys! 60
If in your country wars you chance to die,
That is my bed, too, lads, and there I'll lie.
Lead, lead. ⌜*Aside.*⌝ The time seems long; their
blood thinks scorn
Till it fly out and show them princes born. 65

They exit.

CYMBELINE

ACT 5

5.1 Posthumus, in Britain as part of the Roman army, repents Imogen's (reported) murder and decides to seek death by joining the British army in the disguise of a poor soldier.

---

3. **this course:** i.e., the path leading to **this bloody cloth**

5. **wrying:** erring

6. **does not:** i.e., **does not** obey

7. **No bond but:** i.e., (he is) bound only

8. **Should have:** i.e., had

9. **put on:** instigate

14. **second ills with ills:** i.e., follow one wicked act with another; **each elder worse:** i.e., **each** sin **worse** than the previous (**elder**) sin

15. **thrift:** (spiritual) profit

ACT 5

Scene 1

Enter Posthumus alone, ⌜*wearing Roman garments and carrying a bloody cloth.*⌝

POSTHUMUS

Yea, bloody cloth, I'll keep thee, for I wished
Thou shouldst be colored thus. You married ones,
If each of you should take this course, how many
Must murder wives much better than themselves
For wrying but a little! O Pisanio, 5
Every good servant does not all commands;
No bond but to do just ones. Gods, if you
Should have ta'en vengeance on my faults, I never
Had lived to put on this; so had you saved
The noble Imogen to repent, and struck 10
Me, wretch more worth your vengeance. But, alack,
You snatch some hence for little faults; that's love,
To have them fall no more; you some permit
To second ills with ills, each elder worse,
And make them dread it, to the doers' thrift. 15
But Imogen is your own. Do your best wills,
And make me blest to obey. I am brought hither
Among th' Italian gentry, and to fight
Against my lady's kingdom. 'Tis enough
That, Britain, I have killed thy mistress. Peace, 20
I'll give no wound to thee. Therefore, good heavens,

23. **weeds:** clothes, garments; **suit:** clothe, dress
25. **part:** party, side
28. **Pitied:** i.e., neither **pitied**
30. **habits:** garments
32. **guise:** custom, practice

5.2 In a series of battles, Posthumus (disguised as a peasant) defeats and disarms Iachimo; the Britons flee and Cymbeline is captured by the Romans; Belarius and the two princes enter and, with the help of Posthumus, rescue Cymbeline. Caius Lucius urges "Fidele" to flee.

---

2. **belied:** told lies about
3. **air on 't:** i.e., its **air**
4. **or could this carl:** otherwise **could this** churl or lowborn man
6. **profession:** i.e., as a soldier
8. **go before:** surpass
10. **Is:** i.e., are

Hear patiently my purpose. I'll disrobe me
Of these Italian weeds and suit myself
As does a Briton peasant. So I'll fight
Against the part I come with; so I'll die 25
For thee, O Imogen, even for whom my life
Is every breath a death. And thus, unknown,
Pitied nor hated, to the face of peril
Myself I'll dedicate. Let me make men know
More valor in me than my habits show. 30
Gods, put the strength o' th' Leonati in me.
To shame the guise o' th' world, I will begin
The fashion: less without and more within.

He exits.

Scene 2

Enter Lucius, Iachimo, and the Roman army at one door, and the Briton army at another, Leonatus Posthumus following like a poor soldier. They march over and go out. Then enter again, in skirmish, Iachimo and Posthumus. He vanquisheth and disarmeth Iachimo, and then leaves him.

IACHIMO

The heaviness and guilt within my bosom
Takes off my manhood. I have belied a lady,
The Princess of this country, and the air on 't
Revengingly enfeebles me; or could this carl,
A very drudge of nature's, have subdued me 5
In my profession? Knighthoods and honors, borne
As I wear mine, are titles but of scorn.
If that thy gentry, Britain, go before
This lout as he exceeds our lords, the odds
Is that we scarce are men and you are gods. 10

He exits.

10 SD. **fly:** flee

11–14. **Stand . . . fight:** These speeches address the fleeing Britons.

17. **As . . . hoodwinked:** i.e., **as** if **war were** blindfolded

18. **supplies:** reinforcements of troops

19. **Or betimes:** i.e., either speedily

5.3 Posthumus, still seeking death and failing to find it as a poor British soldier, reverts to his earlier role as a Roman. He is captured by the victorious Britons. Without recognizing him, Cymbeline sends him to jail.

---

1. **Cam'st thou:** The lord's use of the familiar "thou" reflects Posthumus's disguise as a "poor soldier" (5.2.0 SD); **made the stand:** repelled the attack

3. **the fliers:** i.e., those who fled from the battle

6. **But:** except; **fought:** i.e., took Britain's side (See Judges 5.20: "They **fought** from heaven, even the stars in their courses **fought** against Sisera.")

The battle continues. The Britons fly; Cymbeline is taken. Then enter, to his rescue, Belarius ⌜as Morgan,⌝ Guiderius ⌜as Polydor,⌝ and Arviragus ⌜as Cadwal.⌝

BELARIUS, ⌜*as* MORGAN⌝
Stand, stand! We have th' advantage of the ground.
The lane is guarded. Nothing routs us but
The villainy of our fears.

GUIDERIUS, ⌜*as* POLYDOR,⌝ and ARVIRAGUS, ⌜*as* CADWAL⌝
Stand, stand, and fight!

Enter Posthumus, and seconds the Britons. They rescue Cymbeline and exit. Then enter Lucius, Iachimo, and Imogen ⌜as Fidele⌝.

LUCIUS, ⌜*to Fidele*⌝
Away, boy, from the troops, and save thyself, 15
For friends kill friends, and the disorder's such
As war were hoodwinked.

IACHIMO
'Tis their fresh supplies.

LUCIUS
It is a day turned strangely. Or betimes
Let's reinforce, or fly. 20
They exit.

Scene 3

Enter Posthumus and a Briton Lord.

LORD
Cam'st thou from where they made the stand?

POSTHUMUS
I did,
Though you, it seems, come from the fliers.

LORD
⌜Ay.⌝

POSTHUMUS
No blame be to you, sir, for all was lost, 5
But that the heavens fought. The King himself

7. **Of his wings destitute:** i.e., having lost the divisions that made up the right and left **wings** of his **army**

8. **but:** merely

9. **strait:** narrow; **full-hearted:** filled with courage and confidence

10. **Lolling the tongue:** i.e., with **the tongue** hanging out (like a beast of prey)

12. **touched:** hurt, wounded

13. **that:** i.e., so **that**

14. **hurt behind:** i.e., killed as they fled

19–20. **who deserved . . . to:** perhaps, who has merited his country's support for as many years into the future as, in the past, it took to grow his lengthy beard

22. **like:** i.e., likely

23. **country base:** a popular boys' game, also known as prisoners' base

24. **fit for masks:** i.e., so beautiful (or delicate) as to deserve the protection of ladies' **masks**

25. **those for . . . shame:** i.e., **those** (ladies') **faces** masked to protect the skin or for modesty

26. **Made . . . passage:** i.e., secured the pass or exit

27. **harts:** For the connection between **harts** (i.e., deer) and cowardice, see the reference to "England's timorous deer" in *1 Henry VI* (4.2.46) and to "the poor frighted deer" in *The Rape of Lucrece* (line 1149).

28. **fleet:** fly; **Stand:** a command to come to a halt

29. **are Romans:** i.e., will behave like **Romans**

(continued)

Of his wings destitute, the army broken,
And but the backs of Britons seen, all flying
Through a strait lane; the enemy full-hearted,
Lolling the tongue with slaught'ring, having work 10
More plentiful than tools to do 't, struck down
Some mortally, some slightly touched, some falling
Merely through fear, that the strait pass was dammed
With dead men hurt behind and cowards living
To die with lengthened shame. 15

LORD
Where was this lane?

POSTHUMUS
Close by the battle, ditched, and walled with turf;
Which gave advantage to an ancient soldier,
An honest one, I warrant, who deserved
So long a breeding as his white beard came to, 20
In doing this for 's country. Athwart the lane,
He with two striplings—lads more like to run
The country base than to commit such slaughter,
With faces fit for masks, or rather fairer
Than those for preservation cased or shame— 25
Made good the passage, cried to those that fled
"Our Britain's harts die flying, not our men.
To darkness fleet souls that fly backwards. Stand,
Or we are Romans and will give you that
Like beasts which you shun beastly, and may save 30
But to look back in frown. Stand, stand!" These three,
Three thousand confident, in act as many—
For three performers are the file when all
The rest do nothing—with this word "Stand, stand,"
Accommodated by the place, more charming 35
With their own nobleness, which could have turned
A distaff to a lance, gilded pale looks,
Part shame, part spirit renewed; that some, turned
coward
But by example—O, a sin in war, 40
Damned in the first beginners!—gan to look

30. **Like beasts:** i.e., violently, cruelly; **beastly:** i.e., cowardly; **may save:** i.e., you can prevent

31. **But . . . frown:** i.e., only by turning and looking defiant

32. **act:** action

33. **file:** i.e., whole army (literally, list or roll)

35. **more charming:** perhaps, enchanting **more** of the Britons

36. **nobleness:** noble actions, greatness of character

37. **A distaff to a lance:** i.e., a woman into a soldier (literally, a staff used in spinning thread into a military weapon); **gilded pale looks:** i.e., brought a brilliant color to **pale** cheeks

38. **Part shame, part spirit renewed:** i.e., (transformed the Britons) in part through their **shame,** and in part through renewing their **spirit; that:** i.e., so **that**

41. **gan:** began

42. **they did:** i.e., **these three** (line 31) **did**

43. **Upon:** assailing, attacking

44. **retire:** retreat; **anon:** immediately

45–46. **they fly . . . eagles:** i.e., **they** flee like **chickens** (down) the very **way** (path) on which **they** had swooped like **eagles** (Birds of prey are said to *stoop* when they descend swiftly to capture prey.)

46–47. **slaves . . . made:** i.e., like **slaves** (they retrace) the steps they had strode as **victors**

49. **fragments:** i.e., scraps of food

50. **life o' th' need:** i.e., means of preserving **life** in time of **need**

(continued)

The way that they did and to grin like lions
Upon the pikes o' th' hunters. Then began
A stop i' th' chaser, a retire; anon
A rout, confusion thick. Forthwith they fly 45
Chickens the way which they ⌜stooped⌝ eagles; slaves
The strides ⌜they⌝ victors made; and now our
cowards,
Like fragments in hard voyages, became
The life o' th' need. Having found the backdoor open 50
Of the unguarded hearts, heavens, how they wound!
Some slain before, some dying, some their friends
O'erborne i' th' former wave, ten chased by one,
Are now each one the slaughterman of twenty.
Those that would die or ere resist are grown 55
The mortal bugs o' th' field.

LORD This was strange chance:
A narrow lane, an old man, and two boys.

POSTHUMUS
Nay, do not wonder at it. You are made
Rather to wonder at the things you hear 60
Than to work any. Will you rhyme upon 't
And vent it for a mock'ry? Here is one:
"Two boys, an old man twice a boy, a lane,
Preserved the Britons, was the Romans' bane."

LORD
Nay, be not angry, sir. 65

POSTHUMUS 'Lack, to what end?
Who dares not stand his foe, I'll be his friend;
For if he'll do as he is made to do,
I know he'll quickly fly my friendship too.
You have put me into rhyme. 70

LORD Farewell. You're angry.
He exits.

POSTHUMUS
Still going? This is a lord! O noble misery,
To be i' th' field and ask "What news?" of me!

50–51. **Having found . . . hearts:** The language is unclear, but the image presented is of the vulnerable backs of the fleeing Romans.

52. **Some . . . dying:** i.e., **some** of **our cowards** (lines 47–48) who had pretended to be dead or **dying; some their friends:** i.e., **some** who were **friends** of these **cowards**

53. **O'erborne:** overcome; **ten . . . one:** i.e., **ten** (Britons) **chased by one** (Roman)

54. **slaughterman:** executioner, slaughterer

55. **or ere:** rather than

56. **mortal bugs:** implacable terrors

61. **work any:** i.e., perform **any** marvelous acts (wonders)

62. **for a mock'ry:** i.e., as an action (or, perhaps, as a rhyme) deserving of ridicule

63. **twice a boy:** i.e., again **a boy** (in his "second childhood")

66. **'Lack:** i.e., alack, alas

67. **stand:** i.e., withstand, confront

68. **made:** i.e., created

72. **Still:** i.e., always, continually; **noble misery:** with wordplay on "miserable nobleman"

76. **charmed:** i.e., protected as if by a magic spell

79. **hides him:** i.e., **hides** himself

86. **veriest hind:** i.e., merest peasant or lad

87. **touch my shoulder:** i.e., arrest me (In *Comedy of Errors* an arresting officer is called a "**shoulder** clapper" [4.2.42].)

90. **spend my breath:** dispose of my life

95. **a silly habit:** i.e., rustic clothing

96. **affront:** attack, assault

100. **seconds:** supporters

(continued)

Today how many would have given their honors
To have saved their carcasses, took heel to do 't, 75
And yet died too! I, in mine own woe charmed,
Could not find Death where I did hear him groan,
Nor feel him where he struck. Being an ugly monster,
'Tis strange he hides him in fresh cups, soft beds,
Sweet words, or hath more ministers than we 80
That draw his knives i' th' war. Well, I will find him;
For being now a favorer to the Briton,
No more a Briton. (⌜*He removes his peasant costume.*⌝) I have resumed again
The part I came in. Fight I will no more, 85
But yield me to the veriest hind that shall
Once touch my shoulder. Great the slaughter is
Here made by th' Roman; great the answer be
Britons must take. For me, my ransom's death.
On either side I come to spend my breath, 90
Which neither here I'll keep nor bear again,
But end it by some means for Imogen.

Enter two ⌜Briton⌝ Captains, and Soldiers.

FIRST CAPTAIN
Great Jupiter be praised, Lucius is taken!
'Tis thought the old man and his sons were angels.

SECOND CAPTAIN
There was a fourth man in a silly habit 95
That gave th' affront with them.

FIRST CAPTAIN So 'tis reported,
But none of 'em can be found.—Stand. Who's there?

POSTHUMUS A Roman,
Who had not now been drooping here if seconds 100
Had answered him.

SECOND CAPTAIN Lay hands on him. A dog,
A leg of Rome shall not return to tell
What crows have pecked them here. He brags his service 105
As if he were of note. Bring him to th' King.

101. **answered him:** i.e., acted as he did
106. **of note:** i.e., important, distinguished

5.4 Posthumus, in chains, falls asleep and is visited by the ghosts of his dead family and by the god Jupiter, who assures the ghosts that Posthumus will eventually be fine. Jupiter also leaves a written message for Posthumus predicting the future—a message that Posthumus, on waking, cannot interpret. A messenger brings word that Posthumus is to be brought to the victorious Cymbeline.

1–2. **You . . . pasture:** The image is of a pastured animal put in shackles to keep it from straying or being stolen.
3. **a stomach:** i.e., appetite
8. **sure:** reliable, trustworthy
15. **Must I:** i.e., if **I must**
16. **gyves:** shackles for the legs (See picture, page 216.)
17. **constrained:** compelled
17–18. **To satisfy . . . part:** i.e., **if** atonement is central to **my freedom** (of conscience)
19. **No stricter render of me:** i.e., **no** less a rendering up from **me; my all:** i.e., my life

Enter Cymbeline, ⌜*Attendants,*⌝ *Belarius* ⌜*as Morgan,*⌝ *Guiderius* ⌜*as Polydor,*⌝ *Arviragus* ⌜*as Cadwal,*⌝ *Pisanio,* ⌜*Soldiers,*⌝ *and Roman captives. The Captains present Posthumus to Cymbeline, who delivers him over to a Jailer.*

⌜*They exit.*⌝

Scene 4

Enter Posthumus ⌜*in chains,*⌝ *and* ⌜*two Jailers.*⌝

JAILER
You shall not now be stol'n; you have locks upon you.
So graze as you find pasture.

SECOND JAILER
Ay, or a stomach.

⌜*Jailers exit.*⌝

POSTHUMUS
Most welcome, bondage, for thou art a way,
I think, to liberty. Yet am I better 5
Than one that's sick o' th' gout, since he had rather
Groan so in perpetuity than be cured
By th' sure physician, Death, who is the key
T' unbar these locks. My conscience, thou art fettered
More than my shanks and wrists. You good gods, give me 10
The penitent instrument to pick that bolt,
Then free forever. Is 't enough I am sorry?
So children temporal fathers do appease;
Gods are more full of mercy. Must I repent, 15
I cannot do it better than in gyves,
Desired more than constrained. To satisfy,
If of my freedom 'tis the main part, take
No stricter render of me than my all.
I know you are more clement than vile men, 20
Who of their broken debtors take a third,
A sixth, a tenth, letting them thrive again

23. **abatement:** i.e., reduced amount

25–28. **'Tis not so dear . . . being yours:** Posthumus, returning to the coining metaphor he used at 2.5.5, says that his life, while not as valuable as Imogen's, yet was nevertheless **coined** (i.e., created) by the gods, and thus should be accepted by them. (See longer note, page 269.)

29. **audit:** statement of account

30. **cold bonds:** defunct legal documents recording his debts (See longer note, page 269.)

31 SD. **music before them:** perhaps, musicians walking **before them** (with **other music** [more musicians] preceding **the two young Leonati**)

32. **Thunder-master:** i.e., Jupiter, king of the Roman gods and the god of thunder, to whom lines 32–94 are addressed (See picture, page 262.)

33. **mortal flies:** i.e., humans (See *King Lear:* "As **flies** to wanton boys are we to th' gods; / They kill us for their sport" [4.1.41–42].)

34. **Mars:** Roman god of war; **Juno:** queen of the gods

35. **That:** i.e., who

36. **Rates:** vehemently reproves

40. **Attending nature's law:** i.e., waiting for the natural process (of birth)

41. **as:** i.e., since

44. **earth-vexing smart:** i.e., pain that vexes earthly beings

45. **Lucina:** Roman goddess of childbirth

On their abatement. That's not my desire.
For Imogen's dear life take mine; and though
'Tis not so dear, yet 'tis a life; you coined it. 25
'Tween man and man they weigh not every stamp;
Though light, take pieces for the figure's sake;
You rather mine, being yours. And so, great powers,
If you will take this audit, take this life
And cancel these cold bonds. O Imogen, 30
I'll speak to thee in silence. ⌜*He lies down and sleeps.*⌝

Solemn music. Enter, as in an apparition, Sicilius Leonatus, father to Posthumus, an old man attired like a warrior; leading in his hand an ancient matron, his wife and mother to Posthumus, with music before them. Then, after other music, follows the two young Leonati, brothers to Posthumus, with wounds as they died in the wars. They circle Posthumus round as he lies sleeping.

SICILIUS

No more, thou Thunder-master, show
Thy spite on mortal flies.
With Mars fall out, with Juno chide,
That thy adulteries 35
Rates and revenges.
Hath my poor boy done aught but well,
Whose face I never saw?
I died whilst in the womb he stayed,
Attending nature's law; 40
Whose father then—as men report
Thou orphans' father art—
Thou shouldst have been, and shielded him
From this earth-vexing smart.

MOTHER

Lucina lent not me her aid, 45
But took me in my throes,

51. **Molded . . . fair:** i.e., fashioned him so agreeably or beautifully **stuff:** substance from which something is made

59. **dignity:** worthiness; excellence

62. **Leonati seat:** the place of habitation of the Leonatus family

65. **suffer:** allow, permit

66. **Slight:** worthless; untrustworthy

67. **his:** i.e., Posthumus's

69. **geck:** dupe; **scorn:** object of mockery

71. **stiller seats:** quieter regions (i.e., the resting place of souls, identified in line 99 as **Elysium,** in Greek mythology the abode of the blessed and of heroes after death)

73. **That:** i.e., who

75. **Tenantius':** See 1.1.35–36, and Historical Background, page 285.

A man in gyves. (5.4.16)
From Cesare Vecellio, *Degli habiti antichi et moderni* . . . (1590).

That from me was Posthumus ripped,
Came crying 'mongst his foes,
A thing of pity.

SICILIUS

Great Nature, like his ancestry, 50
Molded the stuff so fair
That he deserved the praise o' th' world
As great Sicilius' heir.

FIRST BROTHER

When once he was mature for man,
In Britain where was he 55
That could stand up his parallel
Or fruitful object be
In eye of Imogen, that best
Could deem his dignity?

MOTHER

With marriage wherefore was he mocked, 60
To be exiled and thrown
From Leonati seat, and cast
From her, his dearest one,
Sweet Imogen?

SICILIUS

Why did you suffer Iachimo, 65
Slight thing of Italy,
To taint his nobler heart and brain
With needless jealousy,
And to become the geck and scorn
O' th' other's villainy? 70

SECOND BROTHER

For this, from stiller seats we came,
Our parents and us twain,
That striking in our country's cause
Fell bravely and were slain,
Our fealty and Tenantius' right 75
With honor to maintain.

77. **Like hardiment:** similar courageous exploits

80. **adjourned:** postponed

81. **graces:** favors, privileges

83. **crystal:** transparent; **ope:** open

89. **marble mansion:** perhaps, the marbled or dappled heavens

94 SD. **Jupiter descends:** See longer note, page 269, and picture below.

98. **Sky-planted:** i.e., placed in the sky in position for discharge (To *plant* artillery is to position it for discharge. Military language continues in **batters** and **rebelling.**) See picture, page 262.

99. **shadows:** ghosts, disembodied spirits; **Elysium:** See note to line 71.

101. **accidents:** events, incidents

"Jupiter descends . . . sitting upon an eagle." (5.4.94 SD)
From Hadrianus Junius, . . . *Emblemata* . . . (1565).

FIRST BROTHER

Like hardiment Posthumus hath
To Cymbeline performed.
Then, Jupiter, thou king of gods,
Why hast thou thus adjourned 80
The graces for his merits due,
Being all to dolors turned?

SICILIUS

Thy crystal window ope; look out.
No longer exercise
Upon a valiant race thy harsh 85
And potent injuries.

MOTHER

Since, Jupiter, our son is good,
Take off his miseries.

SICILIUS

Peep through thy marble mansion. Help,
Or we poor ghosts will cry 90
To th' shining synod of the rest
Against thy deity.

BROTHERS

Help, Jupiter, or we appeal
And from thy justice fly.

Jupiter descends in thunder and lightning, sitting upon an eagle. He throws a thunderbolt. The Ghosts fall on their knees.

JUPITER

No more, you petty spirits of region low, 95
Offend our hearing! Hush. How dare you ghosts
Accuse the Thunderer, whose bolt, you know,
Sky-planted, batters all rebelling coasts.
Poor shadows of Elysium, hence, and rest
Upon your never-withering banks of flowers. 100
Be not with mortal accidents oppressed.
No care of yours it is; you know 'tis ours.

103. **cross:** thwart, oppose

104. **delighted:** i.e., (**the more**) delightful

107. **Our Jovial star:** i.e., my planet (Jupiter), the natal planet regarded as the source of joy

111. **tablet:** small sheet or leaf, often of wax-covered wood—or a pair of such sheets fastened together to make a kind of **book** (line 136)—upon which correspondence or legal documents were written with a stylus

111–12. **wherein . . . confine:** i.e., in which **tablet** I secure his prosperity **full:** complete; abundant

115. **crystalline:** In the Ptolemaic universe, the **crystalline** sphere(s) were just beyond the eighth sphere (that of the fixed stars); thus **crystalline** here may indicate the location in the heavens of Jupiter's **marble mansion** (line 89 above). See page xxxvii for an illustration of the Ptolemaic universe.

118. **Stooped as to foot us:** i.e., swooped down **as** if **to** seize **us** with its talons

119. **our blest fields:** i.e., the Elysian **fields** (another name for **Elysium** [line 99])

120. **cloys his beak:** perhaps, scratches **his beak** with his claws

124. **roof:** dwelling place

128. **scorn:** mockery

132. **swerve:** i.e., am wrong, am in error

133. **dream not to find:** i.e., do not **dream** of finding

Whom best I love I cross, to make my gift,
The more delayed, delighted. Be content.
Your low-laid son our godhead will uplift. 105
His comforts thrive, his trials well are spent.
Our Jovial star reigned at his birth, and in
Our temple was he married. Rise, and fade.
He shall be lord of Lady Imogen,
And happier much by his affliction made. 110
⌜*He hands Sicilius a tablet.*⌝
This tablet lay upon his breast, wherein
Our pleasure his full fortune doth confine.
And so away. No farther with your din
Express impatience, lest you stir up mine.—
Mount, eagle, to my palace crystalline. *Ascends.* 115

SICILIUS
He came in thunder. His celestial breath
Was sulphurous to smell. The holy eagle
Stooped as to foot us. His ascension is
More sweet than our blest fields; his royal bird
Preens the immortal wing and cloys his beak, 120
As when his god is pleased.

ALL
Thanks, Jupiter.

SICILIUS
The marble pavement closes; he is entered
His radiant roof. Away, and, to be blest,
Let us with care perform his great behest. 125
⌜*He places the tablet on Posthumus' breast. They*⌝ *vanish.*

POSTHUMUS, ⌜*waking*⌝
Sleep, thou hast been a grandsire and begot
A father to me, and thou hast created
A mother and two brothers. But, O scorn,
Gone! They went hence so soon as they were born.
And so I am awake. Poor wretches that depend 130
On greatness' favor dream as I have done,
Wake, and find nothing. But, alas, I swerve.
Many dream not to find, neither deserve,

136. **book:** See note to **tablet,** line 111. **rare:** splendid, fine

137. **fangled:** foppish, affected

141. **Whenas:** i.e., when

145. **after:** i.e., afterward; **jointed:** fastened, united; **stock:** stem or trunk in which a graft is inserted (but also, progenitor of a family)

149. **Tongue:** say; **brain:** understand; **both:** i.e., **dream** and gibberish

150. **Or:** either

151. **Be what:** whatever

152. **it:** i.e., the **tablet** (line 111)

153. **if but for sympathy:** i.e., **if** only because of the resemblance

155. **Over-roasted:** i.e., not only **ready** (prepared), but kept too long in preparation (like overcooked meat)

156. **Hanging:** wordplay on (1) being hanged; (2) suspending meat in the air to mature or to dry for preservation

159. **dish pays the shot:** i.e., food itself **pays** the bill

160. **heavy reckoning:** wordplay on **reckoning** as (1) **tavern bills** (line 162); (2) account of one's life rendered at death; and on **heavy** as (1) large; (2) distressful, grievous (with the further suggestion of the **heavy** weight of a body being hanged)

162. **often:** i.e., as **often**

164. **want of meat:** lack of food

And yet are steeped in favors; so am I
That have this golden chance and know not why. 135

⌜*Finding the tablet.*⌝

What fairies haunt this ground? A book? O rare one,
Be not, as is our fangled world, a garment
Nobler than that it covers. Let thy effects
So follow, to be, most unlike our courtiers,
As good as promise. 140

(*Reads.*)

Whenas a lion's whelp shall, to himself unknown, without seeking find, and be embraced by a piece of tender air; and when from a stately cedar shall be lopped branches which, being dead many years, shall after revive, be jointed to the old stock, and freshly grow, then shall Posthumus end his miseries, Britain be fortunate and flourish in peace and plenty. 145

'Tis still a dream, or else such stuff as madmen
Tongue and brain not; either both or nothing,
Or senseless speaking, or a speaking such 150
As sense cannot untie. Be what it is,
The action of my life is like it, which
I'll keep, if but for sympathy.

Enter Jailer

JAILER Come, sir, are you ready for death?

POSTHUMUS Over-roasted rather; ready long ago. 155

JAILER Hanging is the word, sir. If you be ready for that, you are well cooked.

POSTHUMUS So, if I prove a good repast to the spectators, the dish pays the shot.

JAILER A heavy reckoning for you, sir. But the comfort 160 is, you shall be called to no more payments, fear no more tavern bills, which are often the sadness of parting as the procuring of mirth. You come in faint for want of meat, depart reeling with too much drink; sorry that you have paid too much, 165

166. **are paid:** i.e., **are** punished

168. **drawn:** emptied, depleted

170. **quit:** wordplay on (1) paid up; (2) freed; **penny cord:** i.e., hangman's rope (literally, a rope worth a **penny**); **sums up:** i.e., finishes off (with wordplay on "reckons" or "counts up") See picture, page 242.

171. **in a trice:** (1) with a single pull; (2) in an instant

171–72. **debitor and creditor:** i.e., accountant; reckoning of accounts

173. **discharge:** (1) payment; (2) dismissal

173–74. **counters:** disks used in computation

174. **acquittance:** (1) release from debt; (2) deliverance from trouble (often used in reference to death)

179. **officer:** executioner

182–83. **Your Death . . . pictured:** The allusion is to **Death** as a death's-head or skull, **pictured** (depicted) with eye sockets but not **eyes. Your:** perhaps the impersonal form of the pronoun, so that **Your Death** refers to death in general

184. **take upon them:** i.e., presume

186. **jump:** risk; **after-inquiry:** i.e., Last Judgment

187. **speed in:** prevail at

189. **none want:** i.e., **none** who lack

191. **wink:** i.e., close them

198. **made free:** i.e., by death

and sorry that you are paid too much; purse and brain both empty; the brain the heavier for being too light; the purse too light, being drawn of heaviness. O, of this contradiction you shall now be quit. O, the charity of a penny cord! It sums up thousands in a trice. You have no true debitor and creditor but it; of what's past, is, and to come, the discharge. Your neck, sir, is pen, book, and counters; so the acquittance follows. 170

POSTHUMUS I am merrier to die than thou art to live. 175

JAILER Indeed, sir, he that sleeps feels not the toothache. But a man that were to sleep your sleep, and a hangman to help him to bed, I think he would change places with his officer; for, look you, sir, you know not which way you shall go. 180

POSTHUMUS Yes, indeed do I, fellow.

JAILER Your Death has eyes in 's head, then. I have not seen him so pictured. You must either be directed by some that take upon them to know, or to take upon yourself that which I am sure you do not know, or jump the after-inquiry on your own peril. And how you shall speed in your journey's end, I think you'll never return to tell one. 185

POSTHUMUS I tell thee, fellow, there are none want eyes to direct them the way I am going but such as wink and will not use them. 190

JAILER What an infinite mock is this, that a man should have the best use of eyes to see the way of blindness! I am sure hanging's the way of winking.

Enter a Messenger.

MESSENGER Knock off his manacles; bring your prisoner to the King. 195

POSTHUMUS Thou bring'st good news. I am called to be made free.

199. **I'll be hanged:** an emphatic expression of denial, taken literally by Posthumus (line 200)

201. **bolts:** leg irons, fetters

203. **prone:** eager

204. **verier knaves desire:** i.e., worse **knaves** who **desire**

205. **for all he be a Roman:** i.e., even though **he** is a **Roman** (and thus a **knave**); **them:** i.e., Romans, who, as Stoics, were indifferent to death

207. **would:** wish

208. **there were desolation:** i.e., that would be the utter devastation

210. **a preferment:** perhaps, an advantage (for me)

5.5 Cymbeline knights Belarius and the two young men in gratitude for their valor, and sends in search of the poor soldier who aided in his rescue. The doctor enters to tell the king that his queen has died, confessing her hatred of Cymbeline and her plans to kill Imogen. Caius Lucius is brought in and told that he and his army will be killed; he begs the life of Fidele, which Cymbeline grants, along with whatever gift the boy might ask. Instead of asking for Caius Lucius's life, Fidele asks to interrogate Iachimo as to where he got the diamond ring he is wearing. (Scene heading continues on page 238.)

---

3. **richly:** splendidly

5. **targes of proof:** impervious shields (See picture, page 234.)

(continued)

JAILER I'll be hanged then.

⌜*He removes Posthumus's chains.*⌝

POSTHUMUS Thou shalt be then freer than a jailer. No 200
bolts for the dead. ⌜*All but the Jailer*⌝ *exit.*

JAILER Unless a man would marry a gallows and beget
young gibbets, I never saw one so prone. Yet, on my
conscience, there are verier knaves desire to live,
for all he be a Roman; and there be some of them 205
too that die against their wills. So should I, if I
were one. I would we were all of one mind, and
one mind good. O, there were desolation of jailers
and gallowses! I speak against my present profit,
but my wish hath a preferment in 't. 210

⌜*He exits.*⌝

Scene 5

Enter Cymbeline, Belarius ⌜*as Morgan,*⌝ *Guiderius* ⌜*as Polydor,*⌝ *Arviragus* ⌜*as Cadwal,*⌝ *Pisanio,* ⌜*Attendants,*⌝ *and Lords.*

CYMBELINE, ⌜*to Morgan, Polydor, and Cadwal*⌝
Stand by my side, you whom the gods have made
Preservers of my throne. Woe is my heart
That the poor soldier that so richly fought,
Whose rags shamed gilded arms, whose naked breast
Stepped before targes of proof, cannot be found. 5
He shall be happy that can find him, if
Our grace can make him so.

BELARIUS, ⌜*as* MORGAN⌝ I never saw
Such noble fury in so poor a thing,
Such precious deeds in one that promised naught 10
But beggary and poor looks.

CYMBELINE No tidings of him?

PISANIO
He hath been searched among the dead and living,
But no trace of him.

7. **grace:** goodwill, favor

13. **searched:** i.e., sought

16. **heir of his reward:** i.e., beneficiary of the **reward** he deserves

21. **Cambria:** the Latin name for Wales

25. **o' th' battle:** i.e., dubbed on the field of **battle**

26. **fit:** supply, furnish

27. **dignities:** honorable offices and titles; **estates:** exalted ranks

28. **business:** distress, anxiety

41. **so please you:** i.e., if it is your wish

"The scepter . . . must . . . come to dust." (4.2.341–42)
From *Todten-Tantz* . . . (1696).

CYMBELINE, ⌜*to Morgan, Polydor, and Cadwal*⌝
To my grief, I am 15
The heir of his reward, which I will add
To you, the liver, heart, and brain of Britain,
By whom I grant she lives. 'Tis now the time
To ask of whence you are. Report it.

BELARIUS, ⌜*as* MORGAN⌝ Sir, 20
In Cambria are we born, and gentlemen.
Further to boast were neither true nor modest,
Unless I add we are honest.

CYMBELINE Bow your knees.

⌜*They kneel. He taps their shoulders with his sword.*⌝

Arise my knights o' th' battle. I create you 25
Companions to our person, and will fit you
With dignities becoming your estates. ⌜*They rise.*⌝

Enter Cornelius and Ladies.

There's business in these faces. Why so sadly
Greet you our victory? You look like Romans,
And not o' th' court of Britain. 30

CORNELIUS Hail, great king.
To sour your happiness I must report
The Queen is dead.

CYMBELINE Who worse than a physician
Would this report become? But I consider 35
By med'cine life may be prolonged, yet death
Will seize the doctor too. How ended she?

CORNELIUS
With horror, madly dying, like her life,
Which, being cruel to the world, concluded
Most cruel to herself. What she confessed 40
I will report, so please you. These her women
Can trip me if I err, who with wet cheeks
Were present when she finished.

CYMBELINE Prithee, say.

46. **Affected:** loved; **by you:** i.e., **by** virtue of her marriage to **you**

47. **place:** high rank

50. **but:** except that

51. **opening:** divulging

52. **bore in hand:** professed, pretended

55. **But:** except

56. **Ta'en off:** done away with

57. **delicate:** finely skillful, fastidious

60. **mineral:** poison; **took:** i.e., taken

62. **By inches:** little by little, very gradually

63. **watching:** staying awake at night; **tendance:** i.e., bestowing personal care and attention (on you)

65. **fitted:** prepared; modified

66. **th' adoption of the crown:** i.e., **adoption** by Cymbeline as his son and heir

75. **in fault:** i.e., at **fault**

76. **Mine ears:** i.e., my **ears** were not at fault

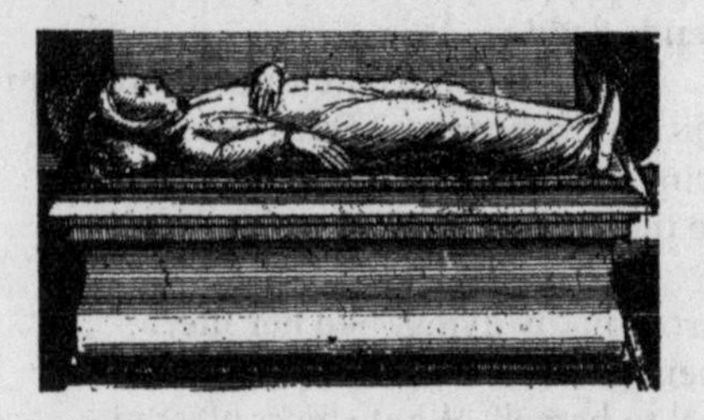

An effigy "in a chapel lying." (2.2.35–36)
From Sir William Dugdale, *The antiquities of Warwickshire* . . . (1656).

CORNELIUS
First, she confessed she never loved you, only 45
Affected greatness got by you, not you;
Married your royalty, was wife to your place,
Abhorred your person.

CYMBELINE She alone knew this,
And but she spoke it dying, I would not 50
Believe her lips in opening it. Proceed.

CORNELIUS
Your daughter, whom she bore in hand to love
With such integrity, she did confess
Was as a scorpion to her sight, whose life,
But that her flight prevented it, she had 55
Ta'en off by poison.

CYMBELINE O, most delicate fiend!
Who is 't can read a woman? Is there more?

CORNELIUS
More, sir, and worse. She did confess she had
For you a mortal mineral which, being took, 60
Should by the minute feed on life and, ling'ring,
By inches waste you. In which time she purposed,
By watching, weeping, tendance, kissing, to
O'ercome you with her show and, in time,
When she had fitted you with her craft, to work 65
Her son into th' adoption of the crown;
But failing of her end by his strange absence,
Grew shameless desperate; opened, in despite
Of heaven and men, her purposes; repented
The evils she hatched were not effected; so 70
Despairing died.

CYMBELINE Heard you all this, her women?

LADIES We did, so please your Highness.

CYMBELINE Mine eyes
Were not in fault, for she was beautiful; 75
Mine ears that ⌜heard⌝ her flattery; nor my heart,

80. **in thy feeling:** i.e., by **feeling** it; through your experience

82. **razed out:** done away with, erased

83. **made suit:** petitioned

85. **ourself:** i.e., I

86. **estate:** (spiritual) condition

87. **chance of:** i.e., the way things fall out in

93. **Sufficeth:** i.e., let it suffice that

96. **my peculiar care:** i.e., concerns for myself

100. **tender over his occasions:** i.e., considerate of his (master's) needs

101. **feat:** adroit, dexterous

102. **make bold:** venture, dare say

105. **And:** even if (you)

107. **favor:** face; appearance

"O, giglet Fortune!" (3.1.34)
From Guillaume de La Perrière, *Le théâtre des bons engins* . . . [1539?].

That thought her like her seeming. It had been vicious
To have mistrusted her. Yet, O my daughter,
That it was folly in me thou mayst say,
And prove it in thy feeling. Heaven mend all. 80

Enter Lucius, Iachimo, ⌜Soothsayer,⌝ and other Roman prisoners, ⌜Posthumus⌝ Leonatus behind, and Imogen ⌜as Fidele, with Briton Soldiers as guards.⌝

Thou com'st not, Caius, now for tribute. That
The Britons have razed out, though with the loss
Of many a bold one, whose kinsmen have made suit
That their good souls may be appeased with slaughter
Of you their captives, which ourself have granted. 85
So think of your estate.

LUCIUS
Consider, sir, the chance of war. The day
Was yours by accident. Had it gone with us,
We should not, when the blood was cool, have
threatened 90
Our prisoners with the sword. But since the gods
Will have it thus, that nothing but our lives
May be called ransom, let it come. Sufficeth
A Roman with a Roman's heart can suffer.
Augustus lives to think on 't; and so much 95
For my peculiar care. This one thing only
I will entreat: my boy, a Briton born,
Let him be ransomed. Never master had
A page so kind, so duteous, diligent,
So tender over his occasions, true, 100
So feat, so nurselike. Let his virtue join
With my request, which I'll make bold your Highness
Cannot deny. He hath done no Briton harm,
Though he have served a Roman. Save him, sir,
And spare no blood beside. 105

CYMBELINE I have surely seen him.
His favor is familiar to me.—Boy,

108. **looked . . . grace:** i.e., brought yourself, through your looks, into my favor
109. **wherefore:** for what reason
110. **Ne'er thank thy master:** i.e., it was not your master's plea that saved you
112. **state:** condition; or, perhaps, rank
118. **alack:** an expression of sorrow or regret
119. **in hand:** going on, in process
121. **shuffle:** scramble, scuffle
123. **Briefly:** quickly
124. **truth:** loyalty, fidelity
125. **perplexed:** troubled
133. **something nearer:** i.e., somewhat closer

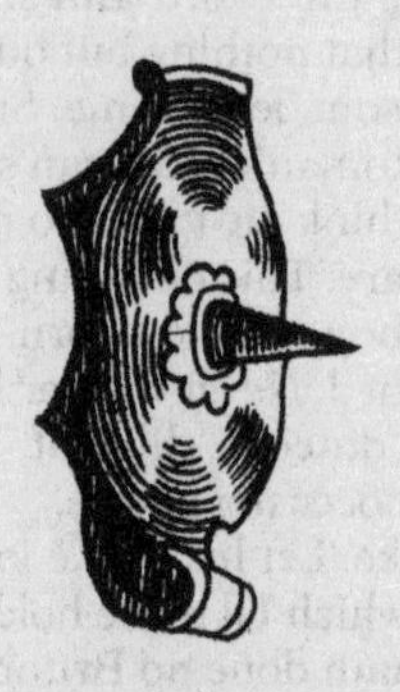

A targe. (5.5.5)
From Louis de Gaya, *A treatise of the arms* . . . (1678).

Thou hast looked thyself into my grace
And art mine own. I know not why, wherefore,
To say "Live, boy." Ne'er thank thy master. Live, 110
And ask of Cymbeline what boon thou wilt,
Fitting my bounty and thy state, I'll give it,
Yea, though thou do demand a prisoner,
The noblest ta'en.

IMOGEN, ⌜*as* FIDELE⌝ I humbly thank your Highness. 115

LUCIUS
I do not bid thee beg my life, good lad,
And yet I know thou wilt.

IMOGEN, ⌜*as* FIDELE⌝ No, no, alack,
There's other work in hand. I see a thing
Bitter to me as death. Your life, good master, 120
Must shuffle for itself.

LUCIUS The boy disdains me,
He leaves me, scorns me. Briefly die their joys
That place them on the truth of girls and boys.
Why stands he so perplexed? 125

⌜*Imogen stares at Iachimo.*⌝

CYMBELINE What would'st thou, boy?
I love thee more and more. Think more and more
What's best to ask. Know'st him thou look'st on?
Speak.
Wilt have him live? Is he thy kin? Thy friend? 130

IMOGEN, ⌜*as* FIDELE⌝
He is a Roman, no more kin to me
Than I to your Highness, who, being born your vassal,
Am something nearer.

CYMBELINE Wherefore ey'st him so?

IMOGEN, ⌜*as* FIDELE⌝
I'll tell you, sir, in private, if you please 135
To give me hearing.

CYMBELINE Ay, with all my heart,
And lend my best attention. What's thy name?

143–45. **One sand . . . Fidele:** The general sense is that **one** grain of **sand** does not resemble another more than this boy **resembles Fidele.** Editors speculate that some words have dropped out of the text.

147. **eyes us not:** i.e., is not looking at us; **Forbear:** be patient

150. **see him dead:** perhaps, **see him** who is **dead** (However, **see** was still sometimes used in Shakespeare's day where we would use "saw.")

159. **grace:** ornament

163. **render:** declare, state

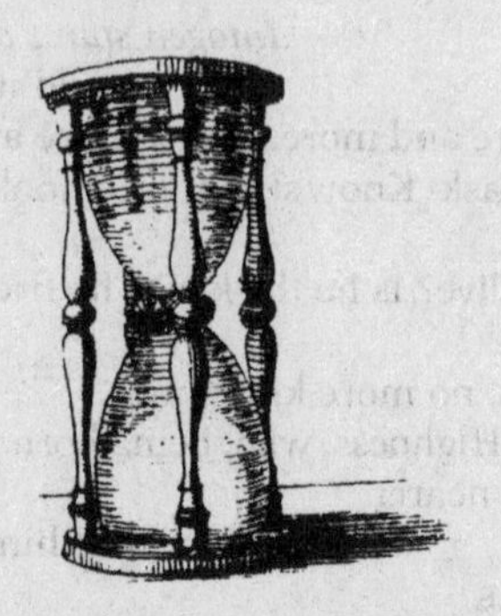

An hourglass. (3.2.76–77)
From August Casimir Redel, *Apophtegmata symbolica* . . . [n.d.].

IMOGEN, ⌜*as* FIDELE⌝
Fidele, sir.
CYMBELINE Thou'rt my good youth, my page. 140
I'll be thy master. Walk with me. Speak freely.
⌜*Cymbeline and Imogen walk aside and talk.*⌝
BELARIUS, ⌜*as* MORGAN⌝
Is not this boy revived from death?
ARVIRAGUS, ⌜*as* CADWAL⌝ One sand another
Not more resembles that sweet rosy lad
Who died, and was Fidele. What think you? 145
GUIDERIUS, ⌜*as* POLYDOR⌝ The same dead thing alive.
BELARIUS, ⌜*as* MORGAN⌝
Peace, peace. See further. He eyes us not. Forbear.
Creatures may be alike. Were 't he, I am sure
He would have spoke to us.
GUIDERIUS, ⌜*as* POLYDOR⌝ But we see him dead. 150
BELARIUS, ⌜*as* MORGAN⌝
Be silent. Let's see further.
PISANIO, ⌜*aside*⌝ It is my mistress!
Since she is living, let the time run on
To good or bad.
⌜*Cymbeline and Imogen come forward.*⌝
CYMBELINE, ⌜*to Imogen*⌝ Come, stand thou by our side. 155
Make thy demand aloud. (⌜*To Iachimo.*⌝) Sir, step
you forth.
Give answer to this boy, and do it freely,
Or by our greatness and the grace of it,
Which is our honor, bitter torture shall 160
Winnow the truth from falsehood.—On. Speak to
him.
IMOGEN, ⌜*as* FIDELE, *pointing to Iachimo's hand*⌝
My boon is that this gentleman may render
Of whom he had this ring.
POSTHUMUS, ⌜*aside*⌝ What's that to him? 165
CYMBELINE
That diamond upon your finger, say
How came it yours.

5.5 (continued) As Iachimo tells the story of how he had slandered Imogen, Posthumus comes forward, reveals who he is, and in his grief calls Imogen's name. She runs to him, but he pushes her away and she falls. Pisanio tells Posthumus that the boy is Imogen. As Posthumus and Imogen embrace and Imogen is reunited with her father, Pisanio explains to Cymbeline about Cloten's journey to Milford Haven. Guiderius finishes the story by telling how he killed Cloten and cut off his head. Cymbeline has Guiderius arrested. (Scene heading continues on page 248.)

---

168. **to leave:** i.e., if I **leave**

169. **to be spoke:** i.e., if spoken

181. **Give me leave:** i.e., permit me (to stop talking, or, perhaps, to sit or lie down)

183. **while nature will:** i.e., to the end of your natural life (literally, as long as **nature** wishes)

185. **Upon a time:** i.e., once (This opens Iachimo's fragmented and heavily embellished story, in which facts—**in Rome . . . Posthumus, . . . Hearing us praise our loves,** etc.—are heavily embroidered with extraneous detail.)

192. **ill:** bad

193. **rar'st:** most exceptional

194–201. **praise our loves . . . the eye:** The basic structure of these lines is "**praise our loves . . . For beauty** [line 195], **. . . for feature** [line 196], **. . . for condition** [line 198] **. . . .**"

196. **feature:** shape, figure

(continued)

IACHIMO
Thou'lt torture me to leave unspoken that
Which to be spoke would torture thee.

CYMBELINE
How? Me? 170

IACHIMO
I am glad to be constrained to utter that
Which torments me to conceal. By villainy
I got this ring. 'Twas Leonatus' jewel,
Whom thou didst banish, and—which more may
grieve thee, 175
As it doth me—a nobler sir ne'er lived
'Twixt sky and ground. Wilt thou hear more, my lord?

CYMBELINE
All that belongs to this.

IACHIMO
That paragon, thy daughter,
For whom my heart drops blood and my false spirits 180
Quail to remember—Give me leave; I faint.

CYMBELINE
My daughter? What of her? Renew thy strength.
I had rather thou shouldst live while nature will
Than die ere I hear more. Strive, man, and speak.

IACHIMO
Upon a time—unhappy was the clock 185
That struck the hour!—it was in Rome—accursed
The mansion where!—'twas at a feast—O, would
Our viands had been poisoned, or at least
Those which I heaved to head!—the good
Posthumus— 190
What should I say? He was too good to be
Where ill men were, and was the best of all
Amongst the rar'st of good ones—sitting sadly,
Hearing us praise our loves of Italy
For beauty that made barren the swelled boast 195
Of him that best could speak; for feature, laming
The shrine of Venus or straight-pight Minerva,
Postures beyond brief nature; for condition,

197. **shrine of Venus:** perhaps, the shape of **Venus,** goddess of love, imagined as a **shrine; straight-pight:** tall and erect; **Minerva:** Roman goddess of wisdom

198. **condition:** disposition, character

199. **shop of:** i.e., store containing

200. **that hook of wiving:** i.e., that which ensnares one into marriage

201. **Fairness:** beauty

207. **hint:** occasion, opportunity

211. **a mind put in 't:** i.e., her intellect included in the **picture** (line 210)

212. **cracked . . . trulls:** i.e., uttered about **kitchen** girls

213. **unspeaking sots:** inarticulate fools

214. **to th' purpose:** get to (or keep to) the point

216. **as Dian:** as if Diana, goddess of chastity; **hot:** lecherous

217. **cold:** chaste

218. **Made scruple of:** raised doubts about

219. **this:** i.e., the ring

221. **In suit:** through wooing

225. **would so:** i.e., **would** have done **so; carbuncle:** precious gem

226. **Of Phoebus' wheel:** i.e., from the **wheel** of the sun god's chariot; **might so:** i.e., **might** have done **so**

227. **all the worth of 's car:** perhaps, equal in value to **Phoebus'** chariot; or, perhaps, **Phoebus'** chariot itself (See picture, page 256.)

228. **Post:** i.e., rush (as if by post-horse)

230. **Of:** i.e., by

233. **Gan:** began

A shop of all the qualities that man
Loves woman for, besides that hook of wiving, 200
Fairness which strikes the eye—

CYMBELINE I stand on fire.
Come to the matter.

IACHIMO All too soon I shall,
Unless thou wouldst grieve quickly. This Posthumus, 205
Most like a noble lord in love and one
That had a royal lover, took his hint,
And, not dispraising whom we praised—therein
He was as calm as virtue—he began
His mistress' picture; which by his tongue being made 210
And then a mind put in 't, either our brags
Were cracked of kitchen trulls, or his description
Proved us unspeaking sots.

CYMBELINE Nay, nay, to th' purpose.

IACHIMO
Your daughter's chastity—there it begins. 215
He spake of her as Dian had hot dreams
And she alone were cold; whereat I, wretch,
Made scruple of his praise and wagered with him
Pieces of gold 'gainst this, which then he wore
Upon his honored finger, to attain 220
In suit the place of 's bed and win this ring
By hers and mine adultery. He, true knight,
No lesser of her honor confident
Than I did truly find her, stakes this ring,
And would so, had it been a carbuncle 225
Of Phoebus' wheel, and might so safely, had it
Been all the worth of 's car. Away to Britain
Post I in this design. Well may you, sir,
Remember me at court, where I was taught
Of your chaste daughter the wide difference 230
'Twixt amorous and villainous. Being thus quenched
Of hope, not longing, mine Italian brain
Gan in your duller Britain operate

234. **vantage:** profit, gain

235. **practice:** plot, stratagem, treachery

236. **simular:** counterfeited, simulated

238. **renown:** good name, reputation

239. **tokens thus and thus:** i.e., various pieces of evidence; **averring notes:** i.e., asserting the existence of visible evidence

244. **ta'en the forfeit:** i.e., gained what was lost through the breaking of **her bond**

251. **justicer:** judge

258. **she herself:** perhaps, **virtue** itself

262. **Be villainy:** i.e., **villainy** (in comparison to my actions) is

267. **Shall 's:** i.e., **shall** we, must we; **scornful:** contemptible

268. **There lie thy part:** perhaps, lying **there** is your role

"O, the charity of a penny cord!" (5.4.170)
From Sebastian Münster, *Cosmographiae uniuersalis* . . . (1554).

Most vilely; for my vantage, excellent.
And to be brief, my practice so prevailed 235
That I returned with simular proof enough
To make the noble Leonatus mad
By wounding his belief in her renown
With tokens thus and thus; averring notes
Of chamber-hanging, pictures, this her bracelet— 240
O, cunning how I got ⌜it⌝!—nay, some marks
Of secret on her person, that he could not
But think her bond of chastity quite cracked,
I having ta'en the forfeit. Whereupon—
Methinks I see him now— 245

POSTHUMUS, ⌜*coming forward*⌝ Ay, so thou dost,
Italian fiend.—Ay me, most credulous fool,
Egregious murderer, thief, anything
That's due to all the villains past, in being,
To come. O, give me cord, or knife, or poison, 250
Some upright justicer.—Thou, king, send out
For torturers ingenious. It is I
That all th' abhorrèd things o' th' earth amend
By being worse than they. I am Posthumus,
That killed thy daughter—villainlike, I lie— 255
That caused a lesser villain than myself,
A sacrilegious thief, to do 't. The temple
Of virtue was she, yea, and she herself.
Spit and throw stones, cast mire upon me, set
The dogs o' th' street to bay me. Every villain 260
Be called Posthumus Leonatus, and
Be villainy less than 'twas. O Imogen!
My queen, my life, my wife! O Imogen,
Imogen, Imogen!

IMOGEN, ⌜*running to Posthumus*⌝ Peace, my lord! 265
Hear, hear—

POSTHUMUS
Shall 's have a play of this? Thou scornful page,
There lie thy part. ⌜*He pushes her away; she falls.*⌝

274. **these staggers:** i.e., this staggering gait (The name **staggers** was applied to various diseases that affected farm animals.)

283. **stones of sulfur:** thunderbolts

291. **approve:** prove

292. **confection:** compound, medicine

296. **importuned:** accent on second syllable

297. **temper:** concoct; **still pretending:** always using as a pretext

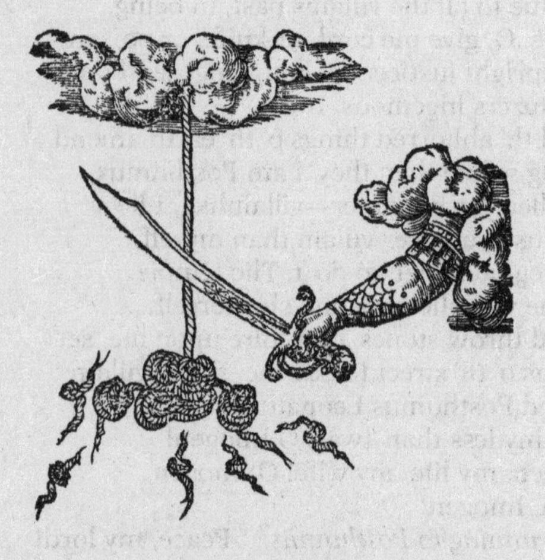

Cutting the Gordian knot. (2.2.38)
From Claude Paradin, *Deuises heroiques* . . . (1557).

PISANIO O, gentlemen, help!—
Mine and your mistress! O my lord Posthumus, 270
You ne'er killed Imogen till now! Help, help!
Mine honored lady—

CYMBELINE Does the world go round?

POSTHUMUS
How comes these staggers on me?

PISANIO Wake, my mistress. 275

CYMBELINE
If this be so, the gods do mean to strike me
To death with mortal joy.

PISANIO How fares my mistress?

IMOGEN O, get thee from my sight!
Thou gav'st me poison. Dangerous fellow, hence. 280
Breathe not where princes are.

CYMBELINE The tune of Imogen!

PISANIO
Lady, the gods throw stones of sulfur on me if
That box I gave you was not thought by me
A precious thing. I had it from the Queen. 285

CYMBELINE
New matter still.

IMOGEN It poisoned me.

CORNELIUS O gods!
⌜*To Pisanio.*⌝ I left out one thing which the Queen
confessed, 290
Which must approve thee honest. "If Pisanio
Have," said she, "given his mistress that confection
Which I gave him for cordial, she is served
As I would serve a rat."

CYMBELINE What's this, Cornelius? 295

CORNELIUS
The Queen, sir, very oft importuned me
To temper poisons for her, still pretending
The satisfaction of her knowledge only
In killing creatures vile, as cats and dogs,

301. **of more danger: more** harmful or dangerous

302. **cease:** end

323. **mother's:** stepmother is

325. **naught:** wicked; **long of:** because of

329. **Now . . . me:** i.e., **now** that I'm no longer afraid

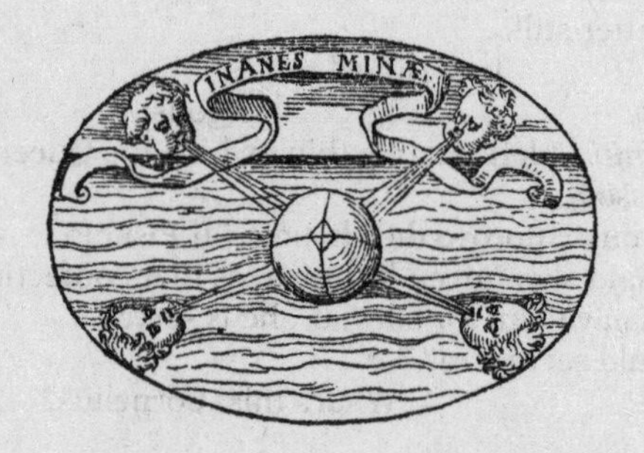

". . . winds of all the corners." (2.4.32)
From Giulio Cesare Capaccio, *Delle imprese trattato* . . . (1592).

Of no esteem. I, dreading that her purpose 300
Was of more danger, did compound for her
A certain stuff which, being ta'en, would cease
The present power of life, but in short time
All offices of nature should again
Do their due functions.—Have you ta'en of it? 305

IMOGEN
Most like I did, for I was dead.

BELARIUS, ⌜*as* MORGAN, *aside to Guiderius and Arviragus*⌝
My boys,
There was our error.

GUIDERIUS, ⌜*as* POLYDOR⌝ This is sure Fidele.

IMOGEN, ⌜*to Posthumus*⌝
Why did you throw your wedded lady from you? 310
Think that you are upon a rock, and now
Throw me again. ⌜*She embraces him.*⌝

POSTHUMUS Hang there like fruit, my soul,
Till the tree die.

CYMBELINE, ⌜*to Imogen*⌝ How now, my flesh, my child? 315
What, mak'st thou me a dullard in this act?
Wilt thou not speak to me?

IMOGEN, ⌜*kneeling*⌝ Your blessing, sir.

BELARIUS, ⌜*as* MORGAN, *aside to Guiderius and Arviragus*⌝
Though you did love this youth, I blame you not.
You had a motive for 't. 320

CYMBELINE, ⌜*to Imogen*⌝ My tears that fall
Prove holy water on thee. Imogen,
Thy mother's dead.

IMOGEN I am sorry for 't, my lord.
⌜*She rises.*⌝

CYMBELINE
O, she was naught, and long of her it was 325
That we meet here so strangely. But her son
Is gone, we know not how nor where.

PISANIO My lord,
Now fear is from me, I'll speak truth. Lord Cloten,

330. **missing:** absence

333. **discovered:** revealed

334. **accident:** chance

335. **a feignèd . . . master's:** i.e., presumably the letter referred to in 3.5 (which was **feigned** in that Posthumus wrote it to deceive her) See note to 3.5.120.

345. **forfend:** forbid

347. **hard:** harsh

348. **Deny 't again:** i.e., speak again in order to **deny** what you have said

351. **incivil:** uncivil, unmannerly

354. **off 's:** i.e., **off** his

355. **right:** truly

357. **sorrow:** sorry

5.5 (continued) Belarius, to save Guiderius's life, confesses to Cymbeline that the young men are the two lost princes. Cymbeline welcomes his new family, Imogen is reintroduced to her brothers, and Cymbeline not only pardons Caius Lucius but also grants a pardon to all and promises to pay Rome the tribute he had earlier refused.

Upon my lady's missing, came to me 330
With his sword drawn, foamed at the mouth, and
swore,
If I discovered not which way she was gone,
It was my instant death. By accident,
I had a feignèd letter of my master's 335
Then in my pocket, which directed him
To seek her on the mountains near to Milford;
Where, in a frenzy, in my master's garments,
Which he enforced from me, away he posts
With unchaste purpose and with oath to violate 340
My lady's honor. What became of him
I further know not.

GUIDERIUS, ⌜*as* POLYDOR⌝ Let me end the story.
I slew him there.

CYMBELINE Marry, the gods forfend! 345
I would not thy good deeds should from my lips
Pluck a hard sentence. Prithee, valiant youth,
Deny 't again.

GUIDERIUS, ⌜*as* POLYDOR⌝ I have spoke it, and I did it.

CYMBELINE He was a prince. 350

GUIDERIUS, ⌜*as* POLYDOR⌝
A most incivil one. The wrongs he did me
Were nothing princelike, for he did provoke me
With language that would make me spurn the sea
If it could so roar to me. I cut off 's head,
And am right glad he is not standing here 355
To tell this tale of mine.

CYMBELINE I am sorrow for thee.
By thine own tongue thou art condemned and must
Endure our law. Thou 'rt dead.

IMOGEN That headless man 360
I thought had been my lord.

CYMBELINE Bind the offender,
And take him from our presence.

⌜*Attendants bind Guiderius.*⌝

368. **Had . . . for:** i.e., **ever** deserved through being scarred in battle

371. **undo:** ruin; remove

374. **spake:** spoke

377. **But I will prove:** i.e., unless **I prove; on 's:** i.e., of us

380. **haply:** perhaps

383. **Have at it:** i.e., let's go for it, let's attempt it; **By leave:** i.e., with your permission; **by** your **leave**

389. **Assumed this age:** i.e., become the old man you see

395. **confiscate:** confiscated (accent on second syllable)

An astrologer. (3.2.28)
From George Wither, *A collection of emblemes . . .* (1635).

BELARIUS, ⌜*as* MORGAN⌝ Stay, sir king.
This man is better than the man he slew, 365
As well descended as thyself, and hath
More of thee merited than a band of Clotens
Had ever scar for.—Let his arms alone.
They were not born for bondage.

CYMBELINE Why, old soldier, 370
Wilt thou undo the worth thou art unpaid for
By tasting of our wrath? How of descent
As good as we?

ARVIRAGUS, ⌜*as* CADWAL⌝ In that he spake too far.

CYMBELINE, ⌜*to Morgan*⌝
And thou shalt die for 't. 375

BELARIUS, ⌜*as* MORGAN⌝ We will die all three
But I will prove that two on 's are as good
As I have given out him.—My sons, I must
For mine own part unfold a dangerous speech,
Though haply well for you. 380

ARVIRAGUS, ⌜*as* CADWAL⌝ Your danger's ours.

GUIDERIUS, ⌜*as* POLYDOR⌝
And our good his.

BELARIUS, ⌜*as* MORGAN⌝ Have at it, then.—By leave,
Thou hadst, great king, a subject who
Was called Belarius. 385

CYMBELINE What of him? He is
A banished traitor.

BELARIUS He it is that hath
Assumed this age; indeed a banished man,
I know not how a traitor. 390

CYMBELINE Take him hence.
The whole world shall not save him.

BELARIUS Not too hot.
First pay me for the nursing of thy sons
And let it be confiscate all, so soon 395
As I have received it.

CYMBELINE Nursing of my sons?

398. **saucy:** insolent

399. **prefer:** advance or promote in rank or fortune

407. **sometime:** once, formerly

408–9. **Your pleasure . . . treason:** i.e., your whim in accusing me of **treason** and punishing me comprises my entire **offense** **mere:** entire

409. **That:** i.e., **that** which

410. **gentle:** wellborn

412. **trained:** brought; **those arts:** i.e., such skills, learning, and accomplishments

415. **for the theft:** i.e., in recompense **for the theft**

416. **Upon:** at the time of; **moved:** persuaded

418. **Beaten:** i.e., being **beaten**

420. **of:** i.e., by; **shaped:** was conducive, tended

421. **end of:** i.e., purpose for

426. **inlay heaven with stars:** i.e., become constellations (enjoying the apotheosis of classical heroes)

429. **Unlike:** unlikely, improbable

BELARIUS
I am too blunt and saucy. Here's my knee.
⌜*He kneels.*⌝
Ere I arise I will prefer my sons,
Then spare not the old father. Mighty sir, 400
These two young gentlemen that call me father
And think they are my sons are none of mine.
They are the issue of your loins, my liege,
And blood of your begetting.

CYMBELINE How? My issue? 405

BELARIUS
So sure as you your father's. I, old Morgan,
Am that Belarius whom you sometime banished.
Your pleasure was my ⌜mere⌝ offense, my punishment
Itself, and all my treason. That I suffered
Was all the harm I did. These gentle princes— 410
For such and so they are—these twenty years
Have I trained up; those arts they have as I
Could put into them. My breeding was, sir, as
Your Highness knows. Their nurse Euriphile,
Whom for the theft I wedded, stole these children 415
Upon my banishment. I moved her to 't,
Having received the punishment before
For that which I did then. Beaten for loyalty
Excited me to treason. Their dear loss,
The more of you 'twas felt, the more it shaped 420
Unto my end of stealing them. But, gracious sir,
Here are your sons again, and I must lose
Two of the sweet'st companions in the world.
The benediction of these covering heavens
Fall on their heads like dew, for they are worthy 425
To inlay heaven with stars. ⌜*He weeps.*⌝

CYMBELINE Thou weep'st and speak'st.
The service that you three have done is more
Unlike than this thou tell'st. I lost my children.
If these be they, I know not how to wish 430
A pair of worthier sons.

437. **curious:** beautifully wrought

438. **probation:** proof

441. **sanguine:** blood-red

446. **his evidence:** i.e., **evidence** of **his** identity

449. **Rejoiced:** felt joy because of; **deliverance:** delivery

450. **starting:** flying; **orbs:** spheres (In the Ptolemaic universe, hollow concentric spheres surrounded the earth and carried the planets and stars with them in their revolution. See note to 5.4.115.)

463. **dram:** i.e., small drink of medicine

". . . the reed is as the oak." (4.2.340)
From Geoffrey Whitney, *A choice of emblemes* . . . (1586).

BELARIUS Be pleased awhile.
This gentleman whom I call Polydor,
Most worthy prince, as yours is true Guiderius;
This gentleman, my Cadwal, Arviragus, 435
Your younger princely son. He, sir, was lapped
In a most curious mantle, wrought by th' hand
Of his queen mother, which for more probation
I can with ease produce.

CYMBELINE Guiderius had 440
Upon his neck a mole, a sanguine star.
It was a mark of wonder.

BELARIUS This is he,
Who hath upon him still that natural stamp.
It was wise Nature's end in the donation 445
To be his evidence now.

CYMBELINE O, what am I,
A mother to the birth of three? Ne'er mother
Rejoiced deliverance more.—Blest pray you be,
That after this strange starting from your orbs, 450
You may reign in them now.—O Imogen,
Thou hast lost by this a kingdom!

IMOGEN No, my lord.
I have got two worlds by 't.—O my gentle brothers,
Have we thus met? O, never say hereafter 455
But I am truest speaker. You called me "brother"
When I was but your sister; I you "brothers"
When we were so indeed.

CYMBELINE Did you e'er meet?

ARVIRAGUS
Ay, my good lord. 460

GUIDERIUS And at first meeting loved,
Continued so until we thought he died.

CORNELIUS
By the Queen's dram she swallowed.

CYMBELINE, ⌜*to Imogen*⌝ O, rare instinct!

468. **Distinction . . . rich in:** i.e., should be elaborately distinguished from each other

474. **your three motives to:** i.e., what motivated you three to join

476. **by-dependences:** i.e., conditional circumstances

477. **nor . . . nor:** i.e., neither . . . nor

482. **object:** i.e., one she sees; **counterchange:** reciprocation

483. **severally in all:** i.e., separately from each to each (everyone looking **with joy** at everyone else)

486. **relieve me:** supply me with nourishment; rescue me

487. **To see:** i.e., so that it was possible for me **to see**

494. **forlorn:** lost, not to be found; wretched

495. **becomed:** suited

498. **company:** accompany

Phoebus in his chariot. (2.3.21; 5.5.227)
From Hyginus, . . . *Fabularum liber* . . . (1549).

When shall I hear all through? This fierce abridgment 465
Hath to it circumstantial branches which
Distinction should be rich in. Where, how lived you?
And when came you to serve our Roman captive?
How parted with your ⌜brothers⌝? How first met them? 470
Why fled you from the court? And whither?
⌜*To Belarius.*⌝ These,
And your three motives to the battle, with
I know not how much more, should be demanded, 475
And all the other by-dependences
From chance to chance; but nor the time nor place
Will serve our long interrogatories. See,
Posthumus anchors upon Imogen;
And she, like harmless lightning, throws her eye 480
On him, her brothers, me, her master, hitting
Each object with a joy; the counterchange
Is severally in all. Let's quit this ground,
And smoke the temple with our sacrifices.
Thou art my brother, so we'll hold thee ever. 485

IMOGEN, ⌜*to Belarius*⌝
You are my father too, and did relieve me
To see this gracious season.

CYMBELINE All o'erjoyed
Save these in bonds; let them be joyful too,
For they shall taste our comfort. 490

IMOGEN, ⌜*to Lucius*⌝ My good master,
I will yet do you service.

LUCIUS Happy be you!

CYMBELINE
The forlorn soldier that so nobly fought,
He would have well becomed this place and graced 495
The thankings of a king.

POSTHUMUS I am, sir,
The soldier that did company these three

499. **beseeming:** appearance, look; **fitment:** preparation

502. **finish:** die

504. **sinks:** forces down

506. **so often owe:** i.e., **owe** many times over

513. **doomed:** judged

514. **freeness of:** generosity from

516. **holp:** helped

517. **As:** i.e., **as** if

518. **Joyed:** delighted

519. **Your servant:** a polite expression of submission

521. **backed:** mounted

522. **spritely:** ghostly, spectral (with possible wordplay on "sprightly, lively"); **shows:** apparitions (though with a suggestion of the more common meaning "displays, spectacles")

524. **label:** piece of paper or parchment; **containing:** contents

525. **from sense in hardness:** i.e., hard to understand

526. **collection of:** i.e., inference or conclusion from

527. **construction:** explanation, interpretation

531–38. **Whenas . . . plenty:** See notes to 5.4.141, 145.

In poor beseeming; 'twas a fitment for
The purpose I then followed. That I was he, 500
Speak, Iachimo. I had you down and might
Have made you finish.

IACHIMO, ⌜*kneeling*⌝ I am down again,
But now my heavy conscience sinks my knee,
As then your force did. Take that life, beseech you, 505
Which I so often owe; but your ring first,
And here the bracelet of the truest princess
That ever swore her faith.

⌜*He holds out the ring and bracelet.*⌝

POSTHUMUS Kneel not to me.
The power that I have on you is to spare you; 510
The malice towards you to forgive you. Live
And deal with others better.

CYMBELINE Nobly doomed.
We'll learn our freeness of a son-in-law:
Pardon's the word to all. ⌜*Iachimo rises.*⌝ 515

ARVIRAGUS, ⌜*to Posthumus*⌝ You holp us, sir,
As you did mean indeed to be our brother.
Joyed are we that you are.

POSTHUMUS
Your servant, princes.—Good my lord of Rome,
Call forth your soothsayer. As I slept, methought 520
Great Jupiter upon his eagle backed
Appeared to me, with other spritely shows
Of mine own kindred. When I waked, I found
This label on my bosom, whose containing
Is so from sense in hardness that I can 525
Make no collection of it. Let him show
His skill in the construction.

LUCIUS Philarmonus!

SOOTHSAYER, ⌜*coming forward*⌝
Here, my good lord.

LUCIUS Read, and declare the meaning. 530

⌜SOOTHSAYER⌝ *reads.* *Whenas a lion's whelp shall, to*

541. **Leo-natus:** lion-born (See note to 1.1.38.)

544. **mollis aer:** soft or **tender air** (Latin), anciently thought to be the origin of **mulier,** "woman"

547. **Answering:** acting in conformity with; **letter of the oracle:** i.e., precise terms of the message (from Jupiter)

549–50. **clipped about / With:** surrounded or encompassed by (*To clip* is also "to embrace.")

553. **Personates:** represents

553–54. **point . . . forth:** indicate

556. **issue:** offspring

"The azured harebell." (4.2.284)
From John Gerard, *The herball. . .* (1597).

himself unknown, without seeking find, and be embraced by a piece of tender air; and when from a stately cedar shall be lopped branches which, being dead many years, shall after revive, be jointed to the old stock, and freshly grow; then shall Posthumus end his miseries, Britain be fortunate and flourish in peace and plenty. 535

Thou, Leonatus, art the lion's whelp.
The fit and apt construction of thy name, 540
Being Leo-natus, doth import so much.
⌜*To Cymbeline.*⌝ The piece of tender air thy virtuous daughter,
Which we call "*mollis aer,*" and "*mollis aer*"
We term it "*mulier,*" which "*mulier*" I divine 545
Is this most constant wife; who, even now,
Answering the letter of the oracle,
⌜*To Posthumus*⌝ Unknown to you, unsought, were clipped about
With this most tender air. 550

CYMBELINE This hath some seeming.

SOOTHSAYER

The lofty cedar, royal Cymbeline,
Personates thee; and thy lopped branches point
Thy two sons forth, who, by Belarius stol'n,
For many years thought dead, are now revived, 555
To the majestic cedar joined, whose issue
Promises Britain peace and plenty.

CYMBELINE Well,

My peace we will begin. And, Caius Lucius,
Although the victor, we submit to Caesar 560
And to the Roman Empire, promising
To pay our wonted tribute, from the which
We were dissuaded by our wicked queen,
Whom heavens in justice both on her and hers
Have laid most heavy hand. 565

567. **vision:** See 4.2.424–28, where the Soothsayer explains the **vision** as a prophecy of Roman victory in the battle.

568. **stroke:** i.e., beginning

570. **full:** i.e., fully, completely

576. **Which:** i.e., who

577. **Laud we:** let us praise

578. **crooked smokes:** i.e., curling smoke (from sacrificial fires)

580. **Set we:** i.e., let us go

582. **Lud's Town:** See note to 3.1.35.

585. **Set on:** go forward

Jupiter, the "Thunder-master." (5.4.32)
From Vincenzo Cartari, *Le vere e noue imagini . . .* (1615).

SOOTHSAYER

The fingers of the powers above do tune
The harmony of this peace. The vision
Which I made known to Lucius ere the stroke
Of ⌜this yet⌝ scarce-cold battle at this instant
Is full accomplished. For the Roman eagle, 570
From south to west on wing soaring aloft,
Lessened herself and in the beams o' th' sun
So vanished; which foreshowed our princely eagle,
Th' imperial Caesar, should again unite
His favor with the radiant Cymbeline, 575
Which shines here in the west.

CYMBELINE Laud we the gods,
And let our crooked smokes climb to their nostrils
From our blest altars. Publish we this peace
To all our subjects. Set we forward. Let 580
A Roman and a British ensign wave
Friendly together. So through Lud's Town march,
And in the temple of great Jupiter
Our peace we'll ratify, seal it with feasts.
Set on there. Never was a war did cease, 585
Ere bloody hands were washed, with such a peace.

They exit.

SOOTHSAYER
The fingers of the powers above do tune
The harmony of this peace. The vision,
Which I made known to Lucius ere the stroke
Of this yet scarce-cold battle, at this instant
Is full accomplished. For the Roman eagle, 540
From south to west on wing soaring aloft,
Lessened herself and in the beams o' th' sun
So vanished; which foreshowed our princely eagle,
Th' imperial Caesar, should again unite
His favor with the radiant Cymbeline, 545
Which shines here in the west.

CYMBELINE Laud we the gods,
And let our crooked smokes climb to their nostrils
From our blest altars. Publish we this peace
To all our subjects. Set we forward. Let 550
A Roman and a British ensign wave
Friendly together. So through Lud's Town march,
And in the temple of great Jupiter
Our peace we'll ratify, seal it with feasts.
Set on there. Never was a war did cease, 555
Ere bloody hands were washed, with such a peace.

They exit.

Longer Notes

1.1.195. **Fie, you must give way:** The Queen may say this line to Cymbeline—before or during his exit—as part of her pretense of support to Imogen, or she may say it to Imogen. For her to tell Imogen that she "must give way" may be to repeat the earlier advice she gave Posthumus and Imogen: " 'twere good / You leaned unto his sentence with what patience / Your wisdom may inform you" (1.1.88–90).

1.6.129. **illustrous:** The spelling **illustrous** is the customary editorial rendering of the Folio's "illustrious," which usually means "lustrous" or "bright." In the present context, the word must mean just the opposite—dull, not lustrous. In order to indicate such a meaning, editors adopt the spelling **illustrous.**

2.3.130. **contract:** Cloten charges that whatever **contract** Imogen has made with Posthumus, "it is no contract" (line 132)—i.e., it is not legal, not binding. Cloten seems to be claiming that Imogen and Posthumus have bound themselves as ordinary citizens were allowed to do—namely, with a private exchange of promises to marry, rather than being married in a public ceremony. An exchange of vows, expressed in the present tense and accompanied with a clasping of hands (a "handfasting"), constituted a legal betrothal even when done privately. Cloten seems to be arguing that such a handfasting, "though it be allowed in meaner parties" (line 133), would not be valid for the heir to a kingdom. His charge, though, and the assumptions that appear to lie behind it are negated at the end of the play, when Jupiter says "in / Our temple was [Posthumus] married" (5.4.107–8).

2.4.103. **Dian:** The phrase "chaste Dian bathing" almost unavoidably brings to mind the most famous story of the bathing Diana—that of Diana and Acteon, recounted in book 3 of Ovid's *Metamorphoses* (lines 160–304 in the 1567 translation by Arthur Golding). According to the myth, the goddess Diana, tired from hunting, removes her clothes and is bathing with her attendants in a special pool in the forest when Acteon, having himself just come from hunting, stumbles unintentionally on "Diana bare." Furious that a mortal has seen her nude, Diana turns him into a stag, who is torn apart by his own hunting dogs. Iachimo's allusion to this story places him ironically in the position of the voyeuristic Acteon, perhaps setting himself up for a terrible fate while emphasizing Imogen's connection to the goddess of chastity.

3.1.30. **baubles:** This reference to the failure of Julius Caesar's "shipping" during his assaults on Britain may have been suggested by Holinshed's "The Historie of England" (1587). Holinshed records that the fourth day of Caesar's first invasion of Britain, his fleet was dispersed by a tempest: "ships . . . were pitifullie beaten, tossed and shaken" (sig. C1). Following the initial battle of his second invasion, his great fleet (800 sail), at whose sight the Britons had fled into the mountains, was itself badly damaged by being driven onto the shore (C2v).

3.1.34. **giglet Fortune:** The queen's implied accusation against Fortune for the British defeat may derive from Holinshed's "Historie" (1587): "At length Cesar sending sundrie other cohorts to the succour of his people that were in fight, and shrewdlie handled as it appeered, the Britains in the end were put backe. Neuerthelesse, that repulse was but at the pleasure of fortune; for they quited themselues afterwards like men, defending their territories with such munition as they had, vntill such time as either by policie or inequalitie of power they were vanquished" (sig. C2v).

3.2.44. **as:** Posthumus's letter, especially lines 42–45, has been widely debated, with some editors suggesting that the letter is written in a deliberately ambiguous way which shows that Posthumus has not been able entirely to suppress his malice against Imogen. These editors point to the anger that may come through in the words "Justice and your father's wrath . . . could not be so cruel to me as you."

4.1.14–15. **imperceiverant:** The Folio's spelling, "imperseuerant," if modernized to "imperseverant," would have meant, in the period, "lacking in perseverance." Since that meaning seems ill-suited to the context of the speech, editors have modernized the word as "imperceiverant," or undiscerning.

4.2.42–43. **Th' imperious . . . fish:** These lines compare that which is bred in the sea with that which is bred in rivers, thus metaphorically comparing the court to rustic life (where she has unexpectedly found "kind creatures"). "Poor tributary rivers," Imogen says, are as likely to provide "sweet fish" as is the ocean, which also breeds "monsters." There is wordplay on *tributary,* which means "paying tribute" to an "imperious" or imperial power and also refers to one river that flows into another.

4.2.145–46. **for defect . . . fear:** Belarius's declaration in these lines that **fear** often arises from a **defect of judgment** has seemed to many editors to contradict what he has just said about Cloten: "he had not the apprehension of roaring terrors"—that is, Cloten suffered from a defect in understanding and, possibly as well, in judgment, but the defect made him fearless rather than fearful (in contradiction to the general case set out here). To repair this possible contradiction, editors have often resorted to emendation, changing **defect** to "th' effect" or, alternatively, changing **cause** to, for example, "cease" or "cure." Others have suggested that the possible contradiction arises because Belarius's remark is interrupted by the entrance of Guiderius, and so texts should read "fear—" to indicate the interruption. Still others have interpreted the lines to mean that a defect in judgment in one person gives rise to fear in others who care about him.

4.2.358. **Upon their faces:** Because Cloten, of course, no longer has a head, this line has been the occasion of comment by editors. It has been variously suggested that **faces** may mean "the front of their bodies," or that **upon their faces** may be an instruction to turn the bodies over so that they no longer lie on their backs, although no reason for turning them over is given in the text. But it may not be necessary to read the line so literally as to make a problem of it.

4.2.406. **To them:** These words may have appeared in the manuscript copy as part of the stage direction and then been mistakenly printed in the Folio as part of this speech. The phrase **to them** often appears at the end of entrances when one group of characters enters after another already occupies the stage, thereby coming **to them.**

4.2.457. **Richard du Champ:** Some editors have suggested that this name is a private joke and that Shakespeare was referring to a fellow Stratfordian, Richard Field, who became a London stationer and printed Shakespeare's long poems of 1593 and 1594. (See "Shakespeare's Life," page xxxi.)

5.4.25–28. **'Tis not so dear . . . being yours:** Using the conventional metaphor that expresses the creation of a human being in terms of the coining of money, Posthumus says that just as men in business transactions do not weigh every **stamp** (i.e., coin) but instead, even when coins are **light** (i.e., below the legal weight), accept them because of the figure imprinted on them, so the gods should even more readily accept his life, even though it is **light** (i.e., of little worth), because he is the gods' creation.

5.4.30. **cold bonds:** Although the primary allusion here is to defunct legal bonds, there is also wordplay on *bonds,* both as the gyves that physically restrain him and as a figure of speech for human life itself, as in *Richard III* 4.4.79: "Cancel his bond of life" and *Macbeth* 3.2.55–56: "Cancel . . . that great bond / Which keeps me pale."

5.4.94 SD. **Jupiter descends:** Elizabethan and Jacobean theaters contained equipment, including a winch and pulley(s), that enabled characters to descend, usually seated in a special chair. Since Jupiter is here described as "sitting upon an eagle," it is likely that the chair would have been disguised so as to look like a gigantic bird. For a discussion of playhouse machinery for "descents," see John Astington, "Descent Machinery in the Playhouse," *Medieval and Renaissance Drama in England* 2 (1985): 119–33.

Textual Notes

The reading of the present text appears to the left of the square bracket. Unless otherwise noted, the reading to the left of the bracket is from **F**, the First Folio text (upon which this edition is based). The earliest sources of readings not in **F** are indicated as follows: **F2** is the Second Folio of 1632; **F3** is the Third Folio of 1663–64; **F4** is the Fourth Folio of 1685; **Ed.** is an earlier editor of Shakespeare, beginning with Rowe in 1709. No sources are given for emendations of punctuation or for corrections of obvious typographical errors, like turned letters that produce no known word. **SD** means stage direction; **SP** means speech prefix; ***uncorr.*** means the first or uncorrected state of the First Folio; ***corr.*** means the second or corrected state of the First Folio; **~** stands in place of a word already quoted before the square bracket; **‸** indicates the omission of a punctuation mark.

1.1

2. courtiers'] ~‸ F
6. wife's] F (wiues)
59. election] F (electiõ)
66–67. them‸ . . . old, . . . clothes‸ . . . other,] ~, . . . ~‸ . . . ~, . . . ~‸ F
80. SD *Enter*] Ed.; *Scena Secunda.* | *Enter* F
81. SP QUEEN] *Qn.* F
91. Please] F ('Please)
136. cere] F (seare)
183. SD *1 line earlier in* F
195. SD *1 line earlier in* F

1.2 0. Scene 2] Ed.; *Scena Tertia* F
37. the∧] ~. F

1.3 0. Scene 3] Ed.; *Scena Quarta* F
12. this] Ed.; his F

1.4 0. Scene 4] Ed.; *Scena Quinta* F
29 *and throughout.* Briton] F (Britaine)
50. not] Ed.; *omit* F
77. Britain] F (Britanie)
78. others∧] ~. F
79. but] Ed.; *omit* F
86. mistress] Mistirs F
89–90. purchase] Ed.; purchases F
110. five] F *corr.* (fiue); fine F *uncorr.*
124. that] rhat F
134. safe.] F *corr.;* ~, F *uncorr.*
134. thousand] F3; thousands F
141. My] F *corr.;* my F *uncorr.*
144. preserve] preseure F
162. provided∧] ~. F

1.5 0. Scene 5] Ed.; *Scena Sexta* F
2, 40, 68. has] F (ha's)
23. human] F (humane)
85. SD *1 line earlier in* F

1.6 0. Scene 6] Ed.; *Scena Septima* F
5. Vexations] F *corr.;* Vexation s F *uncorr.*
7. desire] F2; desires F
31. takes] Ed.; take F
36. mad?] F *corr.;* ~. F *uncorr.*
40. beach,] F *corr.* (Beach,); ~∧ F *uncorr.*
41. spectacles] Spectales F
42. foul?] F *corr.* (foule?); ~. F *uncorr.*
49. opposed] F *corr.* (oppos'd); opos'd F *uncorr.*
61. abode] F *corr.;* aboed F *uncorr.*
65. Continues] F *corr.;* Continwes F *uncorr.*

94. talents] F *corr.* (Talents); Tallents F *uncorr.*
109. your—] F *corr.;* ~. F *uncorr.*
115. do—] ~. F
117. born—] ~. F
119. SP IACHIMO] *Iach'* F
124. Fixing] F2; Fiering F
124. damned] F *corr.* (damn'd); dampn'd F *uncorr.*
129. illustrous] Ed.; illustrious F
132. Encounter] F *corr.;* Eneounter F *uncorr.*
133. fear,] F *corr.* (feare,); ~‸ F *uncorr.*
135. SP IACHIMO] F *corr.* (*Iach.*); *Iacb.* F *uncorr.*
135. himself.] ~, F
188. me] F *corr.;* ma F *uncorr.*
194. men's] F2; men F
196. descended] F2; defended F

2.1 12. curtail] F (curtall)
21. bellyful] F (belly full)
27. your] F3; you F
34. tonight] F2; night F
56. And] Aud F
60. expulsion] F *corr.;* expusion F *uncorr.*
61. husband,] ~. F
62. make!] ~‸ F
63. honor,] ~. F
65. *He exits.*] Ed.; *Exeunt* F

2.2 3. hour] F *corr.* (houre); houe F *uncorr.*
11. me, gods] F *corr.* (Gods); m e, Gods F *uncorr.*
23. lids‸] ~. F
26. design:] F *corr.* (designe.); ~. F *uncorr.*
27. chamber.] ~, F
29. adornment] F *corr.* (adornement); adronement F *uncorr.*

42. A mole] F *corr.;* Amole F *uncorr.*
47. riveted] F *corr.* (riueted); riuete F *uncorr.*
50. Philomel] *Philomel e* F *uncorr.; Philomele* F *corr.*
53. bare] F (beare)

2.3

7. SP CLOTEN] F4; *omit* F
25. *eyes*.] ~∧ F
29. SP CLOTEN] Ed.; *omit* F
29. penetrate] pen trate F
31. vice] Ed.; voyce F
33. amend] amed F
50. solicits] solicity F
97. SD *1 line later in* F
99. fairest sister.] ~, ~∧
112. kindness] kinduesse F
116. Fools] Fooies F
129. father.] ~, F
139. it∧] ~; F
144. besides,] ~: F
146. envy,] ~. F
155. SD *Pisanio.*] ~, F
156. garment] F2; Garments F
165. am∧] ~. F
178. you] F3; your F

2.4

8. hopes] F2; hope F
27. wingèd] Ed.; wing-led F
43. tenor] F (tenure)
45. SP PHILARIO] Ed.; *Post.* F
59. not] F2; note F
71. you] F2; yon F
73. honor∧] ~; F
127. that.] ~∧ F
171. the] Ed.; her F
191. beside] F (besides)

2.5
17. German] F (Iarmen)
17. one] F (on)
28. have a] Ed.; *omit* F
29. all.] ~‸ F
31. still‸] ~; F

3.1
0. SD *Caius‸ Lucius*] ~, ~ F
5, 33. Cassibelan] F (Cassibulan)
22. palèd] F (pal'd)
23. rocks] Ed.; Oakes F
56. be. We do‸] ~, ~ ~. F
80. precedent] F (President)

3.2
8. wifelike,] ~; F
14. to do good] F *corr.;* to go do od F *uncorr.*
17. So much] F *corr.;* Somuch F *uncorr.*
18. *letter‸*] ~. F
21. ink] F *corr.* (Inke); Incke F *uncorr.*
23. here] F *corr.;* her F *uncorr.*
27. thy lord‸] ~~?
50. *Leonatus‸ Posthumus*] F *corr.;* ~-~ F *uncorr.*
63. Wales‸ was] F *corr.;* ~: ~ F *uncorr.*
65. and] F *corr.;* nd F *uncorr.*
70. score] Ed.; store F
73. Madam, 's] F (Madam's)
75. heard] F *corr.;* həard F *uncorr.*
82. SP PISANIO] *Pisa.* F *corr.; Pịsa.* F *uncorr.*
83. me, man.] ~ (~) F
83. nor] F2; not F
83. here,] ~; F

3.3
2. Stoop] Ed.; Sleepe F
12. sport. . . . hill;] ~, . . . ~‸ F
18. service,] ~; F

25. robe] Ed.; Babe F
30. know] Ed.; knowes F
34. known,] ~. F
37. for] Ed.; or F
47. choir] F (Quire)
85. SP BELARIUS] Ed.; *not in* F
90. wherein they] Ed.; whereon the F
93. Polydor] F (*Paladour*)
114. Morgan] F (*Mergan*)

3.4

1. from] F (frõ)
1. the] F (y^{e})
61. men, being heard∧] ~∧ ~ ~, F
86. afore 't] Ed.; a-foot F
97. make] Ed.; makes F
111. out] Ed.; *omit* F
128. struck] F (strooke)
170. haply] F (happily)
180. obedience,] ~. F
194–95. one. . . . this,] ~, . . . ~. F

3.5

0. SD *Lords*] Ed.; *and Lords* F
22. SD *and Lords*] Ed.; *& c* F
39. looks] Ed.; looke F
48. strokes] F2; stroke F
49. SD *Attendant*] Ed.; *a Messenger* F
52. SP ATTENDANT] Ed.; *Mes.* F
54. loud'st] Ed.; lowd of F
68. SD *1 line earlier in* F
84. SD *Queen*] F (*Qu.*)
126. travail] F (trauell)
166. insultment] insulment F

3.6

27. SD *She . . . cave.*] Ed. *Exit.* | *Scena Septima.* F
81. Ay] F (I)

3.7

0. Scene 7] Ed.; *Scena Octaua.* F
9. commends] F (commands)

	16.	supplyant] F (suppliant)
4.1	14–15.	imperceiverant] F (imperseuerant)
	20.	haply] F (happily)
4.2	31–32.	‸Cowards . . . | ‸Nature] "~ . . . "~ F
	49.	answer] auswer F
	59.	shalt] F (shal't)
	59.	SD *1 line earlier in* F *as "Exit."*
	63.	He] Ed.; *Arui.* He F
	75.	patience] Ed.; patient F
	158.	thank] Ed.; thanks F
	171.	humor] Ed.; Honor F
	237.	ingenious] Ed.; ingenuous F
	262.	crare] Ed.; care F
	263.	Might] Ed.; Might'st F
	263.	eas'liest] easilest F
	286.	ruddock] F (Raddocke)
	304.	Euriphile] *Enriphile* F
	363.	is] Ed.; are F
	364.	SP IMOGEN] *omit* F
	393.	Struck] F (Strooke)
4.3	0.	SD *Pisanio*] Ed.; *and Pisanio* F
	48.	betid] Ed.; betide F
4.4	3.	find we] F2; we finde F
	11.	us.] v.. F
	22.	the] Ed.; their F
	24.	And] Aud F
	33.	hard] F (heard)
5.1	1.	wished] Ed.; am wisht F
	10.	struck] F (strooke)
5.3	4.	Ay] Ed; I did F
	11.	struck] F (strooke)
	14.	dead men‸ hurt behind‸] ~ ~, ~ ~, F
	27.	harts] F (hearts)
	46.	stooped] Ed.; stopt F

47. they] Ed.; the F
78. struck] F (strooke)

5.4

0. SD *two Jailers*] Ed.; *Gaoler* F
17. constrained.] ~, F
52. deserved] d seru'd F
69. geck] F (geeke)
79, 80. thou] F (y^u)
83. look] F2; looke, looke F
114. lest] F (least)
120. Preens] F (Prunes)
131. greatness' favor∧] ~, ~; F
173. sir] Sis F
201. SD 9 *lines later in* F *as "Exeunt."*

5.5

7. Our] Onr F
73. SP LADIES] F (*La.*)
76. heard] Ed.; heare F
81. tribute.] ~, F
82. razed] F (rac'd)
161. On. Speak] Ed.; One speake F
186. struck] F (strooke)
212. cracked] F (crak'd)
233. operate] operare F
241. got it] F2; got F
249. being,] ~∧ F
281. Breathe] F (Breath)
291. Pisanio] *Pasanio* F
310. from] fro F
329. truth] F (troth)
377. on 's] F (one's)
408. mere] Ed.; neere F
409. treason.] ~∧ F
425. like] liks F
435. Arviragus,] ~. F
470. brothers] Ed.; Brother F

472–73. whither? These,] Ed.; whether these? F
486. me‸] ~: F
494. so] F2; no F
541. Leo-natus] F (*Leonatus*)
569. this yet] F3; yet this F

Historical Background

Shakespeare's principal historical source for *Cymbeline* was "The Historie of England" in volume 1 of Raphael Holinshed's *Chronicles of England, Scotland, and Ireland*... (1587).[1] Holinshed's account of Cymbeline's reign contains none of the stuff of successful drama; the making of the play consisted in Shakespeare's setting aside his chosen historical source and developing his own fiction. He took from Holinshed little more than hints for his fiction and an array of proper names for the play's characters. Holinshed, drawing on English chroniclers, gave Shakespeare the following biographical sketch of King Cymbeline:

> Kymbeline or Cimbeline the sonne of Theomantius [also called Tenantius] was of the Britains made king after the deceasse of his father, in the yeare of the world 3944, after the building of Rome 728, and before the birth of our Sauiour 33. This man (as some write) was brought up at Rome, and there made knight by Augustus Cesar, under whome he served in the warres, and was in such fauour with him, that he was at libertie to pay his tribute or not. Little other mention is made of his dooings, except that during his reigne, the Sauiour of the world our Lord Jesus Christ the onlie sonne of God was borne of a virgine, about the 23 yeare of the reigne of this Kymbeline, . . . [who] reigned 35 years and then died, & was buried at London, leauing behind him two sonnes, Guiderius and Aruiragus. (sig. C4v)

From this account, Shakespeare took almost nothing but Cymbeline's name and a detail for the king to remember from his past, as, addressing a Roman, he says: "Thy Caesar knighted me; my youth I spent / Much under him" (3.1.75–76).

When, however, Holinshed compares this brief biography from the British chroniclers to accounts of the same era in histories written by ancient Romans, he begins to bring in a hint of the most important political conflict in the play: the refusal of the British king to pay tribute to Augustus Caesar and the resulting invasion of Britain by the Romans. Holinshed notes that according to Cornelius Tacitus and Dion Cassius, Tenantius's and Cymbeline's refusals to pay tribute led Augustus Caesar to plan invasions of Britain on three occasions, though on each occasion he was deterred—on the first, by the need to quell a rebellion by the Pannonians and the Dalmatians; on the second, by the Britons' sending "certeine ambassadours to treat with him of peace" as well as by the necessity to "settle the state of things among the Galles" (C4v); and, on the third, by the need to put down yet another rebellion, this time among the "Salassians (a people inhabiting about Italie and Switserland), the Cantabrians and Assurians" (C5). Holinshed is unconvinced that the Roman story about Cymbeline's refusal to pay tribute is true. He notes that "our histories doo affirme, that as well this Kymbeline, as also his father Theomantius lived in quiet with the Romans and continuallie to them paied the tributes which the Britains had covenanted with Julius Cesar to pay"; he also writes that "whether this controversie which appeareth to fall forth betwixt the Britons and Augustus, was occasioned by Kymbeline, or some other prince of the Britains, I have not to avouch: for that by our writers it is reported that Kymbeline being brought up in Rome,

& knighted in the court of Augustus, ever shewed himselfe a friend of the Romans, & chieflie was loth to breake with them, because the youth of the Britaine nation should not be deprived of the benefit to be trained and brought up among the Romans" (C5).

Despite Holinshed's doubts, Shakespeare may well have picked up the idea of a Roman invasion of Cymbeline's Britain from the reported accounts of the Roman historians, just as he seems clearly to have derived from Holinshed the idea of using the Pannonians and Dalmatians as companion (or rival) rebels to the Britons. Shakespeare's characters twice mention these tribes (3.1.79, 3.7.3), though Roman attention to Pannonians and Dalmatians in the play does not prevent an invasion of Britain; it merely requires that the invading army be augmented by Roman gentry—a device that provides a way of bringing Iachimo (and Posthumus) back to Britain (3.7.7, 5.1.17–19).

Yet another way of explaining Shakespeare's version of Cymbeline's war with Rome is to note that Holinshed records as a matter of fact that both Guiderius and Arviragus in turn refused Rome its tribute and, as a consequence, experienced Roman incursions (C5v–6, C6v–D1). It is possible that Shakespeare simply reshaped Cymbeline's reign by borrowing details from the reigns of Cymbeline's sons. (When Edmund Spenser gives a brief account of these early kings of Britain in book 2 of *The Faerie Queene,* he conflates Cymbeline with Guiderius and has Cymbeline refuse to pay Roman tribute and, as a consequence, die at the hands of the Roman army [2.10.50–51].) Whatever the explanation, the fact remains that the central political action of *Cymbeline*—Cymbeline's refusal to pay tribute, the subsequent war with Rome, the British victory, and the voluntary payment of tribute—is not to be found in Holinshed.

Shakespeare did, however, take many details of the play from Holinshed's *Chronicles.* For example, he reached into Holinshed's "The Historie of Scotland" (N6), a source for *Macbeth,* for the crucial incident in the play's Roman/British war. In an account of a battle between Scots and invading Danes during the reign of King Kenneth, son of Malcolm (976–1000 C.E.), Shakespeare found the story of a farmer and his two sons defeating an army, which he appropriated for his representation of the decisive skirmish in which Belarius, Guiderius, and Arviragus (with help from Posthumus) rally the Britons and defeat the Romans (5.2.10 SD–20, 5.3.17–56). And many scholars have heard—in the Jailer's wish that "we were all of one mind, and one mind good" (5.4.207–8) and in the repeated references to peace and pardon at the play's conclusion—references to the one event of Cymbeline's reign considered significant by Holinshed: namely, that Jesus "was borne of a virgine, about the 23 yeare of the reigne of this Kymbeline." There was a tradition, elaborated by Holinshed, that the world was at peace at the coming of Christ: "it pleased the almightie God so to dispose the minds of men at that present, not onlie the Britains, but in manner all other nations were contented to be obedient to the Romaine empire" (C5).

In "The Historie of England," Shakespeare also found biographical information about Cymbeline's royal predecessors. He read there that Britain's first king, Mulmucius (or Mulmutius), whose reign began in "the yeere of the world 3529," "made manie good lawes" (B2). These details appear in *Cymbeline* in the lines "Mulmutius made our laws, / Who was the first of Britain which did put / His brows within a golden crown and called / Himself a king" (3.1.61–65). Shakespeare also found Cymbeline's immediate ancestry. In Holinshed, King Lud figures as Cymbeline's grandfather, his reign beginning more than 350 years after that of Mulmutius; Lud's many building projects in the city of Troinouant, writes Holinshed, led to its renaming as "Luds towne: and after by corruption of speech it was named London" (B6). Lud appears in *Cymbeline* only in the frequent references to "Lud's Town."

Next among Cymbeline's forebears comes Cassibellan; according to most of Holinshed's sources, he was Lud's brother, who took the throne upon Lud's death in 58 B.C.E. because Lud's sons, Androgeus and Theomantius or Tenantius, were not yet of an age to govern. The Roman invasion of Britain led by the great general and politician Julius Caesar began in Cassibellan's reign (B6); Holinshed dates the subjection of the Britons to the Romans from 53 B.C.E. and records that Cassibellan agreed to pay Rome annual tribute of "three thousand pounds" (C4). The sum and Cassibellan's granting it to Rome are described in 3.1.5–9.

In Holinshed's account, the rule of Cymbeline's father, Theomantius or Tenantius, began in 3921, or 45 B.C.E. There is nothing in Holinshed to indicate hostilities during Tenantius's reign that would provide a military occasion for the death of Posthumus's brothers, though Shakespeare has the ghost of one of them say that they fell maintaining "Tenantius' right" (5.4.75). According to Holinshed, "Theomantius ruled the land in good quiet, and paid the tribute to the Romans which Cassibellane had granted, and finallie departed this life after he had reigned 22 yeares, and was buried at London" (C4v). In accepting Lud, Cassibelan, and Tenantius as Cymbeline's immediate kingly predecessors—the lineage given by Holinshed—Shakespeare ignores the Roman sources related by Holinshed that claim that Britain was not at this time unified under the rule of a single king (C4). (Holinshed cites Julius Caesar as reporting that the Troinouants, Cenimagni,

Segontiaci, Ancalites, Bibroci, and Cassi all submitted themselves to him while Cassibellan was still holding out against the Romans [C3].) Shakespeare also chooses to follow those sources that describe Julius Caesar as having conquered Britain rather than those that represent the Britons as driving Caesar's Roman army back to Gallia (C2, 3v)—though the Queen's contemptuous reference to Julius Caesar's having made no more than "a kind of conquest" (3.1.25) may echo the historians who deny him any victory over Britain.

While Shakespeare depends on Holinshed for Cymbeline's lineage, the dramatist creates an extended family for Cymbeline through purely imaginative acts that play havoc with history. Shakespeare gives Cymbeline a daughter of whom there is no historical record and names her Imogen, the name of the queen of Brute, the legendary founder of Britain (Holinshed, "The Historie of England," A4v). Shakespeare gives Imogen a husband and names him Posthumus, the name of the son of the Trojan hero Aeneas (legendary founder of Rome) born to his widow Lavinia after Aeneas's death; this Posthumus, in Roman legend, was the grandfather of Brute (A4). Shakespeare calls Posthumus's father Sicilius, the name of a British king said to have ruled about three hundred years before Cymbeline (B4). Shakespeare gives Cymbeline a second wife, the nameless Queen, who is also the dramatist's own invention, and then gives her a son named Cloten—the name of Mulmutius's father, according to Holinshed (B2). Finally, Shakespeare creates for Cymbeline's sons, Guiderius and Arviragus, a remarkable story of kidnap, life in a cave, murder, heroic acts of warfare, and ultimately triumphant return to their proper positions as heirs to the throne. All in all, Shakespeare's *Cymbeline* is history only in the loosest of senses, but the play's success as drama is markedly improved by Shakespeare's disregard for anything resembling modern historical accuracy.

---

1. Shakespeare also seems to have consulted other accounts of early British history, among them parts added to *The Mirror of Magistrates* by Thomas Blenerhasset in 1578 and by John Higgins in 1587 that feature Cymbeline's son Guiderius (or Guidericus, as Blenerhasset calls him).

Cymbeline: A Modern Perspective

Cynthia Marshall

Cymbeline shows an unusual, even perverse, interest in sleeping characters. "Playing Imogen," the actress Harriet Walter remarks, "one spends quite a lot of time 'asleep.' "[1] The villain Iachimo steals from a trunk in the bedroom of the sleeping Imogen and breathlessly inventories the attractions of the furniture and of the princess's exposed body. Later in the play, Imogen struggles to consciousness, still groggy from a narcotic potion, to discover a headless corpse beside her. Imogen's husband Posthumus, the play's putative hero, experiences a climactic dream vision while he lies sleeping in prison. Throughout his career Shakespeare was apparently interested by the resemblance between deep sleep and death (one thinks of Juliet, and of Henry Bolingbroke on his deathbed in *2 Henry IV*) and by the seam separating the unconscious mind of dreams from the control of waking consciousness (instanced by the sleepwalking Lady Macbeth, and, in a different key, by Bottom awakening from his forest adventures in *A Midsummer Night's Dream*). But the dramatic possibilities of an actor miming sleep are distinctly limited, and *Cymbeline*'s repeated slowing to a still focus on an unconscious character seems especially odd given the busy complexity of the play's multiple plots. Dramaturgically and thematically, the play engages questions about the relative merits of activity and passivity: Does history happen to us, or do we happen to it? Do individuals direct their own actions, or are they pawns within an encompassing structure? Are we ever entirely awake to life's meanings and complexities?

These questions do not emerge from the characters' philosophical musings—*Cymbeline*'s characters are refreshingly lacking in profundity—but from the play's often sensational efforts to entertain its audiences. Like Shakespeare's other late plays, *Cymbeline,* dating from 1609 or 1610, was written in a fashionable coterie style apparently designed to appeal to audiences at the Blackfriars, the indoor playhouse that Shakespeare's acting company acquired around 1608. These more sophisticated viewers might relish the way the play calls attention to its own theatricality: for example, the courtiers speak with mannered opacity, and Cloten's severed head advertises its status as a stage prop. Posthumus's dream vision, with its chanting spirits and the spectacular descent of Jupiter, suggests the influence of the masque (an elaborate form of court entertainment), while at the same time displaying the theater's technical apparatus for presenting a *deus ex machina.* The play's attention to historical patterning resembles the experimental tendencies of *The Winter's Tale* and *Henry VIII,* late Shakespearean plays likewise skeptical of the reliability of narrative storytelling. Yet the complexity of *Cymbeline*'s plot lines, concluding in a "twenty-four-fold dénouement,"[2] defies the faith in temporal logic evidenced in the other romances: whereas Time the Chorus appears in *The Winter's Tale* to move the play toward a happy ending, outcomes in *Cymbeline* seem more the effect of chance or surprising choices, and judgments are clouded by deception and self-deception.

Defying historical chronology in the manner of dream or myth, the play features three distinct settings: the historical King Cymbeline's first-century B.C.E. Britain, an apparently fifteenth-century Italy, and the remote mountains of Welsh legend. It also incorporates elements of tragedy, comedy, and romance. In creating a play that straddles temporal, spatial, and generic boundaries, Shakespeare drew on a variety of sources. The framing story of war between Britain and Rome originates in Raphael Holinshed's *Chronicles of England, Scotland, and Ireland,* as does the incident in which a man and his two sons defeat an army. The wager plot can be traced to Boccaccio's *Decameron,* a fourteenth-century Italian collection of prose tales (available to Shakespeare in French translation), and to an English version of the same story known as *Frederyke of Jennen.* The notes on a 1611 performance (probably at the Globe theater) recorded by Simon Forman, the early modern physician and astrologer, testify to a confusing array of actions:

> Remember also the story of Cymbeline king of England in Lucius' time. How Lucius came from Octavius Caesar for tribute and being denied after sent Lucius with a great army of soldiers who landed at Milford Haven, and . . . 3 outlaws of the which 2 of them were the sons of Cymbeline stolen from him when they were but 2 years old. . . . And how one of them slew Cloten. . . . and how the Italian that came from her love conveyed himself into a chest. . . . And in the deepest of the night, she being asleep, he opened the chest & came forth of it. And viewed her in her bed and the marks of her body. . . . (spelling modernized)

Forman is an erratic reporter at best, but his difficulty in seizing on a central action to follow has been shared by other readers and viewers.

In an effort to make sense of all this confusion, critics have often inferred an overarching design in the play. Some detect a Christian framework, citing as evidence the coincidence of Cymbeline's reign with Christ's birth and the Jailer's wish for moral unity (5.4.207–8). Others find a political agenda, such as tribute to King James, who fancied himself a force for unity among nations and for renewal at home. Certainly the play's welter of action can make a commentator wish for a grand design, but the case for a consistent pattern of religious or historical allegory seems weak. Though there may be fleeting hints of larger patterns, Shakespeare has arranged the "plot lines [so] that large expectation patterns about the play's action are never allowed to develop"[3]; consequently, no scheme can be said to dominate. For instance, the pattern of *translatio imperii*—the westward expansion of empire—bears a force almost of destiny in the play.[4] Yet the delicacy with which Caius Lucius's ambiguous relation to Britain is presented—he reluctantly declares Augustus Caesar's enmity while being cordially entertained at court, then departs to take the opponent's part—suggests the complexity of the individual's role within the unfolding history of empire, society, or family.

Sometimes called Shakespeare's last Roman play, *Cymbeline* extends the attention shown in *Antony and Cleopatra* to the difficulties of maintaining an empire, with the focus here on the British colony and events seen from that northern perspective. The Queen and Cloten have urged King Cymbeline to renegotiate an earlier agreement to pay tribute, a plot line lacking in historical validity but valuable in demonstrating British subjects' complicated attitude of defiance and deference toward Rome. *Cymbeline* continues the self-conscious interest of the other Roman plays—*Julius Caesar, Coriolanus, Antony and Cleopatra*—in exploring how history is written and dramatized. Postmodern historiographers call attention to the shaping role of the historian in formulating an account of the past,[5] and Shakespeare seems similarly aware that any story is colored by its framework, to the extent that an individual's role may be determined by external forces. So Posthumus submits to a prophetic text he scarcely understands. He describes the tablet left behind by the visiting ghosts as "senseless speaking, or a speaking such / As sense cannot untie," even as he accepts its relevance and validity: "Be what it is, / The action of my life is like it" (5.4.150–52). He seems willing to take his place in a larger action, although its meaning remains inscrutable to him—and to us.

The play's emphasis on plot may account for the flat quality of some of the characters—most notably the Queen, who is foiled in her worst schemes and thus lacks the intensity of passionate malignity. Cymbeline himself is surprisingly passive, a kind of absent center around which the action moves, manipulated by his wife and defrauded by Belarius. However, the insistent motif of the outer and inner person (see, e.g., 1.1.25–27, 1.4.8–10, 1.6.18–20, 5.1.33) provides a clue that in this play, Shakespeare is continuing his exploration of subjectivity. The final scene reunites a hero and heroine who are each doubly disguised: Posthumus, fighting officially for the Roman army but wearing the garb of the British cause he has adopted apologetically, and Imogen, dressed as a boy who has been employed as a page by the Roman Lucius. Fighting for opposite armies and displaced from their own identities, the couple nevertheless manage eventually to recognize each other.

Although the disguise motif assumes the existence of inner truth, the principal characters in *Cymbeline* are not static. Instead, they show a striking capacity for change. One of the most stunning moments in the play is Posthumus's decision to forgive his wife (whom he mistakenly thinks has been unfaithful) "For wrying but a little" (5.1.5). Posthumus does not receive contradictory evidence and no one encourages him to reconsider: he simply changes his mind. The revisionary action is repeated on a grand scale when Cymbeline in the final moments of the play offers to pay tribute to his defeated foe and the battle becomes suddenly inconsequential. The strict logic of cause and effect, winners and losers, is replaced by an endorsement of the metamorphic properties of human experience.

Oddly, the capacity for change is not accompanied by self-understanding. The play's mood is "not introspective,"[6] and even the best-developed characters seem peculiarly unaware of their actions, almost as though they are sleepwalking or drugged. Soliloquies, of which there are many, tend to report feelings and responses rather than to explore them. In *Cymbeline* Shakespeare relies on symbolic and structural means of unfolding character. For instance, Posthumus, whose name announces him traumatically deprived of family (see 1.1.41–47), is psychologically and morally reborn through the dream vision of Act 5, which supplies him the missing nexus of familial concern and support. Posthumus's maliciousness is partially displayed (and displaced) through symbolic doubling: during the play's middle acts, Cloten serves as his psychic stand-in. Different as they apparently are, the play insists on an analogy between them. Cloten, who wishes to take Posthumus's place in Imogen's favor and in her bed, devises a plan to rape her while wearing Posthumus's clothing. Securing the garments from the servant Pisanio, Cloten sets off for Milford Haven, where he is vanquished by Guiderius. That Imogen, awakening next to a headless corpse dressed in her husband's clothing, mistakes Cloten's body for that of Posthumus confirms the physical and symbolic links between the two men. Posthumus's disrespectful gambling on his wife's chastity and his murderous response to Iachimo's false report of enjoying Imogen's body are paralleled by Cloten's aggressive wish: "With that suit upon my back will I ravish her" (3.5.162–63). Through a dreamlike logic, Cloten and Posthumus sporadically merge, and Posthumus's slide from devoted husband to suspicious trickster to murderous misogynist and finally back to repentant noble combatant is made dramatically coherent, even in the absence of dialogue that might provide conscious motivation.

The use of dream logic might alert us to another cause of the characters' apparent lack of self-awareness: this play is remarkably attentive to the role of fantasy in shaping human actions. Contemporary psychoanalytic theory points out how fantasy is particular to the individual yet shaped by ideological forces within a culture.[7] Although Posthumus should know better than to doubt his wife's fidelity, his insecurity, fostered by Iachimo's lubricity, prepares the ground for a vivid, misogynistic suspicion:

> This yellow Iachimo in an hour, was 't not?
> Or less? At first? Perchance he spoke not, but,
> Like a full-acorned boar, a German one,
> Cried "O!" and mounted.
>
> (2.5.15–18)

Fantasy can be a generative force, providing the screen on which a person projects himself; but, as with Posthumus's fantasy, it also carries the danger of reducing other people to objects.

Fantasies likewise drive the villainous Iachimo. In contrast to the boarlike creature of Posthumus's imagination, Iachimo in the bedchamber displays literary sensibility (pointing out the similarity between himself and Tarquin [2.2.15–17]) and an aesthetic appreciation of Imogen's qualities. His breathless sensual admiration necessitates, at line 26, his recalling himself to his dastardly plot:

> Cytherea,
> How bravely thou becom'st thy bed, fresh lily,
> And whiter than the sheets.—That I might touch!
> But kiss, one kiss! Rubies unparagoned,
> How dearly they do 't. 'Tis her breathing that
> Perfumes the chamber thus. The flame o' th' taper
> Bows toward her and would underpeep her lids
> To see th' enclosèd lights, now canopied
> Under these windows, white and azure-laced
> With blue of heaven's own tinct. But my design:
> To note the chamber.
>
> (2.2.17–27)

Iachimo may lack the intellectual subtlety of his dramatic forerunner Iago, but Shakespeare provides ample clues to his unhappy emotional life. The ache and longing that mark his visual violation of Imogen ("Why should I write this down that's riveted, / Screwed to my memory?" [2.2.47–48]) are converted to bravado and bluster when he reports to Posthumus a "night of such sweet shortness" (2.4.54). Eventually a repentant Iachimo will explain how Imogen's virtue left him "quenched / Of hope, not longing" (5.5.231–32). Shakespeare has given us access to the mind of the voyeur, for whom looking provides erotic pleasure; in this sense, Iachimo is not lying when he speaks of the delight he took in Imogen's company.

Of course, as viewers in the theater we necessarily share Iachimo's violation of Imogen's privacy. By positioning Iachimo as an illicit viewer who enables our gaze, Shakespeare uses a technique associated with pornography. He sets the tone by specifying Imogen's Ovidian reading material and adds to the effect by having Iachimo later describe the room's titillating decorations ("Proud Cleopatra," "Chaste Dian bathing," "two winking Cupids" [2.4.87, 103, 112]). The bedroom scene functions as an erotic fantasy, to be both observed and experienced by theatergoers. Lest we miss the point that the episode is a symbolic rape of Imogen, Shakespeare in the following scene shows Cloten scheming to "penetrate her" (2.3.14).

Submission to a fantasy sequence can eclipse a sense of one's own identity—as when Cloten channels his hatred and desire into identification with Posthumus.[8] Cloten's fantasy of raping Imogen while wearing her husband's clothes indicates this pathological identification. Although often played as a buffoon, Cloten displays a frightening capacity for self-hatred: it seems that Cloten desires to *be* Posthumus as much as to *have* Imogen. Again, we are led to ponder the way in which theater, by offering fresh scripts for imaginative involvement, invites viewers to experience compelling fantasies.

To provoke heightened emotional effects, Shakespeare takes large risks in *Cymbeline,* using sensationalism and odd combinations of tone. The funeral obsequies in 4.2, for instance, create a moving impression of grief, with the tender lyric "Fear no more the heat o' th' sun" (331) offset by the realistic details of Guiderius's inability to sing and his impatience with his brother's poetic bent. Viewers will be aware that Imogen is not actually dead (and is not Fidele), and the stage dummy (or disguised actor) representing the headless Cloten is a reminder of an unmourned character. Still, it is a terrifying moment when Imogen wakes beside the corpse to find herself in a nightmare: "The dream's here still. Even when I wake it is / Without me as within me, not imagined, felt" (4.2.379–80). The gothic horror of the mutilated corpse is compounded by Imogen's mistaken identification of Cloten's manly parts for those of Posthumus. Harley Granville-Barker long ago declared the scene a "fraud on Imogen."[9] As in the bedroom scene, the play here solicits our participation in a misogynistic structure, perhaps punishing Imogen for the violent fantasies she has provoked in the other characters, and at the very least creating a difficult challenge for the actress who must maintain intensity and focus while grieving for a beheaded would-be rapist—or the dummy representing him.

With her steadfast devotion, her quaint epithets, and her courageous adaptability, Imogen provides a moral center even as she provokes the play's central fantasies. As such, she was a favorite of Shakespeareans in the nineteenth and early twentieth centuries. Swinburne gushed about her as "the immortal godhead of womanhood," and Arthur Quiller-Couch labeled her "the be-all and end-all of the play."[10] More recent commentators have been less in tune with the virtues of this patient Griselda, whose personal energy is compromised by betrayal and looming threats of violence. The late solidification of patriarchal rule afforded by the return of Guiderius and Arviragus has been seen as a lamentable check on her strength. Nevertheless, Imogen exhibits considerable force, functioning as the central character in tying together the three plots: war with Rome, Posthumus's wager, and the return of the lost princes. Her crucial decision "to begin a new life as Caius Lucius's page" rather than surrendering herself to grief serves as "the turning-point of the whole play."[11]

Notably, a reliable moral compass seems to guide certain characters through the play's surprising plot twists: Belarius, falsely accused of treason, is vindicated for stealing Cymbeline's sons, and Pisanio receives not nearly enough praise for disobeying Posthumus's lethally misguided command to kill Imogen. Their examples contribute to the play's recognition of the importance of individual choice and action. But in general *Cymbeline* emphasizes story more than character, fantasy more than self-knowledge. King Cymbeline retains power despite what appears to be a long history of lamentable rulership. The final settlement, in which "Pardon's the word to all" (5.5.515), erases lines of political opposition. Structurally, *Cymbeline* seems to advocate retreat, such as Belarius's escape to Wales. This escape is repeated within the play's action by the removal of Imogen, and then of the other characters, from the supposedly corrupt British and Roman courts to the remote Welsh wilderness. In terms of the play's genre, pastoral romance finally trumps tragedy or history, thus apparently endorsing passivity and patience. For despite Guiderius's and Arviragus's bluff ethical sensibility and the rehabilitation of Posthumus and Iachimo, ultimately *Cymbeline* does not depict a heroic world in which the characters discover the moral certainty to take up arms against a sea of troubles. To modern audiences living in a global civilization, the pattern of geographical escape presents an inadequate political solution. But pastoral drama has never been prized for its practical relevance; rather, the prospect of contemplation and perspective, heightened here by the fiction's emotional intensity, offers rejuvenation. *Cymbeline*'s meditation on the collision of empires and its scrutiny of the mind-altering function of fantasy continue to hold poignant appeal because the sensational stories the play brings before us are so altogether absorbing.

---

1. Harriet Walter, "Imogen in *Cymbeline*," in *Players of Shakespeare 3*, ed. Russell Jackson and Robert Smallwood (Cambridge: Cambridge University Press, 1993), p. 214.
2. Frank Kermode, *William Shakespeare, the Final Plays* (London: Longmans, Green, 1963), p. 28.
3. Barbara Mowat, *The Dramaturgy of Shakespeare's Romances* (Athens: University of Georgia Press, 1976), p. 78.
4. Patricia Parker, "Romance and Empire: Anachronistic *Cymbeline*," in *Unfolded Tales: Essays on Renaissance Romance*, ed. George M. Logan and Gordon Tesky (Ithaca: Cornell University Press, 1989), pp. 189–206.
5. See Hayden White, *Tropics of Discourse: Essays in Cultural Criticism* (Baltimore: Johns Hopkins University Press, 1978).
6. Harley Granville-Barker, *Prefaces to Shakespeare*, vol. 1 (1946; reprint, Princeton: Princeton University Press, 1974), p. 510.
7. See Slavoj Zizek, *The Sublime Object of Ideology* (London: Verso, 1989), and *The Plague of Fantasies* (London: Verso, 1997).

8. See Mikkel Borch-Jacobsen, *The Freudian Subject,* trans. Catherine Porter (Stanford: Stanford University Press, 1982), p. 39.

9. Granville-Barker, *Prefaces to Shakespeare,* p. 539.

10. Quoted in *Cymbeline,* ed. J. M. Nosworthy, Arden Edition of the Works of William Shakespeare (New York: Routledge, 1969), pp. xlii, xliii.

11. Roger Warren, *Shakespeare in Performance: Cymbeline* (Manchester: Manchester University Press, 1989), pp. 56, 18.

Further Reading

Cymbeline

Abbreviations: *Per.*=*Pericles; Tmp.*=*The Tempest; WT*=*The Winter's Tale*

Belsey, Catherine. "Marriage: Imogen's Bedchamber." In *Shakespeare and the Loss of Eden: The Construction of Family Values in Early Modern Culture,* pp. 55–83. New Brunswick, N.J.: Rutgers University Press, 1999. (The chapter incorporates portions of the author's earlier essay "The Serpent in the Garden: Shakespeare, Marriage, and Material Culture," *Seventeenth Century* 11 [1996]: 1–20.)

Belsey traces the "representation of the emergence of the loving [nuclear] family in three linked fields: Shakespeare's plays, English visual culture of the sixteenth and seventeenth centuries, and interpretations of the book of Genesis in the period." In the chapter on *Cymbeline,* she concentrates on two furnishings in Imogen's bedchamber—the chimneypiece of the chaste Diana bathing and the chamber's wall hangings of the passionate Cleopatra meeting Antony. The difficulty for the play's male protagonists lies in distinguishing these two contradictory feminine stereotypes of modesty and sexual invitation: Posthumus interprets Imogen's chastity as lasciviousness, while King Cymbeline takes the Queen's sexuality for virtue (5.5.74–78). The King's "Who is 't can read a woman?" (5.5.58) seems an apt epigraph for the whole play. Like the iconography, sermons, and marital tracts of the period, which associate the first marriage with the Fall of Man and death and also reveal a dual meaning in the feminine (i.e., Eve as both helpmate and temptress, ideal and warning), *Cymbeline* suggests "a structural anxiety at the heart of the early modern celebration of conjugal love."

Boling, Ronald J. "Anglo-Welsh Relations in *Cymbeline.*" *Shakespeare Quarterly* 51 (2000): 33–66.

There are three major settings in *Cymbeline:* the British court in Lud's Town, Rome, and the vicinity of Milford Haven in southwest Wales. Critics have either ignored the Welsh setting, read it as timeless pastoral, or interpreted it totally in the context of Tudor myth (since Henry Tudor landed at Milford Haven in 1485 en route to Bosworth). Boling, however, finds in the Welsh scenes traces of the "anglicizing process" in early modern Wales, Milford Haven functioning as a "microcosm of contemporary Anglo-Welsh relations." The author moves dialectically between the expansionist "Great British" trope and the insular "Little English" trope to argue that the play depicts the numerous complexities involved in defining the British state. In *Cymbeline,* "Rome is to Britain what in Shakespeare's time England was to Wales." Britain thus plays a double role as "empire to Wales but colony to Rome: as *Cymbeline*'s Wales is anglicized, so *Cymbeline*'s Britain is Romanized."

Crumley, J. Clinton. "Questioning History in *Cymbeline.*" *Studies in English Literature, 1500–1900* 41 (2001): 297–315.

Instead of identifying *Cymbeline* with romances such as *Per.* and *WT,* Crumley classifies it as "a kind of history play [with] something to say about history and historiography." Honoring both the form and content of its historical source (Holinshed's *Chronicles*), even while taking "exorbitant romantic liberties" with it, *Cymbeline* "uses romance to question history." In 3.1, Shakespeare's choice of the play's most repellent characters, the Queen and Cloten, to deliver the highest praise for Britain achieves a "delicate balance between moral sympathies and any nationalistic biases within the audience" (educated spectators would have inclined more toward Rome than Britain). Had the more sympathetic Imogen given the defense, the audience would have been encouraged to support the pro-British position. As it is, Shakespeare prevents one version of history (the Queen and Cloten's account of Caesar's invasion) from outweighing the other (Lucius's) in terms of historical credibility, thus leaving the audience with "something close to historical objectivity."

Cunningham, Karen. "Female Fidelities on Trial: Proof in the Howard Attainder and *Cymbeline*." *Renaissance Drama* 25 (1994): 1–31, esp. 15–25.

A challenge, both judicial and theatrical, in the early modern period was that of "providing a credible story." Cunningham focuses on the "narrative and rhetorical strategies necessary to the provisions of proof" in two distinct but related instances—Katherine Howard's attainder for treason in 1542 and Imogen's "metaphorical trial for promiscuity" in *Cymbeline*. Both tales turn on the issue of female " 'incontinency,' conjuring and containing a wayward female within the discipline of legal and legalistic rituals." Making its claims to truth by following the traditional legal approach of suppressing the notion that proof is something "made," the Howard attainder minimizes the effect of human agency and intervention. *Cymbeline,* however, "wears its status as a simulation on its sleeve, aggressively destabilizing the quasi-legal fictions that generate the 'unfaithful woman.' " Unlike in the Howard attainder, proof in the play maximizes human intervention in Iachimo's production of "Imogen-incontinent." Both texts probe female fidelity "within a more general theory of nationhood and identity—one organized around ideas of the legitimacy of patrilinear purity, unified subjectivity, and secure gender hierarchy—that was asserted, interrogated, and reasserted again and again in law courts and theaters."

Desmet, Christy. "Shakespearean Comic Character: Ethos and Epideictic in *Cymbeline.*" In *Acting Funny: Comic Theory and Practice in Shakespeare's Plays,* ed. Frances Teague, pp. 123–41. Rutherford, N.J.: Fairleigh Dickinson University Press; London: Associated University Presses, 1994.

Desmet uses epideictic rhetoric (the ceremonial oratory of praise and blame) to analyze the characters in *Cymbeline* according to ethical rather than psychological categories. Those who fault the play for its disjointed characterization fail to see that the dramatic agents achieve self-formation through the construction of ethical character, or what the ancients called *ethos.* The First Gentleman's appraisal of Posthumus (1.1.20–27), a "truncated encomium," evinces an "urge to evaluate moral character and the difficulties attendant on moral judgment." Desmet looks closely at three passages—Iachimo's "rhapsody" over the sleeping Imogen (2.2.14–54), Posthumus's rant against womankind (2.5.1–36), and the masque of the Leonati (5.4.32–153)—to demonstrate how *Cymbeline* "dramatizes the tensions that characterize epideictic rhetoric, examining self-consciously the relationship between *ethos* and the decorative rhetoric [hyperbole, metaphor, and other figures of amplification] used for its representation."

Granville-Barker, Harley. *"Cymbeline"* (1930). In *Prefaces to Shakespeare,* 1:459–543. 1946. Reprint, Princeton: Princeton University Press, 1974.

Granville-Barker's frequently cited treatment of *Cymbeline* addresses a wide range of issues: the question of collaboration (there must be a "whipping boy" responsible for the moments of "unresisting imbecility"), the influence of the Blackfriars playhouse, the self-consciously artificial style that permeates every aspect of the play, the construction of the action (the "swift forwarding" of the first part of the story, the "subtle composition" of Iachimo's three scenes, and the elaborate finale with its eighteen surprises are the best parts), the verse (Shakespeare creates a "new Euphuism . . . of imagination rather than expression"), and the characters (primarily Iachimo and Imogen, with some discussion of Posthumus, Cloten, and the two lost princes). Integral to the nature of *Cymbeline* is a "sophisticated artlessness," i.e., an art always on display and never concealed that steers the audience (especially at the conclusion) "between illusion and enjoyment of the ingenuity of the thing." Clumsy at times and full of imperfections, *Cymbeline,* nevertheless, has a "recondite charm."

Kermode, Frank. *"Cymbeline."* In *William Shakespeare, the Final Plays: "Pericles," "Cymbeline," "The Winter's Tale," "The Tempest," "The Two Noble Kinsmen,"* pp. 19–29. London: Longmans, Green, 1963.

Kermode considers *Cymbeline* a dramatic experiment in which Shakespeare is "somehow *playing* with the play" as he continues to explore, thematically and structurally, the dramaturgical element of recognition. Among *Cymbeline*'s peculiar features are a verbal style that is anything but "lucid," an extraordinarily complex plot filled with ambiguities, and a "wanton rapidity" of last-minute revelations that risks evoking farcical associations for the audience. The opening exchange between two unnamed gentlemen (1.1.1–80) exemplifies the "obliquity" that runs throughout the text. In spite of its obscurities, Kermode considers *Cymbeline* a "superb play."

Lewis, Cynthia. " 'With Simular Proof Enough': Modes of Misperception in *Cymbeline*." *Studies in English Literature, 1500–1900* 31 (1991): 343–64.

Lewis contends that of all the plays in the canon, *Cymbeline* is the one most preoccupied with the deceiving of characters and audience alike. The theme of misperception, introduced in 1.1, informs the play's asides, its characters (almost all of whom are "duped" at least once), the repeatedly piecemeal imparting of information crucial to understanding, the building of episodes around incomplete pictures, and the language (which constantly underscores problems of seeing). The play's signature line is Imogen's "Our very eyes / Are sometimes like our judgments, blind" (4.2.374–75). With mercy and love (figured most clearly in Imogen/Fidele) ultimately transcending the strictures of rational systems, faith emerges "as the only viable means to living harmonious spiritual and social lives."

Maley, Willy. "Postcolonial Shakespeare: British Identity and Identity Formation and *Cymbeline*." In *Shake-*

speare's Late Plays: New Readings, ed. Jennifer Richards and James Knowles, pp. 145–57. Edinburgh: Edinburgh University Press, 1999.

Maley reads *Cymbeline,* a text profoundly preoccupied with myths of origin and ideas of union and reconciliation, as "a nativity play" about the birth of Britain and of the "homecoming" of Britishness associated with the reign of King James I. As England moved from a nation to an empire, it looked to the only model of expansion it knew, one that it had earlier rejected: Rome. In *Cymbeline,* Shakespeare works through England's post-Reformation history, "the history of a nation wrested from an empire that copied . . . the thing to which it was ostensibly opposed." At the end of the play, this mimicry is presented positively, "but the covert reintroduction of Catholicism by the back door would be interpreted much less generously and optimistically by those whose insular idea of an Englishness [essentially Protestant] did not extend to Britain."

Mikalachki, Jodi. "The Masculine Romance of Roman Britain: *Cymbeline* and Early Modern English Nationalism." *Shakespeare Quarterly* 46 (1995): 301–22. (A slightly revised version of the article appears in Mikalachki's *The Legacy of Boadicea: Gender and Nation in Early Modern England* [London: Routledge, 1998], pp. 96–114.)

Mikalachki develops George Mosse's work on the "mutually informing" constructs of nationalism and sexuality to argue that the "gendering and sexualizing" of the nation, usually thought to have emerged in the eighteenth century, had come into existence by the early seventeenth century. In *Cymbeline,* the creation of a modern English nation requires "virile bonding" (the battle with Rome in Act 5 serves as a rite of passage for the lost sons of the King), the elimination of the wicked queen (who bears a striking resemblance to the mid-first-century Boadicea, who bravely failed to drive out the Roman conquerors sixty years after Cymbeline's reign), and "the construction of Imogen as a viable alternative[,] . . . a national icon of feminine respectability." The play concludes with the image of an "exclusively male community," from which the savage female (a threat to patriarchal order) has been banished; in her place, the respectable, domesticated ideal remains, still in her male attire. The "convergence of the personal and the national in the forging of masculine identity" helps reconcile two important interpretive traditions of *Cymbeline:* the psychoanalytic and the historicist.

Mowat, Barbara A. *The Dramaturgy of Shakespeare's Romances*. Athens: University of Georgia Press, 1976, esp. pp. 46–59.

In this study of the dramaturgy of *Cymbeline, WT,* and *Tmp.,* Mowat makes *Cymbeline* the focus of her chapter on theatrical tactics and theatrical styles, "because, of all the romances, [it] has been most open to attack or apology because of its 'primitive'—or, as they are called, 'artificial'—tactics." Concentrating on 1.5 as typical of the play's self-conscious theatricality, she examines such presentational conventions as (1) expository direct address to the audience; (2) indiscriminate distribution of soliloquies among major and minor characters alike, which results in the scattering of audience interest; and (3) emphatic entrance and exit cues. Such "obtrusive" devices, when combined with extradramatic monologues that provide long histories of individual characters and suggest the passage of time, yield a narrative structure that sporadically interrupts our sense of dramatic illusion by detaching us from moments of emotional intensity. Mowat claims that Shakespeare deliberately conjoins comedy and tragedy, presentation and representation, and narrative and dramatic modes to create "open form drama," through which he forces the audience "to acknowledge and experience" life's complexity in all its contrarieties and mysteries.

Palfrey, Simon. *Late Shakespeare: A New World of Words*. Oxford: Clarendon Press, 1997.

Palfrey investigates the fascination of *Cymbeline* and its companion romances (*Per.*, *WT*, and *Tmp.*) with "the genetics of speech and writing, and the political mutations of each" in a period of symbiotic linguistic and civic self-consciousness. He contends that in these plays "Shakespeare's febrile use of metaphor, and the diffusion of narrative authority and responsibility among competing voices or agencies, creates a politically restless genre which offers a robust and often irreverent challenge to providentialist or conservative teleologies." The author discusses the "turbid world" of *Cymbeline* in four chapters: "Body Language at Court" (Cloten, who bears much of the play's political dialogue, typifies Shakespeare's "experimental, decentred figurative process of character construction"); "Country Matters" (the Welsh scenes provide "an alternative to established order and, consequently, an environment capable of inaugurations, of beginnings"); "Women and Romance" (the woman's part, as found in Imogen, is one of "ideological disjunction," the archetype of embodied virtue, stalwart in the face of assault, "tak[ing] up a fearful strain"); and "Endings" (the ineffective and belated appearance of the "glittering, meretricious" Jupiter provides only a "simulacrum of closure"). Political imperatives are at the core of Shakespeare's revamping of romance.

Palmer, D. J., ed. *Shakespeare's Later Comedies: An Anthology of Modern Criticism.* Harmondsworth: Penguin, 1971.

This collection includes three influential essays on *Cymbeline:* Philip J. Brockbank's 1958 "History and Histrionics in *Cymbeline*" (pp. 234–47), Emrys Jones's 1961 "Stuart *Cymbeline*" (pp. 248–63), and Arthur C. Kirsch's 1967 "*Cymbeline* and Coterie Dramaturgy" (pp. 264–87). Brockbank focuses on Shakespeare's integration of historical sources (especially chronicle material relating to Brute, the legendary founder of Britain) and "self-confessed" theatrical artifice to create a historical romance depicting the "apocalyptic destiny of Britain": a brazen world transformed through reconciliation and providential design into a golden one. Jones explores the topical significance the play held for its first audience, pointing out parallels between Cymbeline's reign, which carried associations with Christ's nativity and Augustus's *pax Romana* (Roman peace), and the reign and political views of King James I, who regarded himself as another Augustus. There are so many analogues, however, that the play "suffers . . . from being too close to its royal audience." Kirsch contends that *Cymbeline*'s theatrical contrivances, which distance the audience from characters and actions, reflect Shakespeare's experimentation with the dramatic techniques and language of a dramaturgy associated with Jonson, Marston, and Beaumont and Fletcher in their work for the private theaters. The defining feature of *Cymbeline* is the dominant trait of coterie dramaturgy, "deliberate self-consciousness."

Parker, Patricia. "Romance and Empire: Anachronistic *Cymbeline.*" In *Unfolded Tales: Essays on Renaissance Romance,* ed. George M. Logan and Gordon Tesky, pp. 189–206. Ithaca: Cornell University Press, 1989.

Parker's investigation of the Virgilian subtext of *Cymbeline* leads her to conclude that the play's "curious" anachronisms—e.g., the character of Iachimo, who combines an ancient Roman noble with a Renaissance "jay of Italy" (3.4.51), and the superimposing of language suggestive of Italian and English Renaissance merchants on a plot and scene ostensibly set at the time of Augustan Rome—are deliberate, not the result of "bungling error or historical oversight." The conflation of Virgil's *Aeneid* and Shakespeare's last Roman plot is most pronounced in Posthumus, the British Aeneas; both figures are false to the women who love them and are "ignorant" of the larger schemes working to secure their outcomes. Cloten's headless trunk recalls the fall of King Priam, thereby serving as a visual emblem of the fall of Troy itself; Imogen's character holds allusions to the abandoned Dido and the grieving Hecuba, and (in Iachimo's emergence from the trunk) her body suggests "the potential British counterpart to ransacked Troy." At the end of the play, the repentant Iachimo pays tribute to Posthumus in a gesture of submission that, in subtly reversing Cymbeline's gesture of submission to imperial Rome, embodies the passing of true Roman virtue to a Britain that looks ahead to the inauguration of a Jacobean *pax* (peace), itself an echo of the *pax Augusta* (peace of the emperor Augustus). When read in the light of Virgil's epic, the play's anachronisms underscore the theme of imperialism and shift the emphasis from romance to history in the hybrid *Cymbeline.*

Skura, Meredith. "Interpreting Posthumus' Dream from Above and Below: Families, Psychoanalysts, and Literary Critics." In *Representing Shakespeare: New Psychoanalytic Essays,* ed. Murray M. Schwartz and Coppélia Kahn, pp. 203–16. Baltimore: Johns Hopkins University Press, 1980.

"Family resonances" underlie each of the play's three plots: the political story of King Cymbeline and his relations with Rome, the dynastic story involving the loss and recovery of the King's sons and his remarriage to a wicked queen, and the marital story of Imogen and Posthumus. The quest for a viable family matrix, however, is most important to Posthumus's moral growth as a husband worthy of Imogen. Skura views as crucial to this development the vision involving the Leonati and Jupiter (5.4), which Shakespeare psychologizes through a transformation of two theatrical conventions: the *deus ex machina* (or divine epiphany) that "presents the family from above as a sacred revelation," and the "family recognition scene" that presents it "from below as the memory of infantile experiences." The re-creation of his dead family in the dream sequence enables Posthumus to harmonize the tensions "between family inheritance and personal individuality[,] . . . between being part of the family unit and being the head of a new family." In finding himself as son, Posthumus finds himself as husband.

Warren, Roger. *Cymbeline.* Shakespeare in Performance Series. Manchester: Manchester University Press, 1989.

For Warren, the play's most striking theatrical quality is "its capacity to astonish and to move an audience at the same time." The first part of the volume addresses a variety of topics: the challenge in performance of combining theatrical virtuosity with powerfully evocative language in key scenes (1.6, 4.2, and 5.4); the use of myth, pseudo-history, and Ovidian techniques; the role of language in complicating the stereotypes to which the fairy-tale characters seem to conform; the play's "theatrical self-consciousness"; and *Cymbeline*'s stage history from the seventeenth century to the mid–twentieth century. The second half of the study provides a detailed analysis of seven productions spanning the years 1957 to 1988, with Peter Hall's 1957 version at the Shakespeare Memorial Theatre in Stratford-upon-Avon and his 1988 revival at the National Theatre in London framing the discussion. The other productions examined are William Gaskill's (RSC, 1962), Elijah Moshinsky's (BBC, 1982), Jean Gascon's and Robin Phillips's (Stratford, Ontario, 1970 and 1986, respectively), and Bill Alexander's (RSC, 1987). In his later *Staging Shakespeare's Late Plays* (Oxford: Clarendon Press, 1990), Warren devotes a chapter to Hall's 1988 production; he uses the rehearsal process, which he observed, as a means of exploring, scene by scene, the theatrical issues raised by the play ("Spiritual Journeys: *Cymbeline*," pp. 25–94).

Shakespeare's Language

Abbott, E. A. *A Shakespearian Grammar.* New York: Haskell House, 1972.

This compact reference book, first published in 1870, helps with many difficulties in Shakespeare's language. It systematically accounts for a host of differences between Shakespeare's usage and sentence structure and our own.

Blake, Norman. *Shakespeare's Language: An Introduction.* New York: St. Martin's Press, 1983.

This general introduction to Elizabethan English discusses various aspects of the language of Shakespeare and his contemporaries, offering possible meanings for hundreds of ambiguous constructions.

Dobson, E. J. *English Pronunciation, 1500–1700.* 2 vols. Oxford: Clarendon Press, 1968.

This long and technical work includes chapters on spelling (and its reformation), phonetics, stressed vowels, and consonants in early modern English.

Houston, John. *Shakespearean Sentences: A Study in Style and Syntax.* Baton Rouge: Louisiana State University Press, 1988.

Houston studies Shakespeare's stylistic choices, considering matters such as sentence length and the relative positions of subject, verb, and direct object. Examining plays throughout the canon in a roughly chronological, developmental order, he analyzes how sentence structure is used in setting tone, in characterization, and for other dramatic purposes.

Onions, C. T. *A Shakespeare Glossary.* Oxford: Clarendon Press, 1986.

This revised edition updates Onions's standard, selective glossary of words and phrases in Shakespeare's plays that are now obsolete, archaic, or obscure.

Robinson, Randal. *Unlocking Shakespeare's Language: Help for the Teacher and Student.* Urbana, Ill.:

National Council of Teachers of English and the ERIC Clearinghouse on Reading and Communication Skills, 1989.

Specifically designed for the high-school and undergraduate college teacher and student, Robinson's book addresses the problems that most often hinder present-day readers of Shakespeare. Through work with his own students, Robinson found that many readers today are particularly puzzled by such stylistic devices as subject-verb inversion, interrupted structures, and compression. He shows how our own colloquial language contains comparable structures, and thus helps students recognize such structures when they find them in Shakespeare's plays. This book supplies worksheets—with examples from major plays—to illuminate and remedy such problems as unusual sequences of words and the separation of related parts of sentences.

Williams, Gordon. *A Dictionary of Sexual Language and Imagery in Shakespearean and Stuart Literature.* 3 vols. London: Athlone Press, 1994.

Williams provides a comprehensive list of the words to which Shakespeare, his contemporaries, and later Stuart writers gave sexual meanings. He supports his identification of these meanings by extensive quotations.

Shakespeare's Life

Baldwin, T. W. *William Shakspere's Petty School.* Urbana: University of Illinois Press, 1943.

Baldwin here investigates the theory and practice of the petty school, the first level of education in Elizabethan England. He focuses on that educational system primarily as it is reflected in Shakespeare's art.

Baldwin, T. W. *William Shakspere's Small Latine and Lesse Greeke.* 2 vols. Urbana: University of Illinois Press, 1944.
Baldwin attacks the view that Shakespeare was an uneducated genius—a view that had been dominant among Shakespeareans since the eighteenth century. Instead, Baldwin shows, the educational system of Shakespeare's time would have given the playwright a strong background in the classics, and there is much in the plays that shows how Shakespeare benefited from such an education.

Beier, A. L., and Roger Finlay, eds. *London 1500–1800: The Making of the Metropolis.* New York: Longman, 1986.
Focusing on the economic and social history of early modern London, these collected essays probe aspects of metropolitan life, including "Population and Disease," "Commerce and Manufacture," and "Society and Change."

Bentley, G. E. *Shakespeare's Life: A Biographical Handbook.* New Haven: Yale University Press, 1961.
This "just-the-facts" account presents the surviving documents of Shakespeare's life against an Elizabethan background.

Chambers, E. K. *William Shakespeare: A Study of Facts and Problems.* 2 vols. Oxford: Clarendon Press, 1930.
Analyzing in great detail the scant historical data, Chambers's complex, scholarly study considers the nature of the texts in which Shakespeare's work is preserved.

Cressy, David. *Education in Tudor and Stuart England.* London: Edward Arnold, 1975.
This volume collects sixteenth-, seventeenth-, and

early-eighteenth-century documents detailing aspects of formal education in England, such as the curriculum, the control and organization of education, and the education of women.

De Grazia, Margreta. *Shakespeare Verbatim: The Reproduction of Authenticity and the 1790 Apparatus.* Oxford: Clarendon Press, 1991.

De Grazia traces and discusses the development of such editorial criteria as authenticity, historical periodization, factual biography, chronological development, and close reading, locating as the point of origin Edmond Malone's 1790 edition of Shakespeare's works. There are interesting chapters on the First Folio and on the "legendary" versus the "documented" Shakespeare.

Dutton, Richard. *William Shakespeare: A Literary Life.* New York: St. Martin's Press, 1989.

Not a biography in the traditional sense, Dutton's very readable work nevertheless "follows the contours of Shakespeare's life" as he examines Shakespeare's career as playwright and poet, with consideration of his patrons, theatrical associations, and audience.

Fraser, Russell. *Young Shakespeare.* New York: Columbia University Press, 1988.

Fraser focuses on Shakespeare's first thirty years, paying attention simultaneously to his life and art.

Schoenbaum, S. *William Shakespeare: A Compact Documentary Life.* New York: Oxford University Press, 1977.

This standard biography economically presents the essential documents from Shakespeare's time in an accessible narrative account of the playwright's life.

Shakespeare's Theater

Bentley, G. E. *The Profession of Player in Shakespeare's Time, 1590–1642.* Princeton: Princeton University Press, 1984.

Bentley readably sets forth a wealth of evidence about performance in Shakespeare's time, with special attention to the relations between player and company, and the business of casting, managing, and touring.

Berry, Herbert. *Shakespeare's Playhouses.* New York: AMS Press, 1987.

Berry's six essays collected here discuss (with illustrations) varying aspects of the four playhouses in which Shakespeare had a financial stake: the Theatre in Shoreditch, the Blackfriars, and the first and second Globe.

Cook, Ann Jennalie. *The Privileged Playgoers of Shakespeare's London.* Princeton: Princeton University Press, 1981.

Cook's work argues, on the basis of sociological, economic, and documentary evidence, that Shakespeare's audience—and the audience for English Renaissance drama generally—consisted mainly of the "privileged."

Greg, W. W. *Dramatic Documents from the Elizabethan Playhouses.* 2 vols. Oxford: Clarendon Press, 1931.

Greg itemizes and briefly describes many of the play manuscripts that survive from the period 1590 to around 1660, including, among other things, players' parts. His second volume offers facsimiles of selected manuscripts.

Gurr, Andrew. *Playgoing in Shakespeare's London.* Cambridge: Cambridge University Press, 1987.

Gurr charts how the theatrical enterprise developed from its modest beginnings in the late 1560s to become a thriving institution in the 1600s. He argues that there were important changes over the period 1567–1644 in the playhouses, the audience, and the plays.

Harbage, Alfred. *Shakespeare's Audience.* New York: Columbia University Press, 1941.

Harbage investigates the fragmentary surviving evidence to interpret the size, composition, and behavior of Shakespeare's audience.

Hattaway, Michael. *Elizabethan Popular Theatre: Plays in Performance.* London: Routledge and Kegan Paul, 1982.

Beginning with a study of the popular drama of the late Elizabethan age—a description of the stages, performance conditions, and acting of the period—this volume concludes with an analysis of five well-known plays of the 1590s, one of them (*Titus Andronicus*) by Shakespeare.

Shapiro, Michael. *Children of the Revels: The Boy Companies of Shakespeare's Time and Their Plays.* New York: Columbia University Press, 1977.

Shapiro chronicles the history of the amateur and quasi-professional child companies that flourished in London at the end of Elizabeth's reign and the beginning of James's.

The Publication of Shakespeare's Plays

Blayney, Peter W. M. *The First Folio of Shakespeare.* Hanover, Md.: Folger, 1991.

Blayney's accessible account of the printing and later life of the First Folio—an amply illustrated catalog to a 1991 Folger Shakespeare Library exhibition—analyzes the mechanical production of the First Folio, describing how the Folio was made, by whom and for whom, how much it cost, and its ups and downs (or, rather, downs and ups) since its printing in 1623.

Hinman, Charlton. *The Norton Facsimile: The First Folio of Shakespeare.* 2nd ed. New York: W. W. Norton, 1996.

This facsimile presents a photographic reproduction of an "ideal" copy of the First Folio of Shakespeare; Hinman attempts to represent each page in its most fully corrected state. The second edition includes an important new introduction by Peter W. M. Blayney.

Hinman, Charlton. *The Printing and Proof-Reading of the First Folio of Shakespeare.* 2 vols. Oxford: Clarendon Press, 1963.

In the most arduous study of a single book ever undertaken, Hinman attempts to reconstruct how the Shakespeare First Folio of 1623 was set into type and run off the press, sheet by sheet. He also provides almost all the known variations in readings from copy to copy.

Key to Famous Lines and Phrases

. . . his name
Is at last gasp. [*Queen*—1.5.61–62]

Every jack-slave hath his bellyful of fighting.
[*Cloten*—2.1.21–22]

The crickets sing, and man's o'erlabored sense
Repairs itself by rest. [*Iachimo*—2.2.14–15]

'Tis her breathing that
Perfumes the chamber thus. [*Iachimo*—2.2.21–22]

Hark, hark, the lark at heaven's gate sings,
And Phoebus gins arise. . . . [*Song*—2.3.20–28]

As chaste as unsunned snow. [*Posthumus*—2.5.14]

Some griefs are med'cinable. [*Imogen*—3.2.34]

Our cage
We make a choir, as doth the prisoned bird,
And sing our bondage freely. [*Arviragus*—3.3.46–48]

'Tis slander,
Whose edge is sharper than the sword, whose tongue
Outvenoms all the worms of Nile.
[*Pisanio*—3.4.35–37]

By Jupiter, an angel! Or, if not,
An earthly paragon. Behold divineness
No elder than a boy. [*Belarius*—3.6.46–48]

With fairest flowers,
Whilst summer lasts and I live here, Fidele,
I'll sweeten thy sad grave. Thou shalt not lack
The flower that's like thy face, pale primrose; nor
The azured harebell, like thy veins.
[*Arviragus*—4.2.280–84]

Fear no more the heat o' th' sun,
Nor the furious winter's rages. . . .
[*Song*—4.2.331–54]

O, the charity of a penny cord! It sums up thousands
in a trice. [*Jailer*—5.4.170–71]